Forbidden Child

By

James Aiello

D1714810

Forbidden Child
©2014 by James Aiello

Cover Design: Graphic Art Designer, Leonardo Rabathaly

ISBN-978-0-578-14279-1

James Aiello Prouctions Inc.
Vero Beach, FL 32962
jimgil9@yahoo.com

CHAPTER 1. INNOCENCE LOST

It's June 27th, 1989 and my mind is screaming, "Oh my God! How did this happen? Why did I kill him?" I can't believe that I, *'Christina Powers'*, *America's sex goddess* is sitting here in this Las Vegas County Courtroom waiting to be sentenced for the murder of Frank Salerno.

As I sit here pondering my future, I can faintly hear the shouting from the crowds in the streets, "Christina! Christina!" they chant. The sound is maddening.

Trying to gaze into the eyes of these jurors who hold my life in their hands, I can't help but to begin to plead in my mind over and over, "Oh, God! Oh, God! How did it get to this point? Why have I taken this course with my life?"

So many questions are going through my mind. I once thought I knew who I was, where I was going, and how I was going to get there; but it seems fate has a mind of her own. Events are out of my control now and I know I must follow this path wherever it leads. Or has this always been my destiny? I have no answers to these questions.

Sitting here silently waiting for a verdict, it comes to me like a vision in a mirror. "Oh, God" I plead once more. "Oh, yes," my thoughts continue, "It's all coming back to me now."

For you see, it was 1973 when my war with Frank started. I was an eighteen-year-old pop star poised on the brink of super stardom, with two Platinum albums, two Grammy awards and a sure bet to be nominated for my first Academy Award. I felt as though I was on top of the world. As if I had it all. All at the tender, naive, age of eighteen. 'Or so I thought.'

I was also the apple of my uncle's eye, who just happened to be 'Frank Salerno' himself. Uncle Frank was a legendary performer whose entertainment career spanned over twenty-five-years. He was Italian, forty-five-years old, six-feet-two-inches tall, with brown hair, brown eyes, and he weighed about two-hundred-pounds. He had two children Anthony and Debbie. Frank was also the alleged godfather for the entire West Coast of the United States.

Frank was the one person in my life I could always count on. This man was my rock! At that time I was fast becoming one of the biggest stars to be signed on the Salerno Record Label. It was a glorious time for me, for I had always stayed to myself in the past and no matter how hard I tried, I never seemed to fit in. 'Oh, yes! There was Barbara Goldstein,' I can't forget her. We met in 1970 at the Grammy awards just after I won my first Grammy for best new artist of the year. We became close friends and she became my mentor. She was the kind of woman I wanted to be, strong and independent with the voice of an angel. She also happened to be one of the only friends I chose for myself who my uncle approved of.

My mother was Frank's sister and shortly after my birth both my parents died after being in a car crash, 'or so I was led to believe.' I attended exclusive Catholic schools straight through my high school graduation. I never bothered continuing my education after high school because I had a dream; and that was to become a great performer like my beloved Uncle Frank. As for the affection of my cousins, Frank's children, there was none. They made it very clear that I was in their way. I hardly knew any love or even friendship to speak of at all as a child, except for that which came from my uncle himself. Frank always showered me with his love and affection. He took care of my every need, from every song I sang, to every part I played. From my schooling right into my career and every date I ever went on, Uncle Frank had it all planned out. I wanted to be a star, and Uncle Frank was going to take me there. Until the day 'Johnny' came into my life!

It was a beautiful spring afternoon and I was having lunch with Kathy Brown. She was twenty-two, beautiful and her prime time TV show was number one in the Nielsen Ratings. We were paired together to be best friends' courtesy of my Uncle Frank. He felt it would be good for both our careers, to be seen together in public.

So there we were, two of the most desirable and eligible young women in America, having lunch together at Tavern on the Green in Central Park. We were just finishing our meal, when the Maître d' came to our table, "Pardon me, Miss Valona and Miss Brown, the two gentlemen at table eleven would like to give this bottle of champagne to you ladies to have with your meal." *Oh by the way, my name was Christy Valona at that time.*

"Thank you." I replied, "please tell the gentlemen it is not our custom to drink champagne with our lunch, but we will accept the gift if they will join us for some fresh vegetable juice."

"Why did you do that?" Kathy asked with a look of distress. "Now we have to have lunch with two perfect strangers. What are we going to say to them?"

"Sometimes you have to go with your feelings, Kathy." I winked, "Something tells me this is one of those times."

"Well I have a feeling too, Christy, and it's telling me to get the hell out of here."

"Don't you dare leave me here alone with them, I'll slap you, girl." I said with a giggle, half meaning it.

Then it happened. There were two men approaching our table, but I could only focus on one. He was a splendid six-foot-tall, blond haired, blue eyed god! His muscles rippled through his tight fitting baby blue designer sport shirt, which enhanced those blue eyes of his. Peeking through the 'V' of his open collar, the curls of his thick blond chest hairs cascaded across his well-defined physique. He was incredible to look at!

As he reached our table, he stretched out his hand to mine and with a slight southern twang in his voice, "Hi Miss Valona, my name is John Everett. It's my pleasure to meet you." As he touched my hand, I felt it, in that instant I knew I had to know more about this man, this beautiful, seemingly gentle giant who was holding my hand.

He reached over to Kathy, "Miss Brown, it's also a pleasure to meet you." He then gestured toward his dark haired companion, "This is my friend and colleague, Steve Grady."

After we exchanged greetings, I invited them to sit with us. In an effort to break the ice, I struggled with my thoughts for a moment. Trying to be witty, I smiled, "I hope you like vegetable juice, guys!"

"I take mine straight," John said with a boyish smile. Looking straight into my eyes with those baby blues, he added, "I think you're an incredible performer, Christy. May I call you, Christy?"

"If I may call you Johnny?"

"But my name is John."

"I know that, Johnny," I answered with a slightly seductive smile.

With that he gallantly replied, "Whatever my lady would like!"

Our meeting over vegetable juice was going quite well. Kathy and Steve seemed to hit it off nicely, but you could never really tell what Kathy was truly thinking about when it came to dealing with men. As for Johnny and me, it was magic. He told me he was a pitcher for the New York Mets and that Steve was his catcher. He also assured me with great enthusiasm and confidence, the Mets will win the World Series this year.

He seemed to have a real zeal for life. This was something I had felt in myself, but had not seen in anyone else until then. He told me he was twenty-four-years old and he grew up in Virginia. Although he loved the excitement and vitality of life in New York and playing with a major league team, his ultimate passion was to one day return home to work the soil with his own hands. That's where he truly felt as though he was one with God and nature.

As we finished our conversation, the four of us made a dinner date for that evening. Johnny was going to pick me up at eight o'clock and Steve was picking up Kathy. We were to meet at La Shazonz' Restaurant in downtown Manhattan.

I felt a childish anticipation throughout that very long afternoon, as I primped for that evening's rendezvous. I brushed my long wavy dark black hair and made up my eyes with just a touch of blue liner to enhance the blue of my eyes. I slipped into a tight black evening dress, which deliberately had a very low cut neckline. I tied up my hair with a white silk scarf and donned a pair of black leather heels. I was dressed to kill.

"What is this I'm feeling?" I thought. I have met many men in the past three years of being a performer and none of them ever made me feel like this. I actually felt as if I were glowing inside! "Was he feeling the same," I wondered?

Finally the hour came. Johnny picked me up at my Park Avenue penthouse which I purchased with the earnings from my first record album. When I opened the door, he was holding two dozen red roses with one pure white rose sitting in the middle of the bouquet.

His eyes opened wide when he saw me, "Good evening, Christy." Handing me the beautiful bouquet, "You look awesome, tonight."

"Thank you, Johnny." I eyed him up and down, "You don't look too shabby yourself and thank you for the lovely flowers. Red roses are my favorite flowers and the white one makes them a little more special." I smiled, "Would you like to come in for a minute while I place these in a vase?"

He entered the living room as I headed for the kitchen. When I returned he was standing by the fireplace where I kept all my awards. He looked at me through adoring eyes, "I was just admiring your collection, very impressive. You should be proud."

"Thank you," I answered, gracefully. "I am proud of my achievements. I've worked very hard for them."

"Your home, it's beautiful," he turned to gaze at the rest of the room.

"Thank you again. Would you like to see the rest of it? I decorated it myself."

"Yes, I would," he replied enthusiastically.

As I took him on a tour of my home he really seemed impressed with what I had done with it. When we reached the master bedroom Johnny stood in amazement as he looked around the room. My heart started pounding in my chest as I felt my blood pressure rising. I was becoming nervous by my overwhelming feelings of desire for this man I had only met a few hours earlier.

Johnny's first gaze fell on the black marble fireplace which was majestic in size. As he took in the rest of the decor, he noticed the paintings and sculptures of angels throughout the room. "Wow! Someone's into angels, aren't they?" He exclaimed.

"Yes, I am. I've been intrigued by angels since I was a child. They have comforted me and filled an empty void in my life in many ways, and that's why I've decorated this room with them. This is my sanctuary."

He looked over to the canopy bed and stood in awe of the splendid white marble roman column like pillars, which held up each corner of the canopy. The canopy was made of sheer white chiffon drapes, which cascaded down from the ceiling and flowed gently between the columns to meet the pearly white marble floor, inlaid with twenty-four-karat gold. "Your bedroom is out of this world! You have an incredible imagination to have decorated it this way."

"Why thank you, Johnny," I replied with modesty. "But it's getting late, we'd better go. I'm sure Kathy and Steve are wondering what's taking us so long."

He looked at his watch, "Holy cow, 'little angel,' it's 8:15 already! I'd guess we'd better get going." He escorted me to his car, and our evening was on.

Kathy and Steve were already waiting at the bar when we arrived. The Maître d' escorted us to the best table in the restaurant. It had a fabulous skyline view of Central Park West. Dinner was splendid and the four of us got along as if we had known each other for years. Johnny and Steve were so witty together. It was obvious they were best friends. I could not remember the last time I had laughed so much. Johnny made me feel so free that by the time dinner ended, I knew he was special.

We all decided the night was young, and we should go to Furn's for a drink. Furn's was the most exclusive club in town and only the elite were allowed in. As the four of us approached the entrance, the cameras from the tabloids were snapping all around us. The night seemed enchanted. We were led to a table, which was reserved for patrons such as ourselves. To my surprise the diva herself, Barbara Goldstein, was also out on the town that evening. She was seated two tables away from ours with Liza, the famous Broadway star. They were there with two very attractive gentlemen. I was about to ask to be excused for a moment, to go say hi, when she noticed us and came to our table.

"Christy!" With a big smile she embraced me.

"Barbara!" Enthusiastically, I returned her hug, "I didn't know you were back in town. I thought you were still shooting out on the West Coast."

"Not anymore, the film is finally finished and it's time to start promoting it. The premiere is next Friday. It would make me very happy if you would come as my guest."

"I'd love to Barbara, but I can't. I'll be out on the West Coast myself next Friday. Uncle Frank has a script he wants me to audition for at Paramount."

"Is it the script for the film, 'Samantha's Father'?" She asked with wide eyes.

"Yes," I answered, with a devilish look in my eye.

"You know, whoever nails the part of 'Samantha' is going to skyrocket in popularity."

I smiled mischievously, "I know girlfriend, and I want it."

"Oh by the way, congratulations, I hear you're a shoe in to be nominated for an Oscar. That's wonderful, baby! I'm so happy for you. I just know you're going to get it! Your performance in 'Blue Lady' was breathtaking." She turned to Kathy, "Hello, Kathy, it's so nice to meet you, and oh my, my, John Everett and Steve Grady, I just love you guys. You're both such great ball players."

"Thank you," they answered. The four of them exchanged greetings, after which Barbara turned back to me, "Why don't you guys come join us at our table?"

"Maybe another time." I kissed her cheek and whispered in her ear, "It's our first night out together and I'd like to keep Johnny all to myself for a while."

"He's a living doll," she whispered back, "We'll do dinner and you can let me know how it went."

I laughed, "With our notorious appetites? Don't you remember the last time we did dinner? I'm still doing two hours on the stair master every day. I'll call you next week; it's safer for both our figures." We both laughed and as we said our goodbyes I told her to give my love to Liza.

I turned my full attention back to Johnny. The magic between Johnny and I continued. We were in a fantastic dream together as we held each other on the dance floor. We danced till midnight. Finally, we said goodbye to Kathy and Steve, and Johnny drove me home.

When we reached my front door, Johnny took me in his arms and kissed me passionately. "Well, I guess I'd better get going, I have practice in the morning and a game in the afternoon." We embraced again as he softly continued, "May I see you tomorrow, Christy?"

We relinquished our embrace, "I'd love to see you tomorrow, Johnny."

He kissed me once more with such passion I thought I'd melt. He released my lips, "Good night little Angel." As he turned to leave he stopped, turned back, hugged me softly, "Christy I can't leave you, please let me stay the night."

Trembling in his arms, "Johnny, I can't, I've never."

He looked heartbroken as he whispered, "Please forgive me. I've never been this forward in my life. I'll leave; may I still see you tomorrow?"

"Of course you may."

This time as he slowly turned to leave, I felt a fire explode within me burning with a passion I'd never felt before. I reached for his hand, "Johnny, please don't leave me tonight. I don't know what this is I'm feeling, but I have never felt this way before. I want you to stay with me, *please*." As these words flowed from my mouth I thought, "How could you be saying these things?" I had never been intimate with a man before and now I was longing for this man I had only met for the first time this afternoon.

Johnny looked intently into my eyes, "I was praying you felt it too, Christy." He kissed me deeply, "I won't leave you angel. I'll stay as long as you want me to."

He swept me off my feet and carried me into the bedroom. The room was dimly lit with only the light of a splendid full moon filtering in through the bay glass doors, which led out onto the open balcony. He gradually stood me up alongside the bed and we embraced. Slowly and oh so softly he kissed my cheeks as his large hands slid so gently through my hair. My silk scarf floated to the floor as one hand tenderly held the back of my neck, the other hand began to caress my breasts. His lips met mine again and this time I became frightened, so I softly pushed him away, "Johnny, please slow down, I'm scared. I've never made love before."

He gazed so shyly into my eyes and with complete sincerity in his voice, "I've never made love before either, Christy."

Hearing him say that seemed to take all the fear away, as I pulled him to me and kissed him tenderly. I felt so weak in the arms of this man whom I knew at that moment I loved. My body began to softly shiver with a feeling of extreme ecstasy. He began to slowly undo the buttons on my dress and let it slide down to my ankles. As he was undressing me, I found myself undressing him. I had to see him, touch him, taste him and make love to him. The passion swelled between us. "Johnny, oh, Johnny," I whispered in his ear as he laid me on the bed. The heat of our bodies was scorching as his flesh met mine. The fire grew hotter as we touched one another, kissed one another, and loved one another. We caressed each other from head to toe. It was incredible. There was lightning flashing through our souls and then in our hearts. When we were wild with passion and thought we could take no more, he slid back on top of me and held me passionately in his arms.

With a gentle quiver in his voice, "Christy, I love you. I don't understand how I know this. I just do. I love you, I need you. I'll love you now and always."

I held him so close to my pounding heart and cried in a soft voice, "I love you too, Johnny, I love you too." I drew him to my melting body. My soul screamed in ecstasy and pain, as he gently took the gift of my virginity. Gentle soft tears slowly began to drip from his deep blue eyes as he accepted my gift of love. My tears began to flow with his. The love we felt together at that moment was eternal. We sealed our love that night with the fire of our souls. We were one and we knew it. The night was filled with passion and pleasure. So much so I felt as if I had never lived until that moment. We embraced and shared our love throughout that glorious night. Our bodies and souls were one when the rays of the morning sun found us.

"I love you, Johnny." I lifted myself out of his embrace, and looked in amazement at this magnificent man as I softly stroked his body.

"You're beautiful, angel," rising up to kiss me, "and I love you with all my heart."

We embraced again and the fire flared. We had an insatiable thirst we couldn't quench. 'Oh how I loved him so.' As much as we wanted that night's love making to never end, it did, and we knew we had to come back to earth.

"We'd better get up, it's seven o'clock." I kissed his cheek, "Why don't you shower while I fix us some breakfast?"

"Okay, angel," embracing me, "I love you, Christy."

He rose from the bed and headed for the shower. I slipped on my robe and headed for the kitchen, quickly put on the coffee pot and popped some bread into the toaster. I went to the bathroom to freshen up and when I entered the room, I could see his silhouette through the shower doors. He was sliding a washcloth all over his body. "This man is perfect." I thought as I slipped off my robe and entered the shower with him. I took the wash cloth from his hand and began to wash his body. He leaned his back against the side of the shower wall and as I washed him, I watched his large, limp, muscle slowly become enormous. My body shivered with passion. I kissed his lips and slowly slid my tongue from his neck down to his hard nipples. I began to softly massage them with my tongue and the tips of my teeth. As the warm water ran off our bodies, I moved from one nipple to the other. Johnny was moaning and his body began to softly twitch with excitement. I found myself being drawn to his throbbing manhood. My lips began to quiver with anticipation, as I slowly took him into my mouth. Our bodies went wild together in perfect rhythm, until Johnny screamed in ecstasy. As he exploded, I drank from him as if I were drinking from the 'fountains of the gods'. I felt his lightning shoot through the essence of my being, and the heat of my passion exploded within me. The feelings of pleasure and lust were magnificent. We embraced again, "I love you, I love you," was all either one of us could say. Slowly we began to finish washing one another.

We got dressed and headed out to the kitchen to find burnt toast and muddy coffee. We looked at each other and laughed.

"That's okay, angel, I have to go anyway. I have practice at nine o'clock." He grabbed me, kissed me, "Can you make it to the game this afternoon? I'm pitching."

"I wouldn't miss it for the world, what time does the game begin?"

"Four o'clock. If you come to the players' entrance at 3:30, I'll be waiting for you."

"I'll be there, my love," We kissed and I walked him to the door. One last embrace and he left my arms. I closed the door when he was out of sight, leaned back on the door and began to cry.

"These emotions are so strong," I thought, "I could never express them in words." I walked over to the couch, picked up a pen and paper and began trying to compose my thoughts. This was at 8:30 in the morning. By 1:30 that afternoon, I was at the recording studio putting music to the lyrics. Writing was what kept me sane that day as I prayed for afternoon to come. All I could think about was Johnny and I just knew I was all he could think about.

Finally, it was 3:30. I ran to him the instant I saw him and I leaped into his arms. He embraced me and we were whole again; and the flashing of the tabloid cameras caught it all. He led me through the dugout to a seat he had saved for me. It was so close to the pitcher's mound we could see each other's eyes. As the game began, my heart grew with excitement. My eyes were focused on every move he made; they were so strong, smooth, and fast; that I was mesmerized. As I watched, I could hardly believe this beautiful gladiator was the man I loved. My heart began to fantasize deeper and deeper with every pitch. In my mind, I could see myself wipe the sweat from his brow with the tips of my breasts. There we were, the two of us, making love with our eyes in front of the world. He was magnificent that day and to the cheers of fifty-thousand screaming fans he took bows for a no hitter. Steve ran something out to Johnny. It was a bouquet of two dozen red roses with one white one in the middle. Johnny walked over to where I was seated, took a bow, and handed them to me. The crowd went wild.

As we tried to leave the stadium, the press with their cameras, were all around us. It was 7:30, by the time we left the ball park and by nine o'clock that evening, the whole country knew we were in love. We were so high on love, we thought we would live forever, yet so tired and hungry, we thought we would die at any moment. But it was off to a celebration party at the Hilton, to celebrate his tenth no hitter of the season, and Johnny was the main attraction. As Johnny finished receiving all those slaps on the butt from the biggest names in baseball, I slipped away and went over to speak with Patrick Victor. He was the orchestra leader and a friend, "Hi, Pat." We embraced, "Do you think you could do me a small favor?"

"Anything for you, Christy," he answered with a smile. "What is it?"

"I have this copy of sheet music with me. Would you please have someone copy it for your musicians and have them try to play it for me? Pretty, please."

"I'll do my best and let you know."

Thank God they were finally serving hors d'oeuvres, when I rejoined Johnny at our table. To my surprise Kathy was also seated at our table with Steve. I greeted them both with a warm smile and embrace. Steve popped the cork from an expensive bottle of French champagne, "Will you ladies have some champagne with us now?"

Kathy and I looked at each other with a devilish look in our eyes, grabbed for the bottle at the same time and acted as if we were going to splash it all over them. Astonished looks came over their face's and we laughed so hard I thought we'd burst. After our outburst we all started to drink, maybe just a little too much, especially Kathy.

From the stage Patrick Victor announced, "Excuse me, ladies and gentlemen, tonight we have a dear friend of mine here with us. Right now, I'd like to invite her up on stage to do a number for you. Please give a hardy welcome to Christy Valona."

The room began to applaud as I walked to the stage. I was a

little nervous as I took the microphone in my hand, but I wanted to do this, "Good evening, ladies and gentleman. I would like to give a special gift to a very special friend of mine, John Everett. This is a new song I wrote, just for him."

With that the music started and I began to sing. I sang from the core of my heart to the man I loved. I found strength and passion whirling up within my soul as I sang to Johnny. The words burst out of me like fire. I sang like I'd never sung before. I was incredible and the crowd knew it. I got a standing ovation and Johnny met me at the stage when the song was finished. We embraced to the applause of our friends and colleagues. The night was enchanting. We were living a fairy tale and we loved it. It was 2:00am by the time we arrived at Johnny's condo in Tarry-town, just north of the city. We spent the rest of that night with our bodies mingled in pure ecstasy.

In the morning we showered together, AGAIN! Then I made him a real breakfast. Johnny dropped me off at my penthouse at 8:30, kissed me and left for practice. We made plans to meet at 6:00 that evening at my place.

I entered my home to a barrage of phone messages from Uncle Frank. I picked up the phone and called him on his private line at his corporate headquarters in Las Vegas.

"Hello."

"Hi! Uncle Frank," I said with excitement in my voice.

"Where the hell have you been, Christy?" He interrupted my thoughts, "And what the hell is going on out there? My phone has been ringing all night because of your reckless behavior. Have you seen the headlines in today's papers? Photos of the two of you embracing are splattered all over the country. Dammit girl, I thought you were more mature then that! When you asked me on your birthday to let you buy that place and live in the city alone I said yes, because I trusted your loyalty to me. I told you I didn't want you dating anyone unless I approved! Why have you disobeyed me?"

"Please calm down, Uncle Frank," I exclaimed. "It's not what you're thinking. I'm in love, Uncle Frank, I'm truly in love."

"Well, if you're truly in love baby," his voice began to calm, "then how come I'm the last one to find out?"

"It all happened so fast, we only met two days ago."

"Two days ago! Are you serious? What the hell are you thinking? How can you be in love in two days?"

"I don't know how, I only know I am." With enthusiasm, "Wait till you meet him Uncle Frank. He's wonderful! He's everything I ever dreamed he'd be and if you're not happy for me, I'm just going to cry."

"Don't cry baby," he said with a reassuring tone. "Let me just compose my thoughts for a while. I have a hectic schedule today, so there's nothing I can do about this now. I'll be flying out tonight. If all goes well, I'll see you around 11:00pm your time."

"That's wonderful, Uncle Frank, I can't wait to see you. I can't wait for you to meet him. You're just going to love him. I know it!"

"All right Christy, just do me a favor and don't do anything foolish!" he said harshly.

"I won't do anything foolish, Uncle Frank, I promise. I love you so much and thank you for coming. It means so much to me."

His reply was very short, "Okay, okay, I have to go. I'll see you tonight. Goodbye for now."

"Goodbye, Uncle Frank."

As I hung up the phone, I got a very uncomfortable feeling from our conversation. Uncle Frank had never used that tone of voice with me before and it concerned me because I didn't understand it. I decided to dismiss these feelings. I was so happy at that moment and I was not going to let anything take those feelings from me.

I quickly changed my clothes and headed for the recording studio around 9:00am. The crew and I worked furiously that day and by 3:00pm we had recorded a masterpiece; a masterpiece which I wrote in only three hours for my beloved Johnny. I titled it, 'Johnny's Love.' I rushed home with my heart pounding at just the thought of seeing him. I quickly began to prepare for a romantic dinner, accompanied by candle light, champagne, and soft music. By 5:58pm I was out of the shower and dressed to impress. Just then the doorbell rang, and I ran to answer it. I felt like a puppy anticipating the entrance of his master. I opened the door and he swept me up into his arms and carried me to the sofa, kissing me wildly all the way. "I love you! I love you!" He kept repeating as he placed me on the sofa. Our bodies immediately exploded with passion. He was back in my arms and I was alive again.

I finally served dinner shortly after 10:00pm that night. Needless to say it was not very appetizing, but we ate it anyway. The meal really didn't matter because we were living on love. Over dinner, I told Johnny about the conversation with Uncle Frank. I shared my concerns with him over the way Frank spoke to me. I told him he should be arriving any minute. Johnny stood up from his seat at the table, walked over, knelt down, wrapped his arms around me, "Don't worry angel, you're right, he will love me. I'll make sure of that, I promise."

I was so reassured by his words as he held me tightly that I felt encouraged by his strength. I kissed him, "I have something for you."

"You do?" He smiled as he gently tickled my waist.

"Yes, I do." I playfully slapped his hand, "Now let me go get it."

I walked to the living room, opened my purse and pulled out a key. I took it over to him, "Please take this Johnny. It's the key to my home and I want you to have it. I want you to be able to come here anytime you want."

He smiled and took the key, "I guess great minds really do think alike."

He slipped a small sealed envelope out of his pocket and handed it to me. I opened it and inside was a key to his condo. We looked at each other and laughed. Nothing more had to be said. We were giving ourselves to each other with those keys and we both knew it.

Then the doorbell rang and we knew it was Uncle Frank. For some reason my heart began to race as Johnny walked me to the door.

"Relax, Christy, he's your uncle. He loves you and we're going to get along great."

I squeezed his arm, "You're right." But in the back of my mind, I couldn't help but feel concerned, for I was raised by this man. He was always wonderful to me, but I could also remember how frightening he could be, when I was disobedient. So I hardly ever stepped out of line.

As I opened the door, I'll never forget the look of shock on Uncle Frank's face when he saw Johnny standing there with me. He burst into the room, pushed Johnny up against the wall and screamed, "You bastard! You fucked my niece! I should have you killed for this!"

Johnny was in shock! As he held my uncle back, all Johnny could say was, "I'm sorry sir. I'm sorry! Now please try to calm down and listen to us."

I screamed, "Please, Uncle Frank, please stop this!"

He flung his arms free from Johnny's grasp, stood back, straightened his suit and with anger, "Christy, how could you do this to me? And to yourself! Dammit, girl!" He raised his fist to me then dropped it in disgust, "I thought I raised you better than this!" He lowered his voice, "You've brought shame to me."

All I could do was cry. I was devastated. I couldn't stop crying. Johnny grabbed me and held me up as he forcefully said, "Mr. Salerno, I am very sorry you feel this way, but I love your niece and she has done nothing to bring shame upon herself or upon you. I would marry your niece tonight if she'd have me!" I looked up at Johnny and my heart leaped.

"Okay, Okay, I've heard enough," Frank shouted. "I think you should leave now, so I may speak with my niece alone."

"I'm very sorry Mr. Salerno, but I can't do that. We are in love and I'm staying with Christy tonight."

"You're what! Like hell you are! Can't you see you've done enough harm?" He swung his hand toward the door and shouted, "Get the hell out before I throw you out!"

Johnny stepped in front of me, "I'm not leaving!"

Uncle Frank looked straight into my eyes and shouted, "Christy, tell him to leave, **now!**"

My heart froze and as if my mouth was in slow motion, "A! Ahhhh! A..."

Commanding he shouted, "**Christina!** Don't you dare disobey me, or I will walk out that door and you will regret it!"

The tears just flowed down my cheeks as I looked at him and

pleaded, "Please, Uncle Frank, don't do this. Please don't force me to make that choice."

He screamed, "Damn you, **Christy**!" Then he turned, walked to the door and slammed it on his way out.

I buried my face in Johnny's chest and cried. Johnny picked me up and carried me to the bedroom. I clung to Johnny as we lay in bed. He held me so tenderly and stroked my head, as the tears softly fell from my eyes. The wind slowly began to pick up that night. We could hear the rain start to fall out on the patio. The thunder rumbled and the lightning flashed. The storm grew until the wind roared. It sounded so cold that my body felt frozen, as I listened to it right outside my window. I didn't know until that moment that the heart could hurt so badly, and yet feel so full of life all at the same time. As I drifted off to sleep, I felt safety in Johnny's arms, but I also felt fear. For if there was one thing I knew about Uncle Frank, it was no one crossed him and got away with it.

In the morning we woke up still embraced in each other's arms. Johnny slowly lifted himself up, gazed down at me and in the most loving tender voice, "Will you marry me, Christy?"

Looking up into his deep blue eyes, my tears began to flow again, as I grabbed him and cried, "Yes! Johnny, yes! I will marry you."

The rest of that day, I was on cloud nine. I was so happy with the thought of being Mrs. Johnny Everett that I didn't think of Uncle Frank at all. Neither one of us went to work. We got in Johnny's Porsche and drove endlessly. We talked about our love as we drove; our marriage and how many children we would have.

Johnny drove me to his dream house that day. It was a five-thousand-acre farm in Wells, Virginia, just south of Norfolk. There was a beautiful big old white colonial house, with three large barns seated behind it. Johnny told me he played here as a child and how he had saved through the years to buy this place. He told me how he dreamed of one day bringing his bride here. Then we dreamed together of how we would live here. He would run the farm, and I'd be right beside him. We dreamed of having our children and raising our family here. Johnny's dream became mine that day. All I wanted was to be his bride and bear his children. 'Oh, how I loved him!'

The time came to leave the dream, but we took it with us in our hearts. After we left that beautiful farmhouse, Johnny took me to meet his parents. Their home was only five miles down the road. When we got there Johnny introduced me to his parents as his fiancée. His parents hugged us both with excitement, then his mother ran to the phone. After she hung up the phone, she ran to the kitchen and started to immediately put out a big spread. His father stayed and entertained us as his mom ran back and forth in the kitchen. I tried to offer her some help, but she lovingly threw me out.

Within thirty minutes Johnny's whole family came through the front door, his brothers Billy and Mark with their families, then his sister Joanne with her family. By the time dinner was placed on the table, I had met Johnny's whole family.

After dinner, right in front of everyone, Johnny came over to where I was sitting, knelt down in front of me, "Christy, this ring was my grandmother's." He placed it on the ring finger of my left hand, "I love you, angel, and it would honor me if you will accept this for your engagement ring."

I hugged him, "Thank you, Johnny, I love it!" It was just an old thin gold band, but I loved it!

As we were leaving, Johnny's mom was handing all the ladies handbags back to them, which had been thrown in the bedroom on the bed when we arrived. It was quite amusing to watch her fumbling as she gave us the wrong bags.

She looked at me with an expression of pure love, threw her hands in the air and said, **"Oh well, I'll figure it out tomorrow!"**

We had a great time that afternoon. Meeting Johnny's family was wonderful. I fell in love with them and they fell in love with me.

When we arrived back at the penthouse there was one message from Uncle Frank, "Christy, honey, I'm sorry. I do love you baby, so please call me back at the Hampton Estate."

With a great sigh of relief, "Oh, thank God! I want to call him now. All right, Johnny?" I looked into Johnny's eyes for his approval, "You don't think it's too late do you?"

Looking at the time with a smile, "2:00am, nah, it's not too late." He kissed me, "Go call him, you little screwball."

I called Uncle Frank and got him out of bed. We both, very emotionally apologized to each other. After talking for an hour, he seemed to accept the things I was telling him about Johnny and me. I told him of our intent to wed and he was finally happy for us. He invited us to dinner that evening to celebrate. He would have his car pick us up at 7:00pm. I hung up the phone and turned my full attention back to Johnny.

We climbed into bed together and our passion rose instantly. We couldn't keep our hands off one another. The fire of our imaginations eclipsed our souls as we made love, and that night became filled with endless pleasure.

The next morning we started our day the same way we ended our night, making love. Then Johnny was off to the ballpark and me to the studio. I was so inspired by our love I stopped recording, sat down and wrote 'I'm Johnny's Girl' in twenty minutes. The crew and I spent the rest of that day putting music to the lyrics. I insisted 'Johnny's Love', and 'I'm Johnny's Girl' be placed on my new album. I also had the title of the album changed to 'Johnny's love.'

Johnny met me at the penthouse at 6:00pm with a fresh change of clothing in his hands. He dropped his bundle on the floor as soon as he saw me. We embraced and just held one another on the sofa for the first ten minutes. It was such a warm tender feeling to have him back in my arms. Then we got ready for dinner.

Uncle Frank's car was there at seven o'clock sharp, and the next thing we knew we were on our way to his estate in the Hamptons. I could see Johnny was impressed as the guards let us in through the steel gates. We traveled down the two-mile driveway, past the well-lit guest homes, then up the hill to Frank's oceanfront, four story mansion.

Uncle Frank greeted us warmly at the front-door and immediately apologized to Johnny for his outburst of anger the night before. He continued to express his joy and concern over our engagement. We were served dinner in the informal dining room. The meal was exquisite and as we ate Uncle Frank said, "John, I want to be very candid with you, I have had your entire background researched and it appears as though you are a very talented and respected young man. Forgive me for prying into your life, but this is my niece you're planning to marry. I promised her mother on her deathbed, I would give my life to keep her beautiful little angel safe."

My heart was moved by Uncle Frank's compassion as he spoke of his love for my mother and me. At last, I thought I finally understand my uncle's obsession with my life, and it made me love him even more.

Johnny spoke up, "I understand completely, Mr. Salerno, and I would expect no less from myself, if I were in your position."

Uncle Frank interrupted, "Let's stop being so formal, John, please call me Frank."

"Thank you, Frank, and let me assure you, my intention for Christy is honorable. I love her with all my heart."

As I sat there listening to the two men I loved most in the world talk about my future, I felt so safe and secure. I knew nothing in the world could hurt me as long as Johnny and Uncle Frank were by my side. 'Oh boy, how naive I was!'

Uncle Frank said, "All I ask of the two of you is that you hold off on the wedding until after you finish your summer tour, Christy. And by that time John, you will have completed this year's baseball season. I also request that the both of you, please, allow me to take care of all the wedding plans as my wedding gift to you and I hope to have the honor of giving the beautiful bride away."

Johnny smiled, "That sounds agreeable to me, Frank." Turning toward me, "As long as it's okay with you, angel?"

"That sounds wonderful to me too, Uncle Frank, all I ask is my tour schedule be planned to correspond with Johnny's baseball schedule."

"I think I can manage that, baby."

We finished dinner, then talked some more over coffee in Uncle Frank's study. As we were getting ready to leave, Uncle Frank warmly embraced me, "I love you, Christy, and my only concern is your happiness." He took Johnny's hand in his and embraced him with the other arm, "You be good to my little girl son, and welcome to the family." He hugged me again, "By the way, good luck tomorrow with the audition."

"Oh my God," I replied with surprise. "I totally forgot about the audition for 'Samantha's Father.'"

"Well, I hope you're ready for it."

"I'm ready for it, Uncle Frank, but I'm not going to try out for the part."

"You're not going to the audition?" Uncle Frank asked, with a look of surprise.

"Uncle Frank, I really don't want to take the part anymore. All I want to do is get through the summer and then marry Johnny."

Uncle Frank looked at me strangely, "Well, if that is what will make you happy, then you have my blessings." He hugged us again and we walked out the door.

Johnny and I were so happy when we left Frank's that evening. We had our whole lives ahead of us and fate was smiling on us.

That summer was incredible. We traveled the country together. Johnny played ball like a god and I sang my heart out to him. Johnny didn't lose a single game he pitched that summer, and I was there cheering him on every step of the way. The magic of our love seemed to touch the whole nation. We were America's golden couple. We were in every newspaper and on the cover of every magazine in every corner store. Wherever we went, cheering crowds mobbed us and fan letters poured in from all over the country. America loved us, and we loved America. We could do no wrong. We were living a fantasy.

By the time the Mets won their way to the pennant that year, Johnny was the crowning star of the games. At the same time, my career was soaring with 'Johnny's Love' at the top of the record charts the whole summer. My concerts were bringing in record crowds and the money kept rolling in. The amount of money I made that summer was staggering! I couldn't believe one person could make that much money in four months. But that was not my concern. I left that part to my business manager, 'Uncle Frank.'

I was in love!

The summer finally led us to the pennant playoffs. It was September 24th, 1973. The fifth inning of the seventh game of the pennant series was being played. The Mets were playing the Cardinals. The game was being played in New York and my Johnny was pitching. The score was one to nothing, the Met's favor. Johnny was pitching a perfect game up to that point. The tension was high between the players. It had been a hard fought playoff and this was the game that would lead one of these extraordinary teams to the World Series. Joe Rosa was at bat for the Cardinals. There was, what seemed to be, a personal battle being played out on the field between Johnny and Joe throughout the playoffs. Joe was a powerhouse home-run hitter and every time he came up against Johnny, he kept him from hitting even one ball. When Johnny pitched the third ball, it was a wild one. The ball hurdled through the air and hit Joe in the leg. The battle turned physical. Joe ran out on the field with the bat in his hand and swung it at Johnny with all his might. Johnny ducked the bat and jumped on Joe. Both teams ran out onto the field and leaped on them both. I jumped to my feet and screamed in horror, "Johnny! Johnny! Oh My God! Johnny!"

The battle seemed endless. I stood there helpless, frantically looking just to catch a glimpse of Johnny in the midst of these thundering gladiators. Finally, the dust cleared and Johnny emerged unscathed. My heart leaped when I saw him and the crowd went wild. Johnny brushed himself off, picked up his cap, placed it on his head and blew me a kiss with two fingers. *I melted*!

He composed himself and continued the game. Joe Rosa was unbelievably barred from the game for only two innings. In the eighth inning, they were up against one another again. Only this time Joe got what he was after, a home run. The crowd booed as Joe ran the bases. The score was now one to one in the eighth inning, and Steve Grady was at the plate for the Mets. Ralph Lowne was pitching for the Cardinals and doing a hell of a job. Johnny and Ralph had been pitching the whole game. Then Steve slammed the ball over center field for a home run. The crowd went wild again. It was now two to one, our favor. The Cardinals were up at bat. It finally came down to two outs, when the Cardinal's manager called time out. To our surprise, a lineup change was announced and Joe Rosa was up at bat. You could hear a pin drop with the first pitch. "Strike one," shouted the umpire and the crowd screamed. "Strike two," shouted the ump and the crowd screamed again.

The stadium was breathless as Johnny wound up for the third pitch.

"Strike three! You're out!" screamed the ump and the whole place exploded.

The entire team ran out to Johnny, grabbed him and flung him in the air. They carried him around the field screaming and poured champagne all over him. As we screamed, the crowd began to jump onto the field and chase after them. All at once there was a mass of humanity right in front of me. I could see the team go into the dugout and Johnny was out of sight. I sat there for a few moments just crying. I was so proud of him that day and I loved him so much.

I finally made my way to the lockers and waited there with the press for our hero to emerge. Then, there he was, my Johnny coming down the hall toward the waiting room. We ran to one another and I leaped into his open arms. He embraced me, swung me around in the air and shouted for all to hear, "I love you angel!"

I held his arm as the press swarmed us. He was the man of the hour. The entire team came running out from the lockers. When they reached us, they screamed and showered us with champagne. We were soaked. We finally left the press behind and headed for our limo. We were escorted out of the stadium by four police cars with sirens wailing. The car arrived at the penthouse at 5:20pm. We needed a quick respite before heading to the Plaza Hotel for dinner and the celebration party, which was to begin at 8:00pm. As we entered the penthouse Johnny picked me up and carried me to the bathroom kissing me all the way. He placed me down laughing, "You're a little sticky, angel."

I looked at us and began to laugh. We hugged and kissed then took our sticky clothing off and jumped into the shower together. I scrubbed his body and he scrubbed mine. After we rinsed off, he picked me back up still dripping wet and carried me to the bed.

He was so incredibly hot! He was like a wild beast that just killed its opponent for the prize, **'and I was that prize**.' He devoured my flesh over and over again. It was exquisite.

As we dressed, I began to feel lightheaded, like I was going to faint. I reached for the bedpost to hold myself up. Johnny grabbed me just as I was beginning to fall, and as he laid me on the bed, I could faintly hear him say, "Christy, baby! Christy, wake up!" I slowly came back as Johnny held me, "Are you all right, baby?"

"I think so, Johnny." I answered slightly dazed.

"What happened, angel?"

"I don't know I just felt weak. It must be from all the excitement of the day."

"Do you feel all right now?"

"Yes, I'm feeling much better. Let's get going. We can't keep your public waiting, you know."

"We don't have to go any place if you're not feeling well."

"I'm fine now, baby." I answered reassuringly as I gentle squeeze to his shoulder. 'And I was.'

Then it was off to the Plaza. As the limo drove us through town that night, there were people all over the streets. The city was alive with excitement. There were celebrations everywhere. The limo pulled up to the Plaza and we climbed out. We entered the ballroom to a standing ovation. It was Johnny's ovation. I turned to him and curtsied then he bowed to me and escorted me to our table. The cameras were lighting up the room. Steve and Kathy were seated at our table that night and we were glad to see them. We had at least ten different toasts to Johnny and the team before dinner even arrived. By the time dinner was over and the band began to play, we all had plenty to drink, and once again, **especially** Kathy.

Johnny and I danced and danced. The night was divine and our love seemed to outshine the brightest star. Then Steve and Kathy danced between us and we changed partners. I was dancing in Steve's arms, but I could not keep my mind or eyes off Johnny.

As Steve and I danced, I began to feel slightly weak again, so I excused myself and headed for the ladies' room. I washed my face, took a few deep breaths and began to feel better. After a moment, I put my face back on and headed back to Johnny. As I entered the room, I could see Johnny across the well-lit, crowded dance floor. He was uncomfortably attempting to hold back Kathy's drunken advances and Steve seemed embarrassed by her behavior. As I watched her hang her arms around Johnny's neck and begin to whisper into his ear, I also noticed everyone else in the room witnessing this behavior and trying to act as if none of it was taking place. Steve turned and walked out of the room. I on the other hand had fire in my eyes as I walked over to them, grabbed Kathy and pulled her off Johnny. I held her tightly by the wrist, looked her straight in the face and with a sharp tone which echoed throughout the ballroom, "If I ever catch you putting the moves on Johnny again, I'll beat the crap out of you!"

She gave me an evil look, "I'm sorry if you got the wrong impression, Christy." as she pulled her hand from mine, "Don't flatter yourself, I'm not after your man." With that she turned and walked out the door.

Johnny immediately took me by the hand and with a silly smile, "I think you better just dance, 'little lady,' and cool down."

As we danced, "Was she coming onto you? Or was I just acting like a jealous fool?"

"She sure as hell was coming onto me, angel, believe me," Johnny answered with a slight snicker. "But you have nothing to worry about with me, I'm all yours." Then he held me tightly as we danced one more dance.

It was 1:00am when we arrived back home. We were physically exhausted and emotionally charged. Johnny took me in his arms and held me ever so close. Looking lovingly into my eyes, "We're almost there, Christy. Just think, in two weeks you and I will have won the World Series and we will be wed. We'll have the most romantic honeymoon you could imagine. Oh baby, I can't wait to carry you off to our dream. Then we will begin our lives angel, our lives together."

"I love you so much, Johnny."

We slowly walked out arm in arm onto the balcony, "Look at it, angel. Isn't this the most beautiful city you've ever seen?"

The city lights were filling the sky, "Oh, Johnny, It is beautiful."

Johnny kissed me, "And tonight it's all ours."

As we stood there in each other's arms gazing out over this beautiful city, on this glorious night, we knew our love was eternal. We embraced passionately and Johnny slowly began to unhook the back of my gown and it fell to the floor. He slid my bra off my shoulders to expose my breast to the warm night air. As he began to lick my neck I felt a chill run up my spine. He squeezed my breasts together with both his masculine hands and softly buried his face in my flesh so closely he could hear the throbbing of my heart. He slid his head back and forth licking and kissing both my nipples with such warmth and tenderness I thought I would explode. I felt so much like a woman as he grabbed me up in his arms, laid me down on the cool carpeting, and gently finished undressing me. His tongue was hot as he moved down to my navel. Sliding my legs apart he brought his smooth warm lips to my quivering essence, slowly moving his tongue round and round until passionately and wildly he drove it deep within me.

I moaned, "Oh God, Johnny. Johnny, oh Johnny," I pulled him up and began to rip his clothing off. I kissed him madly, "Make love to me, Johnny. Please make love to me." I wanted him so badly.

Slowly he placed the head of his massive manhood gently into the opening of my surrendering body. As he slid deeper, harder and faster into my fiery soul, I cried out in pure ecstasy, "Oh God, Johnny, I love you."

He screamed, "Oh, baby!" as we both simultaneously exploded in a whirlwind of passion and pleasure.

The weight of his body collapsed on mine and we held each other tightly with the sweat of our passion dripping from our bodies. After a while, I slipped out of his embrace. I returned to his arms with a damp washcloth and towel. I washed the sweat from his body that night, and it felt so right. I felt I could never love him more than I did at that very moment. I laid my head on his shoulder and we drifted off to sleep surrounded by the city lights.

We woke up at 7:00am that morning to the persistent

messages from Uncle Frank. He wanted me to call him right away. It was very important. I finally got up, brushed the hair from my face and answered the phone, "Hello, Uncle Frank," I said with a half yawn. "What's wrong?"

"I have to meet with you as soon as you can fly out here."

"Where are you? What's going on, Uncle Frank?" I asked again with concern.

"I'm at the Vegas house and I can't speak about it over the phone. That's why it's imperative I see you tonight. I can't leave here now I'm not feeling well enough, otherwise I'd come to you."

"All right, Uncle Frank, I'll catch the first flight out."

"What's going on, baby?" Johnny asked as I hung up the phone.

"I don't know. That was Uncle Frank. He sounded as if there was something wrong and he needs to see me as soon as possible. He can't leave Vegas so he wants me to fly there today." I hugged him, "I'm sorry baby, but I have to go."

Reassuringly, "I know angel," playfully he lifted me up, "What would you say if I said I'd like to come with you?"

"Could you?" I asked as he placed my feet back on the floor.

"Sure I could. I have the next two days off and I'm all yours."

I booked a 10:00am flight to Vegas for that morning. I called Uncle Frank, told him what time to expect us, and he said he'd have a car waiting.

I was so glad Johnny was with me because my mind went wild with crazy thoughts wondering what the problem could be. During the flight Johnny could see I was concerned. He tenderly took my hand, "Don't worry, Christy. Whatever it is, we'll handle it together."

"I love you, Johnny, but what if it's his health, what do I do? He had a severe heart attack only two years ago. I almost lost him then."

"Try to stop worrying honey. I'll give you some of my mom's famous advice for a good case of the worries. Oh, let me see," putting his hand to his cheek, "She would say something like, 'try not to fix something before you know it's broken.' My mom is filled with little ditties like that."

I smiled as I gazed up into his eyes, "Oh well, I'll figure it out tomorrow. She's wonderful, your mother." We laughed then I placed my head on his shoulder and we stayed that way until the plane landed.

It was 5:00pm when the limo pulled up to the main door of the thirty-three story building which was the headquarters to Frank's empire. When we entered Frank's office, he walked over to me, put his hands on both my shoulders and exclaimed, "Thank God you're here baby, it's almost too late." Turning to Johnny, "Hello, John. I'm sorry but I'm going to have to ask you to wait in the outer office while I speak with Christy."

Johnny looked at me, "Do you want me to stay with you?"

"Yes, I do." I looked at Uncle Frank, "Johnny's my fiancé and I don't want to keep anything from him."

"All right then. Come sit down." He headed toward his desk.

We took the two seats in front of his mammoth desk. He opened the top drawer, took out a large thick envelope and with a wide smile on his face, tossed it to me, "You got it, baby!"

I opened the envelope and inside was the script to 'Samantha's Father'. For a second the blood raced through my veins with excitement. Then I looked at Johnny and remembered our dream. I looked back at Uncle Frank, "You called us out here for this? I thought it was your health! How could you do that to me Uncle Frank? You couldn't tell me this over the phone?"

Johnny glanced down at the package, saw what it was and said nothing.

"I'm sorry I didn't tell you, honey, but I had to get you here. You have to start studying this script right away. Filming begins in four days in LA." He tossed me another envelope, "I also wanted to give this to you myself, baby. You have officially been nominated for an Academy Award."

I didn't even open the envelope. I was so taken aback over getting the part of Samantha, all I could say was, "How is this possible? I didn't even try out for the part."

Frank looked straight into my eyes, "I did it, baby. I did it for you. I called in a lot of favors for this one and we got it!"

I reached over and grabbed Johnny's hand for strength, "Uncle

Frank, I don't want the part."

Frank got up from his chair, walked over to the window, then turned back to face us again, "What do you mean, you don't want this part? Do you know what this part will mean for your career? Do you know or even appreciate what I went through to get you this part?"

"Yes, Uncle Frank. I do know what this part means. I also appreciate what you had to do to get me this part and I love you for it. But after Johnny and I are married, I'm not going back to work. We are going to start our lives together and that doesn't include performing."

Frank walked up to where I was seated, slammed his fist down on the desk right in front of my face, "That's what you think! You have two years left on your contract with me young lady, and you're going to take this part!"

Johnny stood up, "I've heard enough of this. If Christy says she's not taking the part, she's not!" taking my hand, "Let's get the hell out of here Christy."

Uncle Frank yelled, "Don't you dare walk out on me, Christy! You signed a contract and I am holding you to it."

Johnny becoming visibly angered, "You can take your contract and shove it, Frank!" And we walked out the door.

We headed for the airport and caught the first flight back to New York. After the frenzy of trying to get a flight back home eased, Johnny lovingly put his arms around me, "Christy, my angel, I love you. You made me so happy and proud today, when I heard you defend yourself to your uncle. And when I see what it is you are willing to give up for me, it brings tears to my eyes." He kissed me gently, "Baby, are you sure you can leave all this behind to raise a family with me?"

Oh God, my heart melted. I cuddled close and with tears in my eyes, "Johnny, my sweet, wonderful, Johnny. I love you more than life." We finished the flight in each other's arms.

It was 2:00am when we finally climbed into bed. We were physically exhausted, emotionally disgusted and totally in love. I took the phone off the hook and for the first time since the day we met, we fell asleep without making love.

We were awakened at 10:00am by the continual ringing of the doorbell. I threw on my robe and ran to the door. When I opened it, there stood a uniformed officer who thrust an envelope into my partially opened hand and departed without uttering a single word. Not even good morning. I stood there a moment, thinking, "What the hell was that?"

Johnny came out of the bedroom, "Who was that?"

"A police officer, I guess. He stuck this envelope in my hand and left."

"Well, it's addressed to you, maybe you should open it," he chuckle.

I kissed Johnny's cheek as I started to open it, "Good morning, baby. Come on in the kitchen, I'll put on some coffee."

As we entered the kitchen, I was reading the letter, "It's a summons! It basically says, **'I have to appear in court at the City Hall building, room 717 at 2:00pm this afternoon for an informal hearing in front of Judge Christopher.'** It's regarding a suit brought against me by dear Uncle Frank, for breach of contract!" I took a breath, "I can't believe this, it goes on to say, **'if you fail to appear, there will be a bench warrant issued for your arrest.'**" I threw the paper on the floor, "I still can't believe this!"

Johnny held me, "Calm down, Christy. It's going to be okay."

"I hope so, Johnny, I hope so." I answered slightly giggling.

He led me to the table, "Here, you sit down and I'll make the coffee." As Johnny put the coffee on, "How in the world did he get a summons in one day?"

"He can get almost anything he wants in this city. He has that kind of clout."

"Why don't we get cleaned up and go for something to eat. Then I'll come to court with you."

"That sounds great to me, Johnny," with a sigh of relief.

We headed for the shower and as I passed the phone, I placed it back on the receiver. By the time we got out of the shower there were five phone calls for Johnny; two from Steve, two from his coach and one from Stephan Brown the owner of the New York Mets. All saying call now!

I looked at Johnny and I was scared, "He's getting to you now."

He hugged me wearing a smile, "Let's not fix something we don't know is broken," throwing his hands up in the air, "Or something like that," and we both started to laugh.

I couldn't believe he was able to bring some light to such a horrendously dark moment. I just started to kiss him all over his face and we laughed again. In the midst of our fears, we chose to cling to the innocence of our love. After we composed ourselves, Johnny picked up the phone and called Stephan Brown, 'who guess what,' had to meet with Johnny in his office at 2pm promptly 'which by the way,' was across town from City Hall. Johnny hung up the phone, turned to me, "I guess we're on our own, angel," hugging me confidently, "We can do this, Christy. I know we can."

As he said these words, I knew I could be strong without him by my side. Johnny and I were one, whether we were together or not and I was not going to let my uncle intimidate me any longer.

We finished dressing and went for lunch. After lunch we kissed and made plans to meet back at my place immediately after our meetings. We kissed again and went our separate ways.

When we parted that day, we took with us the utmost confidence we would return victoriously. Unfortunately, I was totally dazed when I returned home at 8:00 that evening and to my dismay, Johnny had not yet arrived. I took my clothes off, threw them on the bedroom floor, and headed for the shower. I felt like I had to wash the stench of the afternoon's meeting off my body. After showering I dried off, threw on my robe and headed for the sofa to wait for Johnny.

When Johnny opened the door he looked like a little boy who just received an old fashioned southern thrashing. I stretched my arms out to him, "Come over here, sweetie."

For the longest time we just held each other like two wounded pups. After a while, Johnny said to me with an exhausted tone, "How are you, angel?"

"I could be better."

"Okay, you tell me what happened, and then I'll tell you."

"I don't know if you're ready for this, but here it is," I began with a disgusted tone, "It seems I have no choice but to be on a plane to LA tomorrow morning."

"And if you're not, then what?"

I took a deep breath, "Johnny, my love, first I'll be sued for thirty-million dollars for breach of contract. Second, I will be totally penny-less because Uncle Frank managed to trick me into signing over power of attorney for all of my finances to him." I started to cry, "Third, he would have you pulled out of the World Series games." I held him tightly and with tears still falling from my eyes, "Fourth, if I marry you, all of your financial assets will be frozen to pay off my debts. Including in my uncle's own words, *our little dream house.*"

"That fucker!" Johnny exclaimed angrily, "I got the same thing. We can't let them get away with this baby, we just can't."

"What are you saying, Johnny?"

"Exactly, what I'm saying. What if we just say to hell with them? I'll drop out of the game and we'll take off together."

"Oh God, Johnny, try to be realistic here. We'll be letting him steal all of our dreams if we do that."

Looking slightly puzzled, "What do you mean?"

"Johnny, the World Series, it's your dream; our, dream. Our family on our farm; it's our dream. If we leave, we lose it all. Baby, for a lousy two years it's not worth it. He can only hold me to the contract for two more years and I'm willing to play his game that long, so I can have you and we can have our dreams come true."

"I guess you're right, angel." Johnny put his sleepy head on my shoulder, "So what time are you leaving in the morning?"

I kissed his cheek, "four o'clock honey."

This was the second night we both just fell asleep. It was 3:00am when I got off the sofa with Johnny. I covered him with a quilt and went to clean up. It was 3:45am when I kissed a very sleepy Johnny goodbye. I left a note on my pillow saying, **"I love you, Johnny, with all my heart and I will be thinking of you every moment of the day. Baby, I will call you every free second I have. All my love to you, honey. Love You, Christy."**

Then I was on my way to LA and the shooting of 'Samantha's Father.' The schedule for the next couple of weeks was unbelievable. Johnny was with the team almost 24 hours a day. They were playing the LA Dodgers, so at least I knew Johnny would be coming out to the West Coast. As for me, my shooting schedule was intense. They seemed to be deliberately keeping me hopping. I had ten complete costume changes in one day. The only time I got to see Johnny was at a game. The only place I got to touch Johnny was in the dugout for a few minutes before the team was rushed out to a locked hotel room. The team was forbidden to have any social life at all until after the series was over. In the dugout before the opening game, Johnny gave me a present. I opened it and saw a pendant so beautiful it took my breath away. It was a square, aquamarine stone with baguette diamonds all around it.

"Johnny, it's beautiful!" I exclaimed.

"I chose it because the stone matches the color of your eyes," he replied with an adoring look.

I kissed him passionately, "I love it, Johnny."

Just then, the manager called Johnny back into the dugout and he was out of my reach once more. Johnny pitched the opening game in L.A. that day and I screamed and cheered as he dominantly won the game. The Dodgers won the next two games. The next game the Mets won, making the score two to two. The fifth game was to be held in New York and Johnny was pitching. I was not able to make it to that game and much to my dismay Johnny lost the first game he had pitched since the day we met. This made the score three to two, Dodgers favor, and the next game was crucial.

Johnny finally called me at 2:00am and he sounded so sad, "Christy, I need you. I can't make it without you anymore," started to cry, "I lost the game today, angel, and you weren't there."

My heart hurt deeply as I heard him crying, "Johnny, please don't be sad. I love you so much and it's killing me not to be with you."

"Oh, baby," he replied as we cried together, "I love you, Christina. I love you."

That was the first time Johnny called me by my full name. I felt as if he was crying to me as his equal, because we were both in need of strength, and we gave it to each other over the phone that long dark night.

"Honey, we have to be strong. Remember what you said to me? We can make it through anything together."

"I know, angel! I know. Christy, baby, if we win Wednesday's game I'll be pitching Thursday at 9:00pm. Christy, will you please, please, be here with me? I need you to be here! Baby, this time, I'm the one who's scared."

"Oh yes, my Johnny! I'll be there, baby, I'll be there, I promise."

We fell asleep on the phone that night to the sounds of each other's breathing. It was 6:00am when I woke up. I told Johnny I would call the airport as soon as I hung up. I called and reserved a 1:00pm flight for that Wednesday. I called Johnny back to let him know, and then it was off to the studio. It was Wednesday morning and I was in the middle of shooting a scene when Johnny had an emergency page sent for me. I ran to the phone, "Johnny, what's wrong?"

With panic in his voice, "Christy, they've changed the line-up and I'm pitching! The game is tonight at 9:00pm!"

I looked at my watch, "Honey, don't worry I'll be there! I love you, Johnny." I hung up the phone and called the airport. I told them who I was, gave them a credit card number and hired a private jet to New York. I ran out of the studio, jumped in the rental car and sped to the airport. Just as I got there, I heard my name being paged again. I ran to the phone thinking it was Johnny. My heart was pounding as I answered it, but the voice on the other end was unrecognizable.

I heard, "Christy, it's me, your cousin Anthony. It's Dad, he's had a massive heart attack and he's dying."

My head began to whirl, "Are you sure, Anthony?" I asked with a disbelieving tone.

"Christy," Anthony said with a tone of urgency. "If you want to see him once more before he dies, you'd better come now!"

I looked down at my watch, "Where is he?"

"He's at the Vegas home."

I was torn. What do I do? I looked at my watch again and

figured if I spent ten minutes with Uncle Frank, I would still have an hour to spare. So I went for it. I had the jet go to Vegas first. I had a town-car waiting and I was off to see Uncle Frank. When I arrived at the mansion, I ran to the door and flung it open. I looked around and could not find anyone. I ran up the towering spiral staircase straight to Frank's room and found him standing there. I walked up to him and with all my might slapped him across the face and angrily shouted, "What kind of sick joke is this?"

He began to laugh at me, "You'll never make it to the game now, he'll lose and he'll hate you for not being there, because you will have let that sap down."

"You monster," I shouted! "Why are you doing this to us?"

He screamed at me, "I love you, Christy, and if I can't have you, no one will."

I stepped back throwing my hands in the air while screaming, "I'm your niece, what the hell are you talking about?!"

He slapped me with all his strength knocking me to the floor and shouted, "You're not my niece. I own you!"

I scrambled off the floor, "What are you saying? Am I your daughter?"

"No," he answered wickedly."

"If I'm not your niece or your daughter, who the hell am I?"

"No, Christy, you're not my niece or my daughter. You're mine," Frank said emphatically!

I screamed, "Why do you keep saying that?! Who am I?! Who are my parents?!"

A look of complete insanity radiated from him, "I was in love with your mother. I loved her with all my heart. But she was like you, she didn't love me back."

I stood there trembling, "Who was my mother?"

He gave me an evil look, "You don't need to know that."

I ran over to him, grabbed his arm and with hatred in my voice screamed, **"I DO NEED TO KNOW! I DO!"**

He began to cry like a baby, "I loved your mother. She was a rising star with golden possibilities and we were in love. Until she met **him**!"

"Who were they? Frank, tell me!" I screamed again.

"They had an affair when she was just becoming well known. He was a young state senator from New England. He got her pregnant, but they couldn't be together. She couldn't find it in her heart to kill the child, so she had it. You're that child."

"Is my mother alive," I asked with pain in my voice?

"No, she took her life with an overdose of sleeping pills."

"Is my father alive?" I asked as tears began to flow.

"No, he was assassinated," he replied ruthlessly.

I screamed again, "Who were they? Tell me Frank! Tell me!"

With an enraged expression his jaw clinched, "Your mother was the 'queen of Hollywood' Marilyn Monrow and your father was once the President of the United States, John F. Kenney. And I'm the only person in the world still alive who knows that.

I backed away from him screaming, "Do you know what you're saying? Are you mad?" He grabbed me and tried to kiss me and I screamed, "Stop it, let me go! Let me go!"

As I struggled to break free from his arms he screamed in my face, "You're a **FORBIDDEN CHILD** Christina, and you're mine!"

I screamed and wildly fought my way out of his powerful grasp. I ran down the steps crying all the way, and as I ran, he screamed at me, "You can't leave, your mine! Come back here now! Come back here or you will never perform again!"

I opened the door and ran down to the car. I jumped in and sped away in hysterics. I tried desperately to calm down and compose myself before reaching the airport.

It was 4:00pm when I boarded the jet and was on my way to Johnny. During that very long flight to New York my mind was racing with thoughts of what Frank had said. "Could it be true? Am I truly the daughter of President Kenney and Marilyn Monrow?"

I finally stopped thinking of myself and my thoughts turned to Johnny. My heart almost stopped when it was 9:00pm and we still had half an hour to go before reaching New York. When the plane landed, I had a car waiting and I sped to the game. I turned on the radio and heard the announcer screaming, "The LA Dodgers have just won the World Series!" I cried out, "Oh God, no!"

By the time I arrived at the stadium it had started to rain

heavily. The parking lot was nearly empty. I sped through it madly looking for Johnny's car. When I spotted it, I sped up to it, slammed my foot on the brakes and screeched to a stop. I jumped out of the car into the pouring rain and ran with all my might through the parking lot to the player's entrance. I opened the door and ran down the cold dark hall. I stopped dead in my tracks when I saw him walking toward me. I grabbed him and cried, "Johnny, I'm so, so sorry, baby!" He became weak in my arms and we both fell to our knees.

He cried out, "I lost the game. I failed you. I lost the dream."

I held him so tightly on that cold floor and with desperation, "I'm here now, Johnny, I'm here."

All at once he pushed himself away from me and with disgust in his voice shouted, "Where were you, Christy? I looked for you! I needed you and you weren't there!"

"Johnny! I'm sorry I didn't make it, baby, but Frank . . ."

He cut me off in mid-sentence and as he stood up, he flung his arms in the air and shouted, "Frank! Frank! Frank! I can't take any more of Frank!" Then he turned and walked away from me.

I pleaded, "Johnny, please, I'm begging you." But he just kept walking away. As he moved out of sight, I fainted. I woke up two hours later in the hospital with my doctor standing over me. He smiled, "Good morning, Miss Valona."

I sat up, "What am I doing here?"

Still smiling, "You passed out last night, young lady. I think a woman in your condition should be a little less active."

I looked at him and started to laugh and laugh until finally I could say, "Are you telling me I'm pregnant?"

Still with that stupid smile, "Yes, you are."

I shook my head in disbelief, "Oh God! When you're screwed, you're screwed."

He thought I was nuts and wanted to have me psychologically evaluated, so I said, "Live through a day like I just had and then tell me that."

I signed out against the doctor's advice and left the hospital. As I headed home, I began to think about Johnny. In my heart I realized he loved me. I knew he was probably looking for me that very moment.

I stopped quickly at a florist shop and bought two dozen red roses with one white one in the middle. On the card I wrote, **"Johnny, my beloved, we're going to have a baby!"**

With anticipation, I ran into my penthouse looking for Johnny, but he wasn't there. I drove to his condo in Tarry-town and my heart leaped when I saw his car. I grabbed the flowers and ran up to the door. I opened it and ran in yelling, "Johnny! Johnny my love!"

My heart crumbled when I burst into the bedroom and found him lying in bed with Kathy beneath him. I screamed, "You bastard!" as I drew my hands to my face, "How could you, Johnny? How could you?"

I threw the flowers right in his shocked face and ran out crying. **It was horrible. I was devastated**. I cried frantically as I sped wildly through the streets. I rounded a corner, lost control and plunged down a six-foot embankment to an abrupt stop. I sat there crying in the dark for six hours. As the sun rose, a police car spotted me and back to the hospital I went.

While I was there, everything went through my mind. Johnny, Frank, my mother, my father, my career. They were all gone now. I didn't know what was out there for me, or for a child. Then I thought of the possibility of my child being raised by someone as sick as Frank. That thought, at that moment, caused me to harden my heart so much, that without a second thought, I had one of the first legal abortion performed in our nation.

I came home from the hospital the next day and lay in bed for two days crying. I was surprised on that second day when Johnny walked into the room. He came over, knelt down beside me, took my hands in his and with tears of love in his eyes, "Christy, please forgive me. I'm so sorry. Please tell me you still love me?"

I grabbed him tightly and cried, "I forgive you, Johnny! I love you!" We were back in each other's arms and we felt the love run so deep again.

His eyes began to glow and with an excited tone, "I can't believe we're going to have a baby!"

Instantly, tremendous pain shot through my heart as I began

to cry even harder. Only now they were tears of sadness and with my voice cracking, "*Johnny, I had an abortion.*"

He looked at me and screamed in horror, "You killed my baby? Christina, how could you kill my baby?"

I had no answer, for there was none. I looked at him and saw so much hatred and anger in his eyes that I knew he could never forgive me. I couldn't stand to see him look at me like that, so I screamed at the top of my voice, "Get out! Get out!"

With tears flowing down his cheeks, he turned, walked to the door, opened it and gazed back at me. Then he turned again, slammed the door and walked out of my life. ***My heart and soul died in that split second. And there was no innocence to be found.***

CHAPTER 2. THE AFTERMATH

It was December 10th, 1973, my nineteenth birthday, when finally it all crumbled. At 8:00am I received a call from my attorney informing me the IRS had decided today at 10:00am would be the day they were to arrive to seize my penthouse with all of its contents, for back taxes. He said, "They want your car and the title at that time as well."

I tried to tell him this car was my baby, "They can take my home, my jewelry, my clothes, and my money, but not my car!"

It was a 1972 Pontiac Grand Prix, and was beautiful. It was emerald green with a black vinyl roof. I loved it and Frank hated it, which made me love it even more.

I told him, "This is the first car I bought on my own and I picked it out by myself. Frank picked out everything I ever owned, except for this car and he has taken it all back, but I'll be damned if he'll get my car!"

I hung up the phone and took the only cash I had from under my mattress, which was sixty-six- thousand -dollars. I packed whatever I could fit into two suitcases, grabbed one bottle of champagne, carried them to **my car** and took off. **I HAD, HAD ENOUGH!**

You see, my life was pure hell after Johnny and I broke up. I stayed in my room for seventeen days; I only ate a few bites I could manage to keep down. I could hear the messages on the answering machine, but I could not utter a word. In the midst of the madness of those seventeen days, I felt such shame, I wanted to die! "What had I done?" I asked myself over and over, "How could I have taken the life of our child?"

In the depths of my anguish, I took a blade to my throat and began to slice it. The blood from the first puncture began to drip down the edge of the cold steel blade and touched my hand. I began to shake, I threw the knife across the room and cried, "Oh God I can't do it!" I thought, "You coward! You can kill your own baby without a second thought, but you can't take the life of the murderess." I flew across the bedroom, grabbed the knife and put it to my throat. This time I meant it! I began to slice my throat once again, then I screamed out, "I can't!" as I threw the blade as hard as I could. It struck the mirror, shattering it into a million pieces all over the room. I looked at it, and then I looked at the wall where the mirror had been and I could not see myself. There was nothing there, and I just began to laugh hysterically as I said to myself, "You decide to stay, then you give yourself seven more years of this shit, by breaking the freaken mirror." With that I laughed some more. When I finally stopped laughing, I left that bedroom and decided to make it my life's goal to get Frank!

When I finally listened to my messages, I found out I was in deep **shit.** It seemed I had checks bouncing all over town. **BIG ONES!** I had a seventy-thousand dollar American Express bill for chartering a jet. All of my credit cards were worthless and from out of the blue came the IRS. They were after me for the three-hundred-thousand-dollars in back taxes for 1972 and I hadn't even thought about 1973, yet. Paramount Studios was suing me to the tune of three-million-dollars for walking off the set of 'Samantha's Father' and to top it all off, my checking and savings account balances were **ZERO**, thanks to Frank.

It also appeared that while I was incognito, the papers and the tabloids had a field day at my expense. They read, "**Christy, the Dragon Women who slew the white knight's heart, at his defeat!**" or "**The Temptress, who brought down the New York Mets!**"

All this wonderful press did wonders for my public affairs. I was shunned from the hearts of most New Yorkers, and every time I appeared in court for a summons, it was more than apparent.

When I tried to get work in the field of my dreams, it appeared that had been taken from me too, for I could work nowhere in the entertainment industry. And, on one of my exceptional days, I received a very apologetic note from the chairperson for the Institute of the Academy Awards stating, **"We regret to inform you of a miscount in the votes for the 1973 awards nominations. It appears that your nomination for 'Blue Lady' was one of those that were miscounted. When recounting the votes for your performance, it was not considered to be of Academy Award standards."**

After I read it I crumpled the letter, threw it over my shoulders with a shrug, snapped my fingers and said, "Oh well! I'll figure it out tomorrow."

Then there was my visit from Barbara. She came over sometime around Thanksgiving. I was lying in bed, half a-wake at 1:00pm when the doorbell rang and rang. I finally got up and staggered over to the door. I peeked through the peephole expecting to see a uniformed bearer of 'good news', when there she was.

I opened the door and she said, "What the hell is the matter with you? You don't know how to work your answering machine?" She hugged me, "I'm sorry I haven't been here sooner, Christy, but it's a 'fucking' man's world, and even I couldn't sneak a way to see you before this."

With half a yawn, "Come on in Barbara."

She gave me a strange look and followed me into the very messy living room, "So tell me, Christy, what's going on?"

I leaned over, tiredly kissed her cheek, and bewilderingly shook my head, "It's good to see ya, Barb."

I proceeded to tell her everything. I needed to talk, I needed a friend, I needed to be able to try to trust someone and thank God, it was Barbara! She told me how Frank brought all his muscle to bear on the entertainment industry in order to keep me out and her hands were tied as well. If she, or anyone else in the business tried to give me work, there would be retaliations.

I understood all too well what Barbara was saying that day. At that moment, I decided **'no man'** will ever hold my life in his hands again, and I would live **MY LIFE by MY RULES!**

After Barbara left that day, I found a white envelope in my

bathroom. I opened it and there was one-hundred-thousand dollars cash in it, with a note which read," **Use it with good judgment, Christy, Love Barbara. P.S. don't forget we have a dinner date."**

The first thing I did was pay off all my bounced checks. Then I stuck sixty–six-thousand dollars under my mattress.

So when I pulled away from my Park Avenue penthouse on my nineteenth birthday at 8:30am I was saying goodbye to the past and hello to the future. I drove endlessly that day. It wasn't until 11:00pm that I decided I had to stop and feed my hunger. I pulled into a truck stop off Route 95 south of Thompsonville, South Carolina. I filled the tank with gas for the second time that day, then headed for the restaurant.

When I walked in I felt a little uncomfortable to say the least. The place was filled with southern truck drivers, all looking at me. I ordered a hot pot roast dinner with all the trimmings, I was hungry! While I waited for the feast, I noticed a little jukebox on the wall, right at my booth. As I flipped the nob with my thumb to examine the choices, a title caught my attention. It read, "The Love I lost." I popped a quarter in the slot and punched B8. I could hear through the crackling of the speakers, a male voice singing a country western ballad. He was singing a story of how he had lost the love of his life. It told of his heartbreak and pain, and how years from now he'd still be wondering why. As I listened to his pain, I could feel mine, and I knew I would always feel that void.

She was a cute little waitress in a grease spotted pink uniform who recused me from my memories with a meal fit for a king. As I began to devour my pi'ece de re'sistance, I couldn't help but overhear the conversation going on at the booth next to mine.

It sounded something like this, "Boy she's hot!" One of them said, with mustard hanging off his six-inch beard, which lay on his three-hundred-pound belly.

Then the really dirty skinny one, with the two black teeth, "Shit man, she looks a little like that Hollywood slut everybody is talking about; "You know?" "Christy something, she's the bitch who destroyed that ball player's career. You know? What's his name?"

I wanted to crawl under the table and die. I thought, "Oh my God, even people like that, feel like this about me." I suddenly lost my appetite. I got up and as inconspicuously as possible, walked over to the waitress, stuck a fifty-dollar bill in her hand and walked out.

I found myself gazing out the window of my room at Motel 6, off route 95 at 2:00am. Boy was I depressed. I thought, "How the hell in the world am I going to be able to start a new life?"

The room was dark behind me as I looked over the pool, in the center court of the motel, filled with these thoughts. Out of the corner of my eye, I saw a flash of gold glistening behind me. I felt a chill as I turned around quickly into a dark room. I saw nothing. I moved over to the light sitting on the desk and flicked it on. I looked down and there on the desk was a Bible with a brilliant gold cross carved into the center of it. With curiosity, I flipped the cover open to see an atlas of the world. I could see where someone had taken a red pen and circled the city of Rome. Underneath was written in quotes; "YOURS." I closed the cover, knelt down on my knees, made the sign of the cross, "Lord I don't know how to go on from here so please help me. And thanks for the Bible; I'm taking it with me." Then I climbed into the bed and passed out.

The next morning I was out of the Motel by 9:00am. I drove to the town, stopped at the first record store I could find and purchased a copy of 'The Love I Lost.' Then I drove to the airport. As I pulled into the entrance of the parking lot there was an attendant giving out parking tickets. I took one from him, parked my car, and placed one half of the stub on the dashboard and the other half in my purse. With that I kissed the steering wheel, "I'll remember you, baby." Then I grabbed my belongings and headed into the terminal.

As I waited for the plane to depart, I went to the airport gift shop, purchased an envelope and addressed it to Johnny. I slipped the recording of 'The Love I Lost' and the ring which Johnny had given me into the envelope, sealed it and placed it in the mailbox.

Then I heard over the loud speaker, "All passengers for flight 221 to Rome will be boarding gate 17 in five minutes" **And I was off to Rome.**

CHAPTER 3. JIMMY'S CHAPTER

It was December 15th, 1973, when I started my new life in Rome. First, I changed my name to *'Christina Powers'* then cut my long black hair to just above my shoulders. I wasted no time in getting myself established. I rented a cute one bedroom fully furnished, basement apartment just north of the Coliseum that fit my budget perfectly. The next step was to find employment. Since I did not have much experience at anything I could think of, I took the first position offered to me, which was a waitress at the cafe only two blocks down the road. I was working the evening shift from 4 to 11pm and it was convenient because I could walk to work. The first week, I broke enough coffee cups to last a lifetime. By the end of my second week I was waitressing like a pro.

By the time I was finally established and self-supporting at a level I had to grow accustomed to, it was January 28th, 1974. But I still had sixty thousand dollars under my mattress.

For the first few months, I didn't make many new friends. My mastery of the Italian language, at the time didn't help my social life at all. When I tried to be sociable, unless we were talking about menu items, I didn't have much to say.

It was sometime in early June when I met Jimmy, my sweet Jimmy. He was so cute and funny I couldn't help but fall in love with him. He was a twenty-two-year old, five-foot eight-inch, one-hundred and twenty-pound, ball of energy. He had dark brown curly hair and deep brown eyes. *Boy was he sexy*!

It was a beautiful warm spring night, so after work I decided to go for a walk. The streets in downtown Rome were alive with people. It felt good to feel all the life and energy in the air. It brought back memories of a time past. As I strolled down the avenue around 1:00am, I began to hear the sound of music coming from the building on the corner. As I reached it, I could hear the rhythm more clearly. It was a rhythm I was not familiar with, but I found it very catchy. I gazed up at the neon sign, **"Rome One Discotheque."**

I decided to check it out. I entered the packed nightclub and headed straight for the bar. I couldn't help but notice there were no other women in the place. I thought, "This is strange," but I still took a seat at the bar. The style of the music was just too enticing for me to leave.

The bartender came over to me and shouted in English over the sounds of the music, "Hi, honey! Did you know this is a gay club?"

He screamed it with such dramatics, I felt like an idiot for not knowing. I shout back, "No, I didn't know. May I stay anyway?"

"Sure honey, what can I get you?"

"A White Russian please."

With that he flicked his right hand, just from his wrist at me and shouted, "A White Russian! La, de, da.! You see this crowd, how about a Bud?"

I gave him a slightly puzzled look, as I chuckled to myself, "Sure, a Bud would be fine."

When he returned with my Bud, he introduced himself to me, "Hi, honey, here's your Bud." He leaned over to me and shouted in my ear, "By the way, my name is Jimmy Severino and I'm the queen bee around here. So if you're going to hang out with me, looking that good, we better get that out of the way right now!"

That morning at 4:30am Jimmy took me for breakfast where our bond of friendship, mutual respect and love began.

After that night Jimmy and I became inseparable. Every minute we had free, we were together. And every night Jimmy worked at the Roma, I was there. If they didn't know any better, all the boys at the Roma, would have thought we were lovers. It turned out Jimmy was an American and most of the men who patronized the Roma One Discotheque were American too. And if they weren't, at least they spoke the English language. This fact helped make hanging out at the Roma, a delight. I didn't mind shouting, as long as it was in English. Jimmy was never a good bartender, but the owner kept him on because most of the guys who came in were attracted to him. They all loved him and I swear, I think he slept with them all at least once! Besides Jimmy's jovial disposition, he had many talents. He was a damn good piano player and seamstress. Boy, could he sew. But the talent I loved most of all, came out when he was on the dance floor. He was an incredible dancer. The way he could move his body to this new music style, which was spreading like a wildfire throughout all the gay clubs in Europe was phenomenal. Whenever he would let loose his magic on the dance floor, everyone would give way to *his moves*. He was so good I just had to have him teach me *his moves*. And boy did he! We played and danced that whole summer. It seemed time and living life like a silly school girl was healing the wounds of the past. Or at least I thought so.

It was September 22nd, 1974, at 10:00am when Jimmy entered the front door of my apartment. We had planned a day trip to the Coliseum and when he walked into the kitchen, I was sipping my first cup of coffee of the day. He was carrying an American tabloid in his hands when he sat beside me, "Christina, you're not ready yet, girl?"

I gazed up over my coffee cup, "Oh don't be such a spaz', pour yourself a cup of coffee and sit down with me for a few minutes. It won't take me long to get ready."

As we sipped our coffee, Jimmy began to read the tabloid. I got up, put my cup in the sink, and walked over behind him to kiss his cheek before heading for the shower. As I kissed his cheek, I could see at the bottom of the page he was reading an article which caught my attention. It read, **"The New York Mets' star pitcher, John Everett, was wed on September 1st, 1974, to his high school sweetheart, Mary Wilson."**

I lost it! The pain shot through me like a thunderbolt. I ripped the paper out of his hands and crumpled it. Jimmy watched in disbelief as I fell to my knees and began to cry. Jimmy jumped from his seat, flew to my side and screamed, "Christina, what's the matter, girl? What is it?"

After I finally got a hold of myself, I told Jimmy who I was and then I proceeded to tell him the whole story. He was a big help! He sat there on the floor with me and began to cry. There we were the two of us, sitting on the kitchen floor bawling and I thought, "Well, at least I'm not crying alone."

Looking seriously into my eyes, "You know what you need girl-friend."

"No, Jimmy, I don't know. You tell me."

"To get happy girl!" He pulled a *joint* out of his pocket and lit it up.

I gave him a nasty look, "Get out of here with that stuff, you know I don't smoke pot."

He kissed my cheek, "Well, today you do." Then he handed me the joint. I took one puff, then another. By the time we made it to the Coliseum that day, I was high! We laughed all that day and into the night. I couldn't believe that with only one joint, I was able to push Johnny and the article right out of my thoughts. It seemed like a magical cure for heartache. By the time I hit the bed that night, I considered myself to be a full-fledged advocate for marijuana usage.

During that Fall our partying became more intense and I became the new queen of Roma's. The guys loved me and I hit it off with all of them. It was easy to fit in with all these gay men because I didn't have the concern of someone coming onto me. That was the last thing I wanted. These men, in this bar, gave me a sense of belonging. They helped me feel beautiful again, which was what my ego needed.

It was December 31st, 1974 and the Roma was throwing a New Year's Eve Ball, with a drag show to boot. I was sitting by myself at a table in the corner of this packed, frenzied night club, at 11:58pm. Jimmy was off with his latest love, somewhere on the dance floor, when the clock struck midnight. Suddenly, the place became an explosion of noise and it hit me, "**MY CONTRACT IS UP!**" The thoughts and feelings of entertaining again flared up within my heart and I became overwhelmed with anticipation, "But how?" I asked myself, "Frank would still be able to keep me from working and the people of my own nation have disowned me." My thoughts raced so fast I didn't even notice Jimmy when he grabbed me back into space, time, and the party, with a quick tug on my arm. As I was dragged out to the dance floor, I thought, "Oh well! I'll figure it out tomorrow."

It was 4:00am when Jimmy walked me home. We were, to say the least, stoned out of our minds! When we entered my apartment, Jimmy closed the door, "Do you mind if I stay tonight, Christina?"

"No baby, I don't mind," as I kissed his forehead and headed into the bedroom. I took my clothes off, put on my night gown and I climbed under the covers. Two minutes later, Jimmy climbed into bed with me with nothing on. I looked at him strangely, "What are you doing in my bed with nothing on?"

He answered meekly, "It's too hot in here."

"Go turn the heat down and put something on."

He whined, "I don't want to sleep alone tonight, Christina. Please, let me stay in here with you?"

I thought, "I guess so, it can't hurt, after- all he's gay." So I said, "Okay."

Suddenly I found him clumsily trying to climb on top of me, with an erection no less. Holding back my laughter, "Jimmy, what are you doing?"

With a very shaky voice, he stuck his nose in my face, "If there was ever any woman in this world I would sleep with, it would be you."

Chuckling, "Oh that's sweet Jimmy thank you very much. Now get off of me!"

At that he laid his head on my chest and began to pout, "Oh! Come on, Christina, please just once."

I looked into his big brown, puppy dog eyes and shrugged my shoulders, "Oh well, why not."

The moment his erection touched my leg, I had a flashback of making love with Johnny; and instantly a thought hit me like a ton of bricks! I flew up in the air knocking Jimmy off the bed and onto the floor, where the back of his head hit the dresser and I screamed out, "**I'm a fucking genius**!"

Jimmy looked up at me totally bewildered, and with one hand holding the back of his head shouted, "You're a fucking nut! That's what you are!"

I ran to the kitchen, grabbed a pen and paper and started to write something like this, '**Aa! Ooooo! Ho, aa, imm, imm, oh God.**' Jimmy put his shorts on and followed me into the kitchen. When he reached the table, he looked down at this secret code I was scribbling, "You're a fucking genius, all right." Then he scratched his head, turned and went to bed.

Later that morning over coffee, I handed Jimmy a sheet of paper," Let's put the hottest disco beat we can create to this."

Jimmy read it, looked up at me standing beside him, "What is it?"

I slapped the back of the head and as he yelled, "Ouch!" I said, "It's our new hit single, you dope."

Then it was off to work. The first thing I did was to take the sixty-thousand dollars I had remaining in cash, out from under my mattress. Jimmy and I put music to the lyrics and we knew it was hot! As we were putting together a band to perform our music, I was registering and certifying myself, with the Italian government as Powers Records Incorporated. I now owned my own record label and I was going to make it work!

Within two months, we were ready to go to the Italian public with one-hundred-thousand copies of our first release, 'Ahh Baby! Touch Me Like That!' It was the most sensuous recording ever to be placed on vinyl. The only problem was, it was so hot no radio station in Italy would play it!

With my financial neck on the chopping block again and with no one hearing our new recording, it was time for self-promotion. Jimmy and I planned every detail of my first performance. From my metallic blue eyeliner, bright red lips, flaming red nails, sliver sparkles in my long black wavy hair, black silk chiffon skin tight gown which gently dropped off the upper curves of my breast and down to my ankles with a slit that came up the center to just below my upper thigh, to reveal my black silk-lace stockings and black heels. I was looking hot! Every move was choreographed to enhance the sensuality of the rhythm.

It was finally opening night. Our first performance was at the Roma, itself. It was March 18th, at 12:15am when I was going back on stage for the first time in more than two years. The D.J. was still spinning the last record before calling me to the stage.

I turned to Jimmy with the jitters, "I don't think I can do this Jimmy." and I started to walk away.

Jimmy ran up behind me, grabbed my arm and yelled, "You got us into this, so you get us out!"

"But I can't, Jimmy! I just can't do it!"

He gave me a hug, "If you could perform as Christy Valona, you can certainly perform as Christina Powers, can't you?" I looked up at him sheepishly and nodded my head in agreement, "Well then you shouldn't be afraid to perform tonight."

"I'm not afraid to perform, Jimmy."

"Well then what is it?"

I looked dead in his eyes, "I don't think I can carry this off. It's one thing to pretend I'm making love in a recording studio, but it's another in front of all those men."

Jimmy shook his head, hugged me again, "Is that all it is, Christina? Everyone out there is a friend and besides, they're all gay. So if you can't do the act in front of them when you have the act down perfectly, you'll never do it in front of a straight audience."

I looked at him, "My mind tells me you're right, but my heart tells me I can't be that provocative in front of all these men."

He looked at me and with a flick of that wrist, "Oh, just tell your heart to shut-up and get your sexy little buns out on that stage, girl!" We looked at one another and started to crack up.

He lit a *joint*, passed it to me, "Take a hit off this, then you go get'um girl!"

All of a sudden the dance music stopped and I heard the D.J. begin to say, "Let me have your attention, guys! Tonight we have a special treat. Our very own *Christina Powers* is going to perform her new recording, 'Ahh, baby! Touch Me Like That' for the first time right here at the Roma. Now let's give a big round of applause, to our girl, Christina!"

I swallowed my fears, took one more toke for luck, flicked the *joint* on the floor and slowly sashayed out onto the stage. When I reached the microphone, I was stoned and feeling no pain. I picked up the mike with my left hand and said in the sexiest way I could, "Hi, guys! Are we all hot tonight?"

They all screamed back, "Yes!"

"Great! Now hold on to your seats, because I'm going to make you even **hotter**!"

I waved to the D.J. to start spinning the rhythm as the guys cheered. The stage and dance floor were lit with only strobe lights and the spot light was on me. Swaying my hips as the smooth sensually tantalizing rhythm began to emerge, I moaned loud enough for all to hear, ***"Ahh, baby, touch me like that; Oh yes, yes, touch me like that; I'm in ecstasy, ecstasy, when you touch me like that."*** as I simultaneously and sensually moved my right hand over my head. I let it drift down to my right breast as I gently moved the top of my gown, just enough to expose my right nipple through the black, silk chiffon and moaned, ***"Ahh, baby, touch me like that, I need you, need you, to touch me like that, it's ecstasy, ecstasy, when you touch me like that."*** as my fingernails gently stroked my breast. Then I moved my entire body slowly and smoothly, from side to side slithering down to the floor into a catlike position. Arching my back I swayed my hips and cried out with the voice of an angel, ***"Ahh, baby, baby touch me like that! Touch me like that! Oh yes, yes, touch me like that! It's heavenly, heavenly, when you touch me like that."*** I slowly began to rise from my feline position as I purred. Now standing I slid my hands slowly between my legs, parting the slit in my gown and seductively revealed my sensual black silk stockings up to my thigh. When my hands reached the crease of my swaying hips, I let the slit of my gown gently drift back into place and cried out again, ***"Ahh, baby, baby touch me like that, Oh yes, yes touch me like that."*** Sliding my right hand slowly up my thigh, between my breasts, over my shoulder I reached for the stars, as I lifted my left hand holding the mike close to my lips, tilting my head back so I was looking straight up and sang out, ***"Ahh, baby, baby touch me like that, touch me like that."***

Then the music stopped and I took a bow.

The boys went nuts! Jimmy came running out to me, jumped into the air with his right arm rising up over his head, then pulled it down to his side like a prize fighter, shouting, "Yes! Girl! Yes!" He leaped into my arms and we both almost fell off the stage!

When we arrived home that night, we were on adrenalin high! I hugged Jimmy and said with excitement, "We have to setup a whole European tour now. Oh yes! We need some more songs too." I threw my hands in the air and said, "Oh well, I'll figure it out tomorrow." With that, I turned and headed for the bedroom.

As I walked away Jimmy said, "New songs? How in the world are you going to top 'Ahh, baby, touch me like that?"

I turned to him, gave him my, *'it's no problem look'* with a sexy wink and a girlish tone, "I'll sing." At that point, I went to bed.

By the time we had our tour setup; beginning with all the gay night clubs in Italy, we had a seven cut soundtrack to bring with us. And let me tell you, they were seven of the hottest, sexiest songs Jimmy and I could imagine.

The date was June 1st, 1975. I was so hot on stage; I knocked them dead at every club I played. I became the queen of the gay night life, with groupies to boot!

Our touring schedule was intense and the album began to sell like hot cakes. So much so, that finally in September, it began to filter into the straight clubs. After that it was on the airwaves!

By November 1st, we had the number one selling record in all of Western Europe and the money was starting to roll in. Jimmy, the band members and I were on the road every day and in the clubs every night. When we weren't trying to get some sleep, Jimmy and I were writing and writing. The fame and the music of Europe's new disco queen *Christina Powers*, hit the American shores without me even being there to promote it. The demand to purchase the recording in the United States began to grow in record numbers!

On December 1st, Powers Records Incorporated received a call from Mr. James Smith, the Executive Vice President of Columbia Records Incorporated. He offered to swing a deal which would open up the American markets to Powers Records Incorporated and for their star performer, *Christina Powers*, with only a 60% take on the gross. I informed Mr. Smith I would have to speak with my associates on this matter and I would return his call with a counter offer, as soon as possible. As I hung up the phone, my head was spinning with the thought of heading back home. 'But how?' was still the question. For as soon as Frank discovered I was *Christina Powers*, he would be able to stop me again.

It was 8:00pm December 10th, my twenty-first birthday when Jimmy and I were just getting off the plane at Rome International Airport. We were coming back from a three-night engagement at the 'La Vie en Rose, which was the hottest night club in Paris, when Jimmy said, "I have a little surprise for you Christina."

"You do?" I replied as we walked toward the exit doors of the airport.

As the doors opened, he replied, "Yes, I do!" As soon as we hit the fresh air, Jimmy raised his hand over his head and summoned a limo for us.

I gave him a puzzled look, "What's this?"

He took me by the hand and ushered me into the limo, "This is just the first phase of your birthday gift!"

I looked at my sweet Jimmy as the driver swept us away, "Oh thank you, Jimmy. This is a great surprise." I thought knowing Jimmy as I did, "I hope so!"

He handed me a small wrapped gift, "Happy birthday, Christina!" I opened it and inside was a little heart locket hanging from a delicately woven, gold chain. I opened the heart and inside was a carved inscription which read, "You're a fucking genius! Love Jimmy." I looked at him and we laughed so hard, I thought I'd never stop. I finally had Jimmy snap it on for me.

The driver drove us to the new, much larger apartment, Jimmy and I rented together, back in September. It also happened to be in a much better part of town.

When we entered, Jimmy swiftly led me to the bathroom, pushed me in and with the flick of that wrist and a girlish wiggle, "Dress to impress, girl! We're gonna have a hot time on the old town tonight!"

Laughing I pushed him out of the bathroom, "Okay, sister!

Now get your dramatic little ass out of here."

After we changed, it was back to the waiting limo at 9:30pm destination unknown, and I was dressed to 'the nines'.

As the driver drove us deep within the heart of the city of Rome, I couldn't help but notice the style of the architecture on the buildings around us. They were exquisite! There were angels, gargoyles, lions, naked bodies and heads of gladiators, carved in all of them. It just went on, building after building, until the car stopped at a large, gold plated gate, which just fit between two large buildings. As the gates opened, the driver pulled in and proceeded down a mile long driveway. The walls of these two enormous buildings ran along either side of the driveway.

Instantly I became nervous, turned to Jimmy, "Where the hell are we going? It looks like a **claustrophobic's nightmare!**"

Jimmy Smiled, "Relax!" as the car entered a clearing to expose a thirty-acre flower garden, spread out in front of the most beautiful Italian villa I had ever seen.

At that moment, I became a little suspicious. I grabbed Jimmy by his arm, "What is this? You don't know people like this!"

He interrupted my spasm, "I said, relax! Some of Rome's elite dignitaries are throwing you a surprise birthday party."

I let go of Jimmy, looked around at all the limos and thought, "This might not be half bad after all."

I kissed Jimmy as the car reached the door, "Let's go get'um!"

The second the doorman led us into the main foyer of the villa, I turned on *Christina Powers* as if I were turning on a light switch. With that, I became *Christina Powers,* the sultriest, sexiest, songstress in all of Europe. I played the part to the hilt. Every move, every glance had a sexual connotation attached to it. I felt myself feeding on it and I wanted to become it. This was my ace in the hole.

The foyer was awesome! It had to be a hundred square feet in diameter. The ceiling hovered three stories above the floor. The room was filled with the most well dressed people that I had seen in one place, in a long time, and they were all dancing to *my* music under a ceiling filled with golden chandeliers. The walls had a white background with golden chariots. They appeared to be racing around the room. Directly across the room from where I was standing stood a towering staircase of Italian, white marble. It was breathtaking! At the top of the staircase, I could see the figure of a man beginning to descend. He was expensively dressed with a black silk tux and the rock on his left ring finger, was *blinding*. He appeared to be in his late fifties. I'd say six-feet-tall, two-hundred and twenty-five-pounds, with slightly graying hair filtering back from his temples, into his raven black hair.

As he entered the room, I could see he commanded respect from all who greeted him. As I watched from across the room I thought, "Now here's someone with clout! This is our host?" I wondered, "Who is he?"

So I turned to Jimmy, "Jimmy, who is he?"

Jimmy answered with a smile, "You're not going to believe it, but we were invited here by Dominick Giovannetti, himself."

"You're kidding!" I said, turning back to Jimmy. "But why?" I wondered if he knew who I really was and if Frank had something to do with this. You see, everyone in Italy, including myself, had heard of Dominick Giovannetti, *The Italian Godfather!*

"Because he loves your music and he wanted to meet the woman behind the voice. That's all I know."

"If that's true, this could prove to be a very interesting evening."

As Dominick reached me, I placed my fingers into the palm of his hand and curtsied. The second he looked into my eyes, I knew he had no idea I was Frank's niece. As we were introducing ourselves to each other, my mind was racing and it hit me. "This man could be my ticket back to America," and I was going to be nice to him.

After our greeting, he swept me away from Jimmy and into the heart of the room. I felt a little guilty leaving Jimmy standing by himself in a room full of strangers. Then I thought, "Oh well, he's a big boy." as I charged right into the center of attention with every move I made.

Dominick personally introduced me to everyone in the room. We joked, laughed and flirted our way through the crowd as we sipped champagne from Dominick's private collection. It was turning out to be a fabulous evening after all. Dominick and I were hitting it off superbly as the evening progressed.

It was around midnight when my large beautifully decorated, three tiered birthday cake arrived. The waiters served us tiny little pieces of cake and I thought, "I knew I should have grabbed a bite to eat." When we finished our feast, Dominick led me onto the dance floor. The song that was playing was a very soft Italian love song. We began to dance as the lights dimmed. As we danced so very close, he told me he was a very happily married man with grandchildren and how highly he was viewed by the people of **his Italy**!

So sincerely, he whispered in my ear, "But what wouldn't I do, for a woman like yourself." Smiling, "Would you like to see the balcony?"

Very seductively, "I would love to, Dominick." He escorted me to the balcony which looked out over the well-lit ancient Roman Coliseum. He handed me a small golden wrapped gift box as he kissed my cheek, "Happy birthday, Christina."

I opened the gift gently to heighten the suspense. Within this precious wrapping was the most brilliant ten karat diamond necklace I had ever seen. I was stunned! I looked up into his eyes and seductively winked, "It's beautiful, Dominick, and I'm more than flattered, but the only reason I can accept such a fabulous gift is because it's my birthday. I would never insult such a thoughtful giver by not accepting it."

He kissed my cheek, "I see a woman like yourself does not come frivolously."

I smiled softly, looked up into his eyes sweetly, "You're right, Dominick. You're absolutely right. I don't come frivolously!" I kissed him very gently, "Thank you for the lovely gift."

In that sultry Italian voice of his, he whispered as he bent his head down to kiss me, "I'm pleased you like it."

Before he tried to take advantage of me, "It's getting late and I really must leave now, Dominick. It's been a very long day."

With lust in his eyes, "But the night is young, Christina. I was hoping you would like to spend the evening here with me."

Just to tantalize him, I kissed him tenderly, "Not tonight,

Dominick. I'm exhausted and my heart wouldn't be in it."

He kissed me back, "Would you please have dinner with me tomorrow evening?"

I graciously slipped out of his embrace, "I'd love to have dinner with you, Dominick."

We made plans for his car to pick me up at 7:00pm the next evening.

As our limo drove Jimmy and me home, I thought, "I've got him right where I want him. Now to bait the trap just right."

The next evening promptly at 7:00pm Dominick's limo arrived. I started setting the trap by looking the hottest I've ever looked. When I climbed into the limo, the driver almost fell off the curb as he closed the door behind me. *I was sizzling!* Within thirty minutes, we were pulling up to Dominick's two-hundred-foot yacht, and I was impressed!

He greeted me at the door with champagne in hand and with a distinguished nod of his head, "You look ravishing, Christina."

I handed him my black cape, "Thank you, Dominick. You look quite debonair yourself."

With wide eyes he exclaimed, "Debonair! I was hoping for something more like attractive."

I smiled as he led me to the bar, "You misunderstand me, Dominick. I find the debonair look more than attractive."

He moved close to me, putting his hands on my shoulders, "I'm happy you're pleased, Christina."

I looked up into his eyes, "You have pleased me, Dominick. Just your presence is pleasing to me."

His face lit up with that one, "I have a very special evening planned for us, beginning with dinner in the glass enclosed sky room. Our meal will be more appetizing under the city lights."

"That sounds lovely." I delicately rose from the bar stool and out from under his grasp.

He proceeded to escort me to dinner. I looked around the room, "This is a fabulous yacht. Would you mind taking me on a tour?"

He walked over to me, put those massive hands of his back on my shoulders, "let me lead the way."

As we toured the yacht on our way to the sky room, I had to use the utmost restraint not to knee him in the groin for having his roaming hands all over me. But because I needed him, I was good and I held my temper.

As we shared a lovely filet minion with all the trimmings, he said, "What is it that entices a woman of your caliber?"

I smiled at him *devilishly*, "Power."

"Power, that's interesting, why would a lovely lady like yourself be enticed by power?"

I leaned toward him, "Because I need someone, with power."

"Now that's a dramatic statement. You need someone with power. Why, may I ask, do you need someone with power?"

I reached over with one hand and stroked his temple seductively, "Not just someone with power, Dominick. I need *you* and *your* power."

He took my hand, kissed it, "Do tell, Christina. How can I, with my power, assist **you**?"

I very carefully told him who I was and what I needed from him.

With a look of shock on his face, he exclaimed, "So you're Frank's niece! I heard he had crushed you for trying to break your contract." He stood up, "What's in it for me, if I decide to help you?"

"If you will help me get back to America and keep Frank at bay, I. . ." with the most seductive voice I could muster, "will let you feel what it's like to sleep with the most extraordinary woman on earth."

His eyes opened wide, "That's a powerful offer, Christina. May I hold my decision until the morning?"

Gazing at him with confidence radiating from my seductive eyes, knowing I had him by the balls, "Yes, you may, Dominick. But I promise nothing more than my passion for one night."

With a look of amazement, "That's an offer I can't refuse."

I took him by the hand and led him to the bedroom. As I began to perform for Dominick, I found my thoughts of destroying Frank, feeding my passion. I devoured Dominick with every kiss. With every sensual touch he became mine. I totally violated my innermost being on this dog in heat, as I forced the flames of lust to incinerate my fears and magnify my profound hatred for Frank.

By the time the morning sun shone in through the portholes, I had Dominick wrapped around my finger. That morning, after one more interlude just to ensure my triumph, he held me and assured me he could, and would, put a stop to Frank's influence over my career.

As I was leaving, Dominick kissed me passionately then handed me a card, "This is my private number, use it and I'll be there." As he placed it in my hand, "I only give this number to the special people in my life." Kissing me again, "You are an amazing woman, Christina Powers, and I know you will get whatever it is you want in this life."

I kissed him gingerly, slipped out of his grasp, "Thank you, Dominick I will." With that, I turned and walked away. As I sashayed toward the limo, I knew Christy was gone and I was now, truly, *Christina Powers*, the woman behind the music.

Later that afternoon, I was making arrangements to meet with a representative from Columbia Records, Incorporated, to sign a deal that would open the American markets to Powers Records Incorporated, with only a 10% take on the gross. All of this was possible, thanks to one phone call from my extremely grateful friend, Dominick Giovannetti. With a little more assistance from Dominick's American attorneys, I quietly paid back all the debts I left behind. After that, it was back to work.

On January 2nd, 1976, Jimmy and I released our second album. It was hotter than the first. This time we kept the same sensuality in the lyrics, but we spiced up the rhythm to make them more melodic. By April, the album, 'I'm The Love Master' was number one on the European charts. At the same time my first album, 'Ahh, Baby! Touch Me Like That' was finally soaring across America. In May, my touring of the nightclubs was over and I had advanced to the stadiums. The Europeans loved me! The demand for personal appearances throughout Europe grew and grew. The spotlights, press and cameras were all back. I loved it, but it wasn't America yet!

It was June 1st, when I received a call from Mr. James Smith informing me, "I'm The Love Master" had become number one in just two weeks. He also said the demand from the American public was increasing. They wanted *Christina Powers*! I hung up the phone and just sat there at my desk thinking, "It's time for my return home." Then a feeling of anxiousness shot through me as I thought, "I know they want *Christina Powers*, but will they still want me when they know who I really am?" I shrugged my shoulders and said out loud, "Oh well! I'll figure it out tomorrow."

It was July 23rd, when Jimmy and I were getting ready to leave Rome. Destination, NEW YORK CITY! As I packed, I reflected on how my life here in Rome had taken me full circle, heading back to where I started. I remembered the drawing of a circle around Rome and thought, "How ironic. Ha! Ha! Ha!" Then I grabbed my suitcases, one bottle of champagne and ran out the door for the airport. **DESTINATION, AMERICA!**

CHAPTER 4. THE RETURN HOME

It was July 24th, 1976, at 10:00am when our plane touched down at LaGuardia International Airport, in the United States of America. **MY HOME!** I was so excited I had butterflies in my stomach just knowing that I would soon be back in my beloved city, Manhattan. I was told to expect some reporters, so I dressed for the occasion. As Jimmy and I were exiting the plane, I looked out over the metal detectors and I never expected to see what I saw! The airport was swarming with reporters and the place went wild with screaming fans, as soon as I stuck my head out the door. I was stunned. I couldn't move.

All of a sudden, Jimmy shoved me out onto the ramp, "Come on, Christina, you're holding everybody up!"

When Jimmy finally witnessed what it was that caused me to freeze, he screeched, **"Holy shit!"** as he proceeded to cut off the blood supply to my right hand.

Somehow I got a hold of myself, "Just follow my lead, Jimmy, and please stop breaking my hand."

As we both began to slowly move toward this screaming crowd, we were *freaking!* I immediately turned *Christina Powers* on. As we proceeded to head toward the flashing lights, I posed for the cameras like only the QUEEN of Hollywood, herself, could. It hit me like a ton of bricks, and I knew I was her **daughter!** As I smiled for the cameras and tried to answer a hundred questions for the reporters, my mind raced with thoughts like, "I am her daughter! It's true! Somehow it's true! What does this mean? Are Frank and I truly the only ones in the world who know this? How will this affect my life? What do I do with this knowledge?"

It was starting to drive me mad, right there in front of the whole country! So I stopped my mind from racing and thought, "Oh well! I'll figure it out tomorrow." With that I was able to give my full attention to the reporters.

Finally, we were through the crowd, in the limo and on our way to meet with Mr. James Smith from Columbia Records. We still had to finalize our contract and iron out any last minute glitches with my upcoming American tour.

By the time we reached Manhattan it was already 2:00pm. As the limo drove through the city, I thought of how this city I loved so much, once loved me. Then I thought of Frank. I knew I was within arm's length of him now, but how do I arrange for his demise? I didn't know the answer at that moment, but I knew if I thought about it long enough, it would come to me. It had to be just right.

After an evening of dinner and hobnobbing with the top brass of Columbia Records, Jimmy and I finally arrived at our Fifth Avenue penthouse, which was so graciously provided by Columbia records. It was only 11:00pm when we walked in the door, but we were exhausted. We both went straight to our respective rooms, to wash up for the night. When I finished showering, I put on my robe and headed out to the enticing scent that was drifting in from the other room.

When my nostrils finally found the origins of this aroma, I saw Jimmy sitting on the sofa. He had his legs stretched out and his feet lying on top of the coffee table, with a big bowl of buttered popcorn sitting on his lap. He was watching TV as he stuffed his face with fists full of popcorn.

I gave him a dirty look, "You shit-head! You're having buttered popcorn without me."

I jumped over the back of the couch, which sat in the middle of the floor, and landed on the sofa just next to Jimmy. He fumbled a little as I landed, but he saved the prized buttered popcorn. I lay down across the sofa and placed my head on Jimmy's lap. He placed the bowl of buttered popcorn on my stomach and as I began to eat exactly like Jimmy I asked, "Whatcha' watching?"

"A Star is born."

I lifted up from Jimmy's lap just enough to take a sip from his soda, turned to the TV and looked dead at the star singing on the stage and it hit me! I jumped up off the sofa, knocking the soda and buttered popcorn all over both of us and shouted, "**I'm a fucking genius!**" At that I swiftly ran for a pen and paper; as I ran, I heard Jimmy scream as he tried to frantically wipe the ice cold soda off his chest, "That fucking girl is nuts!"

After I had the items I so desperately needed, I sat down at the big oak desk in the den and began to write. I was writing my thoughts for a screenplay about a young girl who would become a disco diva. It was 3:00am when I couldn't see any longer, so I dropped the pen and staggered to my room. It was dark, except for the light which shone through the sides of the curtains. As I flicked the light switch, I was thinking, "Where in this country would be the best place to build my soon-to-be empire, Powers Incorporated?" But the light didn't come on. So I walked over to the curtains to expose more light. As I reached the curtain, I caught a flash of light glistening in the corner of my eye, and I got a chill. I quickly opened the curtain so I could see the lamp on the night table. I calmly walked over to the table, reached down and flicked on the light. There on the nightstand laid a Poughkeepsie Journal newspaper. I pulled back the covers, climbed into bed, shut off the light and passed out.

I was dressed and on my second cup of coffee, when the phone rang. I could hear Jimmy stumbling out of bed to answer it. I continued to glance through the road map sitting on the table in front of me. As I sipped my coffee Jimmy yelled out, "Christina, where are you?"

I yelled back, "In the kitchen, Jimmy."

He came in carrying the cordless phone, "It's, Joseph Cole, for you."

"Oh yes," I said, as Jimmy brought me the phone. "He's our new orchestra leader, we met him last night, remember?"

Jimmy handed me the phone, "Good morning, Joe. I was just about to call you. What's up?"

"Good morning, Christina. I just wanted to touch base with

you before today's rehearsal and tonight's performance."

"Joe, do me a favor and rehearse the melody with the orchestra today. I have some place I have to go, but I'll be back around 7:00pm for the final rehearsal."

"Are you sure about that?" he asked with concern.

"Trust me on this one, Joe; I'll be there by seven."

He answered with an unconvinced tone, "You're the boss, Christina, so I guess I'll see you tonight."

I clicked off the phone as Jimmy flopped down beside me with a cup of coffee, "What are you doing up and dressed already?"

I took my last sip of coffee, "I'm going to a town called Poughkeepsie. It's about an hour and a half north of here."

Jimmy perked up, "Poughkeepsie, why are you going to Poughkeepsie?"

"Just a feeling," I answered, as I rinsed out my cup.

With a suspicious tone, "A feeling! You know you really are a screwball. Do you realize you have to perform, 'I Am the Love Master,' live on national TV tonight?"

"Yes, Jimmy, I know," I calmly replied.

"Do you want me to come with you?"

I looked him straight in the eyes, "You should know what I want you to do. The stage and lighting for tonight's performance has got to be exactly as we've planned it. When I come back Jimmy, all I want to do is sing."

He gave me a stunned look, flick of that wrist, "Yes sir!"

I kissed his forehead, grabbed the brochure of the real estate brokers in the Poughkeepsie area, which I had sent up to me at 6:00am that morning. Then I walked out to the rental car I had waiting for me, all before 8:00am.

As I buckled myself into the driver's seat, I tossed my briefcase on the seat beside me. It contained four pocket recorders, which I used to record my thoughts. Two for my screenplay and two for new releases. As I drove to Poughkeepsie on that beautiful bright, sunny day, I was wasting no time! You see, I had decided how I would **get Frank** and that would be where it would hurt him the most. **His pocket!**

It was 10:30am when I found the location of the first real

estate agent on my list. I parked the car and headed in. As I
entered the door, I could see a secretary seated at a mid-sized desk
in front of four small cubicles. It appeared as though they were
struggling to survive the slump in the local real estate market,
which I had only discovered two minutes before turning off the car,
from a local radio talk show. I walked over to the secretary and
asked to speak with the first available Realtor.

The Realtor seemed pleasant as she approached me with a
smile. She reached out her hand, "Good morning, my name is,
Terry Baggatta. How can I help you?"

I introduced myself, "I'm looking for a very special piece of
property. It has to be at least eight hundred acres of prime real
estate. I don't want it to be too close to the city, but I don't want it
in the boonies, either. Oh yes, it also has to be in close proximity
to your largest airport."

She looked at me as if she was going to faint, "I don't believe
this. I just received a listing this morning that fits your needs
perfectly."

I smiled, anxiously rubbed my hands together, "When can I
see it?"

Terry said enthusiastically, "Right now if you wish."

Still smiling, "I do wish."

Then we hopped into her car and off we went. It turned out to
be a thousand acres of pure heaven, with a thirty-thousand-foot
riverfront view. It was right on the majestic Hudson. It had
running streams flowing over the creek beds, which led the waters
splashing through the towering pines, on its way down to the river.
This place was beautiful. The property was right off Route 9W in
the town of Milton, N.Y. It was only twenty minutes from Stewart
Airport, which Terry assured me would be a thriving airport in the
near future. As we drove back to Terry's office, I knew this was the
place for my new empire.

Terry and I worked up a thirty-million-dollar offer, on this
seventy-million-dollar piece of property. And I didn't even have the
money yet! But I was still compelled to leave her a deposit check
for one-million-dollars, which was every penny Powers Records
had earned to date. As I signed on the dotted line I thought, "Oh

well, I'll figure it out tomorrow!"

By 4:30pm I was on my way back to New York, and my first American performance as, *Christina Powers*! I was appearing on a national TV show called The Nancy and Dawnett Comedy Hour. The show was being broadcast live from Radio City Music Hall, to honor their one hundredth taping. It was America's number one variety show. I knew all of America would be watching, so it was crucial I be extremely hot tonight!

I arrived for the rehearsal at 6:50pm. As soon as Jimmy and Joe saw me, they dropped what they were doing and headed right for me. They immediately began to inform me everything was set to go. The three of us began to make a quick spot check on everything. The lighting, stage and props were all in place and timed perfectly to the choreographed rhythm of the music and my performance. It was a job well done. Joe assured me the orchestra was tuned to a tee. All that was missing was me. I turned to both of them, "Great job, guys! I'll go change and we can get started." With that, I quickly walked toward the dressing room.

Jimmy came charging after me, hung his arms around my neck and with a girlish excitement to his mannerisms and voice, "Christina! I'm in love! His name is Bobby."

I kissed his cheek as we walked toward the dressing room and with a loving smile, "Again, Jimmy."

He was glowing, "This time it's for real. We met here this morning. He's the lighting director here at Radio City. He's gorgeous! We spent the entire day working together." As we reached the dressing room, he hung onto the door while I began to take off my clothes, "We know we really have a special kind of bond together. I can't explain it, but it's there."

I walked back over to him, "I'm happy for you, Jimmy." pulled him off the door and began to usher him out, "And I can't wait to meet him. Now get out of here and let me get ready for the rehearsal."

With the flick of that wrist, he backed out of the room, "That's great, because I'm bringing him home tonight." With that, he turned and wiggled his chunky little buns down the hall. I shook my head and thought, "Oh well!" as I closed the door to finish getting ready.

When I walked out onto the stage, I was ready for my first and only rehearsal, prior to my live national performance! As Joe cued the orchestra, I began to sweat. The music started and I began to rehearse, 'I Am the Love Master!' The lyrics to the Love Master were one of my most sensual recordings. The rhythm was the fastest and hottest disco beat to date and number one on the billboard charts. My one and only rehearsal was awful! I was tripping over the stage props, my voice was cracking and I couldn't keep up with the orchestra. When we finished, Jimmy, Joe and everyone who had anything to do with the show that night, looked at me in horror! I looked around and saw them all glaring at me as if they had just witnessed a five-car collision.

I dropped the mike on the stage floor and ran off to my dressing room, with my hands shaking as if I were holding a jack hammer. Jimmy came running after me and as we reached the dressing room, I slammed the door and started to cry. Jimmy grabbed hold of me, "Christina, what's the matter with you?"

Uncontrollably I shouted, "Jimmy, I'm so nervous I'm freaking out here. Do you know what's riding on this?"

Jimmy gave me a hardy shake and very calmly, "You can do this, Christina! You know it by heart. We created it."

Still crying, "Jimmy, I know I can. I'm just so nervous."

With a steady reassuring tone, "Just relax, Christina, and tell me what's making you so nervous. Then we can deal with it calmly and logically."

Wiping the tears from my face, "Thanks, Jimmy, I'm starting to feel a little better already."

"Good, now let's talk, girlfriend," he replied with a sigh of relief.

I looked into his comforting eyes, "We have everything riding on this performance tonight." Then, with a giggle as if I were a little insane, "I just gave every dime we've made, one million dollars as a deposit on a thirty million-dollar piece of property."

Jimmy's face appeared as if he had just run face first into a plate glass door, as he screamed, "You what! Are you fucking nuts? How could you?"

With a blank expression, "I don't know! I just took the pen and signed my name."

With that he shouted, "Why in the world would you put all of our money on the line like this, Christina?"

I shrugged my shoulders, "It was just a feeling I had."

All at once he shook me by my shoulders and screamed like someone who had just been driven mad, "Just a feeling! Just a feeling! I can't fucking believe you! You are fucking nuts!"

Just in the nick of time, I was rescued from this man who was about to rip my hair out by its roots, by someone banging on my dressing room door and a bewildered voice screaming, "Are you guys all right in there?"

Jimmy, recognizing the voice dashed to the door, flung it open with full cinematic dramatics, leaped into this man's arms and began to sob, "She's nuts! She's nuts!" This man came bursting into the room and somehow calmed us both down.

After we composed ourselves, I discovered this man was Bobby, Jimmy's newest love.

Jimmy, clinging to Bobby's arm, "Christina, I don't care how you do it, but you had better pull this one off tonight, girlfriend."

"Jimmy, I know that. I just need to relax."

Jimmy looked at his watch and pulled a joint out of his pocket, "You only have 45 minutes to relax. You better smoke this."

I looked at him as if he was nuts, "Jimmy, we're not in the back of a nightclub. Don't you think someone might smell that?"

Jimmy put the joint back in his pocket, shook his head, "Well, I don't know what to tell you then. Just try to relax I guess. We'll get out of here and let you get ready."

Feeling totally drained, I rubbed my forehead with my left hand, "Okay, Jimmy, just let me rest and call me when it's time."

Bobby walked over to me, pulled out a little brown bottle, opened it and took out a tiny little spoon. He scooped some white powder onto the spoon, stretched his hand toward my nose, "I could lose my job for this, but snort some of this and it'll help you relax."

I looked at him then I looked at Jimmy, who was looking at

me, "That's cocaine isn't it?"

Jimmy snapped, "Oh, shit! Don't get moral on us, just snort the crap and let's get through this nightmare. Okay?"

I looked at both of them one more time, and snorted it. Finally they left me alone. I just sat there on the floor trying to calm myself. When I got up, I showered, changed, made up my face and I still had ten minutes to spare.

When the knock sounded on the door, I took a deep breath and swallowed my heart. Then, **'she'** took over and *Christina Powers* walked out onto the stage. As I stood there on stage, waiting for the curtains to rise, I drew a deep feeling of strength up from the depths of my soul and held it captive. Then, I heard it as if it were in the echoes of my dreams, screaming at me, "Ladies and gentlemen, here she is! The Queen of Disco, Christina Powers!"

All at once the lights, sounds, curtains and cheers of the audience, went up simultaneously. I gazed out at this sight while holding my seductive stance in my glistening gold gown, painted up like a queen. Oh, what a rush I felt! Then my performance began. The rhythm and I became one as we began to swirl together with sensual movements, which slowly intensified. The concert hall went black. All the bright intense, flashing lights were on my every move. As I moved, I swayed and slithered every muscle in my body. When I sang out, I sounded like an angel. Then I ripped my angelic, golden gown off my body, to reveal a black leather, gold-spotted leopard, full length skin tight body suit. I danced like a fiery demon from hell and sang out with a voice that was hypnotizing. I hit all the props right on cue. With each prop I hit, the stage flared up with flames and the illusion of silver sparks showered my most seductive moves. The crowd went wild with cheers. They loved it!

When I ended my performance by vanishing while clutching my breasts, into an aqua-blue smoke cloud, the place went mad with passion and deafening screams **for me!** As I stood there above this roaring crowd, I was flying with emotions of incredible power. I left my nation a disgrace and returned a queen! I took bow after bow. That night the world watched the creation of what was to become a **true, 20th century sex goddess**, with all the trappings! It was as if I'd spun a spell of love and lust on everyone watching. From that night on, I made cocaine a part of every performance."

After the show that night, there was a party being held at the Plaza Suite in the heart of the city. It was to celebrate, Nancy and Dawnetts 100th show. As I slipped my right leg out of the limo door in front of the Plaza entrance, I was looking my usual hot self! I performed every step of the way into the Plaza, through the flashing lights and the crowds of beautiful people, all wanting to **meet me!** Jimmy, Bobby and Joe, followed my lead. As I stepped into the ballroom, the applause went up and I was finally **home**!

The party was fabulous and without even trying, I took center stage from my gracious hostess', Nancy and Dawnett. It was like old times. Then, I thought of Johnny and the pain of that flashback made my eyes begin to water, so I quickly changed gears and gave my full attention to the party.

While I was being the life of the party, Mr. James Smith of Columbia Records, came up from behind, touched my shoulder, "Excuse me, Christina, but I'd like to introduce you to a friend of mine."

I turned to acknowledge this introduction, "This is Senator Tom Kenney, from Massachusetts."

I extended my hand to greet this man and thought, as we casually spoke to one another, "Oh my God, could this man really be my uncle? Am I a Kenney?" As our chat continued, I found myself dodging some very sophisticated advances and I thought, "Oh shit! I am a Kenney."

The next morning the whole country knew, *Christina Powers* was once Christy Valona. It was plastered in every newspaper across the country. Beginning at 9:00am that morning, the flowers, cards, letters and phone calls came flooding in. All of them, welcoming *Christina Powers* home, **With Love**.

But the only call I accepted that morning came from Barbara, my one true friend from my past. It was wonderful to finally speak with her again. She grilled me on everything I did over the last two and a half years and I did the same with her. She was out on the

West Coast, so we made plans to spend time together when my tour reached Los Angeles. The rest of that day was spent at the recording studio with all the gang. We had two weeks to finish the third album, before beginning our U.S. Tour.

Needless to say, we worked our asses off night and day to finish it. The title was, 'Love In The Heavens.' It had nine incredible cuts, one hotter than the next, and it was coming with me on tour.

On August 9th, we were getting ready to go on a six-month tour. So I grabbed my suitcases, one bottle of champagne and ran out the door to the waiting caravan of buses. **I was off to see America!**

CHAPTER 5. THE U.S. TOUR

As we toured the nation, my fame grew. I was bringing in the largest crowds ever seen in concert history. The sales of 'Love in the Heavens' my third album, soared to the number one spot its first week. My shows and public appearances also helped to bring new life to my career and increased the sales of my first two albums. The European market was finally being surpassed by the American market and by Christmas 1976, between the concerts and record sales, I was bringing in more than three-million-dollars a week, which was the gross take for Powers Records.

The schedule I kept was intense. While being on the road four nights a week performing, I managed with Jimmy's help to finish my first screenplay, 'Life, Passion and Fame'. We also had an entire sound track to accompany our planned future motion picture. When I wasn't working, I was raking up every high ranking male politician and dignitary across the country, and sticking them in my back pocket for future use. Everything you heard about me in those days was true. I had to seduce them all, especially the ones that were just out of reach. It became an obsession. In my spare time, I purchased the property of my dreams with the assistance of Dominick's American attorneys, for the mere sum of thirty-six million-dollars. There was no grass growing under my feet, as I jockeyed into position to get Frank!

While I was whoring, Jimmy settled down to a one on one relationship with Bobby. Bobby joined our team as head of stage, lighting and props, as well as my personal cocaine connection. My daily life had become consumed with wicked thoughts, passions and behaviors. All fueled by hatred! *Hatred for Frank*! I made sure every step I took brought me closer to destroying him. Somehow, I hid my inner fire from all those who knew me, including Jimmy.

Thanks to Dominick, and my own popularity with the American public, Frank stayed out of my way. But I knew he was out there lurking somewhere. So, I monitored every aspect of my life like a compulsive paranoid dictator. From every penny that came into my hands, to every person I had around me, I had it all under control. I became **THE BOSS**.

My last performance of the tour was February 2nd, 1977, in Hawaii. After the last show, I started a week vacation with Barbara. I needed some time off before I began casting and shooting on the new Powers Motion Pictures and Records Incorporation's first, full length motion picture. Starring, 'yours truly'. But this week was for Barbara and me. We stayed incognito at the Hyatt on the beach. The weather that entire week was perfect, sunny and beautiful with warm breezes. The temperatures ran at a steady ninety degrees during the day and the eighties at night. It was like paradise and this had been the first time I took notice of the weather in six months. It felt rejuvenating to be part of nature again. The heavenly days were filled with blue skies and incredibly starry nights and my soul drank from its pureness.

Barbara and I were having a wonderful time. We were at the beach by 8:00am every day, just soaking in the sun and each other's company. Our nights were started by an early dinner, then out on the balcony to soak in the balmy breezes. We stayed incognito right up to the last night we were on the island, which was a Saturday evening. It was around 8:00pm and we were going to the Governor's Mansion for a formal dinner party. There were about three hundred guests in attendance and you know me, I was **looking hot**.

Barbara and I were mingling with the guests when I noticed a very attractive man on the other side of the room. His presence seemed to be attracting the attention of most of the woman in the place.

I turned to Barbara, nonchalantly pointed him out, "Do you know who that is?"

She glanced toward him, "That's, Tony Demetrees, don't you know him?"

"No, should I?"

She looked at me kind of funny, "He's only America's hottest new leading man in Hollywood. I thought you would have heard he got the leading role in 'Samantha's Father' after you walked off the set. The movie made him an overnight sex symbol!"

I looked at her and with a slight giggle, "You're kidding. That hunk would have been my leading man? Maybe it's a good thing I left the film after all."

He was a looker. He was 6 feet tall, deep black hair, dark blue eyes and from what I could see, he had a body that wouldn't quit!

As we sipped on our champagne, I turned back to Barbara, "I wonder if I should try to get him for my leading man?"

Barbara smiled, "It wouldn't hurt the movie to have him in it, but I hear he's under contract with Frank."

"On second thought, the last thing I need is to have something that good looking hanging around." With a wink I added, "I'd never get the film done." As she laughed, I was thinking, "I'm not ready to come against Frank for anything. Not yet anyway."

Then Barbara asked, "Did you see the finished movie 'Samantha's Father?'

"No, I didn't, why?"

She took a sip of her champagne, "Kathy Brown was given the lead role after you left. The film won her an Oscar. Rumor has it she fucked you out of that part, literally." Her words struck a chord and they cracked the wall around my heart, just a little bit.

Trying to hide my embarrassment, "You mean to tell me everyone heard about her and Johnny?"

Her answer was blunt to say the least, "Christina, if you're coming back to Hollywood, I have to tell you this. Everyone in Hollywood also knows about your abortion."

"You're kidding!" I said with alarm. "Barbara, you're a good friend. I know that wasn't easy, but I love you more for being honest with me."

"I love you too," she kissed my cheek, "Christina, there's one more thing you need to know. Tony Demetrees is engaged to Kathy Brown, and I'm sure, if Tony is here, then Kathy is somewhere close by." Barbara put her arm around my shoulder, "I'm ready to leave now if you are?"

I turned to her firmly, "No, Barbara, I'm not going anywhere. As matter of fact, I just changed my mind. I do want Tony Demetrees for my leading man after all, and I'm going to go get him. Right now!" I grabbed Barbara by the hand, "Come with me, you know it could be bloody if I see her and I'm alone. Besides you have to introduce me to Tony."

With that, I turned Christina on full power, as I seductively charged through this elite crowd toward my prey!

Barbara with an encouraging spark to her tone, "You're so bad Christina I love it!"

I thought, "There is no way Kathy is getting away from me tonight without some damage being done."

As Barbara just happened to bump into Tony she said, "Tony! What a surprise." She grabbed his hand, kissed his cheek, "I didn't know you were on the island, are you vacationing?"

Returning her kiss, "We just finished shooting on Maui, I thought you knew that?"

With a slight chuckle, "I don't catch all the gossip, Tony, just most of it."

Still not noticing me, this sex goddess standing right next to him he said, "It's so good to see you Barbara, you look wonderful."

Smart-ass Barbara, continued her conversation with Tony, as I just stood there. I was ready to kick her when she finally said, with a surprised expression, "Oh, Tony! Please let me introduce you to a dear friend of mine." As she said, "Christina Powers," he turned toward me. When his eyes met mine I smiled softly, winked sensually at this great lady killer and I knew in that moment I'd conquered my prey! Somehow, I could see in his eyes a future beyond the one night stand I had planned for Kathy's fiancée. Catch my drift?

As the three of us continued the conversation, I was so seductive I radiated sensuality with my slightest move. My performance was so subtle no one in the entire room noticed, except him. It felt as if my soul left my body and mingled with his. As we talked, I was hypnotizing him with my eyes. The power I felt over him was incredible, I fed on it and somehow I knew it was real, like witchcraft of some sort, fueled by raging fires of revenge.

Then it happened. Kathy came in the door on Frank's arm. I broke my spell weaving and *froze in fear.*

Barbara quickly jumped in, "I'll go run interference and **YOU,** please go out the side door! This isn't the place or time for a confrontation."

I turned slightly shaking, "I'll meet you back at the hotel." Barbara dashed off to greet Frank as I looked at Tony, "I'm very sorry, but I must leave now."

He took my hand and led me to the side entrance, "I can't let you just leave like this, please let me take you back to your hotel." I graciously accepted his offer. Tony and I slipped around the outside of the Governor's Mansion and sent for his car. Neither Frank, nor Kathy, saw us leave. But I knew it wouldn't be long before they found out. That gave me one shot and one shot only to nail Tony.

We climbed into Tony's car. It turned out to be a vintage 1959, black Cadillac convertible with black leather seats. The car was cool. We drove out of the main gates of the mansion, down the road toward town with the top down.

As we drove, Tony remarked, "Christina, you look absolutely radiant with the wind softly blowing through your hair."

"Thank you very much. I love your car and it feels good to have the top down. I feel like the night sky is right at my fingertips." I ran my fingers through my long black hair, stretched my hands out past the windshield, and straight up to the stars.

Tony smiled, "Thank you, it was my father's car and I have it shipped everywhere I go." With curiosity he added, "That must have been a very awkward moment for you, almost running into both of them like that."

I turned to him, "Well, since my life seems to be an open book, yes I was very uncomfortable." I smiled, "Thank you for rescuing me."

"Christina, I think you're an excellent performer, and I was very disappointed when I learned you were not going to be my co-star in 'Samantha's Father.' I was looking forward to working with you."

"Thank you again, Tony, I truly appreciate the compliment. I hear you're a very talented entertainer, yourself."

We were entering the heart of the city as he said, "Thank you, Christina, I'm not too shabby if I must say so, myself." We laughed, then he asked, "Do you really need to go right back to the hotel now?"

"No, not at all, why, what do you have in mind?"

He gave me a gorgeous smile, "I would never forgive myself if I had the disco diva herself, in my car on a beautiful Saturday night and didn't ask her for just one dance." Then he looked me straight in the eye, "What do you say?"

I looked at him, smiled, ran my fingers through his wavy soft black hair, which was also blowing in the breeze, "I'd love to go dancing with you, Tony."

Just then he pulled, as if it were planned, into the valets' driveway at Platinum's. One of the hottest discos in town. As we climbed out of the car Tony said, "I hear you're the best hustler around."

I laughed, "I'm not too bad." As I said these words I was thinking, "In more ways than you could imagine, Tony."

I kept my innocent smile as he opened the door for me, "I'm not too bad, myself."

When we walked in Tony handed the top bouncer a hundred-dollar bill. We were escorted to a very secluded section of the establishment. We sat at a private bird cage style booth, where we both ordered White Russians. We could hear the music just fine and we could also hear ourselves as we talked. The entire place was decorated in black mirrors with red and gold carpeting. The room where our booth was, was attached to the main bar and dance floor, and separated by a beautiful indoor rainforest with little flowing streams. The only lighting in the rainforest and where we were seated was provided by dim little lights in the ceiling.

As we sat there in this interesting setting sipping our drinks Tony asked, "Do you know your name is the buzz word in the entire entertainment industry right now?"

I smiled, "To tell you the truth, I didn't even think about it until tonight."

With an interested tone, "I hear you're starting casting on your new script and that you just branched out your record label to include films."

I looked at him," Well if I intend to survive in this business for the long haul, I need a solid base to grow on."

He looked at me in awe, "Not only are you beautiful, but intelligent as well. That's very intriguing in a woman."

I smiled again, "I take that as a high compliment." I stroked his hand gently for just a moment, "Since you know so much about me, please tell me a little about yourself."

He reached for my hand, "How about after a dance?" Without hesitation I agreed.

He led me out onto the dance floor, which was lit by brilliantly flashing lights. It felt like magic. It was incredible how well we danced together. We started to dance the Latin hustle on that packed dance floor and people couldn't help but notice. When they realized who we were, they gave us the floor. Let me tell you, we used the entire thing. He spun me one way, then the other. He lifted me up in the air as we spun and I landed on the floor in the split position. Then he lifted me up to my feet. It was as if we had danced together for years. I followed his every lead. We moved together in a perfect sensual rhythm across the dance floor one way then danced as if we were floating on air back the other way. As we danced, we devoured each other's inhibitions, stimulating each other's imagination.

When we finished our dance, everyone began to applaud. I hugged Tony right on the spot, "I want you to play the lead role in my new film. I already know just by one dance, what kind of chemistry we'd have on film."

On the way back to our booth, I held my arm around his waist, as he held his around my shoulders. We walked through the rainforest, over a little wooden bridge which crossed over a small babbling brook. I gazed down at the running water and out of the corner of my eye I saw the shadow of a large man right behind me. I turned quickly to gaze at the figure and there was no one there. I felt a cold chill shoot down my spine, "Tony, do you mind if we leave now?"

I could tell Tony sensed my urgency, "Sure, let's get your cape and get out of here." So we did.

As we climbed into the car I asked, "Do you have to go right home?"

He looked at me, smiled, "No, what do you have in mind?"

I glanced over at him as we drove away, "A nice walk on a secluded part of the beach would be pleasing."

He reached over to me, gently squeezed my hand, "That sounds like a fine idea to me."

He headed out of town along the coastal highway until he found a secluded beach. We strolled hand in hand on the beach that night, with the crystal clear light of a full moon illuminating our path.

As we walked, "Tony, I'm very serious. I would love to work with you on this film."

"Well I might be able to work it into my schedule, if the price and timing are right."

I smiled, "The price I'm sure we can deal with, but what is your time frame?"

"I have six months off before starting the last film, of a five-film contract with, Salerno Pictures. I also have something in the works with Paramount for the next six months."

Intently I asked, "Is your Paramount deal finalized?"

"Not yet."

"That's good, now we can talk figures, because I plan to be releasing the film in only three months."

Wide-eyed he looked at me, "Three months! Boy, when you know what you want you don't waste any time going for it, do you?"

I smiled, "When we were dancing, I knew I had to have you." I paused for a second as his eyes lit up, then emphasized, "For my leading man."

His eyes lost their glow, "You've given me a lot to think about tonight."

I gently squeezed his hand, "Let's stop talking shop now and just take in this fabulous night." With that, we walked and walked for the longest time down the white sandy beach, listening to the crash of the waves on the shoreline.

As we walked Tony turned to me, took me in his arms, kissed me gently and said, "You are the most incredible woman I've ever met." He kissed me again, only this time with passion. We stood there in each other's embrace, with a gentle warm breeze blowing through our hair. I let my full length blue silk cape, drift to the sand, as our gentle encounter, slowly turned passionate.

He began to gently nibble on my ear and whisper, "Christina, I want you, right here right now." He kissed my lips deeply and as we came up for air, "I've never wanted anything more in my life, than I want you at this very moment."

As I slowly surrendered to his passion fueled by mine, I whispered softly and seductively, "Tony, take me. Take my love from me and fill me with yours." We resumed our kissing as we undressed each other slowly and passionately under the canopy of the heavens, until our flesh became one in the soft warm sand. I could hear the wave's crash as we made love and I could not resist the urge any longer. I gently pushed him up by his shoulders, to release our lips and held him there, "Come follow me."

I kissed him again, rolled out from under his body and rose to my feet. In my purest of fleshly apparel, I looked down at him, smiled, blew him a kiss and ran across the sand toward the crashing waves. As I reached the edge of the white foaming shore, Tony was right by my side. He grabbed my hand as we both ran into the sensually stimulating, tingling sensation of the cool ocean water.

As we swam, splashed and laughed, we were drinking in the beauty of our bodies until we could no longer resist one another. We embraced in the midst of the waves. We were so enthralled with one another, neither of us saw the wave that lifted us off our feet and splashed us down into the water on the edge of the beach. As the water rushed over our bodies, he plunged his powerful loins deep into my lusting essence. Our sex was wicked and our surroundings were divine. We consumed one another, over and over, until finally we collapsed on my cape, dripping wet with salt water. As we held each other under the starless sky of dawn's first light I thought, "This is real love, it wasn't just lust." Then my emotions turned dark, "It's not enough to steal him from Kathy for only one night."

As we laid there in a loving and tender embrace, I pulled the wild-card out. I looked deep into his spellbound eyes and with a tone of deepest love, "Tony, marry me! Marry me tonight! We could fly to Vegas and be married by 10:00 this evening. Then we can always be together like this."

I held my breath as he lovingly looked back at me, "Christina, I would marry you this second if I could." With that, we melted into a passionate embrace.

It was 6:30am when we left the beach and headed for my room at the Hyatt. We were totally in love, or so Tony thought. As we drove, we made our plans for the day. Tony was to drop me off so I could pack and make our flight arrangements to Vegas, as he headed to his hotel to pack. Then he would pick me up and off to the airport we'd go.

As we pulled up to the Hyatt, Tony leaned over, kissed me lovingly, "I love you, Christina, and I'll be right back for you."

I kissed him back, "Tony, I love you too and I can't wait to be your wife." I climbed out of the car and watched him drive away. I thought as I walked to my room, "I got him! Now to get him off this island pronto, so I can keep him."

It was 6:48 in the morning when I entered the room I shared with Barbara. When she heard me enter, she came out to find me looking like a drowned rat. She put her hands to her face and in horror, "Oh, my God! What in the world did they do to you?"

I looked at her like she was crazy, "What are you talking about? Nobody did anything to me. I went swimming."

"Didn't they find you?"

"Didn't who find me?"

"Oh, thank God! I thought they found you and tried to drown you." She started to crack up with laughter.

I was still looking at her in bewilderment, "Would you please try to make a little more sense so I can at least figure out what you're saying."

She stopped laughing, "You're right, it's not funny." She looked back at me and started to laugh again.

Shaking my head, "Barbara, we don't have time for this."

She contained herself long enough to say, "Last night about two hours after you and Tony left, one of Frank's men told him you and Tony were seen together at the Platinum's Disco. Frank and his goon left Kathy behind and took off together to go after Tony. I tried to stall them, but Kathy ran interference and rushed them out the door!"

As she was saying these words, I got a cold chill. I remembered the shadow and I thought, "How strange, could that shadow have been a warning of some kind? Ooh! This is too spooky even for me. I think I'll figure this one out some other day." Then I shook my head, "Don't worry about it. We have to pack now. I want you to be my maid-of-honor at my wedding in Vegas tonight. I'm marrying, Tony Demetrees."

Her mouth fell open, "You're not kidding me are you?"

I walked over to her, put my hands on her shoulders, kissed her cheek, "Nope! I'm not." Then I headed for the phone.

As I called the airport, Barbara turned toward me looking dumbfounded, "Isn't this carrying the payback a little to the extreme?"

After I booked the three of us on a 11:00am nonstop flight to Vegas I said, "It's not like that at all, Barbara we love each other."

She burst into hysterics, "Christina, you can sweeten it up with any feelings you want. But believe me girl, we are one in the same and I know you better than you realize." Looking at me with the sincerest expression, "Christina, the stench of revenge cannot be sugarcoated. Take it from someone who's been there."

I smiled at her, "I hear what you are saying, now please hear me." I stopped, looked her in the eyes, "Just be happy for me in the moment, 'cause that's the way I am choosing to live my life. For the moment!"

She embraced me, "I love you, girlfriend, and I am so pleased you've found some happiness, no matter who gets trampled on, because you deserve it." With that, we both slightly laughed a little sadistically. Then we went to prepare for our journey.

As I showered I thought, "If Frank can manipulate people to get what he wants, then so can I. And right now, Frank, I want Tony!"

It was 9:30am when Tony came to the door to pick us up. I had just finished speaking with Jimmy. I told him to have his ass in Vegas and meet me at the Golden Nugget by 7:00pm for my wedding. Then, I just hung up.

When I opened the door, I kissed Tony, "I love you, Tony." I turned to Barbara, "My man is here, now let's go." She came out from her room with two bags and handed them to Tony as she happily greeted him. I grabbed my suitcase, one bottle of champagne and it was **off to Vegas**.

CHAPTER 6. THE DOUBLE WEDDING

February 17th, 1977, we had a double wedding in Vegas. That night Tony and I were wed, Jimmy and Bobby took their vows of marriage at the same time we said ours. It was the first double wedding where one of the couples wed was a same sex marriage in the state of Nevada. It was not legal, but we did it anyway. Barbara stood up for the four of us. After the flashy ceremony, it was back to the airport. But, this time we were flying to LA in Barbara's private jet. We partied all the way back to Los Angeles. By the time we arrived, it was 3:00am, the next morning and we were toasted. The limo took us to Barbara's Malibu beach house, where we all finally collapsed.

The next day we spent recuperating by the warmth of the fireplace, in the glass enclosed family room, which over looked the stormy waves of the Pacific Ocean, on that cold February day. Tony and I clung to one another all that day. It was wonderful to have a strong man's arms around me again. We didn't let the headlines in the LA Times disturb us at all. It read, **"*Christina Powers'* Love Power, Sweeps Tony Demetrees, from the arms of his betrothed Kathy Brown, right to the altar."** The headlines also told the whole free world about our double wedding. As we read these headlines Tony appeared a little sad when he realized what we had done to Kathy, so I kissed his cheek, "We're in love Tony and we mustn't let ourselves feel too bad for her." As I comforted Tony, the only thing I was really concerned about was whether or not this publicity was going to hurt or help my new film. But I shared my concerns with no one.

When we left Barbara's home the next morning, I left an envelope in her bathroom on the back of the toilet tank. It had one hundred-thousand dollars cash in it and a three hundred thousand-dollar gold diamond stick, butterfly pin with a note which read, **"I used it with good judgment, Love Christina."**

Needless to say, Tony and I did not have much of a honeymoon. The next day, we were off to Columbia Pictures to begin auditioning and casting for 'Life Passion and Fame', starring **Christina Powers** and **Tony Demetrees**. We worked out the figures to Tony's liking. I gave him a four-million-dollar contract for one picture. We worked our asses off! Tony, Jimmy, Bobby and I worked almost eighteen hours a day. We would shoot from 5:00am to 9:00pm then, we were off to the recording studio until 2:00am. It was intense, but we knew we were creating a masterpiece, so we were driven. Jimmy and I finally stopped living together, when I moved in with Tony at his oceanfront penthouse in Malibu. But, that didn't mean I saw any less of Jimmy, for he and Bobby rented an apartment together only two blocks from us.

Somehow, amidst this mad pace, Tony and I flew to New York and hired the top architects in the city, and put them to work on the design for the future headquarters of Powers Incorporated. Tony and I worked together like fire. Not only on the screen, but with every aspect of the building of my empire. We also had fun together as we worked, which made all the hard work go faster. The four of us went full steam ahead. It was as if they caught my fire and began to burn with me. We set up a makeshift operation in downtown LA, not far from the studio Columbia Pictures, lent us for the filming of 'Life Passion And Fame'. With the help of an employment agency, along with Jimmy and Bobby, we hired office staff for our new location. Then, they went to work recruiting new talents of all kinds for my final inspection. From writers to singers, we concentrated on our recording label first. It was our moneymaker thus far, but I had full intentions to begin to play with the big boys, right after we made our millions on 'Life Passion and Fame.' I knew this film was a work of genius on paper, but it was up to us to bring it to life on the screen.

Tony and I had extraordinary passion between us and we brought that passion to life on the film with every take. It was magical how we performed together, in more ways than one. Tony and I were becoming one! It was as if my dream became Tony's dream. I slowly began to really fall in love with him and I slowly began to let him, *truly let him,* into my life. When we did find the time to make love, it was honest love! It was beautiful, sensual and passionate. I didn't realize how much I missed this kind of passion in my life. **It was the passion of love.** We lived our lives like this and so did Jimmy and Bobby, from February 20th, to the day we finished the last edit on 'Life Passion and Fame' on June 7th, and it was just in time, because my record sales had begun to slip. Before plunging into the promotion for the release of our film on June 21st, the four of us decided to take a few days off for a much needed rest. So, we were off to our perspective honeymoons' in Lake Tahoe, Nevada leaving all of our cares behind.

The four of us took a cabin together to begin our four days of marital bliss, on a very secluded part of the lake. Our view of this lake, surrounded by majestic mountains, was fabulous. The cabin's forty foot deck jetted out over the crystal clear waters of Lake Tahoe. When you walked in the front door, you entered a large open knotty pine room with living room furniture laid out beautifully around a large fireplace. Off to the left of this room was a completely updated kitchen, on the right was a formal dining room. The entire first floor was open in the back to the deck, which held a captivating view. On either side of the beautiful living room and just before you entered the kitchen or the formal dining room stood two spiral staircases one on each side. The staircases led up to an open wraparound balcony. The balcony looked over the first floor in the front and out over the lake in the back. On either side of this balcony were our rooms with private baths. The whole place was done in knotty pine. We had just enough provisions to last the four days. When we sat down at the kitchen table for coffee that first morning the weather was 'bright' and 'sunny' and already eighty degrees.

As we sat around the table sipping our coffee, Jimmy was reading a brochure on the area's attractions. Tony got up from his chair, walked over behind me and began to massage my shoulders, while looking at all of us, "So what would you guys like to do today?"

Smiling, "What can you do out here in the wilderness except to just take in the beauty of it all?"

Tony kissed my cheek, "There are lots of things to do out here, baby, like fishing."

"Can't we just sit out there on the deck?"

Jimmy spoke up, "No, Christina, I'm not going to let you get us out here just to sit for four days. I want to do something."

With that Bobby said, "I'm with, Christina, I can handle just staying here."

"Oh come on you two," Tony added. "We have to do something fun."

So I replied, "I guess they're right, Bobby. We should do something, after all, who knows when we'll have free time again."

"Okay, whatever you guys want to do. Count me in." Bobby agreed.

Tony asked, "Jimmy, what's in the brochure?"

"Oh, lots of fun things, like boat trips, fishing trips, mountain climbing and sky diving." Then acting a little like a monkey as he jumped up and down in his seat, "Ooh, ooh, ooh, here's one, listen to this. **Come run the white water rapids on your own inner tube down the winding, rolling, Snowy Hill River, until you emerge into the waiting arms of beautiful majestic Lake Tahoe.**"

"That sounds great," Tony said as he slapped his hands together!

Then I said, "Okay, I'm game." Once I did, Jimmy dashed to the phone to make the arrangements.

It was 1:00pm when we grabbed our tubes and headed to the river to begin our ten-mile trip down the white water rapids to the lake.

As I sat down in the middle of my tube wearing my cut off blue denim jeans, I jumped up quickly and shouted, "Oh shit! This water is cold!"

That's when Jimmy spoke up, as he bravely sat in the cold water, "Oh, don't be a pussy! Just get in the water."

"Okay, okay, don't rush me." Then I flopped my ass into the cold water and off we floated down the river.

The four of us started out in a chain, all holding someone else's hand. I held Tony's, Tony held Jimmy's; and of course Jimmy held Bobby's. It turned out to be fun! I couldn't believe floating down a river would be so much fun. The first few sets of rapids we went down were great. They were nice and gentle, with just a touch of the cold water splashing on us.

We were laughing and having a great time, so I yelled out, "Hey, Jimmy, this was a great choice! I know my ass is turning blue, but I love it!"

Then, we started down our second set of rapids. This one was a little faster than the first set and it forced us to break our chain. There was a little more splashing, but nothing I, **jungle woman** Christina couldn't handle! Very quickly we began to be rushed into the next set of rapids. As we hit the first set of rolling water, I noticed Tony, Jimmy and Bobby were drifting off to the left side of the river, while I was drifting off to the right side of the river. By chance, I caught sight of a woman up on a hill just off the river's bank. She was jumping up and down while waving her arms. It appeared she was yelling something, but I couldn't hear her over the sound of the water, until the current brought me closer to her. At which time I could finally understand what this crazed woman was screaming, "Don't go that way! Turn back, it's not part of the **courseeee**," as I sped by!

I looked and noticed the river forked just ahead of me, and I thought, "Oh, my God! Thanks for telling me lady, but how in the hell do I not go that way!" I was being swept away so I screamed out, "Tony! Help me," as I went flying over the rocks, heading the wrong way. I saw Tony as he jumped off his tube, grabbed it and came flying through the rushing water. Then he jumped back on it and headed down after me. I went flying over four foot drops, screaming all the way. I smashed into twenty or more rocks, all head on, clinging to this black inner tube for dear life, and I could not believe what I saw next! I was heading straight for a tree which lay across the entire river. I screamed and held on as I collided with this unmovable beast **and when I did**, I flew head over heels while still holding my ass in the tube, landing in the middle of a five-foot deep whirlpool, which began to swirl me as if I had just been put on the spin cycle of my washing machine. Just as fast, it flung me head first into the ice cold rush of white water. As I struggled to rise from the bottom of this whirlpool, I caught sight of something gold flashing out of the corner of my eye. So when I stood up out of the water, I took a deep breath and when I did, I could see Tony about twenty feet away coming toward me. Then, I dove back into the ice cold depths of the water and found the origin of the gold flash. I reached for a medallion of some sort on the bottom of the river bed and just as I grabbed it, I found myself flying out of the water with such a force it nearly broke my neck, as Tony swept me up into his arms and carried me to the shore.

When we reached the shore, I was banged up and freezing. I just grabbed Tony and held on. As Tony rubbed his hands on my body to warm me up, he excitedly asked, "Are you all right, baby?"

I took a moment to examine my bruises, "I've been better, but I'll survive."

Shaking his head, "What the hell were you doing?"

"What was I doing? I didn't do it. The water did!"

With a bewildered expression, "I don't mean that, I mean jumping back in the water like you did. You scared the shit out of me."

"Look at what I found down on the bottom of the river," I opened my hand to show him the gold piece I had grabbed.

Tony took it from my hand, "This is different, I've never seen a medallion quite like this before." Just then, we heard the panicked screaming of Jimmy and Bobby. I put the gold piece in my pocket and we stood up to see where Jimmy and Bobby were calling. We looked down to the end of the river and there they were. It seemed we only had another one hundred yards to go on this little detour we took, before running back into the main river. So, I climbed on top of Tony in his tube. We floated the rest of the way back down the river, to where Jimmy and Bobby were frantically waiting.

They rushed to our aid, helped us out of the tube and kept repeating, "Are you guys all right?"

When I was finally on my feet with the help of these two bumbling idiots, I slapped Jimmy across the back of his head and shouted, "You and your stupid ideas! We could have been killed."

Jimmy started to cry and sobbed, "I'm sorry, Christina."

I held him, "I'm sorry Jimmy, it's not your fault."

He slowly stopped sobbing, "Well, we can't stop now. We still have five more miles of this."

With that, we all laughed as we climbed back in our tubes. Except for one difference, I was floating on my right side with my body lying next to Tony, as he laid face up. I placed my head on his left shoulder, slid my right leg over his knees, placed my right hand on top of his wet crotch and we floated on his tube just like that. To be honest, I loved the little detour.

As we floated, I could feel the slight throbbing of a growing mass in the palm of my right hand. I immediately felt a warm flash shoot through my body, even though I was still in that very cold water. I quickly raised the temperature of our bodies when I slid on top of Tony and began to sensually shower him with kisses, as I was rhythmically grinding my thighs into his groin. It was becoming quite the hot little ride, when it was abruptly stopped by the river bed. We looked up to see Jimmy and Bobby standing over us.

Tony looked at them, "Don't you guys have something better to do?"

Bobby threw his hands in the air, "You guys should take a look at this, before you get too carried away."

When we stood up, it appeared as if most of the water just vanished. There was only a small steady flow going over the rocks, but not enough to float on. I looked over to the right side of the river bank and there was my tube floating away. We picked up our tubes and started to walk. As we walked, we found ourselves slowly waving our hands in the air at a few annoying horseflies. Then, from out of the depths of hell, came this swarm of demon horseflies. It was un-fucking real! They dive bombed us like kamikaze pilots. They were eating us alive! It got so bad I started

James Aiello

screaming. I thought I was going mad. Then Tony grabbed me, took his big black tube, and started swinging it in the air in a desperate attempt to get them off of me.

I screamed, "Jimmy, if I didn't love you I'd shoot you right now!"

Jimmy shouted as he frantically flung his shorts through the air, beating back the attack, "They're eating me too, you know!"

Once I stopped laughing at the sight of Jimmy, in his wet underpants I shouted back, "That's no consolation Jimmy." Just as I did, I caught my left foot under a rock and went crashing onto the stones again. Tony helped me up and I now had a limp, too!

I turned to Jimmy, "Strike the love part, Jimmy. When I can walk again, I'm going to kill you."

Finally the water rose and we were quickly swept away from our impending doom.

It was 6:00pm when I hobbled into the cabin. I looked like I had fought the Vietnam War by myself and lost. I was black and blue from head to toe and with all the red spots; I looked like I had jungle fever. If I weren't hurting so much, it would have been laughable.

Then I crept over to the spiral staircase, "I'm going for a hot bath, would someone else please think about dinner tonight."

Tony kissed my cheek, "How about Chinese? I could run into town and pick some up."

I kissed him back, "That sounds good to me, baby." Then I slowly proceeded up the steps and right into a hot tub!

After dinner that evening, the four of us sat out on the deck with our Chablis wine. The night was beautifully warm, and it felt liberating just to be sitting there absorbing this awesome display of nature. As we sat there, we were able to look back at the day's events and finally laugh about it. Boy did we laugh!

Then I remembered my find, so I took it off. I had put it on my neck chain shortly after my bath. As I showed it to them, I proceeded to tell Jimmy and Bobby how I came to have it in my possession. We all agreed the piece seemed very old and was solid gold. It was about the size and shape of a man's pocket watch. ***In the center was a carving of a naked goddess standing on top***

94

of a flaming ball of fire, and she appeared to be breaking the chains which bound her to this inferno.

As we remarked on its beauty, jokingly Jimmy said, "Well, if you had drowned, we would have never known of its existence."

With a laugh I said, "Maybe I was meant to find it, it's probably a good luck charm." We all laughed at my words, as I placed it back around my neck.

As Tony and I lay on the soft bed together that night, he looked deep into my eyes, "Christina, honey, I love you. You're the best thing that's ever come my way. Baby, every time I look at you, I gaze in wonder at your beauty, your intelligence and your strength." He kissed me softly and in a gentle loving tone, "You're so full of life Christina and I thank God you are my wife."

I kissed him, "Tony, I love you more every day. I never thought I could feel like this." I kissed him again as I pulled him over to me. Our love soared that night, as we came together in hot passion. He was incredible as he softly caressed my beaten body. I felt no pain! All I could feel was intense love for this man, this magnificent man who was now truly my husband. I surrendered all my emotions as I cried for the first time while making love, since Johnny.

"Oh, God Tony, I love you, I love you. Take me, baby, take me." I cried, and I meant every word. I begged him for more and more and he gave it to me. He satisfied me in ways I thought I'd never feel again. It was lovemaking in its purest form. We were both in heaven together.

I woke up to the chirping of the birds outside our open windows. I looked at the alarm clock and it read eight o'clock. Tony was still sound asleep, so I tip-toed into the bathroom. When I returned, I put on my robe while Tony was stirring in the bed. So I kissed his cheek, "Don't get up, baby, I'll go put on some coffee and bring you a cup."

Returning my kiss, "Sounds good to me, I'll go to the bathroom and meet you right back here." With that, he walked one way and I limped the other.

When I walked out onto the balcony, I couldn't help but notice Jimmy kneeling on the floor on his hands and knees. He was down in the large living room, facing an open door. I could see he had the screen door propped open with a coffee cup. On closer inspection, I could see he was holding a camera in his hands and there were peanuts on the floor, just outside the front door. And to top this whole scene off, Jimmy was only in his underpants, socks and a tee shirt.

Finally, I could resist no longer, "Jimmy, what are you doing down there like that?"

He turned his head almost 160 degrees and in a soft whisper, as he put one finger over his lips, "Look, out there on the porch."

I bent over the rail, "Jimmy, I don't see anything."

With a boyish snicker, "It's a squirrel and it's eating the nuts I'm putting out for it. I'm trying to get a close-up shot."

I whispered back, "Put the nuts a little closer to the doorway so I can see him too."

Jimmy slowly placed a nut just at the doorway and I could see this sweet little squirrel just nibbling on it. It was adorable and we were amazed as Jimmy got his shots.

Then all at once, the wind blew the screen door closed with a **crash!** This sweet little squirrel made a horrifying screech, leaped three feet into the air, at the same time Jimmy let out with a scream and jumped four feet into the air. They both started to slid across the slippery oak floor like cartoon caricatures as they tried to run away from each other.

I cried out hysterically, "Run Jimmy, it could be rabid!" At which time, the squirrel turned and charged right toward Jimmy. Screaming, Jimmy slid across the floor as if he had just gotten hit by a lightning bolt. I screamed in horror as I watched helplessly, "Run Jimmy! He's coming right for you!"

Bobby ran in with the broom and started swatting at it. It jumped, made a turn in midair, landed right on the staircase, and charged up the steps. It stopped at the top, looked straight into my eyes and started running toward me screeching all the way. I shrieked as if a herd of elephants were heading right for me. Turning to run, I saw Tony coming out of the bedroom then he dashed back in. Being left to fend for myself, I flung myself down the spiral staircase in a desperate attempt to escape. As I struggled to my feet, I looked up and there he was still coming after me. I screamed and ran to the sofa Jimmy was standing on, leaped at him and we both went crashing into the coffee table. I looked up quickly to see if the monster was still on my trail, and saw Tony throw a blanket over this flesh eating beast, and let it out the front door.

I stood up in total shock, took a deep breath and shouted, "Jimmy, are you trying to kill me? Or is this your idea of fun?"

He stood there as chicken as I was, "Oh my God, girlfriend! I thought we were goners!" The four of us immediately lost it. We must have laughed a good twenty minutes as we tried to have our coffee and toast.

After we finally stopped laughing, I reached over toward Jimmy from my chair, put my arms around his neck, kissed him and said, "Jimmy, I love you. You're the best friend anyone could want, but I think if I stay here with you in this wilderness much longer, I'll be going home in a casket."

I kissed him again as we chuckled. Then, I turned to Tony as I released my hold on Jimmy. I stretched my hand out, took Tony's hand in mine, "Baby, would you be too upset if I asked you to take me to one of the hotels in town."

Tony looked at me and smiled, "Actually, Christina, I do mind. You see, baby, I have a little wedding gift for you, but I forgot it at home and I can't wait to give it to you. So would you be too upset if I took you home."

I squeezed his hand, "Oh, Tony, that's sweet and no I don't mind going home." Then Tony called the airport and booked us on the 1:00pm flight back to LA. We grabbed our suitcases, I grabbed one bottle of champagne and **it was off to LA.**

CHAPTER 7. AFTER THE HONEYMOON

It was 5:00pm when we loaded the trunk of Tony's black Cadillac with our suitcases at LA International Airport. As we drove toward our home in Malibu, Tony seemed a little excited and he had a childish smile on his face. As I watched him I thought, "What is he up to?" I could take the suspense no longer, "All right, why do you have that smirk on your face?"

His face lit up like a Christmas tree, "What smirk? I don't have a smirk on my face."

I chuckled, "Oh, then that must be a neon sign I see flashing on your face."

As I was saying these things Tony drove past our building, "Where are we going?" Knowing there was not much out past our building, except scenic views.

"I just thought a little ride might be nice."

I slid across the seat, kissed his cheek, "Hmm! That sounds romantic." Then I laid my head on his shoulder as we drove up the scenic Malibu Coast.

Shortly after we passed the gates to Barbara's mansion, Tony began to slow down as if he were looking for something. Then, he pulled into an open gate and proceeded up a winding, wooded driveway, "Where are you going?"

He patted my thigh, "To Barbara's, house."

"If you're going to Barbara's, then you're at the wrong place," Looking at him strangely I added, inquisitively, "What's up? Why are we going to, Barbara's?"

The driveway led up to a brilliantly light tinged, bright yellow, brick mansion with all white trim. Tony parked the car right at the front entrance, "You'll see when we go in." With that, he got out of the car came around to my door opened it, "Come on, she's waiting."

I gave him another strange look, "Tony, this is not, Barbara's house."

He reached for my hand, grabbed it and gently pulling me out, "This is her new place. She said she'd leave the driveway gate open for us."

"Oh," I said with surprise, "I didn't know she was moving."

Then, I looked at this magnificent three-story, brick mansion as we walked up the six steps, of a twenty-foot wide staircase, which was attached to a one hundred foot long, eighteen foot deep, Italian marble front porch and I exclaimed, "Holy, shit! Would you look at this place? It's gorgeous!"

There were six, thirty foot tall, three feet in diameter circular marble Roman style columns holding up, this blast from the past, Greco-Roman architectural styled, front porch. When, we reached the large eight foot double hung doors, Tony slipped a key into the lock. All at once, he flung the big doors open, swept me off my feet and shouted, "Welcome home baby!"

Then, he proceeded to carry a completely shocked woman over the threshold. As he placed my feet back on the floor, he kissed me, "I love you, Christina! I bought it for you. I mean us. Oh, you know what I mean."

I hugged him so-lovingly as I giggled my reply, "Yes, I know what you mean." Kissing him, "Oh, Tony, It's just beautiful and I love you for it! Thank you, thank you my love."

He took my hand tugged my arm with excitement, "Come on Christina, let me show it to you, baby."

As we toured the interior of our new home, I said with a surprised tone, "Tony, this is our furniture. When did you find the time to do this?"

He smiled proudly, "I had it all moved here yesterday. I thought it would do fine for now, at least until we can find the time to decorate it ourselves."

I was so excited; I began kissing him childishly all over his face, "I love you, Mr. Demetrees."

He returned my kisses, "I love you too, Mrs. Demetrees."

The mansion towered majestically on top of a cliff, which overlooked the glistening Pacific Ocean on that early evening sunset. There were lovely flower gardens everywhere and on either side of the mansion, stood two, large water fountains. As you passed through the front doors, you entered a large marble foyer with a six-foot round, crystal, chandelier hanging from the ceiling. Across from the front doors, were two marble staircases which curved up both walls on either side of the foyer to a beautiful landing on the second floor. The inside was Italian marble, slate, wood and stone throughout the entire place. It had fourteen bedrooms, sixteen bathrooms, three kitchens, three formal living and dining rooms, two libraries and three towering balconies which overlooked the ocean. On the grounds were two guest homes, a ten-car garage, a house for the staff and two barns with riding stables, all on two hundred acres. The place was incredible! I had not lived in a place like this since I moved out of Frank's mansion.

After our tour, Tony pushed a button on the wall intercom in the small kitchen and said, "James, would you and Carman, please come up?"

A male voice responded, "We'll be right up, sir."

I looked at Tony, "Who are, James and Carman?"

Before Tony could answer, two people in their late fifties came into the room. At which time Tony said, "James, Carman, I would like you to meet, Mrs. Demetrees." Turning toward me he added, "Christina, let me introduce you to, Mr. and Mrs. James and Carman Pavone. Carman is our cook and housekeeper. James is our chauffeur and gardener. They live in the staff quarters."

We exchanged greetings then Carman said, "It is very nice to meet you, Mrs. Demetrees. Now please excuse me, I have to get back to the main kitchen or we'll be having burnt lasagna for dinner."

With that, she took off down the hall with James still saying, "It's nice to meet you, ma'am," as he ran off after her.

She was walking determinedly toward the kitchen, then she abruptly stopped dead in her tracks, turned and hollered up the hall, "Oh Yes, dinner will be served in the blue dining room at seven o'clock," and just as quickly she ran out of sight.

I turned to Tony, "They seem nice enough, but live-in help. Do we really need them?"

Tony kissed my cheek, "The way you work me, you don't think I'm going to cook and clean up after you too. Do you?"

I laughed, "We'd better bring our suitcases in; we only have twenty minutes till dinner you know."

Tony laughed, "James, has already brought them up and put them in our room."

"Wow!" I replied with a surprise, "Maybe we do need help after all."

Tony chuckled, "Come on; let's go sit on the deck while we wait for dinner."

Tony sat down on a big white rocker, which was part of a twenty-piece wicker set on the first floor deck. I sat on Tony's lap and said to him, as we looked out over the ocean, "Baby, this place is beautiful! But what did you pay for it?"

He gently patted my thigh, "Don't worry about the price. We can afford it."

I kissed his forehead, laughed then replied, "Tony, I'm not worrying about the money, I'd just like to know how much you dished out for me, that's all."

He smiled, "Eight-million and you're worth every penny!"

Wide eyed, "Eight-million-dollars for one house, I'm glad you think I'm worth it!" I flung my legs over the armrest of the rocker, and slipped further down into his lap. I gazed up into his eyes and I sweetly kissed him, "Tony, my love, thank you for my wedding gift. I love it!" I kissed him again, only this time much deeper. When we finally came up for air, "Baby, I have a wedding gift for you too." Gazing lovingly up into his eyes, I softly continued, "Tony, we are going to have a baby."

His face appeared as if he were in shock, "Are you serious?"

I shook my head to indicate yes, smiled, "Yup, I'm pregnant baby."

He held me closely and with enthusiasm, "Oh God, Christina! We're going to have a baby! You have made me the happiest man on earth and I love you with all of my heart." Then, we just laid there holding each other until Carman called us for dinner.

After a scrumptious lasagna dinner, we took a walk arm-in-arm around the grounds and down to the stables. When we got there, Tony said, "I hope you can ride?"

I smiled devilishly, "Nobody rides better than I do. Why don't we go to our new bedroom and I'll show you just how well I can ride?"

He kissed me passionately, "Let's go!" Then we began to walk back to the mansion. As we passed the beautifully fragrant gardens on that warm starry evening, Tony asked me, "So when is our little one coming into the world?"

"I'm not sure, I only found out yesterday when the Doctor called with the results of my test."

Tony turned toward me quickly, "We'd better get you to the doctor then, 'Little Woman'"

I laughed at Tony's, John Wayne imitation, as he said, 'Little Woman'. Then I said, "I'll call Doctor Hedderman tomorrow morning."

"That's good baby. We have to stay on top of these things you know."

As we climbed the steps of the front porch, Tony put his arm around my shoulders, "We're here, Christina." He rubbed my belly, "Our new baby, new home and new life together. May it be filled with lots of love, lots of happiness and lots of babies."

As he said these words I felt joy, which quickly turned into a dim, faint pain in my heart as I thought of Johnny, and what might have been for one brief second. Then, I dismissed the thought and gave my full attention to Tony.

When we reached our third floor master bedroom I said, 'imitating Mae West', as I pulled Tony by his hands, "Come with me little man, I've got something to show you."

He followed willingly as I led him into the bathroom. I turned the bath water on warm and began to undress him. As I unzipped his pants he immediately became aroused, so I knelt down, slipped his pants to the floor and kissed the tip of his beautiful manhood and as I gazed up into his eyes, "Don't get too hot yet, baby. We have a lot to celebrate and all night long to celebrate it."

I finished undressing him and led him to the tub which was nice and steamy by this point. As he climbed into the large four person bathtub, I was gently stroking his beautiful body. I proceeded to continue my seduction of Tony as I climbed in and began to kiss his entire body. I lathered him with a huge sponge; then, he began to wash me and as he did, I felt our passion growing even hotter. That's when I slowed our pace by rinsing and drying us both off. I led him to our bed, pulled back the covers and opened the curtains to a bright starry night. As we fell onto the bed, I began to devour his body with my love. Our bodies soared together in the heat of passion on that brilliant night! It was all so wonderful. As we made love, we were celebrating our new life together as one.

As we laid in each other's arms just before sleep crept over us, I began to think, "That was the closest I came to perfect ecstasy since Johnny." I snuggled a little closer to Tony and thought, "Oh God. I truly do love Tony, so why can't I get Johnny out of my heart?" With that thought I screamed out in my mind, "Stop haunting me Johnny! I don't love you anymore and I want you out of my heart so I can love Tony completely." I felt a tear running down my cheek and I stopped my mind dead and thought, "Oh well! I'll figure it out tomorrow."

The next day, doctor Hedderman informed me to expect a little bundle of joy on October 10th, which just happened to be the same as my true mother's birthdate. After I told Tony, I called Jimmy and Bobby, and told them to come right over as soon as they got back into town. Then I called my office manager and had her send out a memo inviting everyone who was anyone in Hollywood to a celebration party to announce our expected gift. It was to be held at our home that coming Saturday night, June 13th, at 8:00pm which was only two days away. I also invited the press and tabloids. The timing was perfect. One thing I learned from Frank was to never look a gift horse in the mouth. However, I did leave two names off my guest list, Frank and Kathy.

It was Thursday night, June 11th, around 8:00pm when Jimmy and Bobby came to the door just in time for dessert. As soon as Jimmy opened the door he said, "It's no surprise Christina, I saw the house before you did."

I kicked him in his ass as he walked by me, "You did, did you? Why you shithead! How in the world did you keep your mouth shut?"

We laughed as we walked into the living room. While we talked about the house, Carman brought in some coffee and pineapple whipped cream cake.

We were having our dessert and I turned to Jimmy, "Jimmy, I have a confession to make, I lied to you about something."

He looked at me as if he went into shock, "I can't believe you lied to me! I would never lie to you."

"Don't get so melodramatic, Jimmy. Remember I said the test was negative? Well that's what I lied about. I am going to have a baby."

All at once, he jumped up in the air, spilled his coffee all over Bobby and started screaming, "Oh my God! That's wonderful!" As Bobby jumped up and shouted, "Oh my God! That's hot!"

That Saturday night we had the most glamorous party in town. Barbara, Jimmy, Bobby, Joe and Dorothy Cole and the rest of the crew, as well as most of our Hollywood friends were there. They all came to our home to celebrate with us along with the press. Tony and I were dressed to the hilt. He was so handsome in his black tux and I was ravishing in my dark maroon, satin, full length gown. As we welcomed our guests, we opened our new home and our new life, to our friends and our country. We were so proud of ourselves and our achievements that day and the party was a smashing success.

The next day, the whole country knew I was having Tony's baby. Our photos were plastered all over the free world and we planned to keep it that way for the next two months. It was time to get back to work. We promoted the upcoming release of our new film and double record soundtrack, day and night around the entire country. We did TV and radio talk shows, all day and night, in thirty-six cities, in seven straight days. While Tony and I were traveling, Jimmy and Bobby were signing new acts onto the Powers Record Label. It seemed as though the whole record industry was jumping on the disco bandwagon. So, Powers Records started pumping out one disco hit after another. Yes, there were other disco divas in those days, but none like me, for I was the Queen of Disco and the whole world knew it.

Saturday, June 20th, at 7:00pm we held the premier of, 'Life Passion and Fame' at the Palladium, in downtown Los Angeles. We spared no expense to assure we had a lavish opening, with all the Hollywood hoopla! Tony and I looked like a king and queen as we greeted Hollywood's elite at the front door of the Palladium. As the limos pulled up, through the crowds and the flashing of the press with their cameras, we could see from where we were standing, each guest as they climbed out of their limos and walked up the red carpet toward us. I was smiling, happy and proud, as we greeted our friends. Then, I felt the expression on my face turn evil, as soon as I saw Frank and Kathy climb out of one of the limos and start walking toward us. Tony quickly grabbed my arm, "Just relax Christina, we can deal with him."

I turned to him and forcefully, "I've heard those same words before. Believe me Tony, he's a prick and she's his slut, and if they're here, something is up."

Under his breath, "Isn't that a little strong? I still happen to have a contract with Frank, remember? So please don't put me in the middle of this war you and Frank have going."

I looked at him angrily and sharply said, "When you married me you put yourself in the middle of it. So don't try to sugarcoat it with him now, because it won't work."

When they reached us, Frank said, "You look well, Christina and I see.."

I just cut him right off, "What are you doing here?"

He smiled, "I've come to see your work."

I snapped back, "You're both not welcome here."

Frank turned to Tony, "Is this true, Tony?"

Tony quickly answered, "Of course not Frank, please come in."

I stood there trying not to **rip his face off**, as he was inviting Frank in. Then, he continued with, "Kathy, it's good to see you.

You look wonderful tonight." I almost bit my tongue off as I smiled for the cameras. Then finally, the show started.

The premier was a smashing success, but that was not what I wanted to talk about when Tony and I climbed into bed that night. He rolled over to me, kissed my neck, and with anger in my voice, "Don't even think about it! How could you humiliate me like that? In front of all those people no less."

"Me! I was trying to save the moment. Do you realize what you said to Frank Salerno in front of all those people? He's your uncle. You should know better than anyone, what kind of man he is. Nobody talks to Frank like that and gets away with it."

My reply was sharp, "Well I do! He's a no good bastard, and I don't want him in my life, in anyway, at all."

Tony knelt up in the bed and gently grabbed my shoulders, "Christina, I love you and I thought it took a lot of balls for you to stand up to Frank like that. I'm proud of you. You fought the boss-man and won. But baby, I still have to do one more film with that man, so please, for my sake, please don't let him come between us. After the film, I don't care if you stand on the top of the World Trade Center and shout obscenities at him, just please wait until the film is done."

With that, he gave me his little boy look and I slowly melted into his arms. As I did, I said, "Tony, I'm sorry, I should have thought of you, instead of just myself."

I proceeded to gently kiss his shoulders and as I laid my head on his chest, he said, "Baby, I love you! We really pulled it off tonight you know. This film was pure genius and it's going to be a hit for us."

I kissed him passionately, "I love you too Tony, and yes we were like magic on the screen." Then we came together in the tenderness of pure, loving passion.

That weekend, 'Life Passion and Fame', brought in a record breaking sixty eight million dollars and Tony and I became the most popular couple in America. The demand for the two of us to make personal appearances shot through the roof and we did our best to fill them all. Over the next two months, the movie and record sales were bringing in hundreds of millions of dollars worldwide. At the same time, the soundtrack to the movie which was titled, 'Come Lay with Me' was number one on all the record charts. I was singing the number one cut on the album, 'Come Lay with Me' at every appearance. Between traveling and personal appearances Tony and I would write. We started writing the lyrics for my next album and screenplay, as well as the lyrics we sent to Jimmy and Bobby, to be recorded by our new head liners. We also broke ground on the future site of what was now called Powers Incorporated, in Milton, N.Y. The building design we chose for our future home, was the most complete environmentally friendly design of its time.

By August 30th, we were back in the recording studio, working all day on my fifth album entitled, 'Everlasting Love.' All night we wrote our next screenplay entitled, 'Listen to the Wind'. It was a story of two strangers who fell in love in one night, as they talked on the beach. We also found out that day that Tony would have to start filming his next movie with Salerno films, on January 2nd, 1978, in London, England. I was not too pleased to receive this information. I tried to convince Tony to try to break his contract through the courts, but he refused. So I thought, "Oh well! I'll figure it out tomorrow. And if I don't, at least I would have Tony all to myself until then."

We released our fifth soundtrack, 'Everlasting Love' on October 5th, 1977 and I was as big as a house. By now, I was done with being pregnant, but the baby wasn't! I felt like a twenty-two-year-old sex symbol in hiding. I was so fat; I thought I was having a cow instead of a baby. As October 10th, my due date came and went, I hated being pregnant. I thought I would go out of my mind if this kid didn't come out soon." Then I started to get scared. All this talk of breathing the pain away, I knew was all bullshit and it was going to hurt. October 12th, I was really bitchy. Everybody just stayed away as I paced through the entire mansion like a waddling duck with three little spying Indians, following in the distance. The place became an insane asylum. Especially when Jimmy and Bobby insisted on moving in with us until the baby came.

It was October 14th, at 2:00am when my water finally broke and I wet the bed. I turned to Tony, "Tony, I think it's time."

With groggy eyes he looked at me, "Baby, did you say something?"

As I started to climb out of our wet bed I shouted, "Baby, my water broke. I think it's time to go to the hospital!"

His face immediately turned white when he discovered the bed was wet. He flew up out of the bed and shouted, "Oh God, Christina! What the hell is all over this bed?"

He ran into the bathroom and jumped into the shower mumbling, "Oh shit! What is this stuff?"

I looked at him like he was nuts and shouted, "Tony, its only water! So get the hell out of that shower and take me to the hospital!"

I ran out into the hall and yelled, "Jimmy, Bobby, get up it's time!"

I heard this loud screech from Jimmy and he kept it up as he shouted, "Oh shit, Bobby wake up! Christina, hold on! Don't have that baby yet! I'll be right there!"

I shouted as I threw my hands in the air, "What the hell kind of morons are you guys?"

I had finished dressing by the time Jimmy and Bobby dashed into the bedroom. Jimmy grabbed me by both my upper arms, shook me and screamed in my face, "Are you all right?" His head popped around the room like a jack-in-the-box and he shouted again, "Where's, Tony?"

I looked at him, broke out of his crane like grip, "First of all I'm not deaf, second stop trying to shake the baby out of me it's doing a good enough job on its own." Taking a deep breath I calmly replied, "Would you and Bobby, please get Tony, out of the shower while I call the hospital."

He stepped back, put his hands on his hips, "What the hell is he doing in the shower?"

"I don't know!" I answered, as I headed for the phone, "Would you please just get him out!"

I sat by the front door with my bag in hand, ready to go for ten minutes before the three of them came down the steps. Tony got some color back in his face, when he saw I was just fine. When they reached me, Jimmy and Bobby both grabbed me by either arm to help me up, "I'm fine guys, you don't have to hold me let's just go to the hospital and get this over with."

Tony, still not saying much, went for the car. When he pulled the car up to the front of the house he jumped out ran to me and gently helped me into the front seat. As I climbed into the car, I got one! And I screamed, "Oh shit! That hurts!"

Tony flew into the driver's door, stuck his nervous face in mine and shouted, "Are you okay, baby?"

I kissed his cheek, "I've been better, so let's just go."

As Tony drove us the twenty-mile trip to the hospital, I began to get some bad ones. So bad I thought I was going to give birth any minute and I finally screamed out, "Oh, God! I think it's coming!"

Bobby immediately passed out in the back seat. Tony stepped on the accelerator and we all almost broke our necks from the force of the jerk. Jimmy grabbed my shoulder and screamed, "Put your hands down there and hold it in until we get to the hospital."

Then, Tony hit a bump and we all hit are heads on the roof. First, I cried out in pain; then, I screamed, "Tony! Slow down! You're going to make this baby fall out right here on the car seat."

He came to a screeching stop and I almost went through the windshield. As Tony sped up to ten miles an hour, Jimmy was chanting in the back seat, "God don't let it come now! God don't let it come now!"

Tony went over a set of railroad tracks at five miles an hour, to the honking of twenty or so cars behind us, as I cried out in pain again. That's when Tony finally said something, "I can't go any slower."

I screamed at him, "Would you please give this car some gas, and get me to the freaking hospital now!"

With that, he almost broke our necks again as he floored the car. Finally we were at the hospital! Jimmy flew out of the car and ran into the ER as Tony helped me out of the front seat. I noticed Bobby was still out cold on the floor of the back seat. Jimmy run back with a hospital nurse, who put me in a wheelchair, wheeled me into the hospital and straight up to the elevators. When we reached the door to the OB/GYN unit, Tony stopped us all dead, knelt down in front of me and pouted, "Christina, I can't come in there with you."

"What do you mean you can't come in?" I shouted as I looked him straight in the eye. Then I got another one and I screamed, "I don't give a shit what you do! Just someone get this kid out of me!" My driver pushed me through the doors and we left Tony and Jimmy out in the hall.

By the time the doctor came in the room, I was in agony! He smiled at me and with a cheerful tone, "How are you, Christina?"

I looked at him like, **duh**, "I'm having a baby, Doctor Hedderman. How the hell do you think I am?"

He smiled again, looked at his assistant, covered his face with a blue mask, "Now Christina, don't be a testy one."

I got another labor pain and during my pain, I could see panic-stricken eyes popping out through a blue cap and mask. Realizing they were Tony's eyes, I looked at him and screamed, "You idiot! I thought you were staying out!" I screamed out with tears of pain rolling down my cheeks, "Do you see what you did to me?" Tony just stood there like he was frozen solid. I cried out in pain again, "Oh shit! Tony, I'm hurting! I need you!"

He instantly ran to my side, held my shaking hands tightly, and as the sweat poured off our foreheads he said, "I'm here, baby! I'm here."

We heard the first cry of our new baby girl as we buried ourselves in each other's eyes, which were filled with pain and joy. We named our little baby girl, Joy. This little Joy of ours was so precious. She had beautiful curly black hair and a little chubby round face. Her eyes were crystal blue and she was a six pound, ten ounce, little ball of energy. She captured our hearts and we loved her from the instant we heard her first cry.

The next day we were in every headline across the country. The flowers, letters and cards, from well-wishers filled the hospital mail room. America's new golden couple now had a little bundle of Joy, and we instantly became known as America's golden family. That evening we discovered my latest album, 'Ever Lasting Love' shot to the number one spot. When we left the hospital the following day, we ran right into the center of a fanfare, with press and cameras. After a short interview Tony, Joy and I were off to begin our new life together as a family. Oh yes, Jimmy and Bobby came too! They were great. They catered to Joy's and my every need.

The next two months were wonderful. Tony and I stayed home with Joy almost every day. By December 10th, my twenty third birthday I was back on top of the world! We had the best of both worlds. I was in love with Tony and our life as a family, was a dream come true. My career was sky rocketing and it seemed no one could dethrone my music from the top of the record charts. Even though we were home it didn't mean we were not busy. We had six more household staff members and one full-time nanny, which had nothing to do so far. We had two private secretaries, one for each of us. We managed the helm of Powers Motion Pictures and Records, from home. Our wealth and fame kept growing. Powers Motion Pictures was releasing three new films by the first of the year. Powers Records had twenty three-top names signed to our label. We had it all!

After my birthday dinner that evening, Tony received a call from an "old friend," Frank Salerno. It went like this. We had a small gathering of a few friends over to celebrate my birthday with us. We were all gathered in the golden formal dining room chatting over cake and coffee, when Carman excused herself, walked over to Tony and said, "Sir, you have a phone call in your study."

"Please just take a message for me and tell them I will call them later."

"I tried that sir, but the gentleman caller said to tell you he was Mr. Salerno and that it was urgent he speak with you now."

"Thank you, Carman."

Tony excused himself then headed for the study to take the call.

I tried to act nonchalantly over the call amongst our friends, but as the first half hour approached and Tony had not returned, my concern was beginning to show. I finally could take the suspense no longer, so I excused myself and went to find Tony. As

I approached the study, I could faintly hear through the slightly ajar door, what seemed to be the end of Tony's conversation with Frank, "I don't like this at all Frank." I opened the door, "Don't worry Frank, I will honor my contract. Now I really have to get back to my wife's birthday party. Goodbye."

When he hung up the phone, I looked at him and I knew something was wrong, "What did he say to you?"

Tony kissed my cheek, "I'll tell you later, let's get back to our guests."

Later that evening as Tony and I climbed into bed, I turned to him, "So tell me what he said? But first, start with what you disliked so much."

Shaking his head in disgust, "Well baby, you're not going to like it either, but Kathy Brown is my leading lady. Shooting starts January 12th. I need to be in London just as we planned, January 2nd, and the script for 'Billy Boy' will be arriving shortly."

I looked very seriously, "I smell a rat, Tony. This is a setup if ever I saw one and you're right, I don't like it."

Tony took my hand, "Christina, I have no choice, I have to do the film no matter who they co-star me with, I have a contract."

Squeezing his hand, "Why don't you just break the damn contract? So what if we get sued. I'd rather lose everything then to lose you."

Tony pulled me close to his chest, "You're not going to lose me, baby."

With concern, "Tony, you don't seem to understand. She is going to try to get you back. There I said it, I just love you Tony, and I'll go out of my mind knowing she's with you. I've seen her in action before and **she's a bitch**. Please, Tony, I know she wants you back, baby. I have to be honest with you, there has been a sort of rivalry between the two of us for a long time now and there's nothing that would please her more, then to steal your love from me."

Tony looked straight into my eyes, "You mean like you did to her?"

I was taken aback. I could say nothing in reply. He kissed my cheek, "You really don't think I didn't know about your feud with

Kathy, when I met you? I knew, Christina! I knew right down to how Kathy only went after John, because Frank put her up to it." As he said those words, I felt a pain shoot through my heart, which flared up more anger and hatred for them both. "I also knew the real reason you proposed me. The one thing you didn't know was that I loved you long before I met you that night. I was in love with you when you and John Everett were engaged. You thought I just fell in love with you on the beach that night, but the truth is I loved you so much my heart broke when you walked off the set of 'Samantha's Father' before I could even meet you." He squeezed me tightly, "Baby, what I'm saying is, yes, I did have feelings for Kathy, but when you asked me to marry you, you made my dreams come true and you've filled my life with magic every day since then." He pushed me from his chest, looked down into my eyes, "Baby, if there is anyone who should worry about losing anyone it's me, not you. You will never lose my love Christina, never."

Tears of love began to fall, "Tony, I do love you and you never have to doubt that."

He bent down and gently kissed the tears from my cheeks. The love we made that night felt so honest and peaceful that we decided we were going to trust in our love and get through this film together.

January 2nd, 1978, came and Tony left. I slowly began to go mad. There was no chance of Joy and me going with him because that would have made it worse. So on January 3rd, I went straight to the gym and started a rigorous training program. I had just a little too much baby fat left for me to be seen out in public. On January 5th, I was back in the recording studio working on my next release. Tony called every evening to say hi to Joy before I put her down for the night. I would call him back and we would talk for hours. I sent Tony a new photo of Joy and me, once a week. But it was hard, we truly missed one another.

On February 14th, I released my sixth album entitled, 'Love Affair, Long Distance' It was a very special album with four cuts which were each sixteen minutes long. It had a new rock and roll kind of twist, to a very upbeat disco rhythm. It was a ballad of a fairytale love story. But the best thing about the recording was I sang my love to Tony on every cut and he, as well as the whole world knew it.

March 2nd, I heard the news my sixth album topped the number one spot. I also received a letter from the Academy Awards Institute, informing me 'Life, Passion and Fame' had won eight academy award nominations. The ceremony was to be held in Hollywood on March 29th, at 5:00pm. I was also asked to perform the hit single from the film, 'Come Lay with Me.'

Even with all this news I was still going mad. I got a sick feeling every time I thought of Kathy being with Tony. Oh, God! I cringed, at the thought of her touching him! In order to cope with the thought of Tony and Kathy performing love scenes together on screen, I buried myself in work and my little Joy. Then, I had a brainstorm and decided to go on a four month, twenty city world-wide tour. It was scheduled to begin on April 1st, at the London Coliseum because I needed to see Tony and this was the way to do it. I ended at Shay Stadium in New York, on July 4th, with a planned blow-out concert.

March 29th, the night of the Academy Awards, I was back in shape and dressed to kill. As I walked up the red carpet with Jimmy and Bobby, on either arm, through the flashing of the cameras, I wished Tony was by my side. He was nominated for best actor, but his current shooting schedule would not allow him to be present. I also felt a little bad we would miss our nightly call, for the first time since he left. I dismissed my sad feelings and jumped right back into the mood. As soon as we entered the doors I thought, "Screw you, Frank! I made it here without you. Then I got nervous. I turned to Jimmy and in a low voice, "Jimmy! What if I don't win? God forbid! I'll look like a fool!"

As we were escorted to our seats Jimmy squeezed my hand, "Did you bring some cocaine?"

I looked at him as we took our seats, "Yes, I have some."

"Good, now go to the ladies room, snort some and just relax. You'd be doing us both a favor."

I looked at him, Bobby and then at my shaking hands, "You're right! I'll be right back."

Now mind you, I was not a drug addict. I was a municipal user only, but that night was my first exception.

It was 7:00pm when a runner came to me with a note. I was being asked to come backstage, to prepare for my performance. I kissed Jimmy and Bobby for luck, and then followed the runner backstage.

I was looking like a queen in my full length golden laced, soft midnight black satin gown, with my trademark slit up the center seam. I knocked them dead as I sang 'Come Lay with Me!' I ended the song to a five minute standing ovation; then, the announcements came. I won for best song of the year, best screenplay and best leading lady. I was flying so high! I was on top of the world that night! I walked out of there with three Academy Awards for myself and one for Tony. I was so excited and the only person I wanted to see was Tony; so, I decided to skip the celebration party and go home to call him. Believe it or not, Tony was anxiously waiting for my call and we talked one hour past our normal time.

The next morning I was working in my study on my next screenplay with my right hand and playing with Joy with my left hand when I received a call. To my surprise, it was Dominick Giovanetti on the other end of the line. I stopped what I was doing, "Dominick, it's so nice to hear from you."

"Christina, it's good to hear your voice. I want to congratulate you on your great success and your new family."

Happily, "Thank you Dominick that means so much to me to hear you say that. You're a very special friend."

Dominick chuckled, "My beautiful Christina, I'm so pleased you feel that way because I'm in town right now as we speak. I am here to do some business with your uncle, tomorrow night as a matter of fact. That is why I would be very pleased if you would join me for dinner tonight."

I was stunned and all I could say was, "Tonight, Dominick? I have the baby, and I'm trying to get ready for a trip abroad tomorrow. I don't think I can make it."

"Christina, I think tonight would be a good time to renegotiate our contract."

"Would it make any difference if I said, I was happily married?"

He chuckled again, "My dear Christina, could you be turning me down?"

I quickly replied, "No Dominick, you're my guardian angel and I would never turn you down." I swallowed my heart, "Would it be acceptable to you, if I asked you to have your driver pick me up here at 9:00pm after my little girl is asleep?"

With an authoritative tone, "That would be pleasing to me, until 9:00 then. Good day, Christina,"

When I hung up the phone, I grabbed Joy and began to cry. I knew I had no choice but to meet with Dominick and it was killing me.

That night after Tony said goodnight to Joy, I said, "Tony, I have some last minute things I have to straighten out with the orchestra tonight. So don't wait up for me honey. I'll just call you tomorrow before we leave."

"No Christina, I want you to call me no matter what time you get in. You're my wife. I'll miss saying goodnight."

Trying to be reassuring, "Oh Tony, I truly love you with all my heart baby."

His reply was blunt, "You just remember that! I don't like other men being around you without me being there. That's why I wish you would cancel the tour and just come spend some time with me."

"Tony, we need the money. You know the business isn't stable enough to support itself yet. So once again, the mighty buck is still the bottom line."

"You're right and I have to agree with you. I guess that's why I love you so much."

"I love you too Tony. Now, I have to get going if I'm going to get back."

We ended the call and I put Joy to bed. I told Jimmy the same thing I told Tony, when I left the house that night.

I felt like dirt, when I climbed into the back seat of Dominick's Limo. I looked back at our home as the driver drove down the driveway away from the house and my heart screamed out in fear, "Don't leave your home! Stay here safe with Joy in your arms!" But

I knew I could not heed the cry of my heart. I felt myself wanting to scream out, "Tony, help me! God, help me!" But there was no help for me that night as I willingly allowed myself to be raped by this man, over and over.

As I casually glanced at the clock on the nightstand, I thought of Tony waiting for my call. It was 4:00am when Dominick had finally had enough, and it was 5:00am when the limo dropped me off at my front door. I stood there by the door for a short time with my soul wounded, naked and ashamed. It took great courage for me to walk up those steps and open that door.

When I did open the door, Jimmy was waiting in his underwear and ran to me, "Where have you been? Tony has had me calling all over for you."

As he talked, I leaned up against the wall, slid down to my knees and just lost it. I started crying and it seemed like I couldn't stop. Jimmy stopped talking and grabbed my arm, "Christina, what is it, baby? What happened to you?" Starting to cry, "Stop crying and tell me what's wrong?"

I stopped crying, thought very quickly, "I witnessed a car accident last night and the parents of these two little twin baby boys were killed. So I stayed at the hospital with them until they were picked up by child welfare." I thought, "A little over dramatic, but not bad considering all the stress I'm under."

Sympathetically, "You poor thing, why didn't you call?"

"I was so shook up Jimmy, it didn't cross my mind. Would you please call Tony and tell him what happened, while I try to compose myself in the bathroom."

When I left for the bathroom, I was praying Tony would buy the story coming from Jimmy first. I knew Jimmy would elaborate on my state of mind, before I had to talk to Tony. Oh God! I hated lying to Tony, but I knew if I told him the truth I would be pushing him right into Kathy's open arms. And no way was I letting that happen! So I lied through my teeth when I spoke with Tony. He seemed to believe my story and was very concerned for my well-being. But he was still upset for my inconsiderate behavior by not calling; so, I apologized and we made plans to meet at his suite in London at six o'clock the following night. We said I love you and goodbye. I hung up the phone and went to the shower to scrub the filth from my body. Then I went to the bedroom, climbed in bed at 5:57am and cried my heart out.

At 9:00am I grabbed Joy, four suitcases, one bottle of champagne and headed for the airport.

I slept during the whole flight to London that day as Jimmy and Nanny Sue, took care of Joy. I was still tired when we got there. It was 11:00am April 1st, when Joy, Nanny Sue, Jimmy, and I, settled down in Tony's suite at the Regency in downtown London. I searched for telltale signs of Kathy being there and found none. Then I thought, as I waited for Tony to come in, "Oh, God, how do I face him? Will he be able to tell that I have broken the sanctity of our marriage? Will he see it in me, feel it in me?" I stopped my mind dead and thought, "I'll play this one by ear."

Tony did not come in until 2:00am the following morning. When he did come in, I had been sitting up waiting at the door and biting off all my nails, "Hi Tony, I'm sitting here in the living room in the dark."

He walked into the living room, "What are you doing sitting up in the dark?"

"Waiting for you to come in."

"I'm sorry I'm so late. Kathy and I got hung up on a couple of scenes,"

"Until 2:00am?" A phone call would have been nice."

"I just didn't think of it. I was so busy," he replied sarcastically.

"Oh, it's like that, is it? You're just playing some kind of a game because of the other night. Well I think that sucks and I'm going to bed! Goodnight." Then, I stormed off to the bedroom and Tony never came in.

By 5:00am I was crying again. I wanted him to come to me so badly, but he didn't.

Later on that morning, he was playing with Joy when I came into the living room. I kissed Joy and Tony on the forehead, "Good morning Tony. I'm sorry I stormed off like I did last night. It was childish of me."

He picked up his jacket, "I won't be able to see you until after your performance for the Royal Family tonight. So I'll meet you backstage just before we are to be presented to the Queen and Prince."

He turned and walked out the door and I thought, "Oh, God, he must know. Somehow he knows. Could I have been set up by Frank and Dominick? Oh well, I'll figure it out tomorrow. Right now I have to prepare to perform for the British Royal Family."

That evening, my performance was remarkable. Tony showed up right on cue, just as he said he would. We met the Queen, went to Buckingham Palace for a Queen's Ball in my honor and we acted like nothing was wrong. We arrived home at 1:00am, and Tony said, "Christina, I can't stay here with you tonight." The tears started to roll down his eyes, "You're lying to me and I can't stand it. I love you, why did you lie to me?"

I grabbed his hand, "Tony, I love you too and I can't let you walk out on me like this. If we talk, I know we can work it out."

Biting his lip, "I know you were out in a limo and at the Regency the night of your car accident."

My response was quick, "Tony, if you will listen to me I can clear this all up."

"I'm listening."

"Yes, you're right I lied to you and I'm very sorry I did. But it was not for what you're thinking. Do you remember asking me once, how I got away with talking to Frank, like I did?"

"Yes, but what does that have to do with the other night?"

"I'm getting to that. You see when I was in Italy, my Uncle Dominick took care of me. He almost went to war with Frank because of what he did to me. Well, Uncle Dominick was in town that night and since it was the only chance I might get to see him, I went. I just didn't want you to know I had two uncles in the mob."

Tony pulled me to him, "Please don't hide anything from me again."

I kissed him, "I won't Tony, I promise I won't. Now please come to bed with me."

After that, we had an incredible night of love making and we were back together again. We had four more days of heaven together that April. Every time the three of us could be together, we were. The passion and desire of being together again was stronger than ever before. We took courage in the knowledge Tony's film would be finished in eight months and he would be done with Frank's contract for good. That's when we could be a family again.

Then, the time came for the tour to go on the road. As we said our tearful goodbyes, I thought, "If I could get us through that one, I could get us through anything."

We sent Joy back to Malibu with Nanny Sue, and it was back on the road for me and back on the phone for us.

It was 7:00am July 4th,, 1978, when Jimmy and I entered NBC studios, in downtown Manhattan. I was appearing on the Good Day Show, with Jane Smalley. Jane was interviewing me and her questions were to stay on the topics of my July 4 blowout concert at Shay Stadium, and the unveiling of a sixty-foot billboard of me, in a very sensual pose with mike in hand. The billboard was part of the concert promotion, being held at 1:00pm that afternoon in Times Square. She was also to ask me about hosting this year's special summer International Music Awards Ceremony in LA on July 20th, and how I felt about my twelve nominations.

During the interview, I explained to Jane my concert performance was the hottest thing going all summer and I was incredible. I also told her how I arranged and signed a twenty million-dollar deal, the first contract of its kind with HBO. The deal included the live broadcast of my performances exclusively on their cable channel and the recording of the concert live for my next soundtrack. It would have all of my prior number one hits, and two new cuts.

Jane and I were having a very good interview as I gave her all of this information. It had been fun, right up until her last question, "Christina, may I ask you one more question I know the whole nation would like to hear you answer?"

Feeling uncomfortable yet, still smiling, "Sure, Jane."

"How do you cope with the fact, your husband is off in another country filming a very racy movie with his ex-fiancée?"

I smiled confidently, "It's not hard to cope with it at all, Jane. I'm *Christina Powers*! Once a man has been with me, he could never go elsewhere."

"But..."

I stood up before she could ask another embarrassing question, "Thank you Jane, but I must run, I have a lot to do today." I looked into the cameras and winked, "Good Day America."

Once the cameras were off of us, I glared at Jane, "That was the most pressing question you could come up with?" Then I turned and walked out.

Jimmy and I left NBC studios, hopped in the limo and headed for Shay Stadium. It was a beautiful warm, sunny morning around 8:00am, when we went to check on the setup for my performance, before the unveiling of my sixty-foot poster in time square at 1:00pm. I was staying on top of everything. Tonight's performance had to be hotter than anything I'd done yet and I was going to see to it that it was.

The moment the limo left us off at the stadium, I noticed we were standing right in front of the players' entrance and I froze as I was hit with a rush of a thousand flashbacks of the night I ran through the cold New York October rain, across the parking lot to these doors right in front of me to find Johnny in the hall devastated. Jimmy grabbed my hand, looked at me strangely, "Are you all right?"

I took a deep breath, "Yes, I'm fine," as I slapped Jimmy on his ass, "Come on, let's go to work." With that I put it out of my mind and we headed for the players' entrance.

When we reached the doors, we were talking and Jimmy opened one door wide for me to enter. As I began to step in the doorway, I froze again. Only this time as if I saw a ghost! I turned as white as a ghost, when I realized Johnny was standing right in front of me. When our eyes met, we were both stunned. Instantly all the banished forgotten feelings came flooding into my consciousness and I became weak. I reached for Jimmy's hand and stepped back so Johnny could pass. When he came out into the sun light, I noticed he was carrying a small child in his arms. As he passed he calmly looked at me, "Christy, it's nice to see you, you're looking great."

Somehow I managed to say, "John, it's good to see you too."

Then a woman came out of the doorway behind him, reached her hand for mine, "Hi! Ms. Powers, it's nice to meet you." Smiling ear to ear, "I'm Mary Everett, John's wife."

Somehow I snapped myself out of a state of shock, reached out, took her hand and hugged her warmly, "It's very nice to meet you also, Mary." I kissed her cheek, released my friendly embrace, reached for Johnny's free hand, shook it, "Oh my God, John! This must be your son."

Johnny looked at me with the smile of a proud father, "Yes! This is my son, John Jr."

As he spoke, I looked down at Mary's left hand, to see her wedding ring and it wasn't there. My ring! Johnny's grandmother's ring, the one he gave to me, was not on her finger! I quickly glanced up into Johnny's eyes and he acknowledged my discovery with a wink. The moment he did my heart cried out for him. I wanted to hold him and scream out, "Johnny! I love you! I miss you! Please forgive me! I need you!" But I stopped myself because, I could see the same thing in his eyes and our emotions were now forbidden by our new lives.

I reached into my purse, "I would love it if you guys would be my guests at my performance tonight." I pulled out six front row tickets and a card with my personal phone number on it. I gave them all to Mary, "Mary, please take these tickets. There are six of them so please bring some friends." I kissed her cheek again, "And Mary, my personal card is in with those tickets, so if you guys are ever in Malibu or if you ever need anything, please call me."

Mary took my gift, "Christina, thank you. You're just as nice as John's mom says you are and we'd love to come to your show tonight."

We said our goodbyes, and I watched Johnny walk away. As I stood there in a daze, Jimmy slapped me out of it with the palm of his hand on the back of my head, "You didn't even introduce me. You just left me standing there, holding the fucking door like some idiot, as you start having a conversation with your ex-lover and his wife."

"I'm sorry Jimmy. I was completely caught off guard. I never even thought I might run into Johnny, while we were here."

We started to walk through the dark hallways, toward the player's dugout, when Jimmy said, "Are you sure you didn't come here in the middle of baseball season, just so you might run into him?"

I replied a mischievous, "Hmm, I never thought of that. Sometimes your mind is more devious then mine, Jimmy."

Jimmy laughed, "You're right, he is a stud! But I still think Tony is hotter looking."

I gave him no reply as we kept walking. We were just heading out onto the center of the ball-field where the stage was being worked on, when it hit me like a lightning bolt shooting through my body! I could see, feel and hear the whole thing in my mind. It was like some kind of vision or quick dream, in a three-dimensional image, with lights and sound. I turned to Jimmy, grabbed his shoulders and shouted, **"I'm a fucking genius**!" Then I kissed his cheek and shouted, "Quick, come with me!"

As I started to run toward the stage, I could hear Jimmy saying, as he ran to catch up to me, "Here we go again!"

When I reached the stage, I found Ann Markel my stage manager, and started shouting orders at her, like, "Ann! I want you to cut a twelve foot hole in the center of the stage and have it mounted on a forty foot, hydraulic lift. Then run a cable one hundred feet above the stage and mount six super spotlights on it so that they will shine straight down on me as the stage lifts me up. I also want six sets of super spotlights to hit me from every corner of the stadium." Turning to her I added, "And I want it by tonight's show! You got that."

She gave me an overwhelmed look, "You got it, boss."

I found Bobby and told him just how and where I wanted the lights, cameras and stage props to be set up and placed. After that, I ran over to Joe Cole, "Joe, how well do your people have the two new numbers down?"

Joe smiled, "We're right on key with them, Christina."

"Good, because I'm going to have a new number for you guys in one hour and I want it down pat by our 5:00pm rehearsals! You got it?"

He looked at me as if I were nuts, then smiled, "Yes ma'am!"

Then Jimmy and I sat down with pen and paper and went to work. As I started to write on the paper, I first wrote the words down. Then I started to write the music and melody, right over the top of the words. As I did, Jimmy looked at me with amazement, "Oh my, God! You are a fucking genius! How in the world do you do that?"

I looked at him and smiled, "It's not that hard Jimmy, I know the song by heart."

Shaking his head, "You are nuts. You know that? What the hell are we doing this now for anyway? We're supposed to be in the city at 1:00pm, remember?"

I finished writing, "Were not going. Now let's spice these lyrics and melody up and we'll have a hit record by tonight."

Jimmy read the lyrics, "Christina, are you sure you know what you're doing?"

"Yes! I'm writing my third and last encore for tonight's performance. Now shut up, sit down and help me."

He snatched the paper from me, "Where did you get this song from?"

I grabbed it back, "It's a Country Western song I heard a long time ago. Do you remember me telling you about how I mailed my ring back to Johnny, and in the envelope, I also placed a recording I'd heard? Well this is that recording."

With concern, "Do you realize what these words are saying?"

I looked into his eyes, "It's a song, so I don't want to hear one more word about it! Okay?"

Jimmy sat down with a puss on his face, "Christina, I can't let you do this without trying to tell you to please, think about what singing a song like this, might feel like to Tony?"

I grabbed his hand, looked deep into his eyes, "Jimmy, this is the last time I am going to say this. It's just a song." And on that note, we went to work.

It was as if I were possessed. I had to have it done, and perfected, for that night's show. Johnny was going to be there and that was my driving force. By 5:00pm that afternoon, we were rehearsing 'The Love I Lost' and we were rehearsing it the way only *Christina Powers* could. I had everything set to go, from my wardrobe, to every step I made on the stage. It was all choreographed, timed and setup by everyone working that night and it was done down to my every detail. We had the rest of the show down pat, so I had us all working on and perfecting just this one song for that nights show. We worked on that project from 10:00am, that morning and by eight o'clock that night we had a masterpiece ready to go.

The show started at 9:00pm on the dot and it was turning out to be exactly the way I planned it. The **hottest** show I had ever performed. I kept one-hundred-thousand fans, all screaming for more. And I gave it to them! One hot set after another. I could see Johnny and Mary sitting with Steve Grady, his date and another couple. I could hardly keep my eyes off Johnny as he watched my performance with amazement.

Then it was time for my third and last encore of the night and the stage curtains opened for me one more time. I stood there looking like a goddess, in my emerald blue skin tight, full length gown, with a slit up the center seam. My long wavy black hair was draped over my shoulders and I wore tear shaped diamond earrings. My makeup was divine and I had on blue high heels to match my gown, with clear silk stockings.

Then the orchestra started to play and as the whole country and most of Europe, watched on HBO, I began to sing my heart out just to Johnny! The rhythm started very slowly with the string section of the orchestra. I began to sing very slowly and softly. The lyrics recalled a fiery and gentle love, of a time passed. As I sang, I gently floated around the stage with all the stage lights flashing on me. As the tempo of the rhythm increased, so did mine, until I was belting it out with every ounce of my strength, how the love of my life was destroyed with such devastation I could never rebuild it. I sang I would always love this man with all my heart, which I had lost and I would look back after all the years and lovers of my life and ask myself why? As the song went on, I sang of how I would be strong and somehow make all my dreams come true without him. Then, the thunder of the orchestra's tempo increased again, and I looked deeper inside myself to find the strength to match its rumble with that of my angelic voice. All at once the center of the stage began to rise with me on it. As it reached its full span of forty feet, the edges of the circle began to spin with thousands of red and white sparkles, which showered down upon the stage below. As I screamed my last angelic note and held it, the super spotlights all hit me at once and my emerald blue gown began to glisten, as it lit up the night. With the help of mirrors an image of me still singing rose up off the platform as the lights appeared to be lifting me. Then my image just disintegrated as if I were being beamed up by angels into heaven. With that the skies above the stadium became filled with grand finale fireworks, which lasted for twenty minutes. The whole place went wild! People were screaming and passing out all over the place. The crowd grew so excited the guards had to block the stage to keep them from coming after me. I had to be helicoptered out of the place before they could quiet the crowd down and manage a safe evacuation. It was an incredible performance!

Johnny knew I was singing to him and so did anyone who knew anything about my life. And that was the whole free world! Later that night back at my hotel room, I received a bouquet of two dozen red roses, with one white one in the middle and a note, which read, "Ditto!" I held those flowers in my hands and cried. When I finally got around to calling Tony, it was 3:00am. There was no answer, so I drifted off to sleep. The next day the fame of my performance made me a first class, worldwide bonafide sex symbol! And every radio station in the nation wanted 'The Love I Lost' as soon as possible.

I flew back to the West Coast, to my little Joy and to prepare for hosting the 1978, International Music Awards, on July 20th, I tried to reach Tony all week, but he was never in and he never called me back. Then on July 17th, it was spattered all over the front page of every tabloid in the country. The headlines read, **"Tony Demetrees and Kathy Brown appear to be having a very**

explicit public affair, as they hit the nightspots all over London!"

When I read them, it felt like a knife piercing my soul. Then I called the London studio and told them who I was, then said, "I want Tony on the phone, 'Now!' It's an emergency." After having to wait ten minutes, I was steaming even hotter, when someone came to the phone and said that he was not in, but I could reach him at Miss. Brown's personal number. I asked for it and the bastard wouldn't give it out. If I could have reached through the phone, I would have strangled the asshole. I hung up and called my attorney, Lesley Stine, "Lesley, I want you to serve Tony with divorce papers, 'Now!'" I was humiliated for the entire world to see and I was not taking it lying down, if you get my drift.

July 19th, at 1:00am, the phone rang. I picked it up, "Hello."

It was finally Tony, "Christina, what the hell are you serving me with divorce papers for?"

"Now you call? You son of a bitch! After I've served you with divorce papers! Well, now I don't want to speak to you."

With a desperate tone, "Christina, wait! Please don't hang up on me. We have to talk."

Angrily, "There is nothing left to talk about. You made your bed with that bitch, now sleep in it. Do you know I have to host the I.M.A.'s tomorrow night and because of your behavior I somehow have to be able to hold my head up high, in the midst of my disgrace. So why don't you just talk to my lawyer?"

He cried out, "Christina, I love you, baby. Please talk to me!"

I shouted back, "You should have thought of that before you climbed into bed with that slut." Then I hung up the phone, took it off the hook, laid down on the bed and cried my heart out. I was so hurt by the fact Tony slept with Kathy that I was blinded by anything I might have done to cause it.

It was July 20th, at 9:00pm when I walked out onto the stage of the Crystal Palace, in the heart of LA to host the 1978, special summer International Music Awards. I was dressed to kill! I wore a milky white, silver trimmed Stargenzy Original, full flowing, calf length gown, with a diamond tiara in my hair and matching diamond earrings with silver high heels.

I caught sight of the audience and my heart became filled with surprise and warmth, as the audience rose to a cheering standing ovation. All my friends and colleagues in the entertainment industry as well as the whole country were applauding and supporting me. The lights of the cameras flashed wildly every time I came on stage. I also swept the awards that night with an unprecedented twelve International Music Awards. It was a fantasy lived.

As I walked through the mob of screaming fans and hundreds of press, with their flashing cameras I had Jimmy, Bobby and Joe, all around to buffer me from the onslaught of press and their questions. From out of this mass of confusion, came Tony. He grabbed my arm with forceful power. Then right there in front of all these people he shouted loud enough for most to hear, "Christina, you have got to listen to me."

I calmly replied, "Tony, this is not the place or the time, for this. Can't we discuss this later?"

"Only if I'm coming home with you tonight, Christina, baby, I walked off the set. I'm home for you and Joy now."

With that statement I really got pissed off, "Tony, you're not coming home with me tonight and now is not the time to walk off the set. I'm not going to be here to pick up the pieces for you."

With a disbelieving tone, "Why did you do this to us? I loved you! I trusted you."

Anger radiated from my eyes, "You got it wrong, Tony. You did it when you slept with that tramp."

"No, Christina, I'm not the one who slept with their ex-lover first."

I snapped back in anger, "I never slept with anyone but you since the day we were married."

His voice began to break up, "What about the song you sang to him?"

"It was just a song Tony. I didn't sleep with him."

Tony cried out, "Just a song! Just a song! You cried your heart out to him for the whole world to hear. You told the world I'd always be second best in your heart! Your second choice! How did you think I'd feel? Happy, because maybe you'll sell a million copies? No Christina, you humiliated me! You broke my fucking heart and then you ask me why I slept with her. You put me in her bed and I'm just as fucking human as you are! I'm begging you baby, forgive me and I'll forgive you!" Tears fell from his eyes, "I love you Christina, and I don't want to live without you. Don't do this to us, don't destroy our family."

I looked so lovingly into his eyes and I thought, "Tony, I never wanted to think about how you might feel over the song. I'm sorry too baby and I will take you back." Then I looked at the mob of reporters all around us and thought, "Not in front of all these people, I have to be the Queen." I felt as though I was still being humiliated, so I ripped my arm out of his hand, "Just get away from me right now, Tony." Then I turned and began to push my way through the crowd.

As I did I heard a blood curdling cry, "Christina, I love you!"

I slowly began to turn, as if in slow motion and I heard someone yell, "He's got a gun!"

My eyes caught Tony's and he had a gun in his hand. I screamed, "Tony, no!" At that moment he pulled the trigger, **bang**! The blood from his head splattered everywhere. I screamed! **"Tonyyyy! Nooo!!!"**

I ran to his side with my heart exploding in pain and I cried out, **"Tony! My love! No! No! Tony! What have I done to you my love? Tony!"**

I was in *hysterics;* as I tried to stop the blood with my white gown. My Tony was lying in a pool of blood and he was dead. I was screaming and shaking wildly until someone tried to take me from his side. With that I lost it and started to fight everyone who came near us. Then, four strong men tackled me and I felt a sharp pain. After a few more minutes of fighting these men, I began to feel dizzy. **Then there was nothing**.

CHAPTER 8. THE DEVASTATION

I woke up three weeks later in the hospital. It seemed I had gone temporarily mad, and they had to keep me sedated. Every time I did come out of my sedation, I became physically and verbally combative, so they would shoot me back up with the tranquilizers. I guess it was the only way my mind could cope with what I saw, felt and experienced. There are no words for it. It was simply horrendous. How I lived through Tony's death and the state of shock I went into was a miracle in itself. When I did finally regain my senses and realized I was in a hospital bed, I also realized at that same moment, somehow I had to face what I had done. I quickly looked around that hospital room and thought, "If I had only said what I truly felt, I'd still have my Tony here with me now. If I had only!"

But the millions of what if's I had done this or said that which ran through my mind didn't make a damn bit of difference. They couldn't change what happened. Nothing could bring Tony back to me. He was dead and I was alone with Joy. This was my reality and I knew it. I thought, "Oh, God! How do I face my own daughter? I killed her father. How do I hold her in my arms and tell her that her mother is the murderess who caused the death of her father? How do I go on? Why should I go on? How do I get anywhere from here, when all I want to do is die?" As I lay in that bed, I knew I had no answers, to these questions.

I was discharged on August 20th, 1978, from the hospital, one month to the day of Tony's death. My discharge came only after one week of convincing my new psychiatrist, I was able to handle going home. He put me under constant surveillance for that week, but he was sweet about it. He truly cared about me as a patient and I know he felt what I was going through. He tried so desperately to help me in that week and I appreciated that, but at the same time he wasn't letting me go home until he was sure I could handle it, and that, I didn't appreciate. By the end of the week I had him semi-fooled. I told him all the things I knew he wanted to hear in order for me to be discharged; only I was never truly candid with him. I just wanted out. So finally, He felt it would be beneficial for my recovery to send me home, but only under the close supervision of my dear Jimmy. I was also put on a regiment of anti-depressants and three office visits with the Doctor per week.

When Jimmy picked me up in the limo that day at 10:00am from the hospital, he came alone. This was at my request. I had to speak with Jimmy alone. After my chair was wheeled through the hospital, even though there was nothing wrong with my legs, I was swamped by what seemed to be every camera and reporter in the nation, all shouting at me! I buried my face under Jimmy's arms as we pushed our way to the waiting limo, where we flung ourselves into the back seat. As our limo drove away from the mob, I was shaking! When we were out of sight, I reached over and grabbed Jimmy's hand. I looked deeply and sincerely into his eyes as my tears slowly rolled down my cheeks, "Jimmy, you have got to help me. You're the only person in this world I can count on now." My tears began to fall faster, "Because Jimmy, I can't handle this. I'm out of the hospital, but I still can't handle this. I don't know how I'm dealing with it and I don't know how I'm going to. So please, Jimmy, please be with me!"

Jimmy's tears began to fall with mine and as he looked back at me through his tears, "Christina, I love you. This is me, your Jimmy! I'll always be here for you, you're my girl. I'd never let you down."

We embraced, "Thank you Jimmy, but you have to do me another big favor."

"Anything Christina, what is it?" He cried.

I pulled back from him, turned away feeling just a little bit *ashamed* of myself, "You have to keep taking care of Joy for me."

He pulled my cheek back toward him to once again make eye contact, "Of course I'll keep taking care of Joy, Christina. Bobby and I have already moved in lock, stock and barrel. We're also on top of everything at Powers Incorporated, so don't you worry about anything but getting better. Okay?"

I kissed his cheek, "Jimmy, it's not just that. I need you too." I stopped. I could hardly say the words, but I knew I had to, "Jimmy, you have to keep Joy away from me. I can't see her."

He looked at me strangely, "What do you mean you can't see Joy?"

I grabbed his hand desperately, "I can't explain it to you because I don't understand it myself. I just can't look at her. I can't touch her. I can't smile at her." Then, I lost it and really started to cry.

Jimmy hugged me sobbing, "All right Christina, all right."

As we held each other tightly I said, "Thank you Jimmy, I love you." I stayed in Jimmy's strong comforting embrace the rest of the way home.

The limo entered the opening gates and proceeded through the wooded, winding, driveway up to my wedding gift. Once James brought the limo to a stop in front of the mansion, I had Jimmy go right in to make sure Nanny Sue and Bobby were not downstairs waiting for me with Joy. When the coast was clear, I opened the limo door and slowly climbed out. When I looked up at the mansion, I realized I was standing at the same angle as the day Tony lovingly pulled me out of his `59 Caddie, to see Barbara's so-called new home. That's when I began to feel a little shaky.

Jimmy ran over to me and helped steady me on my feet. Then, *Oh God!* I began walking up those steps and over the threshold which Tony carried *me* over. Then it was into the house Tony led me so happily through by my hand. The same furniture was still there. My heart began to **break** when I remembered how we had planned to decorate it together. I could not hold back my tears any longer; they just streamed down my face as I walked through every room. I had no expression, no sound, just tears. Every room I went into I saw Tony's face, I felt Tony's touch and I smelt Tony's scent. I walked straight into our room to the bed where Tony and I slept, played, talked, made love and first fell in love. I took all my clothing off, laid down on Tony's side of our bed, squeezed his pillow tightly and cried, "Oh God, Tony! Forgive me!"

Jimmy came in every few minutes to check on me and see if I needed anything. But I would just wave him out. Then, I cried even harder. The pain was so unbearable! I missed Tony so much. I finally cried myself to sleep sometime around 11:00pm that night.

The next morning, I felt a gentle shake on my shoulder as I heard Jimmy say, "Christina, come on its 10:00am, time to get up. I have a nice breakfast here for you, eggs, bacon, toast and hot coffee."

I woke up from my tear induced sleep, stretched, yawned and wiped my eyes, "Oh Jimmy, why did you wake me?"

Jimmy kissed my forehead, "I didn't want to wake you, but you have a doctor's appointment at 1:00pm so you really do have to get up."

I sat up in bed, "Oh shit, I don't want to go see the Doctor, I don't want to do anything."

Jimmy encouraged me, "Come on, get up and eat something. Then go get cleaned up and you'll start to feel a lot better. You know you have to see the doctor or you might have to go back in the hospital."

Shaking my head, "I'll try Jimmy, but I can't make any promises."

Sadly he said, "The hospital sent over your mail. There is a bedroom full of cards and letters all wishing you well. Would you like me to bring some in for you to read?"

Sarcastically I replied, "Wishing me well! I don't need anyone to wish me anything."

Jimmy wore a nervous expression, "Christina, I have some bad news for you."

"Bad news! Ha! Like that's new. What is it?" I asked with disgust.

He walked over by the windows and opened the curtains. I could see it was a cloudy dark dreary morning and that made me want to stay in bed all the more. Jimmy walked back over to me, sat on the bed and very sadly said, "The whole horrible scene was caught by Hollywood Tonight's news team on video. It has been replayed all over the country, maybe even the world."

I instantly got a sick feeling, "Thanks Jimmy, I really didn't need to know that right now did I? Now get out of here and let me get ready."

Jimmy shook his head sadly, "I had to tell you. They played the film again last night along with some footage of us leaving the hospital yesterday. I just don't want you to see it by chance, without knowing the film is out there."

Realizing how hard that had to be for Jimmy to tell me, "Thank you Jimmy, I don't mean to snap at you."

Jimmy kissed me sympathetically then left me alone. When he closed the door I got out of bed, threw on some old blue jeans, a gray sweat top, an old pair of black sneakers, ran a brush through my scraggly hair and I was ready to go.

It was 2:30pm when I climbed into the limo after my useless appointment with The Doctor. As James began to drive us home, I pushed the button to bring down the partition glass so I could speak directly to him, "James, did you go to Tony's funeral?"

James glanced at me through the rear view mirror, "Yes ma'am, I did."

"James, would you take me there now?" I nervously asked.

Politely he answered, "Are you sure you want to go there by yourself ma'am?"

"Yes James, I'm very sure."

"Whatever you wish, ma'am."

His reply was as dignified as always, but for some reason I felt uncomfortable with it now, "Two things I would like to request from you James. First, please call me Christina from now on. Second, please tell me what Tony's funeral was like?"

His eyelids lifted nervously, "Thank you, I'd be honored to call you Christina." Then as if he felt totally comfortable calling me Christina, he gave me a fatherly wink as he glanced back at me through the mirror and calmly added, "Christina, it was a beautiful funeral. Thousands of his friends and fans came to show their love and respect. When they all left, a small group of close friends and family stayed behind to pay a special private homage to his memory. We all prayed for your speedy recovery as well."

"Thank you James, I needed to know that."

James pulled into the cemetery, drove to some burial sites, and stopped, "We're here, Christina. It's the third row in on the left and the ground is still loose. The missus and I stopped by yesterday."

"Thank you, I will be back shortly," I climbed out of the limo and headed for Tony's burial site.

As I walked past the headstones looking for Tony's, a soft rain began to fall. When I reached the third row in; I turned to my left and there it was, Tony's grave-site. The stone read, **"Here lies Tony Demetrees, who was all heart. This man was loved by millions!"**

I knelt down in front of that stone, "Tony, I'm so sorry." As soon as I said these words my tears began to fall. Then I took off the medallion I had found in Lake Tahoe, scooped up some dirt and began to bury it with my Tony. As I patted the last of the dirt down over the medallion, I cried out, "Tony, can you hear me? I'm sorry baby! Oh God, help me! I want my Tony back!" At that moment I became a grieving widow. I threw myself on the loose wet soil and shouted at the dirt, "Tony! Please come back! Please Tony, I can't live like this without you! Tony, Tony, *pleaseee* forgive me *MY BELOVED!*"

As I screamed and cried these words, the drizzle turned into a torrential downpour. I lied there in the mud wailing my crushed heart out, until James grabbed me, pulled me up out of the mud, "Let's go home, Christina."

He led me back through the pouring rain, to the limo. When James opened the limo door for me, I tried to head back to Tony, but he grabbed my arm, "He's not there, Christina. He's in a better place now."

I looked at him through my muddy tears and somehow I knew he was right. Tony was not in that grave. Then I climbed into the car and I didn't say another word as we drove away from the cemetery.

For the next two weeks, except for my six visits with the psychiatrist, I did nothing but stay in my bedroom. I did not want to talk to or see anyone. Jimmy was great he made sure everyone just gave me my space.

It was about 6:00pm on a Friday, when I just couldn't take the silence and those freaking anti-depressant pills any more. Just taking the damn pills was depressing me. So I threw them in the toilet and flushed it. I opened the medicine chest, reached up to the top shelf to a prescription bottle, opened it and took out my little brown bottle of cocaine. Then, for the first time since I started to use cocaine, I used it for more than just my shows. This time I was using it for me and I took two snorts, one in each nostril. I climbed into the shower, cleaned up, put on some jeans, one of Tony's red flannel shirts, grabbed my purse, the keys to Tony's `59 Caddie, and I was going out.

I tried to sneak out through the mansion to the garage, but as I reached the garage door, Jimmy caught me, "Christina, you're up! Where are you going?"

"Hi Jimmy, I'm just going out for a ride. I have to get out of here for a while; I'm starting to go stir-crazy."

Jimmy smiled, "That's great, Christina. You need to get out. So where are you going?"

"It looks so nice out this evening I thought I'd go shopping for some new clothes."

Jimmy's smile grew wider, "That sounds like fun. How about I come with you?"

I kissed his cheek, "Jimmy, I really want to go alone. You don't mind do you?"

His smile disappeared, "That's Okay, I don't have to come with you. Just be careful, all right?"

I kissed his cheek, "I love you Jimmy, and I'll be fine." Then I opened the door and headed for the Caddie.

When I pulled out of the driveway I was heading for Rodeo Drive, and all the best shopping in Hollywood. As I turned onto Rodeo Drive, I noticed a blood red Mercedes Convertible sitting on top of a six foot high platform. I quickly turned into the car lot of a Mercedes dealership and drove over to it. I climbed out of the

Caddie and walked over to the car on the platform. I walked around it then I went up the ramp to see the inside of this gorgeous car. It had two bucket seats and they were black leather. By the time I walked down the ramp, a tall, fairly attractive, blond haired man, in his late twenties, was standing there waiting for me. He shook my hand, "Hi! My name is Eddie Smith. Here's my card. I'm the sales manager here at, Smith's Mercedes. Can I help you with anything?"

"This car," pointing to the convertible, "I'll take it."

Eddie cleared his throat as he looked at me in my old blue jeans, "Miss, this is an eighty-thousand-dollar automobile. Are you sure this is the car you want?"

I gave him a dirty look, "Mr. Smith, don't patronize me, just sell me the car. I'll pay you for it now and I'll have it picked up in the morning."

Eddie immediately apologized, "Please forgive me, Miss? I'm sorry I offended you."

My smile returned, "You're forgiven, Eddie. Now sell me the car."

He waved his arms graciously toward me, "Well follow me this way Miss, and I will draw up the paper work."

When we reached Eddie's office he invited me to sit down, "Okay, the first thing I need is for you to fill out this paperwork."

I put my hand on my hip impatiently, "Eddie, I really don't have time for this. May I please just sign my name and pay for the car. Maybe you could fill them out for me?"

"It depends on how you want to pay for the car."

"Well I can give you a check now, or give you a credit card."

He smiled his reply, "If you put it on a credit card, then I can take care of it all for you." He looked at me 'kinda' funny, "You look very familiar Miss. Do I know you?"

I put down my Master Card as I winked, "Have you ever heard of *Christina Powers*?"

With a look of surprise, "I sure have and I can't believe I didn't recognize you." Then he ran my card through his little machine, "Miss Powers, I hope you will forgive me for my bluntness, but I must say something." Looking a little nervous, "I am sorry for your recent loss and I know you're still grieving, but I would like to ask you if maybe when you're feeling a little better, I might be able to take you out for dinner some evening?"

I looked at him strangely, "Eddie, that was a number one move and it took a lot of balls to make it." I took my credit card out of his hand and turned away leaving him speechless. When I reached his office door I turned back, took a card out of my purse and flicked it on his desk right down in front of him, "Eddie, call my personal secretary for the information you need. Then, take my address off the card and pick me up tomorrow at 7:00pm for dinner, and bring my car with you." Then I turned and left.

The evening was still young, so it was off to the biggest designer clothing center of the West Coast. By 11:00pm that night I had treated myself to a three-pound lobster feast, at Captain Ed's Seafood Palace. I also happened to spend thirty-thousand-dollars, on a whole new designer wardrobe, of the most outrageous styles of the day. I arranged for it all to be delivered the next morning. It was around midnight when I arrived home, so I left a note for Carman to deal with the morning's delivery. I told her to place the stuff in the guest room closet closest to my room for now. I went straight up to my bedroom and began to go through Tony's belongings. I thought it was time to give some of his things away. As I went through Tony's things I came across some photos of us rafting at Lake Tahoe. I looked at the photos and my eyes began to water. But, I just could not put the photos down. I just kept staring at them. I held them along with a pair of his pants to my breast, laid down on the bed and said as the tears fell, "Tony, I'll be with you soon my love." Then I cried myself to sleep again.

The next morning and most of that day I spent going through the rest of Tony's things. I packed up most of it and had it put away in storage up in the attic. Those I wanted to keep, I left in the closet. Like the suit Tony wore the night I met him and his bikini briefs. I just couldn't find it in my heart to pack these things away. As I was doing these things, sometime around 4:00pm Jimmy tapped on my bedroom door, "Christina, it's me, can I come in?"

I hollered out, "Come on in Jimmy, the door is unlocked."

He opened the door, stuck his head in, "Christina, I have Joy in my arms and she's been looking for you."

I felt my heart begin to race and with fear in my voice, "Jimmy, please don't bring her in here. I can't see her yet."

"Christina, I am bringing your daughter in to be loved by her mother."

I got off the bed and ran into the bathroom, "Jimmy, get her away from me right now or I'll walk out of this house and never come back."

I heard Jimmy say to Bobby, "Here, take Joy back to Nanny Sue." After that he came over to the bathroom door and tried to open it. I opened the door for him, and he said, "What the hell kind of mother are you? Joy is your and Tony's daughter. Now straighten up your act and go see Joy, before I do something I will regret."

I started to cry, "Jimmy, get out of here and stop trying to help me. I can't see her now. Why can't you understand that?"

"Because it makes no sense to me at all," he shouted. "Christina, she's your child and she needs her mother."

I screamed at him, "Jimmy, don't push me! Can't you see I killed Tony? I killed her father! How can I look at her and tell her that? I can't see her now! I just can't! So don't ever do that to me again! I just need some time and I'm begging you to give me that time." I closed the bathroom door and said, as I cried, "Just go away Jimmy, please."

I heard him say, "Okay Christina, I'll give you your time," as the bedroom door shut.

I cried in that bathroom for the next hour. Then I reached for my cocaine, took four snorts, climbed in the shower and was ready for my dinner date by 6:45. Let me tell you, I was looking wild! I had my hair all flared out like I stuck my finger in a light socket, and I wore a blood red designer outfit. It was an all leather pants, vest and jacket, skin tight suit with chains connecting the slits on the sides of my pant legs and vest, along with my new red high heeled patent leather biker boots and I still looked hot. I snuck through the mansion and down to the front door. I snuck out because I was trying not to run into Jimmy.

As I walked around the front yard waiting for Eddie to come with my new car, I took two more snorts of cocaine. By the time Eddie pulled up the driveway to where I was standing, I was feeling no pain. He looked at me, smiled and said, "You look fantastic!" He climbed out of the driver's seat, "Here is your new 1979, Mercedes LX 750 Convertible."

"Tony, oh I'm sorry. Eddie, would you please drive?"

He escorted me to the passenger's door, opened it and held it for me. Then he closed it behind me and went back to the driver's seat. It was a beautiful, warm, evening, and Eddie had the top down. As he drove away I asked, "So Eddie, where are you taking us?"

"I hope you like seafood," he enthusiastically answered. "I made an 8:00pm dinner reservation at Captain Ed's Seafood Palace, on Rodeo Drive,"

I smiled, "Well, you picked the right place, because I sure do like a good seafood dinner."

"You sure bought yourself a nice car here. It handles great." Eddie said as he looked over at me with adoring eyes.

"Thank you, Eddie." I looked up at the sky with its shades of red sunset rippling through the clouds, "It is such a beautiful evening, I could just lose myself in those clouds."

He glanced over at me, "Don't do that, I don't want you to miss any part of our date."

"I'll try to stick around for the good parts, Okay?"

Wide-eyed he replied, "Whoa! You are good." Then he laughed and proceeded to tell me all about himself, all the way to the restaurant.

Over dinner Eddie remarked on how well I could eat a three pound lobster without getting messy. I told him it was only because we were in public and I started to laugh a little. I stopped because he didn't even crack a smile, and I thought, "He didn't get it! Oh boy!"

At that, he proceeded to tell me about his two cats, three dogs, four horses, five pigs and six chickens, that he had grown up with on his parents farm in Ohio. By the time we finished dinner I didn't know if I was out with a down home country boy like Old

MacDonald, or a sophisticated lady killer like James Bond. The one thing I did know was, **he could talk**.

As we waited for the valet parking attendant to bring the car, I took the parking receipt out of Eddie's hand, "This time I'll pick the place if you don't mind?"

He looked at me like I just stepped on his manly right to control the date, "I guess so, it's your car."

It was 10:00pm when I pulled out of the restaurant driveway and onto Rodeo Drive. I was looking for the first disco I could find. All I wanted to do was move my body on a dance floor. I was so filled with penned up emotions I couldn't release and I hoped that dancing would be my relief. Besides that, I was still full of spunk and ready to go from the cocaine. I also didn't want to hear this guy talk about himself anymore.

Finally, around 10:30pm I spotted the Pink Flamingo Disco. I pulled into the parking spot, "Well Eddie, we're here." We climbed out of the car and went in. It wasn't too busy yet, so I found a table right by the dance floor, and close enough to the speakers so I didn't have to listen to him ramble on and on. Then I sent Eddie for a White Russian and I went to the ladies room. While I was in the ladies room I decided to take two more snorts of cocaine.

When I returned to our table Eddie was not there. All of a sudden he came up from behind me and grabbed my arm. I jumped, ripped my arm from his grasp and turned quickly. Then he yelled, "Sorry! But come with me." So I followed him to another table less noisy and he said, "I thought I'd sit us over here, so we can hear ourselves talk."

I took a mouth full of my White Russian, "Good thinking." I took another gulp of my drink and Eddie's eyes opened wide as I drank it down, placed the glass down in front of him, "Eddie, would you please give me a refill?"

He took the glass, and looked up at me strangely, "I hope you don't drink as much as you eat." Then he went for my drink and I thought, "Screw you asshole," realizing what I was out with!

Eddie returned with my drink, put it down on the table in front of me, "Here you go, this time try to come up for some air before you down this one. There is a line at the bar."

I took a gulp, "Thanks," grabbed his hand, pulled him up, "Come dance with me." Then, I dragged him out on the dance floor. Oh boy! Did I dance! I went wild on that dance floor. I danced rings around him and everyone else on the floor. I felt like I became part of the music and lights, I lost myself in the rhythm of each song. The only reason we stopped was because Eddie was about to pass out. When we got back to our table I needed another drink, so I caught my breath as I waited for Eddie to bring it to me. When he did, I took it, drank it down like water and very sweetly, as I gave him a peck on the cheek, "Eddie, would you please get me another?"

He picked up my glass with frustration and headed right back to the bar. I knew that would keep him busy for another ten minutes at least. When he returned with my drink, I drank it down, took his hand and led him back to the dance floor. At first he was reluctant to come, so I grabbed his balls, looked dead in his eyes, "Eddie, if you don't want to lose **these things**, then you better come with me." After that he was right on my tail, if you catch my drift.

I was so high when we walked back onto that dance floor that I went into overdrive. I was dancing so hot, I was becoming a spectacle on the dance floor. Then, I got hot on Eddie. I was all over him. I was dancing so seductively around him, underneath him, backing into the side of him and rubbing up against him, that I had him throbbing on the dance floor. He took me in his arms as we danced and began to kiss me as he rubbed his hard groin against my thigh. I was beginning to lose myself. I kissed him deeper and rubbed my thigh harder up against his. We were almost at the point of having sex on the dance floor. It was hot! And I was getting hotter! Then the music changed again. This time they played 'The Love I Lost' by *Christina Powers*. I heard the rhythm and then I heard my own voice begin to sing the song which caused the whole awful thing. I broke away from Eddie's hot embrace and screamed when I realized what I was doing. I ran out the door and down to the car. I opened the door, climbed in, put the key in the ignition and started it. I just started to cry my heart out. I truly thought I was in Tony's arms and he was kissing me and telling me how much he loved me. I saw Eddie come running toward the car, so I put it in gear and pulled away.

I hopped on the interstate and headed toward home as fast as I could go, which was about 100 mph. As I remembered it, I think it was around 2:00am when the flashing red lights appeared. When I pulled over, I was shaking and my face was full of tears. Then a female California Highway Patrol Officer came up to the driver's side, flashed a light in my face and said as she saw my condition, "Miss, are you alright?"

I looked up at her with tears falling from my eyes, my hands shaking, "Officer, I don't think so I just have to get home."

"Do you know how fast you were going, miss?"

"Fast."

"I need to see your driver's license, registration and insurance card," she flashed the light all around the car, "Have you had anything to drink tonight miss?"

I took my driver's license from my purse, handed it to her along with the registration and insurance card, "Yes, Officer. I have had a few drinks tonight."

She opened the door, "Can you please step out of the car, miss?"

I pleaded, "Please, don't make me get out of the car." Then I looked straight into her eyes and with all sincerity, "Miss, I'm a woman who is going through a very emotional time in my life. Please just call me a cab, so I can go home."

I heard a male voice coming from the other side of the car, "Ma'am, get out of the car now and put your hands up."

I turned quickly and raised my hands at the sight of a gun pointing at me then I dropped my hands, "Go ahead and shoot!"

"Hold on Sam." The female officer said. Then she looked at me, "Miss, please wait here." She walked around to the back of the car and I heard her, "Sam, do you know who this is?"

"No, who is she?"

"Look at her license. It's *Christina Powers*."

"Holy shit, the movie star!"

"Yes the movie star. But not just that, she's also a human being who just tragically lost her husband."

"Your right," Sam replied sympathetically.

"I'll tell you what Sam; let's not radio this one in. You follow me and I'll drive her home."

"You got it partner."

Those two wonderful officers drove me home and saw me safely inside.

The next morning I woke up around 9:00am to a beautiful, sunny, Sunday morning. I showered, threw on a pair of cut-off-jeans, a tank top and a pair of sneakers. I grabbed a pen and paper and headed for my Mercedes. The top was still down when I climbed in. I started it up, opened the garage door and took off for unknown places. I stopped about one hour down the coast to gas up the car and myself, with a Big Mac, fries and a large coke. Then it was back on the road, still heading south on Route 5. I decided to stop at a place called Imperial Beach, just before Tijuana and found a place to park. Then I took my pen and paper and went to sit on the beach. As I sat there on the beach that day watching all the people having fun, I started to write. From 1:00pm till 5:00pm I unconsciously wrote the lyrics for eight of the most sexually, tasteless, lyrics I had ever written. It was almost as if I had made a conscious decision right there on that beach to become, America's bad girl! But, I made no decisions at all.

Monday morning September 1st, at 7:00am I went into my office at Powers Incorporated and called all my top people into the number seven recording studio. For the next two weeks, we all worked on my eighth album entitled, 'America's Bad Girl!' All of my music had always been very sexy, sensual, and hot. After all, I was the disco queen. But, those were nothing like the eight new singles I was about to release on my new album. The first track on the recording was titled the same as the album, 'America's Bad Girl!' The second track,, 'The Queen Of 42nd Street!' The third title, 'Ladies' of Fire in the Night!' The fourth, 'Ecstasy in a Wet Dream!' The fifth, "Love on the run!" and so on. This album was called hardcore disco by most of its critics. But when I released the finished cut on the airways on September 22nd, it only took one week for it to make the number 3 spot on the billboard charts. It was poised to take the number one spot away from 'The Love I

Lost', which had kept the number one spot from July 21st, and stayed there until October 21st, thanks to my tragedy. After releasing the album, I went right to work on shooting our already casted screenplay. It was the one Tony and I wrote together for each other to play. It was titled, 'Listen to the Wind'.

We started shooting 'Listen to the Wind' on September 24th, and I had everyone working sixteen hour days. As I threw myself into work all day, I also threw myself into the hottest discos in LA, all night. The press began to call me the 'Queen of the Night' and I lived up to my reputation. During this time in my life, I also kept my new cocaine supplier well fed. I released my second film, along with my ninth album, both entitled, 'Listen to the Wind' on December 10th, my twenty-third birthday. As soon as the film hit the theaters, I began a three-month concert tour on December 15th, to push the film and album. It turned out to be my hottest tour ever. The last encore of my performance, I stripped right down to a 'g' string and two feathers, which I held over the tips of my breasts. I left them all screaming for more. The hotter my music and performances became, the more my public begged for them to be even hotter. So I gave them what they wanted, one song hotter than the other and one performance sexier than another. It became an obsession to top myself with each creation. My ultimate goal was to have each project earn more money than its predecessor and for the last nine albums and two films **I had been doing it**. There was one thing different with my approach, in the way I had been achieving this goal since my day on the beach, and that was I had become a total bitch at work. I was smiling for the cameras and my fans, but everyone who worked around me began to hate me. I became a true Hollywood *ice queen*. I shouted orders out like Hitler. I told them what I wanted, how I wanted it done and when I wanted it done, which was usually immediately, and it had better be done right the first time! Not only that, but during the eight months between July 20th, 1978, the date of Tony's death, and March 18th, 1979, when I returned back home from my concert tour, I did not see Joy once.

The limo pulled into the driveway of my Malibu mansion, at 6:00pm. I had called Jimmy ahead of time to let him know I was returning home and to have Joy out of sight. Joy was now eighteen months old and I had not even acknowledged her first birthday which was October 14th, 1978.

As I approached the steps to the house, I was greeted by Jimmy who was standing at the foot of the front porch, "Welcome home Christina."

We hugged, "Hi Jimmy, it's good to see you."

"We have to talk about Joy, Christina."

I shook my head 'no', "Not now Jimmy, I'm tired."

Then I headed for the front door as Jimmy, raising his voice in anger, "We need to talk right now Christina. This can't wait anymore."

I stopped on the sixth step, turned, "All right Jimmy! What the hell is so urgent?"

"What!" He replied sharply, "I tell you I want to talk to you about your daughter, and you ask me what the hell is so urgent. The real question Christina is what the hell is wrong with you? Bobby and I have been taking care of everything here, including Joy and Powers Incorporated, while you've been whoring all over the country. Every time I'd look in a newspaper, there was something written about you and your nightly escapades."

I turned back toward him and sarcastically snapped, "What I do Jimmy, is none of your business and just for the record, I have not slept with anyone since Tony. So I don't care what the papers say, I didn't go to bed with any of those men."

He shook his head in disbelief, "Christina, whether you've been fucked is not the issue. Joy is the issue, and how many times you've seen her in the last year. Christina, Bobby and I have decided to leave you here alone with Joy. Bobby is upstairs with her now and no one else is here."

I dropped my suitcase on the steps and headed for the garage, "Jimmy, I'm leaving! I can't see her now and if you try to force me to be with her, I will put her up for adoption."

I reached the garage door with Jimmy right behind me, "Go ahead Christina, run and keep running. That will solve everything."

As I reached the garage door, "Jimmy, I am sorry, but I can't see her!"

I opened the door and headed for the Mercedes. As I climbed in the car Jimmy grabbed my arm, "You know what Christina, I don't care what you fucking do. I don't even like you anymore."

I pulled my hand away, turned the car on, opened the garage door and took off.

As I drove away from my own daughter that evening I felt like I was dead inside. I didn't feel anything at all for Joy and I couldn't even cry about it anymore. I headed for the Hyatt Regency Hotel in the heart of downtown LA and took a room for the night. I had nothing to change into, to wear out dancing that night, and I was definitely going dancing. I went to the dress shop in the lobby and bought myself a new outfit. Then I went up to my room, showered, got dressed in my new three hundred-dollar, baby blue three piece sequined blouse and jacket suit, with clear stockings and black heels. Once I was looking hot, it was back downstairs to the Park Place Restaurant in the lobby by 8:30pm.

As I ate my dinner I noticed five men at the table next to mine, all dressed in business suits. They seemed to be talking about how important personal computers were going to become to the growth of our nation's economy in the years ahead. I found the conversation to be very interesting and I also found the man doing most of the talking, very interesting as well. Not because of his looks, for he happened to be the least attractive man at his table. He appeared to be in his early forties, about five feet, eleven inches, maybe 190 pounds, brown hair and eyes with wire-framed glasses. He also had a mustache and he was slightly balding on top. What I found so interesting about him was the things he was saying and how he was saying them.

As I nonchalantly listened to their conversation, every guy at that table looked over to check me out at least three times, except for the one doing the talking. He didn't look my way once and I thought, "Maybe he's gay. Shit! Even gay men check me out at least twice. Hmm, maybe I should meet this guy?"

Just then I realized these men had finished their meal and were getting ready to leave. So I thought quickly and as he passed my seat I deliberately knocked my White Russian on the floor and all over his shoes. I quickly stood up with my napkin in hand, "Oh no! I'm dreadfully sorry I messed up your shoes. How clumsy of me. Please let me help?" I just pushed him down into my seat, knelt down in front of him and started to wipe off his shoes with my napkin.

I knew he was taken aback by my heroic behavior when he said, "That's not necessary miss, I can clean them myself."

I quickly rose to my feet and acted as if I didn't realize I was on my knees wiping a strangers shoes, "Oh, how embarrassing," I said coyly. "Please forgive me again. It was just a natural reaction to help, I guess."

He smiled, "I appreciate that very much, but I'm fine."

I looked at him apologetically, "At least let me pay you for your shoes."

He stood up, "You don't have to do that, I have another pair in my room. Well, I better catch up with my colleagues."

I reached my hand out to him, "Please, at least let me introduce myself. I'm *Christina Powers*."

Without the slightest change in his expression, "It was very nice meeting you, Christina Powers, and my name is Lee Bradford. Now I really must go."

Then I thought, "Can this guy really not know who I am?" So I said, "Well at least let me buy you a drink in the lounge."

He looked at me strangely, "Well, I guess so. I'll meet you in the lounge in about an hour. Say 10:30."

Smiling, "That sounds great, I'll be there."

I finished my meal, went back up to my room for a few lines of cocaine, and it was back down to the lounge.

It was 10:40pm when I arrived at the Starlight Lounge in the hotel lobby. As I entered the door, I saw Lee sitting at the bar with the same four guys from dinner. The Starlight Lounge happened to be where most of LA's elite business crowd gathered. The lounge was quite large and spread out with a stage and dance floor. The atmosphere was still warm and cozy even though the lounge was large. The lighting was dim, but all the mirrors and fresh flowers made it seem brighter than it really was. I noticed there was a nice sized crowd which appeared to be 90% men. When Lee noticed me entering the lounge, he came over to meet me and said as he began to escort me to the bar, "Ms. Powers, I'm so glad you came. After I realized who you were, I didn't think you would show up."

"Thanks a lot! What kind of person do you think I am?"

He looked apologetic, "I didn't mean to be derogatory. I guess what I'm trying to say is, you're *Christina Powers*, and I'm-well nobody special. Why would you want to have a drink with me, instead of one of my colleagues?"

I looked at him strangely, "Lee, let's get something straight right now. First, I didn't spill a drink on any of their shoes. Second, I didn't come down here for anything but to show you a kindness, for your graciousness, over my clumsiness. Now I would still like to buy you a drink, if you would allow me."

His face turned slightly red, "Yes of course, and please forgive me, Ms. Powers. I'd enjoy a drink with you, and the guys are dying to meet you."

I gently grabbed his hand, "Lee, would you mind if we sat at a quiet booth. I just came off an intense tour, and I'm really not up to a group conversation tonight."

He stopped walking, "I don't mind at all Ms. Powers, but the guys sure will."

I looked at him sweetly, "Please call me Christina, and how about if I take a seat at that booth over there," I pointed to a booth way in the back, next to the restrooms, "while you make my apologies to your friends for me. Please tell them I'd be more than happy to meet them all another time. I'll just be waiting at that table for you."

"That sounds fine to me, and I'll be right back." Then I went off to the booth, while Lee went to the bar.

Within two minutes Lee was taking a seat on the bench across from me, "I'm back and once again Christina, please forgive me. It's just that I never had a beautiful woman like yourself ask to have a drink with me."

I chuckled, "Well thank you for the compliment, that's very nice of you to say. But you should really think more of yourself than you do. I think you're a very attractive man."

He smiled, "Well thank you Christina, but maybe you should use my glasses."

I laughed, "That was cute Lee, you're so witty, and I can't tell you the last time I laughed." I reached over, patted his hand, as I noticed a barmaid coming, "Well what would you like to drink?"

"Scotch and water."

The barmaid reached our booth, "What can I get for you folks?"

"We would like a Scotch and Water and a White Russian," I answered.

She replied with a smile, "Thank you and I'll be right back with your drinks."

I turned back toward Lee, "So Lee, tell me when you realized who I was?"

Appearing somewhat embarrassed, "Well to be honest with you Christina, I didn't know who you were until my colleagues told me you were a big star."

I looked at him strangely, "You really didn't know who I was, even after I told you my name?"

"Please don't be offended I just don't have much time to go to the movies and I only listen to classical music."

I chuckled again, "I'm not offended Lee, just surprised. I thought everyone knew me. So you really never heard any of my music?"

"I wish I could say yes, but I can't, because I don't believe I have."

"What is it you do that keeps you so busy," I asked inquisitively?

"I work with and design new computer programs."

"That sounds very interesting Lee. Please tell me more about what kind of programs you design."

He smiled, "I can tell you I am working on a new prototype of a home based personal computer and that's all I can say. There happens to be a lot of people who would like to know exactly what I'm working on in my lab, but that has to remain top secret."

"Top secret, now I'm really intrigued. Do you work for the government?"

With that the barmaid came over to us and placed our drinks down on the table. I handed her a twenty, "Thank you and keep the change."

In answer to my question Lee said, "Well, yes and no. I work for myself but the government has purchased many of my inventions for national defense purposes, as well as the space program."

"Your work sounds very exciting Lee, and I am somewhat familiar with computers. In my line of work we are beginning to use computers for more and more things every day. But why would a home based personal computer be considered top secret?"

He leaned close to me and in a low tone, "Because the first company to come up with a small inexpensive, home based personal computer, which will have versatile applications and be user friendly, will change the way we live and work forever, not to mention the monetary gains for such a revolutionary invention."

As I listened to Lee speak about his work, he began to become more technical as he went on, until he finally lost me completely. I found myself in awe at this man's intelligence and I slowly became a little more interested in the man as well as in his words.

We had been so involved in our conversation that neither one of us noticed the lounge slowly filling up with people. Then we heard someone over the loudspeaker say, "Ladies and gentlemen it's 11:30 and we are about to begin our comedy show, which will be hosted by a special surprise guest tonight. So without further ado, please give a hardy welcome to the incomparable, Kathy Brown."

As soon as I heard her name my blood began to boil. Then I saw Kathy walk out on the stage. I totally lost complete interest in everything Lee was saying and went into a dead stare at Kathy, until Lee said, "Christina, are you all right?"

He shook my hand, which snapped me out of my trance, "I'm sorry Lee, what did you say?"

"I said are you all right?"

"Actually Lee, I'm not. Do you know anything about my life?"

"I'm sorry I didn't mean to monopolize our conversation. And once again, I don't know anything about you."

I smiled, "Lee, you have nothing to be sorry for, I was truly enjoying our conversation. As a matter of fact, I could listen to you talk all night. I find you to have a very dynamic personality. But, since you don't know anything about me and my life, you could not realize who that woman on the stage is."

He looked for the first time at the stage, "No, I don't know who she is, should I?"

With that I really laughed out loud, "I'm sorry for laughing, but that woman and I have had bad blood between us for years. If you've ever read a Hollywood tabloid you would know that."

"If her presence is making you uncomfortable we can leave. I'm sure there must be someplace else we can go close by."

I patted his hand, "Lee, please forgive me, but I'm not going anyplace. I have a score to settle with that women and I have just decided tonight is going to be the night I'm finally going to settle it. So if you would like to leave now, I'd understand."

His face appeared nervous, "I'm not sure what you mean when you say you have to settle a score with her, but there is no place I'd rather be than here with you right now. So maybe I can help you somehow?"

As Kathy was giving a small monologue I said, "Lee, there is nothing you can do to help me, because I don't need any help. But I can at least tell you a little about what happened."

With that I told him the whole story of how she slept with my husband and helped to cause his death. Afterward he said, "I'm sorry to hear that Christina, it sounds like it was a very intense situation."

"To, say the least!" Kathy finished her monologue and introduced the first comic.

Lee patted my hand assuredly, "I don't know what you have in mind for your revenge, but I do feel that if we stay here this could become another newsworthy story." Taking my hand, "Please Christina let me take you out of here. I don't believe you're thinking very clearly right at this moment and you might be compelled to do something I'm sure you will regret later."

I shook my head, "Oh shit! You're right, let's get out of here."

As we were getting ready to leave, Kathy walked right by us on her way to the ladies room without even noticing me and I thought, "Are you kidding me! This is too good to be true."

I immediately excused myself and went into the ladies room behind her. There were two woman seated at the make-up table and I could see Kathy's shoes from under the stall. The two women stood up and started to walk out so I followed them to the door. As they exited the ladies room, another woman was trying to enter. I put my hand on her chest to stop her from entering and she said, "Hey! What do you think you're doing?" as I closed the door and locked it.

I walked over to the front of Kathy's stall to wait for her, as this woman kept knocking on the door.

When Kathy opened the door her mouth dropped to the floor the moment she saw me standing there and I felt fire in my eyes as soon as I saw her face. I grabbed her and flung her into the sinks behind us and shouted, "Hi, Kathy! You bitch! I'm going to give you what I promised a long time ago and beat the living shit out of you."

She tried to run so I grabbed her and punched her right in the face. She punched me in the stomach with all her might and at that moment, I realized I had a formidable opponent, but I knew she could not overcome my tomboy childhood, as I belted her left jaw knocking her into the sinks. She bounced off the sinks and pushed me back into the stall door as she screamed, "Fuck you, Christina! You're the fucking bitch! If you had just left Tony and me alone he'd still be alive today."

That was all I had to hear! I leaped at her, grabbed her by the hair, put her in a headlock and began to belt her in the face. She was screaming like I was killing her and believe me I think I was! She kneed me in the crotch and knocked me into the sinks. She grabbed a can of hair spray and began to hit me over the head with it. I grabbed her hand and twisted it around her back and put my other arm around her neck. I held her with my body and pushed her forward smashing her face right into the paper dispenser on the wall, and I heard '**Snap**' as her nose broke. Blood began to run all over us as she screamed and tried to break free.

She slipped out of my hold and bit down on my hand like a Doberman Pincer. I swung her around and punched her with all my might right smack in the nose. She reached out and dug her nails right in the back of my neck and pulled. "You bitch!" I screamed, than I walloped her again.

As we fought like two wild animals, we could hear people were trying to break down the door. She grabbed my right breast through my blouse, dug her nails in again and ripped my blouse off, taking my skin with it. I grabbed the can of hair spray and back-handed her right across the head and she fell to the ground screaming. I leaped on top of her and proceeded to smash her face into the floor, as she screamed, "Help! Help! Somebody Help!" and that's when the door finally gave way to the constant pressure. Someone then grabbed and pulled me off of her. I turned and it was Lee, holding me back from killing her.

Someone else helped Kathy up off the floor and she yelled, "Someone call the police, this fucking bitch tried to kill me!"

I yelled, "Kathy, don't you think you've been humiliated enough. Call the police in on this and you'll never live it down. But on the other hand, I will become the heroine. So go ahead, call!"

She looked at me with tears and blood running down her face, "Don't call the police, I only fell." Still looking dead into my eyes, "Christina, if you want to kill someone, it should be Frank, not me. He put me up to sleeping with John. I never wanted to try to break you two up, but you know how convincing Frank can be at getting his way."

I looked at her with disgust in my expression and said nothing. I just turned and held my blood stained head up high as I walked out past the crowd of on-lookers.

As I reached the front door, Lee was right behind me with my jacket and purse, which I totally forgot about. He opened the door for me, "Christina, please let me take you home."

I turned to him, "I'm staying here tonight, so you can walk me to my room if you'd like?"

"I wouldn't dream of letting you walk through here alone, especially after that fight! So yes, I would be happy to walk you to your room."

We proceeded to my room and as we entered the elevator Lee said, "Are you all right, Christina? You look like hell."

First I looked at myself, then I looked at the three men in the elevator with us who were staring at me, I looked back at Lee and started to laugh. I didn't stop laughing until we reached my room on the 16th floor. I turned the key, "Lee, won't you please come in for a few minutes? I could sure use someone to talk to right now."

"I have no place to go and I'd rather stay with you until I know you're all right."

He came in behind me and as I closed the door I said, "Lee, would you please excuse me for a few minutes while I clean up and change."

He eyed me again, "Sure, you go clean up. I'll entertain myself until you return."

As I showered I thought about everything Kathy said, and I realized for the first time since Tony's death, I did not kill Tony. He pulled the trigger not me. I had been blaming myself for months now for Tony's death and that realization made me decide right there in that shower, I didn't have to blame myself anymore. I thought about the last thing Kathy said and it made me hate Frank even more. I didn't think I could ever hold as much hate in my heart as I held there for Frank, but I did. I was now more than ever driven by my hatred to crush Frank and I knew my day for revenge would come. I turned off the shower and began to dry off. As I was drying I began to realize what I had just done to Kathy. I was so angry I think I could have killed her with my bare hands if Lee hadn't pulled me off of her. I began to shake at the thought I could actually get angry enough to kill someone. As I trembled, I threw on a robe and went out to speak with Lee with a towel in my hand, still drying my hair.

When I came out of the bathroom, Lee was sitting on the sofa with two cups of coffee and some Danish. As I sat down on the other side of the sofa Lee said, "I took the liberty of having room service bring us a snack; just in case you were anything like me when you're upset. I usually head for the first thing I can eat."

I wrapped my hair up in the towel, "That sounds great Lee, thank you. Please excuse the towel; I didn't want to leave you while I took the time needed to dry my hair."

"Don't excuse yourself to me, the towel looks like a queen's turban on you."

"Thank you Lee that was a very nice thing to say, especially since I have a black eye to go along with it. Maybe you need your eye glasses checked," we both laughed.

When I reached for the coffee cup my hand started to shake from the weight of it and I almost dropped it. Lee steadied my hand, "You're not all right at all are you? Christina, are you sure you don't need to go to a hospital?"

I laughed, "Oh, God! That's all I'd have to do. Tomorrow the whole free world would know, even you." We laughed a little more, "Lee, I'm really not hurt too badly, I'm just a little shaky. After all that was a hell of an adrenaline rush, let me tell you."

"I guess so, from what I could hear I thought you were killing each other."

"Lee, we were trying to kill one another. The bad blood runs deep between us. That's why I thank God you broke in when you did. I might have actually killed her and she's not worth it. In the scheme of things, she's small change." Then I reached over, touched his hand, "Thank you for being here for me, you could not imagine how alone I feel in this world. I have isolated myself from my own daughter, as well as all the people in my life who mean anything to me. Lee, I have been hurting for so long now, I can't remember what it feels like not to hurt." My tears began to run again and I could feel them stinging my eyes, "Please forgive me again Lee, I don't mean to be crying on you."

"Would you please stop apologizing to me and just let it all out. Christina, if there is one thing I know it's this. If you keep everything locked up inside yourself, you will never be able to start the healing process." He moved closer to me and gave me a gentle hug, "I have a big shoulder and it's free for you anytime you need it."

I looked up into his kind eyes, "Come to think about it, I could use a big shoulder right now." He placed his left arm around me and I laid my head on his chest.

We sat on that sofa for the longest time just like that. It felt so good to finally feel the warmth of a man's arms around me again. I started to feel alive again and I found myself slowly nuzzling closer to him. I gently moved until my lips found the flesh of his neck and I began to softly kiss him. I felt my passion begin to grow as I slowly began to unbutton his shirt. In a soft voice Lee said, "Christina, I know you're not in your normal frame of mind right now, so before we go any further I have to ask you if you're sure this is what you want?"

I looked up at him and with a tender loving voice said, "Lee, if for only one night, will you make love to me?"

He leaned down and began to softly kiss me. I let myself melt into his kisses and the passion slowly began to flow between our lips. Our fire was beginning to crackle when I broke from his embrace. I stood up in front of him and with only the dim light of the lamp on the end table I took the towel off my head and threw it on the arm of the sofa. I gently untied my robe and let it fall to the floor. I could see his heart in his throat and a bulge in his pants as soon as my robe fell. I stood him up and began to undress him, starting from his suit jacket, to his socks and I saved the pants for last. As I unbuckled his pants and began to bring down his zipper, I could hear his heart pounding through his chest. I led him over to the bed, held him and began to kiss him deeply. Slowly I let his pants fall to his ankles, reached down and slipped his underwear over his nicely curved cheeks and then over his throbbing erection. I sat him down on the bed, knelt down in front of his loins, slipped his feet out of his clothing, brought them up and laid him down flat on the bed. I climbed up on top of him and proceeded to make love to every inch of his body. I needed to feel him, I needed to feel the passion, I needed to feel alive. I needed the fire for life back again and I needed the sex! I was incredible! I nearly killed the man, but he kept up with me, if you get my drift. That night of love making was rejuvenating and it definitely was love making. I felt a connection to this man as we made love and all I wanted was to make him feel my love and passion. After we climaxed, we held each other and I said, "Lee, I want you to know we were truly making love and you were wonderful. I also want you to know no matter what you may say about your looks, I think you are extremely attractive. Thank you for making me feel so loved and wanted. I will never forget this night." Then I kissed his lips and we fell asleep.

I woke up at 5:00am that morning and Lee was still asleep. I looked at him sleeping there and thought, "He's not a great looker, but he's sure a sweetheart and not too shabby in the sack either."

I quickly dressed, took a pen and paper and left Lee this note. **"Lee, you are the nicest man I've met in a long time and I had an incredible time with you. So much so, that I know I could get to like having you around. But, for your own safety I am not going to leave you my number. Have a good life Lee, Love Christina**."

I decided not to pursue Lee because I knew deep down inside myself it would only be because I wanted to get in on the ground floor of the up and coming computer age. So for the first time in a long time, I put the personal feelings of another before my own desire for power and revenge." **Then I headed for home.**

CHAPTER 9. FOR THE LOVE OF JOY

I walked into Joy's room at 5:45am on Sunday March 19th, 1979. Joy was now, one-year-five-months and five-days-old. It had been one day short of eight-months since the last day I saw my sweet loving Joy. I looked down at her sleeping in her crib like an angel and I felt a warm feeling come over me. I quietly moved the reading chair closer to Joy's crib and sat beside her. As I watched her sleep, tears began to roll down my cheeks. I guess I fell asleep myself because I did not hear Nanny Sue come in the room. I was surprised when she touched my shoulder and said in a low tone, "Mrs. Demetrees, its 8:00am, I usually wake Joy up now. Would you like to get her up instead?"

I looked at her and answered in a soft low voice, "Thank you, Nanny Sue. I would like that very much." I stood up, reached into the crib, picked Joy up, "Joy, honey, Mommy's home."

She looked at me, started to smile, "Mommy!"

I held her close, "Your Mommy loves you Joy, with all her heart and I will never desert you again." We played and laughed as I washed and dressed her.

I was down in the family kitchen feeding Joy her breakfast when Jimmy and Bobby walked in. They both almost fell over when they saw me, and Jimmy joyfully yelled, "Oh my, God! Christina, you're back! And look Bobby, she's feeding Joy. It's so good to see you with her."

I gazed up at them both, "Hi guys, what would you think about the four of us going to Disneyland today?"

Jimmy jumped into Bobby's arms and shouted, "Thank, God! Our girl's back, Bobby." They both came over to me, and the four of us had a warm group hug.

As we hugged, Bobby looked at me with curiosity, "Christina, do you have a black eye?" I looked at them both staring at my eye and I started to laugh.

As I laughed Jimmy asked, "So what's so funny about a black eye?"

I stopped laughing long enough to explain, "I kicked the hell out of Kathy Brown, last night." Then we all started to laugh. When we finally stopped laughing, I told them both about my accidental run-in with Kathy. After that we all had our breakfast and it was off to Disneyland for the day.

It was a beautiful, warm, bright, sunny day when James drove all of us including Carman and Nanny Sue, to Disneyland in the limo and the seven of us went in together.

I was dressed very inconspicuously with blue jeans, black tee shirt, sneakers, baseball cap and wide sunglasses. I also carried Joy most of the day as we walked through the park.

About halfway through the day, we came across the haunted castle and of course, everyone wanted to go in. But, I decided to wait outside with Joy who was too little to enter, while everyone else went in.

When I said I wasn't going in Jimmy said, "Christina, you have to come in with me." Then he turned to Bobby, "Honey, would you please stay out here with Joy, so Christina and I can go in together?"

Bobby knelt on the ground and said like, 'Dan Acroyd' might, "Oh gee Dad, do I have to?"

We all started to laugh, "No Bobby, you don't have to, I'd rather stay here with Joy anyway."

"No Christina, I'm only kidding. You go ahead with Jimmy, I happen to like my arms without black and blue marks anyway. You know how he is with those hands of his when he gets nervous"

I laughed, "I know what you mean."

Jimmy came over to me with his puppy dog eyes, "Please! Please! You have to come with me. We haven't done anything crazy together in months."

I looked at him with his hands up like a begging poodle, "All right, you talked me into it."

I handed Joy over to Bobby, and Jimmy and I got in line with James, Carman and Nanny Sue. When we finally reached the end of the line, the chairs for the ride would only fit two adults comfortably, so Jimmy and I took a seat by ourselves. As the ride began to take us into the screaming, pitch black darkness, Jimmy and I were both starting to get scared. Things were popping out at us from every angle and we were screaming and having a great time. Jimmy and I were holding each other tightly to help intensify our fear, when a figure of Frankenstein's bride came running toward us with her three-inch long finger nails coming right for our faces, and we both screamed at the top of our lungs. Then it hit me like a charge of dynamite and I flew up out of the seat almost knocking Jimmy out of the chair and yelled, "Ahhh! **I'm a fucking genius!**" as Jimmy screamed out in horror, "Ahhh! What is it?" and grabbed at his chest.

When Jimmy could breathe again, he shouted, "I told you girl! You're a fucking nut! And you'll always be a fucking nut!"

He hugged me and shouted, "Hey world, she's really back!"

Joking around I slapped his hand, "Shut up, you asshole!" Then I kissed him, "Jimmy, you are truly my best friend and I love you."

It turned out to be a wonderful day and I was finally back to myself and my family. We had arrived at the park at 10:00am and we went on all the rides and saw all the shows. Finally, we left at closing time which was 9:00pm right after the fireworks. When we got back to the limo, Joy was sound asleep in my arms. It felt so good to have my baby back in my arms again and I knew I no longer had to hide from her.

The next morning, I decided to take two months off from work. I spent every minute of Joy's waking hours with her during those two months and when she slept I was writing. First, I wrote the lyrics and melody to an entire album of ballads which came from my deepest innermost feelings of love for Tony and Joy. There were nine cuts on the album. Each one told the world just what I went through after Tony's death, and how the love of Joy saved me from myself. This was my tenth album, and I titled it 'For The Love Of Joy.' After I finished it, I sent it into the studios with Jimmy. I wanted everything set up and ready to start recording as soon as I returned to work. At the same time I started writing my third and most brilliant screen play with movie soundtrack, to date. The idea came to me while I was on the ride with Jimmy in the haunted castle at Disneyland. They were both to be titled, 'Halloween In Hell!'

During that time Joy and I had the chance to come to know one another all over again. We had so much fun and I took her everywhere with me. We laughed, played, and I found out I could truly be a good mother.

One day during my vacation, I received a call from Tom Davis, who was one of the attorneys I had hired in New York, to oversee my building project in Milton. He informed me the project was going well and the builders had reached the point of building the first stage of my planned construction. This was the completion of six of the main studio buildings, which was the point I had requested to be informed, so I could make a personal inspection.

The plans were to have the project built in three stages. There was to be three main developments on the property which would be considered individual industrial parks. Each of these three parks would have six large campuses like buildings, spread out amongst the woods. Each park would have its own master control center, to monitor the activities throughout the three parks. There would also be offices, recording studios and movie lots. In addition, each park would have buildings set aside, as well as its own twenty-acre area for future ventures and endeavors of Powers Incorporated.

So, on April 16th, 1979, it was off to New York to inspect the progress of the future home of Powers Incorporated. When Joy, Nanny Sue and I left L.A. it was hotter than hell. The summer had come early to California and we already had two weeks of 90+ degree temperatures. But when we got off the plane in New York at

6:00pm we walked straight into the beginnings of a freak spring **blizzard**. It took the limo nearly four hours to get us from LaGuardia airport to the Plaza Hotel in downtown Manhattan. Then we spent the next two days snow bound in our suite.

Finally on April 19th, Tom Davis who was a very attractive six-foot tall black man, and I took the ride upstate by ourselves, because it was still too cold to take Joy. When we finally reached Milton we drove through the town until we found the sign that read, "**The future home of Powers Incorporated.**" We turned down a sloppy, muddy road and headed to see the completion of stage one of my dream. Tom drove us from one building to the next in his four wheel drive Ford Bronco. After a six hour detailed inspection of the interior and exterior of six very large buildings, I found myself feeling extremely pleased with the work that had been completed.

Just before we left, I stood in one spot and looked all around me at this dirty, muddy, winter wonderland and thought, "You must be freaking nuts, Christina. What the hell are you spending six-hundred-million-dollars, out here in the freaking wilderness for? You asshole, everything you need is in Hollywood and that's where you live." I looked at Tom who was standing beside me patiently waiting to leave and I shrugged my shoulders and said, "Oh well! I'll figure it out tomorrow."

Tom gave me a strange look, "Whatever you say, Ms. Powers."

I looked at him and started to laugh, "It's an inside joke Tom." Then I gave him the okay to continue work and it was back to the city.

The rest of my time with Joy went too quickly. Before I knew it, it was May 15th, time to go back to work. When I arrived at my office in the temporary headquarters of Powers Incorporated in southern LA, I immediately called all my personal staff off the other projects we had them on. Then, with only working nine hour days, we still released a completed album on June 1, entitled 'For The Love Of Joy.'

On June 5th, it was full steam ahead for all of us, on my third film and eleventh album as *Christina Powers*. As I said, I entitled it, 'Halloween in Hell!' I knew 'Halloween in Hell' was going to be an ambitious and expensive sixty-million-dollar gamble. I also knew if we could pull it off before this coming Halloween, we'd make at least a half a billion. Be assured we worked day and night for the next four months, so that we'd be able to release our film to the world on October 5, and we did it!

The film was about a young nursing student who finds herself caught up in a macabre situation on Halloween Night, in the year 2000. It turns out that she must do battle with the demons from hell to keep them from releasing Satan himself on mankind at the stroke of midnight. If she failed, Satan would enslave the whole human race. The film was full of nonstop action and horror, with high speed auto chases, plane crashes and the murders of all the heroine's family and friends by horrifying demons.

The pace of the film was intense right up to the unpredictable terrifying ending, where myself, playing the heroin, is finally defeated and possessed by all the demons of hell at 11:45pm Halloween Night. At which time I started to dance the dance of the demons, to open the gates of hell and summon forth Satan himself, at the stroke of midnight. I danced and sang for the last ten minutes of the film, just like I was truly possessed. Miraculously, at 11:59 the heavens opened above me, and angels flew down and released me from the demons, just as Satan rose up from out of his fiery, smoky hole in the ground, at which time I grabbed a sword one of the angels lost in their battle with the demons, and I plunged it into this hideous creature's heart. He explodes and I saved the human race from everlasting torment, with a little help from my angelic friends.

On September 14th, we finished the last day of shooting on 'Halloween In Hell' and it was time to start promoting our ahead of schedule release date of October 1st, for the new 'Christina Powers' film. I knew it would be a winner because the film and my performance were phenomenal. I also knew the accompanying soundtrack would be the only other album released that year by any performer, to knock 'For The Love Of Joy' out of the number one spot on all the record billboard charts. After 'For The Love Of Joy' was released my fan club membership went from ten-million worldwide to forty-six-million. This number turned out to be the largest fan club ever, for any performer in entertainment history. My fans and I seemed to create a personal and loving relationship through the years. The whole world knew I was telling them all I would survive my heartbreak through the lyrics on that album. Even though 'For The Love Of Joy' had none of my typical dance songs on it, it still became my best-selling album to date. I also had to increase my fan club staff from ten employees to thirty employees, just to keep up with the mail that came in every day.

Finally it was October 1st, at 8:00pm and I was hosting my premiere night at the Palace Theater in downtown LA. I was dressed in a black full length gown, which ran all the way to the floor. It had a three foot long train, which slid along behind me as I walked. It was similar to the gowns 'Elmira' might wear today, on her 'Horror Night' TV shows. I planned it to be a formal invitation bash. I had all the top brass of Hollywood on my invitation list. All but Frank of course.

Jimmy, Bobby, and Barbara, were with me at the front entrance of the theater greeting all our guests as they came in, when to my astonishment I saw Frank walking up the red carpet toward us. He had Kathy Brown on one arm and another bimbo on the other. He also had two of his well-dressed goon's right behind him.

The lobby of the theater was nearly full with most of my influential guests when they reached us, and Frank said, "Christina, you look lovely tonight, and your attire suits you. I didn't receive my formal invitation, which I assume was an oversight by your staff, so here we are."

I looked him straight in the eye, "There was no oversight and you know it! So, please just turn around and leave right now."

He looked at Barbara, "She must be mistaken, don't you think so, Barbara?"

Before Barbara could say anything I interjected, "Frank, Tony is not here tonight, so if you don't leave now and quietly, then I will be forced to call your bluff and make a scene neither one of us will live down for a longtime. So make your choice and make it quick, because I'm becoming more and more nauseous the longer I have to look at you."

I could see the veins in his neck begin to bulge as his anger grew, "Frank, take your looks of admiration and get out, now! Because this is my last warning and I know you want to cause a scene with me a lot less than I do with you."

"Christina, I'm very sorry to disappoint you, but I don't think I want to sit through another one of your over hyped movies after all." Then, he turned and walked away with his entourage bringing up the rear.

Barbara turned to me, "You have some set of balls, girl." And the four of us immediately started to laugh.

The premiere was a complete success, and everyone loved the film. Jimmy, Bobby, all the crew members and I, were flying higher than a kite that night at the celebration party. It was held in the ballroom at the Regency Hotel which was adjacent to the theater. It was about 11:00pm as I stood there with my crystal glass of champagne in hand. I was talking with Barbara and a group of five or six other people. All of a sudden I heard Tony's voice echoing in my mind like a crash of thunder shouting, **"Christina**!" I quickly turned to look behind me and for a split second, I actually saw Tony standing there. I looked into his tear filled eyes and I saw he was holding the limp body of Joy in his arms. Then he was gone.

Instantly I dropped my glass and screamed in horror, "Ahhh!" As I started to shake, everyone came running to me. I screamed out again, "Jimmy! Jimmy! Where are you?"

Jimmy and Bobby both came running through the crowd yelling, "What is it?"

I looked at Jimmy with panic in my eyes and screamed, "We have to get home now! Something's wrong with Joy."

I grabbed their arms and the three of us ran through the crowd and down to the parking lot, to where James would hopefully be waiting with the limo. When we reached the parking lot, Bobby shouted and pointed across the line of limos, "There he is over there!" We ran across the parking lot to where James was waiting.

James almost went into shock when he saw us running toward him shouting, "James, hurry we have to get home now!" He ran around the limo and jumped into the driver's seat. I jumped into the front seat with him, as Jimmy and Bobby jumped into the back.

I caught my dress and tore it at my knees on the door as I slammed it shut and shouted, "James, step on it and get us home NOW!" Then I tore the rest of my dress off from my thighs down, as Jimmy was opening the partition between the front and back seats. When it was completely down Jimmy, yelled frantically "What's going on, Christina? I'm having a fucking heart attack her!"

I looked at them all, "I don't know how I know it, but something is terribly wrong at home."

We raced through Los Angeles toward Malibu on Route 1. When we reached Topanga Beach, James said, "Oh my God! Christina, look at the sky ahead."

We all looked up and to our horror the sky was bright red. Then James really gunned it. We were doing 90 miles an hour down Route 1, toward what was becoming the biggest brush fire we had ever seen. When we reached Rambla Pacifica Road, we were stopped by a state police road block and the officer said, "The Santa Anna Winds have flared up a whopper of a forest fire for the next ten miles in, and no one is allowed past this point."

I stuck my head out the window over James' lap and shouted, "I'm *Christina Powers,* and my daughter is up that road, we have to pass."

He shook his head 'no', "If she's up there the rescue squad will surely get her out, so please just turn around. We have to keep the road open for emergency vehicles."

Panicking and not caring about any emergency vehicles, I pushed my foot down on the accelerator and shouted, "James, drive! Drive!" and we flew right past them.

As we got closer to the mansion, we found ourselves in the middle of a raging fire on both sides of the road. James had to drive over downed burning tree limbs in order to reach our driveway. He sped up the driveway until we were stopped by burning trees about three-hundred yards from the mansion. We jumped out of the limo and ran up to the house. We could hear the sounds of sirens but there were no fire trucks to be seen. As we rounded the bend of the driveway, I could see the entire right side of the mansion was engulfed in flames, and I screamed, "Oh, God, no!"

As we reached the front porch, Carman and two other employees came running out of the half burning front door. They were coughing so bad they could hardly speak as they ran down to us in the front yard. When they reached us, I screamed in horror, "Where's Joy, Carman? Where is she?"

Carman cried out, "I tried to get to her and Nanny Sue in the nursery, but the fire and smoke is everywhere."

"Oh my God!" I screamed, "Joy is still in there!"

I started to run and James grabbed me, "No Christina, you can't help her now."

I ripped myself from him and shouted, "The fire is on the right side of the mansion and the nursery is on the left." I took off and ran up the steps of the porch right through the partially burning front door and straight into an inferno in the foyer. The entire right side of the staircase was engulfed in fire, but I could still make it up through the flames which were burning on the left side. I charged up the staircase and headed through the thick smoke until I reached the nursery. When I entered Joy's room the smoke was so thick I could hardly breathe. I was coughing and shouting, "Joy! Joy! Where are you? Nanny Sue, Where are you?"

I fell to the floor and crawled over to where her youth bed would be. When I found it, I felt the bed for Joy, but she was not there. So I frantically searched the floor on my hands and knees praying to find her, until I finally felt her little hand under-mine. My blood raced through my body with all the force of Niagara Falls as I picked up her limp, lifeless, body.

I pulled her close to me and screamed, "Joy! Joy! Wake up!" But there was no response. I tried to give her mouth-to-mouth resuscitation, but the smoke was too thick. I turned to try and crawl my way back out the same way I came in, but I could see the flames were now at the bedroom door. I stood up in the center of that mass of smoke and started searching wildly with my right arm flinging through the air, looking for anything that would help me find my bearings. I found the iron reading chair, and holding Joy in my left hand, I flung the chair with my right hand with all my might toward the direction of where I hoped the window would be. The chair went crashing out of the bedroom window and as soon as it did, the flames came bursting into the room as the smoke poured out of the window.

I stuck my head out of the second story window and screamed out, "Jimmy! Somebody! Help us!" But no one was on that side of the mansion to hear me over the roar of the fire. I looked behind me at the approaching flames and I had no choice. I held Joy as close to me as I could and I jumped out the window.

When my feet hit the ground, I lost hold of Joy and we both went flying into the broken glass, just missing the iron chair I had thrown out the window. Then I ran to Joy, picked her back up and started giving her mouth-to-mouth resuscitation again. I started to run toward the front of this burning inferno to where I prayed help would be. When I reached the front of the mansion, I could see Bobby and James, struggling to hold a fighting and screaming Jimmy back, from running into a fiery death.

I screamed out as I ran toward them, "Jimmy! Help us!" When they finally heard us, they all turned to see our smoke stained, bloody and partially singed bodies, running toward them. They all started to run toward us. The minute they reached us, there was a series of large explosions which knocked us all off our feet and the heat, smoke and sound of the fire grew so quickly we almost didn't get away from the mansion fast enough. We all stopped running when we reached the driveway which was about one hundred yards from the house.

Jimmy grabbed me and yelled, "Christina, let me take her!"

As Jimmy took Joy from my arms he looked at Bobby and yelled, "Bobby, help Christina, I'll continue C.P.R. on Joy."

Bobby grabbed my left side which I was limping on and shouted, "Come on everybody, we have to keep running, the fire is beginning to encircle us."

I looked at him frantically and shouted, "Let's help Jimmy, Bobby. I'm all right."

At that we all made a mad, one mile dash through the burning woods, away from the crumbling mansion and toward the main road. We could not run up the driveway because it was in flames and so was the limo.

That one mile run through the woods burning all around us, was the longest and scariest run any of us had ever made in our entire lives. I clung to one side of Jimmy, as Bobby clung to the other side of him. While Jimmy continued to give Joy C.P.R., Bobby and I were dragging Jimmy in one direction then the other, as we ran whatever way we could to get through the flames. Right behind us was James and Carman, but we were not able to see the other two household employees.

When we finally reached the main road, we found ourselves right in the middle of more flames and it was closing in on us from all directions.

I desperately looked around at this hopeless situation and screamed out, "**Oh, God! Please help us!!**" Then from over the roar of the fire, we could hear the whirling of a helicopter's blades as it approached us. We all started to jump and scream as the 'chopper' began to descend toward us.

When it landed, two medics jumped out and ran over to us and I shouted, "My daughter! Please help her!" Then one medic took Joy from Jimmy's exhausted arms and began to work on her, as the other one helped us into the 'chopper' and it was off to LA Memorial Hospital.

I pleaded with God in my mind to save my baby, as the medics began to artificially breathe for Joy with a black breathing bag. Then they proceeded to evaluate her condition and radioed their findings to the hospital. We were all in a state of shock by the time the 'chopper' landed on the roof of the hospital. As soon as we landed, the emergency crew came running to us. They grabbed Joy, and disappeared with her before I could even get out of the 'chopper'. We were taken to the emergency room, and the E.R. staff began to evaluate us for injuries.

Panicking again I shouted, "Where is my daughter?"

A doctor came over to me, "Are you the mother of the child just brought in on the 'chopper'?"

"Yes!" I answered desperately, "Where is she?"

"She's in the triage burn center, which is the best burn center in the world. What I need from you is to sign a release form so we can legally treat your daughter. Also, if you're up to it, I need to ask you some questions about your daughter's health."

I signed the form he had and answered all of his questions. Afterward he said, "Now please let us treat your wounds and we will inform you of your little girl's condition."

"I want to be with her now!" I demanded.

"I'm sorry, but I can't let you do that. It is a very sterile area and it would be impossible to let you go in there in the shape you're in now."

After we were treated, they sat us in a waiting room and Bobby looked at me and in a somber tone, "Did you see Nanny Sue, Christina?"

I looked at him sadly, "No."

The five of us sat in the waiting room for what seemed to be an eternity for some word on Joy's condition. Finally at 3:15am a doctor walked into the waiting room and said, "Is Mrs. Demetrees here?"

Jimmy and I stood up, ran to him and I said, "How is my baby, Doctor?"

He had a desperate look on his face, "She is still hanging onto life and we have done all we can do at this point. She is now on a respirator, but her lungs are badly damaged. The next few hours will be crucial for her if she's going to survive."

My tears immediately started to fall, "May I please see her now?"

He answered sympathetically, "Yes, you may, come with me and I will take you to her."

Anxiously Jimmy said, "I'm her father and I need to see her too."

The doctor looked at him strangely, "You may come also Mr. Demetrees, but only one person at a time and for only **five minutes each**."

We followed him to the intensive care unit of the burn center. When I reached Joy's room, I walked up to her. Her precious little body was hooked up to a respirator, I.V.'s, and life support monitors. She was enclosed in a large see-through plastic container. They had her suspended in the air, by what looked like wires in the center of this enclosure. I put my hands on the outside of the container, and cried because I couldn't even touch my baby.

My five minutes with Joy passed too quickly, when a nurse came in, "Mrs. Demetrees, I must ask you to leave so Mr. Demetrees may come in."

I kissed the plastic container, "Joy, it's Mommy honey, I love you my little angel, and I will be right here when you wake up." I turned to leave. When I came to Jimmy, I hugged him tightly, "Jimmy, I'm going to the chapel for a few minutes, if anything happens come get me."

Then I left to find the hospital chapel. When I opened the door to the chapel, it was dimly lit with only two lights. One semi-bright light was over the door as you entered and one small light on the other side of the room was glowing over the top of a statue of the figure of Christ. I walked the twenty feet or so to where the statue was and I knelt down in front of it. I began to pray out loud, "Dear God! I don't ask you for much and I know I don't go to church anymore, but please save my daughter's life. She is so little and helpless, she needs me and I need her!"

I felt a sense of urgency and I started to cry and scream out, "Please, God! I'm begging you to help her. Tony, Tony, I know you can hear me! Please save our daughter!" Just then the door opened. I turned quickly to see the tall figure of something or someone standing there. With the tears flowing from my eyes it looked as if I was seeing a glistening angel from the light shining over the door behind this dark figure. I wiped the tears from my eyes and begged, "Can you save my daughter?"

This figure began to come toward me and in a strong, stern voice, "*Christina Powers*, you're a sinful woman and you must repent for your sinful ways before God will answer your prayers and save your child." I reached out to touch this heavenly image, but it was just a man.

I stood up and shouted, "What are you talking about? If God will only save my daughter after I've repented for sins I don't believe I've committed, then I don't want anything to do with your God."

"You dare to blaspheme God, while you plead with him to save the life of your daughter? What kind of an abomination from hell are you?"

I slapped him in the face with all my might and this six-foot man went flying into the pews. I ran out of the chapel and continued to run back to Joy's room. When I turned through the opened doors of the burn unit, I saw Jimmy walking toward me with tears pouring down his face.

I stopped and shouted, "**Jimmy is Joy all right**?" All he could do was shake his head 'no'.

I screamed, "Oh God, no!" Then I fell to my knees in the middle of that hall and cried my heart out, **as another piece of my soul died**.

CHAPTER 10. THE NIGHTMARE

As I was sitting on that cold floor in the hallway of the hospital crying my heart out, I felt a warm soft breeze flow over my body and immediately a sense of peace came over me. Somehow, I knew Joy was out of pain and safe with Tony. I felt someone touch my shoulder as they knelt down beside me, "Jesus is speaking to you, Christina, please listen to what he is saying."

I turned toward the voice and it was the same man who was in the chapel. I felt so weak I just leaned my head on his shoulder as my tears began to subside, "Would you please help me up? I need to go to my daughter."

As this stranger was helping me off the floor Jimmy and Bobby came over to us and Bobby said, "Thank you sir we'll help her from here."

Then with Jimmy and Bobby on either side of me, we walked toward Joy's room. As we headed slowly down the hall this same man came up to us, placed a card in my hand,, "Christina, this is my card. Please call me anytime you want to know what Jesus is trying to say to you."

He then turned around and left without saying another word. I slipped his card in my partially torn and burnt bra, and continued walking toward Joy's room with Jimmy and Bobby.

When we reached Joy's room and opened the door, there were two nurses in the room with Joy. They were washing her, and one of them was holding Joy's little arm way up in the air, so high that it lifted her little body just enough to reach her hand under Joy's back. When she saw us open the door, she stopped washing Joy, came over to us and said in a very rude tone, "I'm sorry, but you're not allowed in this room until we have prepared the body."

I looked at her sternly and sharply replied, "Miss, you're washing my baby and I don't like how you're doing it. So I will take over from here."

She looked back at me angrily, "I can't let..."

I interrupted her immediately, "You can stop talking right now, or I will have your license in the morning."

I walked over to Joy, took the wash cloth from the other nurse's hand and began to wash my baby's bruised and singed little body.

As the two nurses left the room, Jimmy came over to me reached his hand down into the wash basin grabbed the other wash cloth and began to help me wash her. We looked into each other's tear filled eyes, as we washed our little girl, "Mr. Demetrees, I truly do love you."

When we finished washing Joy, we put her little hospital gown on her. I turned to Jimmy and Bobby, stretched my arms out to them both and they came over to me and we just held one another. There was a tap on the door and as it opened, a young nurse was standing there and she politely said, "Please excuse me. I'm Sue Sereikis and I'm the nursing supervisor for the burn unit. I just wanted to see if there was anything I could get for you folks?"

The three of us broke our embrace as I said in a very low sad voice, "Sue, can you please tell me where my baby's body will go from here?"

She answered me very sincerely, "Mrs. Demetrees your daughter will be held here at the hospital in a safe, clean cooler, until your funeral director comes to pick her up."

"Thank you, Sue." Then I bent down, kissed Joy on her forehead, "Its Mommy honey and I love you baby with all my heart. You will be with me in my heart every day of my life, until I can hold you again." I kissed her again, "Joy, honey, you go with Daddy now." I could no longer hold back my tears, "Daddy will be taking care of you now my baby." **Oh God! How my heart broke as I said goodbye to my baby. It was the hardest thing I ever had to do.**

Then the three of us slowly turned and walked out of her room together. We held each other up as we walked in a dazed state down the hall, where we met James and Carman in the waiting room. We all just looked at each other with no one knowing what to say and everyone trying to hold back their tears. I said in a totally defeated voice, "Since the five of us have no place to go, I suggest we take a taxi to the Regency Hotel. I think we should try to get some rest."

James spoke up, "Why don't you four sit here and I'll get us a ride. Then I'll come back and get you guys." So that's what we did.

I rented a three-bedroom suite for one week at the Regency. James and Carman took one room, Jimmy and Bobby took the other, and I went for the last bedroom. It was 6:00am when my head hit the pillow. As exhausted as I was, I still could not fall asleep. So I got up at 8:00am on the dot and called Hess funeral home which was the same funeral establishment Jimmy hired to do Tony's funeral. I made an appointment with the owner, Mr. Hess, for 10:00am to make the arrangements for Joy's funeral. After I set the appointment time, I had Mr. Hess promise me he would go immediately to the hospital and pick Joy's body up. I could not handle the thought of Joy being left in the hospital morgue any longer.

I called my Senior Personal Secretary, Judy, at her home and had her send clothing to the hotel for all of us, along with a new limo. I also put her to work on finding us all temporary housing at one of the more elite apartment buildings in town, at least until I could try to think about permanent living arrangements. As soon as I hung up the phone, I went to the shower to clean up and get ready for my appointment with Mr. Hess.

About ten minutes after I finished my shower, the clothing which Judy had sent to the hotel for us arrived. I placed all the clothing out on the sofa with a note telling the others to go through the clothes and find what fits. I also told them where I was going and that I would be back as soon as possible. I dressed and walked down to my limo, which I had waiting to take me to my appointment with Mr. Hess. As the limo driver left L.A. and headed toward Malibu, we could still see the smoke in the sky from the fire.

When we reached Hess Funeral Home on Route 1, I climbed out of the limo, took a deep breath and slowly headed into the funeral home. I knew this was going to be a hard thing to do, but I didn't realize how hard until Mr. Hess took me in the back room and began to show me some tiny coffins. When I saw them, the realization I was actually going to have to place my child in one of those coffins made me begin to feel faint. I grabbed onto Mr. Hess' arm to steady myself, "Mr. Hess, I can't do this right now. Would you please pick out the best one you have for Joy?"

He helped me back out of the room, "Mrs. Demetrees, if you would please send me something for Joy to wear, then I can take care of everything else for you."

I looked at him sincerely, "Thank you Mr. Hess, I would truly appreciate that and I'll have a dress sent to you this afternoon. And please call me Christina."

He nodded his head, "Thank you Christina. I need to know one more thing. When would you like to have the showing? We can hold it tomorrow afternoon and evening and have the funeral the day after, or we could wait another day."

"Let's have it tomorrow, I don't think I can handle waiting another day." Then I gave him a hug, thanked him one more time and left.

It was October 4th, 1979, at 11:00am when the funeral procession pulled into the cemetery. The weather was cold and rainy that day. This was the first rain we'd had in months and I was burying my little Joy ten days before her second birthday, in that cold rain. This was also the second time I was at this cemetery in the past year, and as I recall, it was raining then too.

As the men started to lower Joy's golden coffin into the ground right over her Father's, I realized I would never attend my own daughter's birthday party, for some reason it hit me right there as she began to disappear from my sight. **I had missed her first birthday party**. I had been fairly strong through all of it up to the point when Joy completely disappeared out of my sight. That's when I lost it. I began to scream and cry, "No! No! Joy! God, why did you take my daughter from me?" With all my closest friends around me, I turned to them and shouted, as the rain poured down, "What the **fuck** is life all about? Why would God take my child from me?"

Jimmy put his arm around me and softly said, "Christina, none of us truly know the answers. All I know is we are still alive and we must go on living. Maybe there is something we need to learn from death, or maybe not. Christina, if we are to learn something from Joy's death, then we will. For right now let's just let some time pass before we start looking for the answers." Then he hugged me, lifted his eyebrows just a bit, "Okay?"

I wiped my eyes and calmly sighed, "Okay."

I bent down, grabbed some dirt to toss on the casket and in my hand was the Medallion I buried with Tony and I thought, "Well I guess you want me to have." Then I brushed it off and stuck it in my pocket as Jimmy placed his arms around me and said, "Come on baby, let's go back to the hotel," and with that we turned and walked away, leaving Joy and Tony behind.

The next morning I received a visit from a Detective Fred Ulrich of the California State Fire Investigation Bureau. I learned from Detective Ulrich that three other people lost their lives in the fire that night. He said Nanny Sue's body was found where the nursery once was. He also told me the bodies of the other two employees, Flow and Mark Sentamore, who came running out of the burning mansion with Carman that night, were found in the woods about two miles from the mansion. Detective Ulrich also needed some information on all of my household employees. I answered what I could of his questions, I gave him my Secretary's number and told him if he needed anything more to call her. I was a little curious, so I asked, "Detective Ulrich, why do you need information on all of my household employees?"

He answered very officially, "It's all routine Ms. Powers, nothing to be alarmed about." Then he added, "I'd like to thank you for your help, and if I might say, it has been a pleasure meeting you." I thanked him and walked him to the door.

Shortly after Detective Ulrich left, I decided to take a ride out to the mansion. I could not believe what I saw when I rounded the bend of the driveway. There was nothing left to that once magnificent building but rubble and ashes. I stepped out of the car and slowly walked up the sidewalk toward what once was my home. When I reached the porch steps, I decided I had to look through the rubble for anything that belonged to Tony and Joy. I slowly and carefully climbed down into the ashes and began to look through the debris. I spent the next three hours rummaging through the burnt ashes and all I could find was a slightly singed bottle of champagne. I picked up the bottle, wiped it off and thought, "Oh my God! That's all that's left...'one bottle of champagne,' nothing left to the life Tony and I made together. **NOTHING AT ALL!"**

All of our personal photo albums, every stitch of clothing I saved of Tony's, along with all of Joy's things were gone. It was as if there was nothing to confirm I ever lived that life with Tony and Joy. Just then a breeze picked up and the ashes started to blow away in the wind. As I watched the wind blow I realized everything I loved was gone and that I was alone in the world. Sure I had Jimmy, but he was not Tony. When I could no longer take the pain of my hopeless search, I climbed out of the ashes and decided somehow I would rebuild my life.

When I got back to the hotel that evening, Jimmy and Bobby had just returned with two boxes of great smelling pizza. They had gone into the office that day and also went to look at the six-bedroom penthouse Judy had found for us as a possible rental. James and Carman went to stay with their daughter. This was only a temporary living situation for them, because I gave them both some needed time off. James and Carman were going to leave my employment because Carman felt responsible for Joy's death. I convinced her there was no one to blame and that I truly felt like they were a part of my family; so, they decided to stay on with me. Boy was I glad, because I really would have missed them as family members first, then as trusted, irreplaceable employees. They were going to move back in with Jimmy, Bobby, and me, as soon as we were reestablished in semi-permanent living quarters. After I washed the champagne bottle, I went into the living room to where Jimmy and Bobby were. When I entered the room, I noticed they already had opened one of the pizza boxes. I walked past them, placed the bottle on the mantel, then I walked over, poured myself a glass of Coca Cola, grabbed a piece of sausage and mushroom pizza and said, "This was a great idea guys, mmm, it's good too!"

Jimmy was downing a piece of pie as I sat beside him and when he swallowed he said, "Christina, the penthouse was great so we went ahead and rented it. It's on the 16th floor of the Elsmere building, which happens to be the most elite building in LA for the city's gay population."

I laughed, "That sounds great guys. Maybe it will be like our old days in Roma, Jimmy."

He laughed, "Not exactly like those days I hope."

Over our pizza Jimmy and Bobby gave me the rundown on the ten motion pictures and twenty albums we had in the works at the studio. Afterward, Jimmy said, "Everything is running smoothly right now Christina, so if you need more time off go ahead and take it."

"No Jimmy, I think it will be better for me, if I just go right back to work. So I'm going to try to get some sleep tonight, and go in with you guys in the morning."

The next day when I went into my office I discovered, 'Halloween in Hell' had grossed a phenomenal two hundred million dollars in its first weekend. It seemed the news of how I somehow knew something was wrong with Joy, and how I ran out of the premier to try to save my daughter's life catapulted 'Halloween In Hell' to be the most financially successful motion picture of all time.

The album which accompanied the film had shot to the number one spot the very next afternoon. The six days since Joy's death, the gross earnings for the film and soundtrack were five hundred ninety six million dollars worldwide. In those six days the stock of Powers Incorporated soared to a whopping fifty-two-dollars a share.

The newspapers, tabloids and television, all told story after story of how people lined up for blocks and waited hours to see the film. Then there were the stories of how people were fainting in the theaters and there were about six deaths by heart attack, blamed on the film. They also told how the Christian community had condemned the film, my performance in it, and how they had organized a protest to ban the film. However, I think it only helped feed the film's fire. It appeared that the whole world was talking about 'Halloween in Hell' and the horrendous death of my daughter, which just happened to take place on the premier night of this extremely horrifying and emotionally charged film.

Around 10:00am I went into one of the empty soundtrack mixing rooms, put on a set of headphones and began to really listen to my soundtrack of 'Halloween in Hell.' As I listened to one song after the other, I began to feel a chill. The titles to the individual cuts were, 'Halloween In Hell', 'Dance Of The Demons', 'Dark Demon Lady', 'Bride Of Satan', 'Demon Temptress', 'Death On Route 666' and the one with the scariest lyrics of all, 'The Fiery Queen Of Hell Has Come.'

As I listened I thought, "How in the world could I have written all of these lyrics? Each song I sang glorified Satan. What if that man in the hospital was right? No, it can't be. All I did was create another money maker." I shrugged my shoulders to accompany my thoughts, "Shit, if Mickey Mouse can scare the hell out of people, so can I. That guy was just an asshole. Now the true question is, how in the world do I top this one?"

When I finished in the mixing room, I went back into my office. I walked over and sat down at my desk where I started to try and come up with my next money maker.

That night I climbed into bed and tried to fall to sleep, but I could not stop my mind from replaying over and over again the things I discovered that day. I thought about the film and the way I performed in it. I thought about the lyrics I sang on each cut on the soundtrack. I thought about how my fans have reacted to the film, versus the way the so-called Christian community had. Then, I thought about what the man in the hospital said to me. I didn't think I was ever going to fall asleep that night, but finally, I drifted off.

All of a sudden I heard a horrible scream! I flew up out of the bed to find myself once again running at night through a burning forest, only this time without a stitch of clothing on. My feet were blistering, as I ran over the hot burning cinders. It seemed like the fire was screaming at me. It was wailing horrifically as the flames reached out for me from the burning tree limbs. As I ran, the fire was trying to grab hold of me by my bare skin with its flaming hot claws. Then, the fire all around me began to take on the forms of hideous burning men. These horrifying burning beasts began to leap off the trees and started to run toward me from all directions. I screamed in horror as they began to encircle me, chanting in a horrible screeching tone, "Christina! Christina!" With every step I took, the sound became louder and more horrifying.

The fire raged into an inferno as they made a complete circle around me. I had about twenty feet left before I'd be consumed by their flames. Then all at once, a bright light began to shine from over my head. I looked up to see Tony and Joy coming toward me and I screamed out, "Tony! Help me!"

He reached out his hand to me and started to yell, "Christina, grab my hand!"

I stretched out my hand to him, but I could not reach him. Then I heard Joy yell, "Mommy, take Daddy's hand."

I jumped up as high as I could, but I still could not reach Tony's hand. Just as these fiery beasts were about to grab me, I screamed out with all my might, "God, please help me!"

With that there was a great thunder and the fire was gone. The light began to grow so strong that I covered my eyes with the palms of my hands, but I could still see it. I heard the rumble of a voice so strong that I fell to my knees in fear. The voice shouted, "Christina, you have blasphemed my name and sinned against me! Yet you dare plead to me for your life!" As the voice of God spoke to me I became so terrified I dug my finger nails right into my legs, causing them to bleed profusely. The voice echoed through my body, "Christina, the punishment for your sins have been decided. You shall never be allowed to see Tony, or Joy again for all of eternity and you are to be banished into the fiery flames of hell until the time I remember you!"

Then the light began to fade and I could once again see the flames of the fiery beasts approaching me. I screamed out from the depths of my soul, "God no!" With that I felt the fiery hands grab me and I began to fight wildly as I screamed, "No! No!" Then I heard more yelling,

"Christina, wake up! You're having a nightmare! Wake up!"

My eyes flew open and I saw Jimmy and Bobby trying to wake me up. I screamed out, "Oh God, Jimmy. It was horrible!"

I, along with the entire bed was soaked from sweat. I grabbed hold of Jimmy and just held him as I sobbed. After about ten minutes, I was finally able to calm myself and tell Jimmy and Bobby all about the dream.

Jimmy kissed me, "It was a horrible dream, that's for sure. But it was only a dream Christina, so why don't you try to put it out of your mind and go take a shower while Bobby and I change the bed." When I emerged from the shower my bed was ready and I finally fell back to sleep around 3:00am that morning.

I woke up at 6:00am to the annoying sound of my alarm clock. I turned the alarm off, stretched and climbed out of bed. After I dressed, I walked over to the nightstand drawer, opened it and took out the card that was placed in my hand by the stranger at the hospital. It read, "**Evangelist Reverend Timmy Swinebert, Spiritual Leader of the Swinebert Full Gospel Church and President of Swinebert University of God, in Greater Dallas, Texas.**" Included on the card were two phone numbers, a business number and a hand written personal number.

At 6:45am I placed a call to Mr. Swinebert at his personal number and he agreed to set an appointment to meet with me at 1:00pm that afternoon, in Dallas. I thanked him and hung up the phone. I placed his card in my purse and headed out for breakfast. Over breakfast I told Jimmy and Bobby I decided not to go into the office with them. After Jimmy and Bobby left for work, I headed for Dallas. I did not tell them where I was going, because I knew Jimmy would have something to say about it, and **I didn't want to hear it.**

CHAPTER 11. MY REBIRTH

I caught the 9:00am flight on October 15th, at LA International, and I was on my way to Texas. The day was bright, warm, and beautiful when I got off the plane in Dallas. I headed straight for my waiting limo and it was off to my meeting.

The time was 12:40pm when I arrived at Mr. Swinebert's University. I was becoming fairly impressed as we drove past a dozen or so buildings on the campus. It appeared as if Mr. Swinebert's ministry was doing quite well. When we reached the three story administration building, I climbed out and headed for my meeting.

As soon as I opened the office door I was immediately and graciously received by Mr. Swinebert's secretary. She rose from her desk and came to greet me with a bright smile and outstretched arms. I was taken aback a little as she hugged me and said, "God bless you, Sister Christina! It's so nice to meet you."

I stepped back and replied, quite officially, "It's Ms. Powers, and I'm here to see Mr. Swinebert. I have a 1:00pm appointment with him."

She laughed like a little scatterbrain, "Silly, I already know that, Sister Christina, I've been expecting you. Come with me and I'll take you in to see Brother Swinebert."

When we reached the massive, solid oak double doors of Mr. Swinebert's office, my jovial guide tapped twice on the door. Then, she opened it just enough to poke her head through and said with a slight giggle, "Brother Swinebert, Sister Christina is here."

I heard him reply with an excited tone, "Show her in, Sister Nancy." As Sister Nancy opened the door I could see Mr. Swinebert coming toward me. He was well dressed in a black three piece suit. He was about six feet tall, two hundred and ten pounds and fairly muscular. I'd say he was forty five years old and he had the beginnings of gray mixed in with his well-trimmed, soft, brown hair. His captivating, sparkling brown eyes helped to enhance his distinguished look, which I found to be slightly appealing. As he reached me, he took my hands in his, smiled and with a southern twang to his manly voice, "Miss Powers I'm so glad you've come."

I pulled my hands away, and replied very politely, but formally, "Mr. Swinebert thank you for seeing me on such short notice, and please call me Ms. Powers, not miss."

Still smiling, "Of-course, please come on in Ms. Powers."

He led me into his large office which I noticed immediately had eight stuffed and mounted trophies of wild animals, two on each of the four walls around his office. Scattered between these were numerous photos of Mr. Swinebert, with hundreds of other people. We walked the thirty foot span toward a group of bearskin style covered office chairs. A petite woman in her thirties with curly shoulder length, dyed blonde hair and brown eyes, wearing a Donna Reid style Polka dot dress, stood up from one of the chairs, hugged me and sweetly said, "Hi, Sister Christina, I'm Sister Tammy Swinebert, Timmy's wife! It's so nice to meet you."

I smiled cordially, "Hello, It's nice to meet you as well."

She gasped, put her little hands to her mouth, "Oh my! Sister Christina, proper 'Christians' never greet someone in that manner. Saying hello to someone is like telling them to go to hell, you know, hell is low?"

I looked at her strangely, "What are you talking about?"

Mr. Swinebert quickly interrupted, "Sweety, Ms. Powers, is not a Christian yet."

Her face immediately took on a very sad expression, "I'm sorry, I thought you became a Christian the night of your daughter's death."

Feeling quite offended and without my smile, "Mrs. Swinebert, I am a Christian. I was baptized a Catholic as an infant."

She clutched her hands to her chest and gasped, "Gee, I'm messing everything up here. I'm so sorry."

I smiled, "Thank you for the apology. I think the problem is we are both on two different channels." Then I laughed, as she looked at me with a blank stare and I thought, "She didn't get it, oh boy!"

Mr. Swinebert hugged his wife, "Tammy, sweetie, I'm sure Ms. Powers is a very busy woman. So why don't you say goodbye now and leave us be."

This time she only shook my hand, as she said, "Well, I hope we meet again, Ms. Powers."

When she finished shaking my hand I answered very sweetly, "It's nice to have met you, Mrs. Swinebert."

As she left the room Mr. Swinebert said, "Please take a seat, Ms. Powers."

"Thank you," and I sat down in one of the furry chairs. Mr. Swinebert took the seat next to mine, "Please Ms. Powers call me Tim."

"Of course I'll call you Tim, and please call me Christina."

After taking a sip from his glass he inquired, "Now tell me Christina, how I can serve you today?"

Looking seriously at him, "Tim, you told me Jesus was trying to speak to me. I've come all this way today, because I would like to know what you mean by that."

He took my hand in one of his, squeezed it, then he put his other hand in the air, closed his eyes and quite loudly, "I praise you Jesus! God of all power and might; for you have called another child out of the fires of hell and into your salvation."

Astonished at what he was saying, I pulled my hand out of his, "Would you please stop this, you people are freaking me out here. I came to ask a question, not to be mauled and insulted."

I got up to leave and Tim begged me, "Please Christina, forgive my outburst. It's just that when I see the Power of God's Hand at work in another child's life, I become filled with the Holy Spirit and I must proclaim the glory of Christ. So please stay and allow me to answer your question."

I sat back down, "I guess I can understand that."

"Christina, Jesus is telling you He loves you. He wants you to look at your life and judge it for yourself. Then give your life to him and let him help you change your evil earthly ways."

Feeling offended again, "Are you saying God would take my daughter's life, to make me change my ways?"

He grabbed his Bible, opened it, "Do you believe in the Bible?"

"I'm not sure; I have never really read it."

He looked at me with concern, "Please allow me to read some scripture to you I feel God wants you to hear. In James, 2:11, God has said, **'Do not commit adultery and do not kill. Now if you commit adultery and kill, haven't you become a transgressor of the law? Then by denying your transgressions, you blaspheme my name. Now you shall have judgment without mercy, for you have shown no mercy. And mercy rejoiceth against judgment**.' He closed the Bible with force, "Do you understand what Jesus is saying?"

He looked as if he were looking right through me, "Yes, I think I do know what He is saying, but what does God want from me?"

He smiled, "In Acts 8:22 God says, **'Repent therefore of this thy wickedness and pray God, if perhaps the thought of thine heart may be forgiven.'** Turn your life over to Jesus so you may have all eternity with your loved ones in the presence of the Lord. If not, then you choose Satan, and eternity in the flames of hell."

As he said these things I thought of the dream and I knew I wanted to be with Tony and Joy. I also knew I didn't want to be burning in hell for one second, no-less an eternity. I took a deep breath, "So what does it mean to give your life over to Jesus?"

With authority, "It means you become born again. Jesus said in John 3:3, **'Except a man be born again, he cannot see the kingdom of God.'** He also said, **'Except a man be born of water and spirit, he cannot see the kingdom of God.'**

Curiosity made me ask, "I have heard the term born again, but what does that mean?"

His eyes lit up, "You must first repent for your sins then be baptized in the name of Jesus Christ and change your life. God wants to use you, Christina, to reach the world with his message of salvation."

I looked at him as if he were nuts, "Whoa! You said a mouthful and I don't know if I can swallow it all, especially since I don't even know what you're talking about."

"Christina, have you ever seen my television crusades?"

"No Tim, I can't quite say that I have."

This time he looked at me like I was nuts, "You haven't? Well I just happen, 'Praise God' to be holding a crusade tonight in Houston. Why don't you come and see what I'm talking about for yourself?"

I shrugged my shoulders, "Why not! All right I will take you up on your offer."

He grinned from ear to ear, "Good, because we have to leave right now if I'm going to be ready for tonight."

"May I first use your phone? I need to call my office."

"Of course, why don't you use the phone in the back room for privacy?" He pointed to a door on the other side of the room. I got up, walked over to the door, opened it and headed for the phone to dial the number, "Hi Jimmy, I just want to let you know I don't think I'll be home tonight. I'm also checking up on you. How are things?"

With concern he said, "Where are you?"

I answered evasively, "I'm in Dallas checking something out, and I'm not sure what it is yet. Right now it's just a feeling."

With a nervous tone, "Just a feeling! Well, whatever it is, please don't throw every dime we have into it like the last time you had a feeling."

I laughed, "It's nothing like that."

With a sigh of relief, "Thank God! So how can I reach you?"

"You can't right now, I'll have to call you back."

"Okay. Well just in case I don't see you tomorrow, I'll leave your penthouse key with the building security officer. We are moving in tonight you know, now, with no help from you, thank you very much."

I chuckled, "I'll give you a kiss when I come home darling. Will that do?"

We laughed a little like old times, "It will do for now. Do you know where the Elsmere building is?"

"Yes and I'll see you there. So don't worry about me, I'm doing fine."

"I love you girlfriend, so you keep in touch."

I replied in kind, "Same here." I hung up the phone and headed for Houston, Texas with Tim Swinebert.

As we flew on Tim's private jet to Houston, Tim talked more about the Bible and his personal relationship with Jesus Christ. He read scriptures which told what it meant to be a born again child of God. He articulated his message with such warmth and gentleness, I truly felt touched.

When we arrived at the Houston Coliseum, I witnessed a transformation take place with Tim, from this soft spoken teddy bear, to suddenly becoming more like myself, a strong demanding perfectionist. He took charge of the entire set up, which happened to be quite impressive.

The minute we entered the work area, he started giving orders. There was a thirty piece orchestra to back up a sixty member choir, stage lighting, sound, and television crew setups. Everything had to be perfect for that evening's crusade. I could see by the way Tim was handling things, he knew exactly what he wanted for every minute of his sermon.

As the evening approached, the coliseum was becoming a-buzz with life. There were Christian radio and newspaper reporters all interviewing Tim. Then when one of the reporters realized who I was, this nice, peaceful, well-mannered interview, suddenly turned into the frantic ones I'm used to. With the blink of an eye, they all charged towards me and started shouting questions at me simultaneously. But Tim swiftly managed to reestablish control over the interview.

Afterwards, we met with dozens of local church leaders. I just quietly followed Tim as he introduced me to them all. When we reached one of the gentlemen there, Tim introduced him to me as his father, The Reverend Timmy Swinebert Senior. I discovered this sixty-year-old, tall, heavy set man, was the founding father of Tim Junior's Christian empire. He was a very pleasant man upon our meeting, but there was something about him which put me on my guard. After we finished speaking, Tim Senior called us all into a twenty minute prayer, which I thought would never end, asking for the service to be blessed. Finally it was time for Tim Junior to take center stage.

Tim opened his sermon with a prayer, followed by thirty minutes of everyone in the Coliseum singing of their love with praises to Jesus Christ. I didn't know what to make of these thousands of people all around me, all doing something different. Some were singing and dancing, while others were jumping up and down crying and screaming.

Finally, Tim calmed them down and began his sermon. He started by talking about how our sins affect everything in our lives. He said, "In order to see the power of sin in our lives, all we have to do is look at the first sin, which was the sin of Adam and Eve. Because of that first sin, now all mankind must suffer the penalty of that sin which is death. This is why we all must die. So, when you sin and think it does not matter, think again; because it influences everything that takes place in your life." He went on to say, that Jesus died on the cross, paid the penalty for that first sin, for all of us. He said, "This was done because Jesus was a perfect sacrifice. So, when Jesus died he gave us all the opportunity to come to him and be born again. When you die, you are assured eternal life in the presence of Christ and with all your loved ones."

Then he jumped around the stage praising God and working the crowd up into a frenzy of crying and praising God. After that he said, "You must all come to the altar, for now is the time to accept Christ as your Savior. Then, He will forgive your sins and accept you as his child. This is how Christ will open the doors to Heaven for you." Suddenly music started playing and Tim began to cry with real tears as he begged people to come to the altar. He shouted, "Give your lives to Christ now, before it's too late!"

I found Tim's performance to be quite hypnotic. So much so, I almost walked to the altar myself. Suddenly Tammy Swinebert came over to me with a big smile, grabbed my hand and shouted over the crowd of wailing people, "Come Christina, Jesus is calling you! Please let me walk up with you."

A little leery of her aggressiveness, "Thank you Tammy, but I'm not ready to take such a long walk."

Her eyes grew wide as she lowered her voice, "If not for yourself, then give your life to Jesus for your daughter's sake."

At that point I had had enough, and I shouted at her, "Please, Tammy, I don't like someone trying to convince me to do something I already said no to once." I pulled my hand from hers, "I need some fresh air I feel like I'm being suffocated in here. I'll meet you out by the limo." With that I turned and walked away from her as fast as I could and thought, "This one could get on my nerves fast!" After that I waited for Tim and **Tammy** to come out.

It was 11:00pm when Tim finally walked toward the limo driver and me as we were chatting about Jesus. When he reached us he said, "Christina, I must stay here tonight at the Hilton. Shall I reserve a room for you?"

"No, thank you!" I answered quickly. "I must catch the first flight back to L.A. so if you would provide me with a ride to the airport, I would be very grateful."

He sighed sadly, "I wish you could stay, but I understand." He looked at the chauffeur and added, "Billy-Joe, take us to the airport please."

"Where's Tammy, Tim?"

"She is going to the hotel, and I'm taking you to the airport. I'll have my jet take you back to LA right away."

"Thank you, that is very generous."

As the limo pulled away Tim said, "Please tell me Christina, did you feel the power of God this evening?"

I looked into his big brown eyes, "I felt something this evening Tim, but I can't say it was God. What I can say is, I will start to read my Bible because of it."

He grabbed my hand, moved close to me and said, as I thought I was going to be kissed, "Praise God! Christina, God has just told me to be your spiritual teacher."

With that we pulled into the airport, where the private jets are kept and I replied, "Thank you Tim, please let me think about your offer. I'll call you in a few days."

When we climbed out of the limo, Tim took me in his arms and hugged me very nicely, "God speed to you Christina, and I will be waiting for your call."

Graciously, I thanked him, and it was off to LA on Tim's private jet. As the plane took off I thought, "You know, he was not that bad and a lot of what he said made sense." I also felt a sense of peace from within my heart as he talked. I could have listened to him for hours.

It was 3:15am when I opened the door to our new home in the Elsmere building. The lights in the foyer were on, so I closed the door behind me and walked right into the living room. When I flicked on the light, I could hear some noises from the back room. As I headed toward the dark hall I looked for a switch to turn on the light, but I could not find one. The noise became louder. It sounded like someone screaming while being choked. Instantly I became alarmed and thought, "What the hell is going on?"

I saw a light coming from under the doorway and I jumped in the air when I heard another really loud scream, making me run toward the sound. As soon as I reached the door, it flew open and I screamed, "Ahhh!" as this green faced monster screamed, "Ahhh!" at the same time it reached out for me. I kicked it right where it hurts, knocking it back into the light of the room and I heard a loud squeal. I ran into the room ready to do battle, only to find Jimmy bouncing around on the floor holding his balls, with a green facial mud mask on screaming, "Oh fuck! Oh shit! Oh fuck that hurts!"

I wanted to laugh but Jimmy was hurting so much, "Oh my God! Jimmy, are you all right?" I reached down to help him, "I didn't know it was you, all I heard was screaming and choking and I thought someone was being killed."

When I heard the choking again, I turned to see Bobby coughing so hard, his face was turning red. I helped Jimmy up, then I walked over to Bobby, "Bobby, let me look at you."

He replied with a rough voice, "Hi, Christina, I'm not feeling too good."

Bobby started to cough again as Jimmy said, "I was just going to get him a drink and some more cough medicine, when you attacked me."

As we talked I felt his forehead and exclaimed, "Shit Bobby, you're burning up." I turned to Jimmy, "What's his temperature?"

"I don't know, I didn't take it yet."

I gave him my 'Duh' look, "I'll look for a thermometer while you get him the medicine."

I went into the main bathroom, opened the medicine closet and as I suspected, there was a first-aid kit there. I knew Judy would think of everything, so I took the kit back to the bedroom where Jimmy was giving Bobby his medicine. I opened the first-aid kit, took out the thermometer, and shook it down, "Open your mouth Bobby, and place this under your tongue."

As we waited, Bobby was struggling not to cough as he held the thermometer in his mouth. When I pulled it out, it read, **"104.6 degrees**."

Thinking, "Shit, that's high!" I said, "Maybe we should call the doctor."

As soon as I said that, Bobby began to cough again. This time he was coughing up blood. I grabbed a handful of tissues and helped Bobby catch the blood and said, "Jimmy, come here with Bobby, I'm calling an ambulance."

Jimmy ran over to me and took the bloody tissues from my hand. I turned and went to call for help.

I washed the blood off my hands and waited for the ambulance. When the medics came to the door, there were two of them. One tall and skinny, the other short and fat. I greeted them, then led them to the bedroom where Bobby and Jimmy were. As we walked, I told them his temperature and that he started to cough up blood. When they entered the room behind me and saw Jimmy holding Bobby up, so that he didn't choke on his own blood, their faces went white. They stopped walking and the tall thin one asked, "Miss I know this is a gay building, but is he gay?"

I replied with annoyance, "What are you talking about? 'Is he gay?' He's sick."

With a tone of fear, the short fat one, "I'm sorry, but you're going to have to take him to the hospital yourself."

In shock I replied, "You guys must be joking, my friend is sick, now do your job and help him."

Again the fat one spoke out, "Look lady, your friend probably has that new 'gay plague', that's killing gay men all over the country. And I'm not going near him."

They started to walk out, "Listen guys, I'm *Christina Powers* and I don't know anything about a plague. But I promise you both, if you don't help my friend, I will have your heads in the morning."

They looked at each other, turned around, walked back into the bedroom and helped Bobby. Then they took us to the hospital without saying another word.

When we arrived at the hospital, Bobby was asked if he was homosexual. When he said, "Yes", to my horror we began getting more of the same treatment from the hospital staff. Even so, I thank God it was not on such a dramatic scale as our two paramedic friends. Just the same, there was fear in most of the faces of the staff members we came in contact with that morning. When the ER doctor finally came in, he hardly touched Bobby at all as he tried to examine him. I could see he was not doing anything for Bobby, and Jimmy was beginning to get upset, so I quickly spoke up before Jimmy lost it and asked this doctor to call Doctor Heddermen for me. He stopped what he was doing, "Is he your family doctor?"

"Yes he is," I answered. "And I would like to see him as soon as possible."

With a tone of relief, "Great, I'll go call him right now." With that he quickly left the room.

It took him fifteen minutes to come back to our room and when he did, he only stuck his head in the door, "Doctor Heddermen will be in soon." Then he closed the door and left without saying another word.

As we waited in our little room for Doctor Heddermen to come, I could not believe the treatment we were getting. I finally turned to Jimmy, "Jimmy, did you hear anything about a new gay plague?"

He looked at me with a worried expression, "Just last week. I read something about it in the 'Gay and Lesbian Herald.' It said there were an alarming number of gay men who were coming down with some rare disease and dying. The paper also said it was a 'conspiracy' which was being covered up by the government to wipe out the gay population. So, when I read that part of the story, I didn't think it was real."

I lowered my voice, "Well, Bobby is finally sleeping so let's wait and see what Doctor Hedderman says before we get crazy."

When Doctor Heddermen arrived, he examined Bobby then said, "Bobby, you have pneumonia and from what I can see, your coughing is what caused the bleeding. You ruptured a blood vessel in the back of your throat."

Jimmy asked, "Doctor Heddermen, does Bobby's pneumonia have anything to do with this new disease, everyone is calling the 'gay plague'?"

Doctor Heddermen laughed, "No Jimmy, and there is no new disease killing gay men either."

I spoke up, "Then someone better tell your co-workers."

With that I told him everything that happened and he said, "From what I know, there has been some unexplained illness and deaths popping up around the country. But it's not an epidemic. The reason the staff is so jumpy is because we have had two cases in the last week."

I shook my head with concern, "Well, I think you should have a meeting with your people then, and tell them there is no epidemic. Even if there was, they need to treat their patients a lot better than they treated us."

"I think I'll do just that." Then he turned back to Bobby, "Now Bobby, I'm going to keep you here for a couple of days. I'll send a nurse in with something to help stop the cough. I'm also going to order an IV. I want you on an antibiotic drip for a few days and we'll see how you respond to that."

Bobby nodded trustingly, "Whatever you say doc."

Doctor Heddermen turned to Jimmy and me, "It's going to take about an hour before Bobby gets a room; so, why don't the two of you go home and get some sleep."

"Jimmy, he's right. Why don't we go home?"

Jimmy looked at me through faithful loving eyes, "You go ahead Christina, I'll stay here with Bobby."

"Okay, why don't you take the day off? I'll go into the office today." Then I kissed them both, and headed back to the apartment.

Bobby stayed in the hospital on I V antibiotic therapy for two weeks before he was able to come home. When he did, I gave him and Jimmy the next two weeks off from work.

As for me, well, I went back to work. Over the next few weeks, I checked up on every project we had in the works, and reviewed all of our future plans. I read fourteen scripts for movies, and the lyrics for sixty-two albums. I ended up rejecting most of them. However, I did put my stamp of approval on six films and twenty-six albums. I put a stop to the ones I rejected, and had the writers start from scratch with new ideas. I also found the time to double check all the books. I wanted to make sure my hand picked staff in the accounting offices were doing their jobs. Thanks to a huge shot in the financial arm by 'Halloween in Hell', the net cash worth of Powers Incorporated had soared to a whopping two-billion-dollars and still climbing.

On December 1st, after my verification of this great financial news, I had my New York and LA attorney offices prepare to send their best representatives to my office to meet with myself and my top management. The meeting was set for December 7th, at 10:00am. This would also be the first day Jimmy and Bobby would be returning to work. I wanted to be on top of every aspect of my business before I left. You see, I had made arrangements to go away for the first two months after Jimmy and Bobby returned to work.

Between doing all this, I still made time for studying the Bible. I needed to know for myself what God was saying to mankind through the Bible. If I thought of Tony, Joy and the dream once a day; then, I thought about them a thousand times a day.

On December 3, at 9:00am, I received a call from detective Fred Ulrich. He asked if I could meet with him sometime that day.

I looked at my schedule and set up an appointment with him for that afternoon at 5:00pm, here at my office.

It was 2:00pm when Judy paged me and told me Barbara Goldstein was on the line for me. I had her patch the call into Studio 9 where I was working, then I picked up the phone and said, "Hi hot stuff, how are you?"

She replied with a sincere tone, "I'm fine, but how are you doing?"

I chuckled a little, "I'm getting through it Barbara, it's not easy, but I'm doing it."

"That's good news and I'm glad to hear it because Christina, this is not just a social call. I wanted to ask if you had seen Detective Ulrich recently."

I replied with curiosity, "No, but I received a call from him this morning. He said he needed to speak with me, so, I set up an appointment with him for this afternoon at 5:00pm. Now tell me why you're asking?"

"Good," Her voice intensified, "I'm glad I got to you first."

"So what's up?" I asked with concern.

"I think we need to talk before you meet with him, but not on the phone," she said mysteriously.

"Well you've roused my curiosity. So where and when do we meet before 5:00pm?"

"Can you meet me out in front of your office in ten minutes?"

"I don't think I have a choice here, so I'll be right out."

As soon as I walked out of the front door, Barbara pulled up in a limo, opened the back door from the inside, and said, "Climb in." So I did, and off we went down Hollywood Boulevard. I looked at Barbara, who had a very concerned expression on her face and I said, "The intrigue has got me Barbara, and that look on your face is starting to spook me. So start talking."

She took my hand in hers, "Okay, there are two things Christina, but you never heard them from me, you got it?"

"I got it baby, this conversation isn't happening."

"All right then, first, I just heard from a good friend, who happens to be an inside source. This person has informed me you have some kind of insurance policy which allows you certain freedoms Frank would like to take from you."

With wide eyes, "I guess you do have an inside contact."

"It seems that Frank is trying to work around that policy and it has something to do with the laws which govern the stock market. Frank is pumping millions of dollars into trying to influence certain congressman to help pass a new set of laws to govern the stock exchange. My sources say once these laws are enacted, Frank intends to instantly maneuver a corporate takeover of Powers Incorporated, just so he can throw you out of the entertainment industry once again. He wants to make an example of you for anyone who dares to challenge him."

Alarmed, "But how? Powers Incorporated is not listed on the public stock exchange. I have never sold any of the stock."

"I don't know much about it myself Christina, but I do know if Frank wants you, he is going to try anything to get you."

"Holy shit," I exclaimed! "I thought I was covering all the angles and the bastard can still out-fox me."

"Christina, there's more." Her look of concern intensified, "Now promise me you will hold on to your rage, because you're not going to like this one."

She stopped talking for a moment and I said, "I'm already freaking out now Barbara, so you might as well get it over with!"

"You have to promise me you'll stay calm!" She begged, "Or I'm not talking."

"I promise I will not lose it." I reassured her.

She proceeded cautiously, "Christina, listen to me very closely and please heed what I am about to say, before you do anything." Shaking her head, "Okay kiddo, here it comes." She slapped her hand down on her knee with frustration, "Shit Christina, this is going to hurt you, and I don't know how to tell you so it doesn't."

She started to cry, so I squeezed her hand, "Stop it now Barbara and just tell me for God sakes. I'll handle it, whatever it is!"

She took a deep breath, "Detective Ulrich is going to inform you of the fact that the fire was the work of a well-planned arson. The way the fires were started they were assured to incinerate both of our properties." I 'gasped' as Barbara continued, "I have already spoken to Detective Ulrich and he asked me about the disagreement we had with Frank at the theater the night of the fire." At that I grabbed the edge of the leather seat and began to squeeze it with all my might.

Barbara let go of my other hand, reached out and put her arm on my shoulder, "Then he asked if I knew how come you went running out of the party like you did. Now there is more. I heard Frank put the word out to torch our homes as soon as he walked out of the theater that night. But there is no way to prove it."

Horrified, "Are you telling me Frank had the fire set that killed my daughter and there's nothing I can do about it?" I shook my head, "I'll tell the detective what I suspect. There must be something he can do."

Desperately she pleaded, "Christina, listen to me. I believe in my heart what I was told is true, but I also know no one can prove it. That's why I am telling you this now, before the detective does. I want you to think about the best way to get Frank without trying to kill him yourself. Because Christina, I know you and I know you could lose it and actually kill Frank. I just don't want to see you in prison. So before you act baby, please think about it first."

"So what am I supposed to do, nothing?" I asked in desperation.

"Right now Christina, I don't know what you can do, I only know what you should not do. Christina, you're a bright woman and I love you, so just don't throw it all away. Now, I'm going to slip away as fast as I came."

That's when the limo stopped and we hugged. I kissed her cheek and said, "I love you Barbara, and thank you. I'll never forget the things you have done for me."

She smiled with love in her eyes, "When you need me, just call."

I climbed out of the limo and she drove away. I took a deep breath and headed back to my office. As I walked through the halls, I thought about everything Barbara had said, then I thought, "If no one can prove Frank gave the order for the fire, what can I do?" As I entered my office I didn't know how to react to Barbara's news. All I felt was weak, confused and overwhelmed. Not just by what Barbara told me, but by everything that had happened to me. I sat down at my desk and thought, "Oh well! I'll figure it out tomorrow!" With that in mind, I opened my safe and took out the bottle of cocaine I had stashed in it and for the first time since I went home to Joy, I took two lines of cocaine and I instantly felt a sense of relief.

Once I was feeling a little more relaxed, I remembered the feelings of safety and peace I felt when I was with Tim Swinebert that night in Houston as we talked about God. So I picked up the phone and called him.

When Detective Fred Ulrich did show up, I answered his questions to the best of my ability. After my questioning I invited Fred to join me for dinner, which he graciously accepted. After dinner, I asked him to drive me home, so he did, at which time I invited him in for a night cap. As we sipped our champagne out on my balcony, I decided it was my turn to question him. So with a tone of sincerity I said, "Fred, I need to talk to you. I need to ask you for your help."

With a slight look of disappointment he replied, "What is it, Christina?"

I looked deeply into his eyes, "Fred, I think Frank Salerno may have caused the fire that killed my daughter. The only problem is I don't know how to prove it."

His look turned suspicious, "So what is it you're asking, Christina? I'm not sure what you mean."

I replied innocently, "I want to know if you have any clues as to who started the fire?"

"I have a few leads."

"Can you please tell me if any of them include Frank Salerno as a suspect?"

He looked at me guardedly, "Yes, I have thought of that myself. I have researched both of your pasts and I think you may be right."

"Oh boy! I'm glad to hear that. All I'm asking Fred is that you please find out the truth for me, and if it was Frank then please see that justice is served."

He leaned over gently kissed my check, "Christina, I promise you I will solve this case."

"Thank-you Fred," I answered sincerely. After that we continued to spend the rest of the evening together just chatting on the balcony. Fred actually turned out to be a nice guy and I felt I could really trust him.

On December 7th, 1979, at 10:00am in the main conference room, I called attention to our meeting by saying, "The first thing I wanted to say is congratulations and thank you. This year Powers Incorporated has seen such a phenomenal increase in our financial success that it means we have graduated to a full-fledged player in the Hollywood game." I received a round of applause after which I said, "Although we are doing quite well it doesn't insure we will be here tomorrow, especially if we can't surpass 'the competition.' That's why I would like to vote on and hopefully pass a few amendments. First, I make a motion to pass a 20% pay increase across the board to all our employees, at a cost of ten-million-dollars a year. Second, even though we will eventually base our corporate headquarters in New York, I move we purchase this building outright to keep for our California headquarters, at a cost of thirty-million-dollars, a one shot deal. Third, I move we purchase two corporate jets. One for my personal use as President of Powers Incorporated the other to be used by the Top Brass, meaning all of you, at a onetime cost of forty-million-dollars, per purchase. Then with an estimated two-million-dollar annual operations cost; the total cost for my proposed expenditures for the year is one-hundred and twenty-two-million-dollars; leaving cash on hand of seventy-eight-million-dollars. The best part is this will only increase our annual expenditure by twelve-million-dollars a year, and 'gang' I think we need these things for the company's future growth."

Upon completion of my report we took a vote and my proposals passed unanimously. As I passed out copies of our financial report for the year I added, "This year belongs to us all. Most of you here came on board with Jimmy and I back in the beginning, that's why Powers Incorporated belongs to us all, not just Jimmy and me. Yes it's true that I hold 70% and Jimmy holds

20% of all the stock, leaving 10% held by the rest of you. But, I want you all to know you still have a voice and we want to keep hearing from you because Powers Incorporated belongs to everyone in this room, and we all hold the only stock to our dream. Now, I must tell you we are facing a big challenge to the survival of Powers Incorporated. I can't tell you exactly what it is right now, but I would like to inform you of what I intend to do to meet that challenge." I took a deep breath, big gulp of water, looked at Judy who was taking notes, "Ready, Judy?"

"Go for it, boss."

I smiled confidently, "We need to learn everything there is to know about the stock market. So, I move we hire the best 'broker' on Wall Street, to keep us on top of the game. I want a few insiders in Washington because we need to know what bills might be in the works to change the laws concerning the market. I also want to know who might be sponsoring these bills, and who or what committee is writing them. I want a personal Press Secretary for all of our headliners. I want as much control of the news going out of this place as possible." I stood up and added, "Listen closely 'gang', I don't want any of our business dealings slipping out of this room by anyone." I then handed out different assignments to each of them in groups of three, because I had decided earlier who I wanted doing what. When I regained their attention I added, "I really need to make sure you all follow these instructions to the letter. I know everything I have on some of your lists may not make sense now, but it will in the future. Now that we are done, I am leaving Jimmy and Bobby at the helm. I will be out of the office for a few weeks doing some research. If you need me, Jimmy will be able to get in touch with me. Thank you again ladies and gentlemen and hopefully you'll have completed your assignments, which I expect to find done and ready for me when I return two weeks from now." I said my goodbyes to them all, grabbed my re-stocked stash of cocaine, and it was off to Texas.

I had decided to accept Tim's offer to tutor me on the scriptures, so I rented a suite at the Dallas Hilton and began my personal Bible lessons with the 'master' himself, the great Reverend Timmy Swinebert.

For the next two weeks, I spent almost fourteen hours a day with Tim. Tim put his whole agenda and family on hold for me during those two weeks and he taught me as much about Jesus Christ and the Bible, as one person could possibly comprehend in a two-week span. Tim not only made learning the Bible easy, he also made it fun. We studied in the car as we drove all over the state of Texas during my entire stay. We studied from the beaches to the mountain tops. We studied the Bible on horse- back, on bicycles and on a five mile hiking trip. To the ultimate Bible study of them all, a thousand feet up in a hot air balloon! For the first time since Joy's death, I was alive and I didn't feel the pain. I felt free and I began to feel a oneness with Jesus Christ as I learned of his will.

Before we knew it, our last day had come, and we were on our last outing together. We were having a lovely picnic basket lunch on South Padre Island Beach, on the southern tip of Texas. The day was sunny and warm and the sky was a bright turquoise blue, with beautiful, big, white, fluffy, clouds which were scattered about like giant marshmallows suspended in the air. It was my kind of day. We had our swim suits on and we were sitting on a big beach blanket. As we ate our lunch, the warm breeze blowing over my body, along with the sounds of the water crashing on the beach, and the four lines of cocaine I did in the restroom, all had an erotic effect on me. As I watched and listened to Tim talk, I started to notice in a swimsuit the preacher looked pretty good. I caught my thoughts, "Christina, stop it! This man is a man of God! How could you start to look at him in that way?" Then I thought, "God, forgive me! Here I am trying to learn about your word Lord, on how to stop sinning and what am I doing? I start thinking of seducing the man who is teaching me. What am I? Am I an evil person? God, I hope not! Please help me stop thinking like this, God. I don't want to have these thoughts." I took a deep breath as I thought, "Okay, stop it right now Christina, and pay attention to what Tim is saying." So that's what I did.

When I came back down to earth, Tim was saying, "Christina, Jesus loves everyone, even the worst of sinners. The reason why He died on the cross for us was because he knew we were all sinners. But, once we come to know Jesus and are born again He takes the power of sin from us. This is why we know we are saved and will go to heaven with our loved ones."

Curiously I said, "Tim, when you speak to me of God's will for my life, I can truly feel the love Jesus has for me. It makes me love Jesus more every day for what he did for us all, by dying on the cross."

Tim grabbed my hand and moved closer to me with a look of romance in his eyes. I looked deep into his eyes and I felt my willpower instantly fading, so I found myself sliding over to meet him anticipating a warm kiss, but none came, "Christina, God is calling you! Can't you hear him? He's calling you to act now and be born again. Jesus wants you to lead the world to his saving grace and to turn the people from the sins of the world; the sins which you have helped to create by your once immoral lifestyle. Now, you can make up for your sins by saving others with the 'Word of God' and bring them to Jesus Christ." All of a sudden he hugged me, "Christina, you have that power because of who you are. God can use you to reach millions of lost souls. Please, Christina, realize the truth and become born again; then, come with me and leave your world of sin behind. Just think you and me, teaching the 'Word of God'. We can tour the world together and bring the lost sheep back to Jesus." He released our embrace and looked deeply into my eyes, "Christina, I'm serious. Don't go back to Hollywood, come with me. I am beginning a six-month, nationwide crusade next month. Come with me and tell the world what Jesus Christ has done for you. How his love and power has changed your life for the better. You can be an example of the mercy of God for the entire world to see." At that he kissed me and with enthusiasm added, "If you do this, then I will call you Sister Christina, and you can call me Brother Tim."

I hugged him joyfully, "Tim, I do want to be baptized. Right now as a matter of fact, in the ocean."

He threw his hands in the air and exclaimed, "Praise the Lord!" Afterward he kissed me again, took hold of my arm, "I will baptize you, but not here. It must be special." Then he grabbed my hand and pulled me up off the blanket, "Let's get going. We can be back in Dallas by 5:00pm if we leave now. We will hold a special baptismal ceremony this very evening. We don't want to keep Jesus waiting any longer." So off we went back to Dallas and my baptismal ceremony.

On December 21st, at 8:00pm at the Timmy Swinebert, Full Gospel Church of Christ, in Dallas, Texas, I prepared to be baptized by Timmy Swinebert himself. Tim had his whole congregation show up to encourage me as I took my baptismal plunge. 'Oh, by the way, a photo showed up on the front page of every newspaper in the 'Country' the very next day.' Still, it was wonderfully spiritual and I was giving my life to Jesus Christ, and that's what really mattered.

Tim led me to a pool which was set up on the stage and said the words that would change my life forever! "Christina, I baptize you in the name of Jesus Christ. Receive the power of the Holy Spirit." He then submerged me into the water and I came out of the water to the cheers of everyone. When I took my first deep breath, I felt something shoot right through my body. At that very moment, I knew I was touched by the Holy Spirit and it was real. Or else it was the shock of hitting that ice cold water. Well, it was one of the two.

When I could breathe and see again, I saw and heard all the Elders of the church who were standing all around me. They were all talking at the same time and I couldn't understand one thing they were saying. Then Tim said to me in front of the entire congregation, "Sister Christina, did the Holy Spirit speak to you as you were baptized?"

I shouted with astonishment for all to hear, "Yes! I think so! I think he wants me to learn all the languages of the world!" And they all looked at me like I was nuts.

After that, everyone began to sing and dance. It was incredible. I decided that night I was going to begin to learn every language I could for Jesus Christ. I would take them one at a time, until I mastered them all. No matter what they thought.

I returned to my suite at 11:00pm and I walked straight over to the dresser and took out my stash of cocaine. I thought, "You don't need this anymore, you're born again. Jesus has freed you from this."

With that in mind, I went to the bathroom and began to dump it in the toilet. As I started to see it falling out of the jar I stopped, I could not dump it. I went back into the bedroom and put it back in the dresser drawer. After, I knelt down beside my bed and began to pray, "Lord Jesus, I'm tired! I'm only twenty-four years old and I can't deal with my life anymore." I felt my tears begin to fall, "Lord, please help me! I can't take the pain of Joy's death any longer. And I can't keep this hatred I have for Frank in my heart anymore, it's destroying me. Jesus, I can't fight any more battles, I give up and I give my burdens to you. Lord, I chose to give you my life when I was baptized, and my life is out of control. I look all right on the outside, but I'm slowly dying on the inside. Please give me the strength to do your will Lord, because I have no strength of my own left. Amen."

I got up, opened the dresser drawer and cut four lines of cocaine. As I looked in the mirror at myself snorting the cocaine, I said out loud, "Lord Jesus, please forgive me, I don't know why I'm doing this, but I am."

After snorting, I sat down with pen and paper and proceeded to write six of the most beautiful songs of praise and love to God, 'I could imagine'.

The next morning, I flew back to LA and it was back to work. For the next two weeks, we worked like dogs to release my twelfth album entitled, 'The Power of His Love' before I was to leave again. But I had not, as of yet, informed anyone of my plans to take a leave-of-absence. So as soon as we finished the soundtrack, I called Jimmy into my office, "Jimmy, I am going away for a while and I'm leaving you in charge."

"Again! Where are you going now?" He exclaimed with irritation.

"Well Jimmy, I have decided to join Timmy Swinebert, on his nationwide crusade for the next six months."

Jimmy's mouth dropped to the floor as he shouted, "What? You can't do that! What's wrong with you, Christina? You need to be here now. What about the things you have us all working on?

You have us all preparing for a war with a corporate giant, and you're going on a fucking holiday."

I calmly replied, "Jimmy, none of that, matters anymore. What matters is that we are able to stand before Jesus Christ on Judgment Day, and be declared worthy to enter heaven. So Jimmy, I have to do what God is calling me to do and right now that has nothing to do with this place at all. I have a *Higher Calling and I have to answer it Jimmy*." I reached my hand out, touched his and added, "Jimmy, you will be able to reach me at any time and when you need me, I'll come back. But, I must do this first."

Jimmy pulled his hand away from mine, and with a sharp tone responded, "Oh God, Christina! Here we go again. You go ahead and do what you have to do. I'll take care of everything, just like I usually do." Then he got up, walked to the door and slammed it on his way out. After he left, I grabbed my things, and on February 1, 1980, I was off to the airport, where I climbed onto my new private jet, and flew to Texas.

On February 3rd, I began my nationwide crusade with Timmy Swinebert in Las Vegas, Nevada. At the onset, Tim talked about conquering sin in our lives with the power of the Holy Spirit.

After his sermon he said, "Now I would like to introduce to you a new born again child of God! She is a true witness of the power of Jesus Christ. Brothers and Sisters, please welcome, *Christina Powers*."

I walked out on the stage and received a standing ovation. When they calmed down I proceeded to proclaim to the fifty-thousand people in front of me, as well as the whole country on TV, how the power of God's unconditional love had changed my life. I told them how Jesus Christ had saved me from the depths of hell and had freed me from a life of sin and now he has called me into a life of service; where-in, I will serve my Lord and Savior for the rest of my life.

After that I said, "Brothers and Sisters, I tell you now Christ can save you too. So come to the altar and give your life to Christ." With that, I watched in amazement as everyone in the whole place came to the altar that night.

The next morning the papers read, "***Christina Powers, Hollywood's Bad Girl, gives up her glamorous life in Hollywood, to serve Jesus Christ as a 'Born Again Christian!'***"

After the story hit the headlines, Tim's usual crowd of fifty-thousand people a night, turned into an amazing, one-hundred-thousand people every night. The crowds swarmed the crusades just to hear me witness. So, I gave them what they wanted, HOPE! Every night I got up and sang my songs of love and praise to Jesus, and then I'd proclaim the miraculous power of Jesus. What I didn't proclaim was the fact that in order for me to get out on the stage and give them what they wanted, I had to get stoned on cocaine first.

As I toured the country with Timmy Swinebert, I kept in touch with Jimmy back at the office once a day. I helped guide Jimmy's every decision over the phone. Then I would preach to him for the last ten minutes of how happy I was now that I found Jesus.

During our April 16th, phone conversation, Jimmy said, "I have some bad news for you. First, I haven't said anything to you Christina, but Bobby has been sick all month. Finally, Doctor Heddermen admitted him back into the hospital last night. Christina, I'm really concerned about Bobby. Now he has some kind of mouth fungus. It's so bad he hasn't been able to eat any solid foods for the last two weeks."

He stopped speaking and I could hear him start to cry. Realizing he was upset, "Jimmy, relax! Bobby is going to be fine and I will try to come home next week. So just take some time off to be with Bobby, and I will handle everything over the phone with Judy. When I get home, we will take care of Bobby together."

His voice broke up, "Christina, can't you please come home now? I really need you."

With a tone of certainty I replied, "Jimmy, I will pray for Bobby and he will be fine. You just have to believe God answers the prayers of the faithful. That's why I can't come home now and I must remain a faithful servant."

His voice became sharp with anger, "Fine, Christina, you keep praying and while you're at it, pray for your new album, because 'The Power of His Love' is losing money. I had to stop production on the album last week. We're already over stocked by three-million copies."

I was taken aback by his statement, "How can that be Jimmy? When we released it, the sales were climbing fast."

"Well two weeks after you told the world you were a Christian, the mainstream radio stations stopped giving it air play. They branded it a Christian album and tossed it off the air."

I became angry, "That album is fantastic! How could they do this to me? I never thought I would be kept off the air again. I'm *Christina Powers*; they can't just toss one of my works out the window."

"Christina, face it. If the album was what your fans wanted, the stations would be playing it."

"No Jimmy," I insisted. "Even though the album is not my normal style, if people were hearing the music, I know it would still be selling."

Sarcastically, he admonished me, "Of course, you're right again! Well I have to go, remember Bobby? He's not here today, he's sick again."

"Well give him a kiss for me, tell him I'm praying for him; so goodbye for now Jimmy." And on that note we hung up.

On April 29th, I received a call from one of my New York attorneys, Tom Davies. When I answered the phone he said, "Hi, Christina, I have some information for you. As of yet there are no new proposals being sent to congress which have anything to do with the stock market. The only thing I could find out was that Mr. Salerno has been and continues to be, working very closely with Senator Davage, from Nevada, Wesly, from Texas and Relm from South Carolina, all Republicans! What they're working on, I don't know yet. Even with all that, I still don't see how he can touch you. You have no open stock on the public market."

"I don't know either Tom, but thanks, you've done well. Just make sure you keep your feelers out. I don't want to be surprised."

"They won't sneeze without you knowing about it."

After we hung up, I sat there for a minute and realized I still had to figure out what that snake Frank was up to. Then I thought, "Oh well, I'll figure it out tomorrow."

On May 1, one hour before the start of our New York crusade, I took Tim to the side, "Tim, I can't do this anymore."

With a surprised expression, "What do you mean, Sister Christina?"

"I can't go out there any longer and profess to these people Christ has saved me from sin, especially when I am still addicted to cocaine and I have not been able to stop using it." I hugged him, "Tim, please help me! The more I pray to God to stop, the more I find myself needing it. So, until I truly feel God working in my life and I stop using cocaine, I can no longer lie to the world."

"Christina, my sister, I love you!" He exclaimed, "And I will not let Satan defeat you anymore."

Immediately, he called all the Elders who were traveling with us, and had them meet us in a back room behind the stage. They all laid their hands on me and began to pray. As they prayed for me, I could feel my body begin to shake. Probably, because I had not received my high for the day yet, and as I trembled, Timmy Senior said, "Jesus, we ask you to deliver our sister from the bondage of the demon of cocaine. We rebuke you, demon of cocaine and exorcize you from the depths of our sister's soul, in the name of Jesus Christ."

As I knelt on the floor with all these men encircling me, Timmy Senior poured oil all over my head and shouted, "Through the power of the Holy Spirit, I cast you out in the name of the King of Kings, Jesus Christ."

All at once like a miracle, the desire for cocaine, as well as my shaking left me and I jumped up and shouted, "Praise God! I'm free from the demon of cocaine! I felt it leave my body." After that announcement we all held one another and praised God some more.

When I walked out to witness to the crowd that night I was flying high, but on Jesus Christ this time. I proceeded to glorify Jesus Christ for his gift of mercy and love, after which I confessed to the crowd, as I witnessed to them by saying, "Brothers and sisters, I need to speak candidly to you. I am ashamed to say this to all of you, but I must. You see, I have been less than honest with you all. As I have been witnessing with Brother Timmy

Swinebert, of the power of Christ in my life, I was still addicted to and using cocaine." The crowd gasped, "But I praise God; because Jesus Christ has just freed me from my cocaine addiction and I can truly say, I no longer have the desire, or the need, to use cocaine any longer. Jesus has truly set me free!"

The crowd went wild praising God and once again they all answered the altar call that night. As they came up to the altar by the thousands, I knew I was truly serving God now.

As time passed on our tour, I began to notice things which started to bother me. Tim would get on the stage every night and preach hell fire for all those who didn't know Christ, as well as those who did know Christ and still chose to live in sin. He preached against alcoholism, but at the same time, I had seen him under the influence of alcohol more than once after a crusade. He condemned womanizing and looking with an eye of lust, but I had suspected that the looks I was getting from Tim were more than just spiritual for a long time now. One night after he had a little too much to drink, he made advances towards me. Since I knew he was under the influence of alcohol, I chose to dismiss it. I had also caught him more than once checking out other women with eyes of lust. After that, he condemned lying and yet I had caught him in two or more lies. As I thought of these things, I began to become concerned and I thought, "What's going on here?" Then rationalizing it, I thought, "Christina, he's only human. So stop looking at the negative things and look at how he is getting the word of Christ out to the world. Besides, if God can forgive my sins, then I guess I can overlook Tim's little indiscretions.

We were in Albany, New York, on July 1, when I received a call from Jimmy in my hotel room at 9:00am. He immediately started screaming into the phone, "You know what, Christina? You are a self-consumed lying bitch. You dared to call me your only family when Joy died, but I know now that was just because you needed me, and I like a fool was there for you. But when I needed you, you never came. I've been waiting for you to come home since April, when you said you would be home the following week." Starting to cry, he yelled, "You lied! You said you would pray for Bobby. Well Christina, Bobby is dying. He has a rare skin cancer and the only people who have been getting this cancer are the ones who are dying from the 'gay plague'."

Now crying myself, "Oh God, no! Jimmy, I'm so sorry. I will be home today Jimmy, I promise. I will leave right now! Please don't hate me Jimmy, I do love you both." I hung up the phone, immediately called Tim and said, "Tim, I must leave now. A family member of mine is ill and may be dying; so, I am leaving right now."

"Christina, you can't leave now," he demanded. "We have a crusade tonight. Why don't we just call in the Elders and we will pray for your family member. Then you can leave after you do God's work tonight."

Bluntly, "Tim, I said I have to leave, so goodbye." Then, I hung up the phone and headed for home. When I arrived, Jimmy was taking care of Bobby at home, because the hospital would not readmit him. Jimmy told me before we went in to see Bobby that the fungus in his mouth came back and once again he was not eating any solid food at all. He also said Doctor Hedderman had him on a diet of something called 'Ensure' and that every time he gave Bobby some, he started to throw it up.

When we walked into his room, I was shocked. It had only been five months since I saw Bobby last and he looked **horrible**. He had dark red and black skin blotches all over his face and body and he had lost fifty-pounds. He could hardly sit up in the bed. I could tell he was in a lot of pain, just by the look on his face. I could hardly believe what was happening to him. I hid my feelings of shock as I sat on the bed next to Bobby, kissed his forehead and said, "Bobby, listen to me. I believe I know how to help you."

Jimmy asked, "How, Christina? No one else seems to know anything about this disease."

I looked at them both with the deepest sincerity, "Come with me and I will have the Elders anoint you with oil Bobby, as we pray for Christ to heal you. Jesus can take this disease from you, I know he can."

Jimmy was angered by my statement, "Please Christina, I've seen what your prayers can do and we don't want them!"

Bobby patted Jimmy's hand and softly whispered, "Stop it Jimmy!" Then he grabbed my hand, looked me straight in the eye, "Christina, for as long as I have known you, you have always had a special gift for knowing things. So, if you truly believe this will help me, then I believe it too." He reached his other hand toward Jimmy and guided him to sit down beside me on the bed. As the three of us held hands he continued, "Jimmy, I trust Christina, and I want to do whatever she says."

Jimmy had tears in his eyes as he kissed Bobby, "You're right Bobby, our girl is back and the three of us will be fine now."

We all hugged and it was back to the crusade, which was now in Hartford, Connecticut. When we arrived in Hartford, we took a three bedroom suite at the Radisson. The weather was so perfect it was almost impossible to believe that three people could be so depressed on such a glorious day. As soon as we checked into our room, I called Tim, "I'm here with my step-brother. He is dying, so would you please call the Elders together for him so we can anoint him with oil and lay hands for God's healing on my brother."

"Is he able to come to the Coliseum, Christina?"

"Yes, Tim, he can make it."

Assuredly, "Good, I will call together the Elders and meet you in the sound room at the Coliseum. Let's see, its 10:00 now, so say around 1:00pm."

I sighed, "God bless you Brother Tim. I love you so much for doing this." I hung up the phone and proceeded to joyfully tell Bobby and Jimmy, we were going to pray that very afternoon.

When we walked into the prayer group of Elders, I held the door so Jimmy could push Bobby in his wheelchair. I introduced the two of them to the Elders and Tim asked Bobby what his illness was.

Bobby replied, "I have something called 'Kaposi's Sarcoma'."

Instantly, one of the elders rudely interrupted, "Excuse me, but isn't that the skin cancer which is caused by the 'gay plague'?"

Bobby answered innocently, "Yes it is."

All of a sudden Tim's face turned as *white as a ghost* as he looked down at Bobby. Then he looked up at me, and at all the other 'Brothers,' who were looking down at Bobby, and he asked abruptly, "Are you a homosexual?"

Once again Bobby answered innocently, "Yes I am."

Sternly, Tim shouted, "Do you denounce your homosexuality, repent for your sins and accept Jesus Christ as your personal savior?"

Instantly Jimmy piped up with, "We accept Jesus Christ as our personal savior, and we repent for our sins." With that flick of his wrist, "But we cannot denounce our homosexuality, because that's part of who we are."

Tim went into shock and adamantly cried out, "Then may God help your brother, because I can't." Outraged he slapped his hand down on his knee and shouted at Bobby again, "Damn you boy! Are you stupid? You can't accept Jesus Christ as your personal savior, repent for your sins, and still be a homosexual!"

I was horrified and about to slug him when Bobby said, "I'm sorry! But I can't change who I am."

Outraged at Bobby's honesty Tim yelled, "Well then I cannot pray for you."

That's when I couldn't take it anymore, "Now just wait a minute, Tim! This is Bobby's life, we're talking about here! Isn't it God's will that we pray for and love every one! Don't The Ten Commandments tell us to love thy neighbor as thyself?"

With a stunned expression on his face Tim replied, "Christina, I would do anything for you, but this is asking me to go against God. This would be a sin to pray for someone who openly admits to being a homosexual and refuses to repent for it. If we were in the ancient times of the Bible, I would have no choice but to order your brother stoned to death, right now."

I was shocked and my face showed it, but before I could say anything, Jimmy shouted, "Christina, this is who you call, **loving Christians**? This is what you think is **Godly**? Well I think you're all sick." Then he grabbed the handles on Bobby's wheelchair and said, as he turned away, "You can keep your prayers, because none of you pray to the Jesus Christ I know. Now if you will excuse us, we're getting out of this 'hellhole' of 'hypocrisy' right now."

With that he headed out the door like a bolt of lightning. I looked at Tim and all the Elders, then I looked back to see Jimmy leaving the room and I didn't know what to say. So I charged out of the room after Jimmy and Bobby. When I reached them, Jimmy was helping Bobby into the rented town-car and they were both crying. I grabbed Jimmy by the shoulders and pleaded, "I'm so sorry! I had no idea they would act like this." After I finally calmed them down I continued, "Please wait here, I have to give Mr. Timmy Swinebert a piece of my mind, right now."

I stormed back into the Coliseum and I was **'Pissed'**! When I reached the door to the room where I left Tim and all of the Elders, it was partially opened. I stopped at the door before going in, because I could hear them talking about us. Timmy Swinebert Senior was saying, "Brothers, listen to me. I think my son may have over-reacted."

I heard Tim Junior say, "Dad, I won't pray for a fagot. He deserves to die."

Tim Sr. replied, "Son, don't you realize how valuable that girl is to our ministry. If she walks out on us, we lose millions of dollars. So I say you go after that pot of gold and apologize to them all. Tim, I don't care what it takes for you to bring her back here, but you bring her back. Then we say a prayer for that boy. Shit son, I don't give a damn if he lives or dies either. The prayers don't work anyway. Just as long as she thinks the prayers work, and she thinks we're doing it for her, that's all that matters. So if it keeps her under our control, then, who the hell cares if we pray for a fagot."

I felt fire in my eyes and I was about to burst in, when I stopped myself. I turned and quietly walked away, without being seen by anyone. As I walked through the parking lot toward the car, I thought, "God this can't be happening! How in the world could I be deceived like this without realizing it? Christina, this is a travesty! You can't allow this to continue. They are deceiving millions." When I reached the car, I told Jimmy and Bobby what I'd just heard and on the ride back to the hotel I said, "Jimmy, I need your help to stop this wickedness."

With a malicious tone he replied, "Start talking girlfriend! I'm listening."

Deviously I told Jimmy exactly what I wanted him to do.

As soon as we entered the room, I picked up the phone and called Tim. When I got him on the line, he was so apologetic, it was **sickening**. Before I could say anything he immediately said, "Sister Christina, Praise God! You called. I have heard from Jesus and he convicted my heart. Jesus has told me I was wrong, and if we pray for your brother, Jesus will be faithful to our prayers and heal him!"

With enthusiasm, "Praise God, Tim! I thank you from the depths of my heart."

With a tone of authority he continued, "If you bring your brother to the service tonight we will heal him."

Sounding desperate and needy I begged, "Please Tim, can you come over here now. I need to speak with you before tonight's crusade. I'm in the penthouse suite on the top floor of the Radisson Hotel. Can you please come now? I need you."

"Yes Sister Christina, I'll be right over."

The suite we had was on the top floor and it had a direct access to the roof of the building where there were a number of well-maintained flower gardens, which were scattered throughout a Kentucky blue grass lawn. When Tim arrived it was 4:00pm and I had Jimmy hiding out on the roof. When I opened the door, I had two glasses of scotch in my hands, which happened to be Tim's preferred drink. As soon as he entered the room, I handed him one of the drinks, hugged him and said, "I need a drink and I don't want to drink alone."

He took the drink, "Are you all right Sister Christina?"

"Do you mind if we talk out on the roof, it's such a beautiful afternoon?"

"No, I don't mind, that sounds nice."

I led him out onto the roof, and as we gazed out over downtown Hartford I said in a sensual tone, "Tim, look at it. We are on top of the world you and I, and God is giving it to us." I moved close to him, "Tim, just think of it, you and I reaching the whole world together for Jesus Christ." I placed my glass down, hugged him, looked passionately into his eyes and seductively said, "Tim I think I'm beginning to have sexual feelings for you." Then I put my lips next to his ear and softly whispered, "Tim, I think I'm falling in love with you and I don't know what to do about it."

As soon as I said these words, he became a mad man full of passion and he was all over me. His lips were everywhere. I began to push him off as I said, "Tim slow down. I think we should talk about this," but there was no slowing him down! As he began to rip my clothing off my body, I knew there was no way I was stopping him now. I saw Jimmy coming out of hiding, so to stop him from blowing his cover I waved him away with a hand motion. Then I began to rip Tim's clothing off as I gestured to Jimmy to stay hidden. Swallowing my heart, I began to rape Tim as viciously as he was me. The lust between the two of us was unbelievable. As we laid our naked bodies down on the soft blue, green grass, the demons of lust exploded within us both. Our bodies burnt as we quenched the fires of our fleshly lusts. It was the most degrading and demoralizing thing I had ever done, but I had to do it, if only to expose Tim and his organization for the **hypocritical monsters** they were!

At that evening's crusade, Tim had the audacity to preach on the sin of homosexuality. He said, "People, the penalty of the sin of homosexuality is death. I warn all those who are homosexual, God will not be mocked. That is why he has sent the 'angel of death' to visit all those who are homosexual with the new 'gay plague.' This is why the plague is only killing homosexuals. God has told me he will slay all those who dare to sin in such a vulgar manner."

His words incited a chant of hatred toward all of those who are gay and praises to God for bringing his hand of justice to them in this so called divine plague. It was so frightening I thought I was in Germany during Hitler's reign.

Then, it was my turn to minister to the enraged crowd of one-hundred-thousand spectators. As I picked up the mike to sing, the crowd was giving me a standing ovation and I said, "Brothers and sisters, I have something different to say tonight. I want to tell you what I discovered this very day. That is, that Mr. Timmy

Swinebert is a filthy swine. His ministry is full of lying thieves. He preaches against one thing then he goes out and does it. The next thing he'll probably do is go have sex with some guy in the back of a bookstore."

Stunned, Tim screamed out, "I rebuke you, you lying beast from hell! Depart from Sister Christina's, body."

The crowd thinking I was possessed, started to scream out in unison, "Depart from her you demon! Depart from her you demon!"

I shouted, "I don't need to be exorcized Tim, **you do**!"

He started to walk from the other side of the stage toward me, as I pointed to him, "Ask your 'god' here, how come he committed adultery with me, just this very afternoon!"

That's when the crowd gasped as Tim screamed, "Blasphemer! You are a demon from hell and a liar!"

I shouted, "Tim, I'm way ahead of you. I knew you would say that. That's why I have photos of the two of us to prove it. So take me to court for defamation of character why don't you?"

I turned to the crowd as Tim stopped dead in his tracks, "People, this is nothing but a tax free, money making, lying, scheming, brain washing organization and I can no longer be a part of it!"

Tim turned to the crowd and began to cry with tears pouring down his face. Then he screamed with all his might, "She is a harlot from hell and she seduced me with her witchcraft. Brothers and sisters please forgive me for falling into the web of demons, with Satan herself."

After that display of alligator tears I shouted, "Tim, you should be asking God to forgive you, not your bank roll. People, he squanders your money on private jets, mansions, fancy meals and young woman. This whole ministry is a farce, and I only allowed him to seduce me to prove it to you. I hope for your sakes, you will be able to see the truth for yourselves. Brothers and sisters please listen to me, what we as Christians do not truly understand is that the blood Jesus shed for us is priceless. It covers all of us, even if we happen to be gay, lesbian, or transgender. God loves us all and all he wants is for us to have a personal relationship with him. To come and discover why he paid such a high price for us to have eternal life with him. We as the body of Christ have to start letting God be the judge not the church. God does not take pleasure in religious leaders standing on pulpits condemning anyone. When all that really matters is what it says in John 3-16 and 17, "For God so loved the world, that he gave his only begotten Son, that whosoever believeth in him should not perish, but have everlasting life. For God sent not his Son into the world to **condemn** the world; but that the world through him might be saved."

Then I put down the mike and walked out through a shocked mob, as Tim cried in hysterics in front of the whole world. After the release of the photos, in a worldwide scandal, it seemed I had brought the fifty year Swinebert Empire, crashing down into a pile of rubble, **and all in only one day.**

CHAPTER 12. BOBBY'S BATTLE FOR LIFE

Around 3:00am the morning after I slew the Swinebert ministry, the three of us found ourselves still quite shook up. Jimmy, Bobby and I, were in the air on our personal jet, which we paid for from honest money, somewhere between Hartford and LA. We were sitting together in the living room compartment all on one big sofa with me in the middle, when I reached out, took one of each of their hands, "Guys, I love you both and I'm really sorry for having put the two of you through this."

Bobby glanced at me lovingly, "Christina, don't apologize. The way they reacted to this disease and my sexuality had nothing to do with you. What you did was out of your love for us and we know that."

We all hugged and I said with sensitivity, "Listen to me guys, even though Timmy Swinebert and his ministry is a farce, that doesn't mean there is no God. Bobby, I believe in Jesus Christ, and I believe if it's his will God can heal you. So why don't the three of us pray?"

Jimmy quickly grabbed two pencils which were on the coffee table, stuck one up each nostril and said, "Ha! Like, God has time for the likes of the three of us." We lost it and started laughing like crazy.

After our outburst I said, "Come on guys, let's get down on our knees and pray it can't hurt." So, that's what we did.

After two days of rest and reflection on what we had just lived through, it was time to get back to work. There were four things which needed my immediate attention. My first priority was Bobby and the so-called 'gay plague' which was killing him and hundreds of others like him. Second, to somehow absolutely find out if Frank had anything to do with Joy's death; if it turned out he did, then justice would be **MINE**! Third, was to figure out how to out fox, the fox on the Wall Street scene, before he could pounce down and devour Powers Incorporated. Fourth, I had to start writing my next manuscript. It would tell the world the story of a young female performer, who gets caught up with fraudulent religious leaders and how she exposed their inner den of iniquity.

Oh, by the way, two weeks after my incident with Timmy Swinebert, the album, 'The Power of His Love', did the impossible and beat the unbeatable. The sales of 'The Power of His Love' soared past the top selling album of all time, 'Halloween in Hell'. And once again the money was pouring in, our stock were going up, and my popularity was soaring. There were thousands of letters pouring in every day, with 98% of them telling me how much they loved me and how sorry they were to hear what happened to me. There were letters from little old ladies who told me they were sending Tim money from their SSI checks every month. They actually thanked me for exposing the Swinebert Ministry for what it truly was.

It was overwhelming to me. There were millions of people from all over the world, all telling me they loved and cared about me. As I realized these letters came from the hearts of real people, it finally meant something to me, which was more than just the money I was making off of them. It was more than my desire for revenge, which was the driving force behind everything I thought and did. It was as if blinders were taken off my eyes and for the first time in my life, I truly began to look at others first, instead of just myself. I could see there was a great need in the world around me. I realized there were other things happening around me, outside of my world. I had always lived as though my life was the whole universe and everything revolved around me. I finally realized it didn't and that in the scheme of things I meant nothing. I was just a speck in time and what truly mattered was the world around me. This awakening of mine changed my focus and I knew

I had to use my popularity to truly make this life here on earth a little better for as many people as I could.

There was that 2% of the mail which told me I would burn in hell for what I had done. There were also a few death threats, which I decided to take seriously. So, I hired a private security firm to supply eight full time bodyguards to be around me on a twenty-four-hour basis. Something told me not to take any chances. After all, look at my true family's history. I wanted the security, but I still needed my privacy. So, I requested they work two per shift and they had to stay where I wouldn't have to be aware of their presence.

All of a sudden, on the morning of August 26th, Bobby began to go downhill. He was having horrible coughing bouts and I knew he had once again come down with pneumonia. I called Doctor Heddermen who told me to meet him at the hospital emergency room with Bobby as soon as possible. Bobby was admitted into a private room in the intensive care unit. He was intubated with a feeding tube and given mega doses of IV antibiotics. He was also put on a morphine drip to help lessen the pain. It was horrible to see him dying like this and we were helpless. Jimmy and I took turns staying with him because we could not find one private duty nurse willing to take the case. It was so frustrating, no one really knew anything about the disease and if they did, they shunned it because it was a 'gay' thing. I truly wish I did not have to say this, but in August of 1980, the hospital staff was incredible in their attempts to steal whatever dignity Bobby had left. No one wanted to go near him. Everyone was afraid.

I tried to understand what everyone was feeling, so I never complained. As for Jimmy, he was feeling so belittled by the stares he received every time he entered the hospital that he wouldn't complain for fear of some sort of retaliation against Bobby. All that changed when one night Jimmy came down with a fever and I stayed home to look after him. I called the hospital to inform the nurses in the intensive care unit no one would be in that evening to care for Bobby. I asked, "So please look after him for us and I'll be in to stay with him in the morning."

The weather was rainy, cold, and damp on that fateful morning of August 31st, as I drove to the hospital. When I went into Bobby's room, I found Bobby lying in his own feces and the bed was sopping wet with cold urine. I went ballistic as I stormed to the administration office ranting and raving all the way. When I reached the office, I demanded to see the hospital administrator at once!

When I entered Mr. Mallard's office, I told him the condition I found Bobby in, the treatment he had been receiving since we arrived at the hospital, and I was disgusted with the reaction of the hospital staff members. Mr. Mallard said, "Ms. Powers, please try to calm down. I do understand your feelings, but I also want you to understand something too. The only reason Mr. Shaw was admitted into this hospital in the first place, was as a courtesy to you. So if you're not satisfied, I suggest you take him to County General where all the other patients with his disease reside."

I was shocked when I heard his words and my expression showed it as I swiftly replied, "You mean to tell me, you're not accepting patients into this hospital because of a certain type of illness?"

Very sarcastically he replied, "It has become our policy for the time being, not to accept these patients until we know more about this disease. We are in a very delicate situation here, because, if we accept these patients we risk losing our regular patients, who have informed us they will not come here if we have patients with the 'gay plague' admitted into this hospital. The problem is the other patients and the staff are afraid. Due to our financial situation and our main contributors, our hands here in the administration office are tied. So you see Ms. Powers, we are actually being forced to send these patients to County General and like I said, if you're dissatisfied, I'll be more than happy to transfer Mr. Shaw to County General.

I felt fire in my eyes as I replied with indignation, "Well thank you ever so much Mr. Mallard, but we're not going to County General. Los Angeles Memorial is going to take care of Bobby and you are going to have your staff take care of him with dignity and respect, or I will be on the local news this evening telling the public how your hospital is discriminating against certain patients. Now the choice is yours. Speak with your staff and take care of Mr. Shaw, or do I create a public scandal for the hospital? So what's it gonna be, Mr. Mallard? The ball is in your court!"

He was shocked by my response and his face showed it, "Ms. Powers that is not going to accomplish anything except to cause hard feelings between the hospital and yourself."

I sarcastically snickered, "Ha, ha, ha. You know what? I think it will accomplish something more, like destroy the reputation of your hospital."

He grew angry and I knew he was biting his tongue, "Ms. Powers, we don't have to carry this incident to such an extreme. I will talk to my staff, and Mr. Shaw will receive proper care."

Confidently staring him straight in the eyes, "Thank you very much Mr. Mallard, I was sure we could come to some kind of mutual agreement."

I left his office and headed back to Bobby. When I returned to Bobby's room, he was still in the same condition he was in when I left, even after my screaming at the nurses! I grabbed some linen off the cart in the hall and proceeded to clean him up. I must be totally truthful here, I was slightly afraid of catching what Bobby had, but I was not going to let that stop me from helping someone I loved very much. Two minutes after I finished, a nurse entered the room and asked me if I needed anything. I asked her to page Doctor Heddermen and have him stop in to see me. She said she would, and then she left the room.

Doctor Heddermen entered Bobby's room shortly after the noon hour, and proceeded to examine Bobby who was in a semiconscious state. Afterward he turned to me, "Christina, have you had lunch yet?"

"No,"

"Why don't you take a break with me and we'll talk over lunch, my treat." I accepted his invitation and walked with him to the hospital cafeteria.

Over our lunch, I explained to Doctor Heddermen what had transpired that morning and how I felt about it. He said, "Christina, I think it's time you call me Robert." Then reaching across the table and taking my hand in his, he continued, "I heard the whole story ten minutes after it happened. I must ask you as a friend, to try not to get so upset with the reaction of the staff. Christina, please try to understand the situation the hospital is in."

"I can sympathize with the hospital's situation, but I do not agree with the way the hospital is handling the problem. We are talking about the lives of real people, not some inanimate objects which can just be thrown away and forgotten."

He replied with conviction, "You have every right to disagree with hospital policy, all I'm asking you is let the medical community deal with this disease."

I slid my hand out of his, "Robert, what is truly going on here with this disease? I can't believe it's really only killing gay men. Common sense tells me that."

"Christina, I wish I knew. The plain truth is no one knows what's going on. All we know for sure is that people have been dying for the last two years from all types of opportunistic diseases. It appears to destroy the immune system in each of its victims. There have been thirty-two cases locally and all of them have been gay men. That's all we have to go on right now."

I shook my head with concern, "So what's being done about it?"

"The Center for Disease Control, along with private laboratories are working night and day to answer that question."

I sighed, "That sound's great, but it seems to me no one is telling the general population about this disease. I have heard nothing about it in the 'straight' press. The only ones talking about it at all are those in the gay press and the medical community."

"Christina, the nation is consumed right now with the Iran hostage situation. The last thing the President, or the public wants to hear, is a suspicion there might be a new disease killing people. There is another thing to consider, and that's the reaction of the general public to such a story."

With alarm, "Are you telling me, no one is willing to admit there is anything going on out there?"

He answered quite sincerely, "Until we know what it is, there is no scientific proof that there is a new killer loose on the general public. So yes, you're right. At this time, no one is going to admit to what the whole medical community believes to be true, in an official announcement. It could cause a panic and destroy careers."

My reply showed my alarm, "Oh my God! Robert, this is unbelievable. I guess the world has no choice, but to let you guys do your job."

As Robert walked me back to Bobby's room, I asked him, "Robert, please tell me the truth, how long do you think Bobby will survive like this?"

When we reached Bobby's door, Robert hugged me warmly, "I'm sorry Christina, but I don't think he'll last the night."

"Thank you Robert, for being so candid with me."

I gowned up to enter Bobby's isolation room. When I walked back into the room, his breath was so labored, I felt compelled to call Jimmy, even though I knew how sick he was himself. When I called home, Carman answered the phone and within a moment put Jimmy on, and I said, "Jimmy, how are you feeling?"

He coughed to clear his voice, "I still have the chills and I can hardly talk, but I'll live. How's Bobby?"

Trying not to frighten him, "Jimmy if you're up to it, you should come over here."

"What's happening Christina?" he asked with fear in his voice.

"He's taken a turn for the worse, Jimmy."

Jimmy said nothing at first, then, "Okay, I'll be right there."

"Jimmy, have James drive you over here. I don't want you driving by yourself."

"All right, we'll be right over."

As I waited for Jimmy, I sat down on the bed beside Bobby and held his hand. I began to stroke his forehead, "Bobby, I want you to know how much your friendship has meant to me. You have touched my heart and I will always remember you." I started to cry, "Bobby, I'm sorry; I know you wanted me to help you and you believed I could, but I can't. I wish I could, but I just don't know how to help you. Forgive me please." With that I kissed his forehead and just held Bobby's hand as I waited for Jimmy to arrive.

When Jimmy entered the room, I looked up at him and he just started to cry. He came over to me with his arms stretched out. I stood up to hold him, "Christina, I don't want to lose him."

Sadly, we both began crying, "Jimmy, I know baby, I know."

Jimmy looked down at Bobby and as we released our embrace, he fell to his knees beside the bed, laid his head on Bobby's chest and cried even harder.

My heart broke for Jimmy. I could feel his pain as I watched him cry for his love, "Bobby, oh my Bobby, I love you, I love you Bobby. Please don't leave me. I'm going to miss you. I need you Bobby. I need you. Please don't leave me. I can't make it without you."

As Jimmy pleaded, I could see Bobby open his eyes and gaze into Jimmy's eyes. As they looked at each other, Bobby took one last breath and he was gone.

Jimmy cried horribly as he laid on Bobby's body. All I could do was to kneel down beside him and hold him as we both cried.

After what seemed like hours of crying there on our knees I said, "Jimmy, I'm here for you baby. I love you and we will make it through this together." Just then James entered the room and with his help, we finally were able to leave Bobby behind. No one said a word as James drove us home that day; because we had just lost another piece of **our hearts on that rainy day in August of 1980.**

CHAPTER 13. A NEW DIRECTION

Two weeks after Bobby's funeral, the Ellesmere Building Tenants Association called an emergency meeting. Since 90% of the tenants were gay, the meeting was called to discuss this new 'gay epidemic'. Jimmy and I attended the meeting, which was held at 8:00pm on September 18th, 1980. Everyone in the building had the opportunity to speak. It was obvious everyone was on edge and that something had to be done.

Billy Williams the President of the Tenants Association said, "I have been trying to call attention to what is going on in the gay community with local-press and politicians, but no one is listening. It's like everyone is putting their heads in the sand on this one." He looked directly at me, "Ms. Powers, we here in the building, as well as the entire gay community, would like to ask for your help in this matter."

Billy lived on the same floor as Jimmy and me. We had become friendly passing in the hall, so I said, "Please Billy, call me Christina. Now, exactly what type of assistance would you need from me?"

He smiled eagerly, "We need someone with your kind of celebrity status, to help our voices to be heard and to find out what's being done medically and scientifically about this disease."

I walked over to stand at the podium, "Good evening neighbors. I understand exactly what you're asking and before I answer, please let me share some information with you. I have spoken with one of the top people in the medical field and I've expressed the exact same concerns to him which I'm hearing here tonight. I have been assured the CDC, along with private sector laboratories are working night and day on this thing. I was told if I were to raise the issue in public now, before anyone really knows what's going on, I could quite possibly cause a public panic. The medical field believes the backlash of such a panic would slow the progress of the scientific field, by causing them to divert more manpower to solving the panic, rather than finding the cause of these deaths. After my discussions and a lot of thought, I decided that the medical field is most likely correct in their assumptions. Now, after saying all this, I'm sorry, but at this time I feel I must remain silent on this matter. I believe we live in the greatest nation on earth, with some of the greatest minds in the world. I also believe we must first give the government and the scientific community time to work this out their way. I think we have to trust them, but I will stay on top of the situation. I want to know what's going on just as much as everyone else here, and I will. I can guarantee you all that!"

Once the meeting ended, Jimmy and I returned to our apartment. I went straight to the shower to clean off the day's work. After I dressed, I picked up the phone and called Detective Fred Ulrich, "Hi, Fred, this is *Christina Powers*, I haven't heard from you, so I thought I would check in. Are you any closer to solving the case?"

"Hi Christina, I wish I could say that I am, but I'm not."

"You're not telling me you've given up, are you?" I asked bluntly.

With a reassuring tone he answered, "No way, as a matter of fact I was out at the scene just yesterday."

"Why were you out there?"

"A few days after the fire, we found some tire tracks on your property. I had a mold made of the tracks and I finally learned more about the tires. So, I attempted to measure the width of the access road the truck took through the woods to enter your property."

"So, what were your findings?"

"I'm now sure we have the vehicle. So with any luck at all, it will lead me right to the arsonist."

"Fred, that's great news, I don't know how to thank you. Please keep up the good work and when you're done, I will have to think of a very special way to thank you."

We ended our conversation and I walked toward the living room. I was wearing my blue terry cloth robe and slippers, when I sat on the sofa beside Jimmy, who was in a tee shirt and tight fitting jockey shorts, eating popcorn and watching the 1:00am local news. I reached for the remote control and flicked it off. Jimmy slapped my hand, "What's the matter with you? I was watching that.

"Jimmy, we have to talk."

He looked at me with concern, "OOH! That sounded serious, start talking, girlfriend."

I smiled a little, "Well, I think it might be. I think we should move from here."

Jimmy gave me a strange look, "What do you mean move from here? Bobby's still here with me, I can't move."

I took his hand, "Listen to me Jimmy, I have to be up front with you. I'm afraid to stay here any longer. I have nothing against the gay lifestyle, but until the world knows what's going on with this disease, I don't feel like living with six-hundred gay men. Common sense tells me this is not the healthiest place to be living right now, for either one of us. After all, we lost Bobby in this building."

Jimmy's eyes lit up as if someone had just turned on a light switch, "Oh shit! I never thought of that, what the fuck is wrong with me."

Bluntly I said, "The only thing wrong with you Jimmy is that you miss Bobby. I know that feeling better than anyone. That is why I don't want to take any chances of something happening to either one of us."

Jimmy put the bowl of popcorn down on the coffee table, looked at me very seriously, "You're right, so where do we go?"

As soon as he said those words, the phone rang. I looked at him, "Who would be calling us at this time?

"I don't know, pick it up."

"Hello, who's this?" sounding a little annoyed.

"Christina, its Tom Davies, from New York."

"Hi, isn't it 4am out there, what's up?"

"I'm sorry to be calling you so late."

I chuckled, "That's alright; we were only getting ready for bed."

"Forgive me, I'll let you go and call back later."

"Well, can you sum it up, quickly?"

"Sure. First, the building is complete and we need you here in New York as soon as possible. Second, I have come up with some very interesting information I'm sure you will find it quite useful."

With interest I asked, "What is it?"

"I'd rather keep this under wraps until I see you in person. How soon can you get here?"

"I'll be there tomorrow," I answered in haste.

I hung up the phone, turned to Jimmy, "Well I guess I know where we're going."

He looked at me strangely, "Who was that?"

"It was our attorney, Tom Davies, and we're leaving for New York in the morning,"

"What about this place?"

"Screw it Jimmy, let's just get what we can out of here. I can't deal with this right now."

The next morning at our offices, I called Judy my Executive Secretary, her husband Mike, my Account's Office Manager and Ann Markel, who I had appointed Head Studio Coordinator for stage, lighting, and props into my office. Once they came in, I informed them Jimmy and I would be leaving that night for New York. I explained that we needed to open our new offices. I proceeded to promote the three of them to studio executives. I knew I could trust them all, so I left them in charge of my California operations. I also gave Judy and Mike 1% of Powers Incorporated Stock. I gave Ann Markel 2% of the stock and appointed them all a seat on my board of directors.

When Jimmy and I got off the plane in New York, all I had of my personal belongings were two suitcases and one *singed* bottle of champagne. When we reached our waiting limos, we had them take us to our suite on the 20th floor of the Plaza, in downtown

Manhattan. I took the entire floor, because I had a small entourage of hand-picked staff with me.

Friday, September 29th, I had made plans for Jimmy and me to meet with Tom Davies the next morning, at 9:00am in Milton, New York. We would be touring the new headquarters of Powers Incorporated. After that, we had scheduled a dinner engagement at the Turf Restaurant in the Kingston, New York, Holiday Inn. It seemed that Jimmy and I were being welcomed to the area by the Hudson Valley Business Association.

The following morning was a glorious one! The sun and the sky were so bright, they illuminated the day. Yet, there was no glare in my eyes as I drove Jimmy and me in our rented town car up the New York State Thruway, to the New Paltz exit, because I was slightly apprehensive over making this move. But thank God, my confidence returned the moment we arrived. The speed limit dropped to 20 miles per hour as soon as you entered the heart of Powers Incorporated, via the new four lane main thoroughfare. It wound its way five miles through the three main complexes on the banks of the majestic Hudson River. I was in awe of the landscaping. It was magnificent! There were flower gardens all along the roadway. Everywhere you looked, all you could see was nature. The towering pine forest was alive with the sounds of wild life. There were two beautiful waterfalls in site of the main thoroughfare. As we passed each turnoff into one of the three main complexes you could not see a building through the trees until you reached it. This masterpiece of nature, landscaping and modern building technology, which was finished down to my every wish was completed by Joyce Baggatta and her son Lonnie. They were the architects who helped make my dream come true when they drew up the plans and oversaw the building of my Empire.

Jimmy and I met Joyce and Lonnie at the main security house which was nestled in the center of the three main complexes. Joyce informed us Tom Davies would be delayed and would meet us at the Holiday Inn around 7:00pm. The two of them proceeded to take us on a complete tour of the complex. As we toured, I realized after seven-years and two-billion dollars, I had my Empire! It was a phenomenal feeling to behold what I had created and at that moment I knew I could have anything in this world that I wanted. Then, I thought, "You're next Frank! I did all this for one reason, for you to taste my revenge!" Immediately I felt a cold, hard, rush of hatred go through my soul, as I stood in the heart of this garden of Eden-like paradise, and thought, "I'm coming, you bastard!"

Later that afternoon around 6:30pm Jimmy and I checked into our rooms at the Holiday Inn in Kingston, New York. Ten minutes after I entered my room, the phone rang and it was Mrs. Sally Lou Schaffert-Brown, the President of the Hudson Valley Business Association. She welcomed me with warmth in her voice, as she told me of the evening's events. There was to be a welcoming meeting in the D-conference room of the hotel at 7:30pm; followed by cocktails at 8:30pm in the lounge for one-on-one meetings with local business leaders. Dinner would be from 9:15 until 10:00. Then back to the lounge for cocktails and dancing. She informed me she would be my personal guide for the evening and that Mr. Davies is in route. I thanked her and agreed to meet her in the lobby at 7:15pm.

As soon as I hung up the phone, I rang Jimmy's room, "Jimmy do we have any more of those peanut butter and jelly sandwiches left?"

"One, why?" He asked guardedly.

"Well you have ten minutes to dress and get your ass over here with half of that sandwich before we start this evening. Dinner isn't until 9:15 and I'm not taking any chances. I want something to munch on now."

Laughing he said, "I'll be right there, girlfriend."

Jimmy and I met Sally right on time and our greeting was overwhelming. She was a wonderful woman, intelligent, warm and witty. After our ten minute personal introductions, she led us into the conference room. The place was packed with all the most influential business people in the area. Sally opened the meeting by welcoming all the members of the Hudson Valley Business Association. After her little speech she said, "Now I would like to introduce the President and Vice-President of Powers Incorporated,

Ms. *Christina Powers* and Mr. James Severino!" With that we headed up to the podium together, to a standing ovation.

Jimmy spoke first, "Hello, I'm James Severino, but please call me Jimmy, and as you know I'm the vice-president of Powers Incorporated. I thank you for your kind welcome. Now I would like to turn this mike over to the real wizard of Powers Incorporated, my boss and best friend, *Christina Powers."*

As Jimmy returned to his seat, I said, "Good evening everyone, I'm so thrilled by this gracious welcome to your beautiful Hudson Valley. I would like to say at this time, I truly look forward to joining everyone here, in creating a new financial Mecca in the Hudson Valley Region. I know with all of us working together, this region's economic growth will rival the worlds."

I received another standing ovation as I finished my speech. Then it was off to the dining room for dinner. I looked around for Tom Davies, but he had still not arrived. I began to become a little concerned. This was not like Tom, so I shared my concern with Sally who also knew Tom well, then asked, "Do you think you could have someone try to contact him for me?" She agreed, beckoned a young man to her and arranged it immediately.

Without hesitation Sally began to introduce us to as many people as she possibly could in half-an-hour. As we mingled, from the corner of my left eye, I saw him turn toward me. I recognized the smile immediately. His big brown eyes gleamed as he said, *"Christina Powers,* I know everything there is to know about you and I'm madly in love with you."

I gently hugged the man, who made love to me more than a year ago, "Lee Bradford! What a surprise. I had no idea you lived in New York."

He winked, "As I recall, we never got that far."

We parted our embrace, "So what do you do here in the Valley?"

With a smile that was now glowing, "I'm the President of Bradford Computers Incorporated. Our main offices happen to be right across the river from yours."

I smiled in my subtle, seductive way, "Well I guess since you know so much about me, maybe I should take the time and get to know you a little better myself."

His eyes lit up, "That can be arranged." All at once the light in his eyes dimmed, "I was truly sorry to hear of your recent personal tragedies."

"Thank you Lee, I appreciate that," I replied with sincerity. "But, please don't look so sad, I'm surviving."

Just then we were called to dinner, and Lee just happened to be seated on my right side at a beautiful garnished round table. Sally was on my left and Jimmy on her left, with a vacant seat for Tom Davies who was on Jimmy's left. Lee and I were getting along splendidly over our shrimp cocktails, when finally Tom Davies showed up. He came to my side, greeted everyone at the table and apologized for his tardiness. He knelt down, so that his lips were close to my ear, "Christina, may I see you in private for a moment?"

"Sure."

We excused ourselves and I followed Tom to a private corner of the lobby, "I'm sorry I'm so late, but I was waiting to personally verify this information myself. First, just this afternoon I had my source present in a meeting which was held by Frank and all his sinister friends. The bill is finally finished, and they are going to hold off trying to pass it until they see if Ronald Feagan wins this November's election. If he does, they plan to bring their proposal to the Senate floor for a vote in April of 1981."

With curiosity, "What does the bill consist of?"

"I don't know that, but there is one man who might know. He's running for a Republican Senate seat here in New York in this November's elections. He also happens to be the most sought after mind on Wall Street."

With excitement in my voice I asked, "Who is it?" as I thought, "Ah, a challenge!"

Lowering his voice just enough to heighten the suspense, "You happen to be sitting beside him tonight."

With a look of surprise, "Do you mean to tell me Lee Bradford is running for the Senate, and he's also the top man on Wall Street?"

Proudly he replied, "You got it, Boss!"

I kissed his check, "Good work Tom, you can expect a nice bonus for this one. Please, would you do me another favor?"

This beautiful, strong, intelligent, black man, looked at me through eyes of pure infatuation, "You name it Christina, and I'll do it."

"Great! I want to know everything there is to know about Mr. Lee Bradford." On that note, we returned to our table.

As I took my seat beside Lee, I mischievously thought, "This is too good to be true! I don't even smell a challenge! This one is going to be like taking candy from a baby."

Over dinner, Lee once again enchanted me with his brilliance, as well as his remarkable command of the English language. As we spoke, the fact that we were attracted to one another was once again beginning to flare-up between us, as we found ourselves remembering one very romantic night, not so long ago.

After dinner, Lee and I were dancing romantically in each other's arms, when, with a look of deep sincerity he said, "Christina, I have dreamed of a moment like this since our night together. You are truly the most remarkable and beautiful woman I've ever had the honor of meeting."

I gazed warmly into his eyes as he spoke these words, then seductively thanked him, "Lee that means so much to me coming from you. I think you're pretty special too." I kissed him tenderly, "I have remembered our night quite often myself."

We were arm in arm, as we walked off the dance floor, and when we reached our table after that dance, we could see no one else.

As Lee slid my chair out for me I asked, "Do you live around here, Lee?"

"I have a home in a quaint little town called Gardener."

"That sounds like a lovely town, are there gardens all around?"

"A few, would you like to see them?"

Devilishly I grinned, as I moved my head close to his to whisper, "That and much, much, more."

"Well, what are we waiting for?"

I laughed playfully, "For you to get around asking me!"

We informed those at our table that we were departing for the night and proceeded to walk out through the crowd together smiling all the way, which unbeknownst to us, became the talk of the rest of the evening, according to Jimmy.

When we reached Lee's car in the parking lot, it was a cute silver sports car, with red interior. As I buckled my seat belt I said, "This is a nice car Lee, what kind is it?"

He pulled out of the hotel driveway, "It's a 1980 Honda Prelude."

I looked at him strangely, "It's very nice Lee, but a foreign car? Couldn't that be politically embarrassing for you, considering I hear you're running for a seat in the U.S. Senate?"

He laughed, "When the American companies start building better cars I'll start buying them again. It's my own little protest and I'm a man who stands on principle."

I smiled, "You've made your point quite well, I'm impressed," and we laughed.

When we arrived at Lee's home, it was an elegant, two storied old white farmhouse. As we got out of the car, a 'town car' pulled in behind us and Lee said, "I wonder who that is?"

I replied nonchalantly, "It's only my bodyguards; I pay them to tail me."

"Not bad!"

Then we entered his home. Our tour went from the front door to the bedroom where I proceeded to passionately rip his clothes off with one hand, mine with the other hand, while my lips were glued to his. It wasn't easy, but I was triumphant.

The rest of that night was spent in sexual and emotional bliss. It felt familiar, warm, and exciting to be making love to this man. The heat of our passion was so intense that Lee began to cry with tears of joy as he said, "Christina, I love you with all my heart. I have since my eyes first met yours."

With those words I melted, and I knew I would be safe from Frank in the arms of this powerful, gentle, loving man, and I found myself replying to his words of love in kind, "I love you too, Lee, I have also known that from the beginning."

After I told Lee that I loved him too, he went wild with passion. Our love making was phenomenal and we became one in the heat of our passion that night.

The next morning, we found ourselves on Lee's personal jet. We were heading to Las Vegas, to be wed that very day. When we returned to New York, we were newlyweds. It was Monday morning when I called a meeting of my staff in my suite at the Plaza. Jimmy almost fell off his chair when I introduced Lee to them all and announced that we were just married. Jimmy turned red as a beet as I began handing everyone in the room a list of assignments and said, "These are all the things I want done by December 10th, you all have detailed assignments and I'm leaving Jimmy in charge while I go on the campaign trail with my new husband."

That's when Jimmy interjected, with his jaws clenched tightly, "May I speak with you for a minute please Christina? **In private!**"

I followed Jimmy into the master bedroom and he went off, "Have you gone off the fucking wall again? I can't believe you married him! What the hell is the matter with you?"

Quite innocently I replied, "First of all that was very rude Jimmy and second I'm in love with him. So now what's your problem?"

He looked at me like I was crazy, "Give up the act, *please* Christina, you're only kidding yourself. I spoke with Tom Davies the other night. I know how important this Lee character is to you. Can't you see you *did it* again?"

"What are you talking about, Jimmy?"

He shook his head, "It sounds very familiar Christina, it's the same reason you married Tony. Just because he was someone you could manipulate. Shit! It seems like I'm talking to myself here!"

"That's not fair Jimmy," I protested. "I have never judged your actions. I have always stuck by you and loved you, no matter what you did." I looked at him with hurt in my eyes, "I always thought you felt the same way about me."

"I'm sorry Christina it's just that you do this to me every time. You get us in over our heads with work, then you leave me a list of orders and off you go on another tangent."

I kissed him lovingly, "That's because I know you can handle it. I'm being called in another direction right now Jimmy, but I'll be back."

He returned my kiss and with that flick of his wrist said, "Go follow your dreams, Christina. I'll be waiting here for you because I love you, girl."

"I'm not going away, Jimmy, I will be coming in to help you. I just won't be moving into the new house on the complex grounds with you, but I'll still only be ten minutes away. I'm moving in with Lee and the campaign is only in New York State." We said goodbye and I was off with my new husband on the **New York State campaign trail**.

CHAPTER 14. I REMEMBER LEE

On Tuesday, October 2nd, 1980, the day we should have left for our honeymoon, it was straight to the campaign trail with my new husband instead. Lee was an incredible man, and I was determined to make this relationship work. I truly wanted to be a good wife to Lee. I thought, "This wonderful, loving, gentle, powerful man loves me, and he deserves the best I can give him." Then my thoughts turned to revenge, "Besides, Lee doesn't know it yet, but he's going to be my ace in the hole against Frank."

You see, Lee was the owner of one of the most profitable corporations in the world, and he was one of only a handful of men who were wealthy enough and smart enough to defeat an all-out corporate assault from Salerno Incorporated. This little bit of information I discovered via a phone conversation I had with Tom Davies **from Lee's home,** the Sunday morning just before I proposed to Lee and swept **his ass off to 'Vegas'** to be wed.

It all happened like this. That Sunday morning after our night of love making, I climbed out of Lee's bed at 8:00am and went to find the kitchen so I could surprise him with breakfast in bed. As I was cooking, something told me to call Tom Davies at the Holiday Inn in Kingston, so I did.

Tom did not seem happy when he answered the phone with a groggy, "Hello."

But he perked up with my cheerful, "Good morning Tom. It's me, Christina! Sorry to wake you, but I just had a feeling I should call you."

Clearing his voice he excitedly said, "Great, I was hoping you were going to come back last night."

"I had something to do; so, what's up?"

His voice held an air of urgency, "I received a call last night and discovered what the bill contains."

With a pleased excitement I exclaimed, "That's great Tom! Tell me, what does it say?"

"I'll sum it up like this," he began. "Right now, as the law stands, no corporation has to be listed on the stock exchange unless it sells stock to the public first. The other main provision in the law is that anyone can hold as much of a corporation's stock as they wish. This gives a holder of 51% or more of a corporation's stock, controlling interest in that corporation and the right to sit as the Head of the Board of Directors." Then he stopped, "Are you still with me?"

"I'm with you Tom, keep talking."

He spoke direct and clear, "The new law if passed will make every corporation with cash holdings of at least five-million-dollars, register on the public stock market. Then it will require that no one officer of a corporation be allowed to hold more than 49% of a corporation's stock, thus leaving no one officer, or stock holder, in total control of any corporation."

Through a voice of deep concern I asked, "So knowing this Tom, what do you think Frank's up to?"

With a reply of disbelief he continued, "It's so simplistic it's ingenious. Once he gets this law passed, you will be forced to scale down your personal stock to a holding of only 49%, which leaves you with only a 49% controlling interest of the corporation as well. Then he will attempt to acquire the remaining 49% for himself, with probably one of his puppets acquiring at least 2% of the stock, or as much as they can get, thus giving him controlling interest in Powers Incorporated. Then he could conceivably throw you out on your rear, leaving you humiliated."

Through intense anxiety I exclaimed, "Holy shit! Is there any way we can stop him?"

He sighed, "Well first, before the law is passed, make damn sure you give your stock to someone you can trust, because

Salerno Incorporated has a cash holding of somewhere around sixty-six-billion-dollars. This gives him the financial power to convince most stock holders to sell. He also has been known to use other means of persuasion in the past. He's no one to play with. If he gets this bill passed Christina, he could crush Powers Incorporated in one day on the open stock market."

Feeling overwhelmed, I asked in desperation, "So what should I do?"

His reply was less than comforting, "First, I guess would be to try to stop the bill from passing. If you can't do that, then you need to be asking Mr. Bradford that question. He happens to be one of only a few men on Wall Street with the clout and smarts to stop Frank."

With a slight sigh of relief, "Thank you again, Tom. I'll take it from here, but keep your eyes and ears open.

After that conversation I thought, "I do have a few Senators I could call on and it couldn't hurt to be married to one." So I proceeded to serve Lee breakfast in bed and I once again made passionate love to him. After which I proposed. Don't get me wrong! That's not the only reason I married Lee, but that is why I married him as fast as I did. You see, I knew all along I had a love for Lee. I also knew it could grow in time and I wanted it to. To be truthful, I was tired of fighting, and I was still afraid of Frank. I needed someone to love and take care of me for a change and I knew Lee was that someone; or I would not have married him. I also knew I could help him win his bid for a senate seat. Well, I was banking on it anyway.

When I joined Lee's campaign as Mrs. Bradford, he was six points behind his opponent, the incumbent Senator Joe Olympus. But within two weeks of our marriage and my joining Lee on the campaign trail, he was 10 points ahead of his opponent. Lee and I toured the state together, from the tip of Long Island to Niagara Falls. We campaigned in every city across the state, and the size of the crowds we drew was unheard of for a senate election. It was a wonderfully exciting experience to be on the campaign trail with Lee, because Lee was brilliant! He knew all the issues and he addressed them with finesse every time.

When he was finished wooing the crowds, I would take center stage and add my unique style and glamor into the arena. Lee's distinguished charms and the fact that the incomparable *Christina Powers* was now his new wife helped to attract the attention of the whole world to us as a couple. It felt great to be in a positive spotlight for a change. I got high on it!

It's true that the entire month of October we worked night and day, but it didn't stop me from 'seducing' Lee, every chance I got. Being around Lee's powerful and brilliant energy all day long left me electrified all night long. Lee was proper with everything he did, even during our love making. I found myself having to be the aggressor every night, but once I got him started he was a tiger.

One night after one such encounter, we were lying in bed together and Lee's body felt tense. I grabbed some hand cream, rolled him on his belly and began to massage his back. After a few minutes of this I asked, "Is this helping, Lee?"

He turned around to look up at me and lovingly replied, "It sure is, Christina! I love it, and I love you," as he ran his hand through my long, thick, black hair.

I leaned forward, kissed him softly, "I'm so happy you love me Lee, because your love has given me a reason to live again."

He had a glow in his eyes, "We make a great team together, you and I." Then he kissed me again, "One day I plan to be President of this country of ours and you will be the First Lady. Together we will make this nation greater than it has ever been. Christina, I truly believe our government needs to be run like I run Bradford Computers. That's why I decided ten years ago that I would make the Presidency be my life's goal, and now that we are together I am more determined than ever to achieve that goal."

As he finished speaking words of love, I gazed tenderly into his eyes, "I do love you Lee and I admire you so much. I truly believe that you will achieve that goal and I will be right beside you all the way to the White House. I promise." I kissed him, "Now you get some sleep. We have a busy day tomorrow."

He returned my kiss, "Goodnight," and rolled over.

As Lee drifted off to sleep, I started to do what became my nightly ritual. First I spent one hour on my manuscript, then I would plug in my language tapes and for the next hour I'd study a new language.

Then it came, November 4th, Election Day 1980 and by 9:00pm that night Lee was giving his acceptance speech to the cheers of the crowd, with me standing right beside him. He was elected senator by a whopping 62%, of the total vote. The celebration which followed Lee's speech was spectacular and the party was held at the corporate headquarters of Bradford Computers in Fishkill, New York. It was sometime around 11:00pm when Lee and I snuck out of the party and headed for Lee's car. Lee had decided his staff could handle the party from here; because he wanted to take me to his beach house in New Hampshire, for a one week honeymoon.

As we drove, we spoke with renewed vitality of our future dreams. We were high together on Lee's victory and our love was stronger than ever.

We arrived at the beach house sometime around 2:00am and we were wide awake. There was a brisk, cold, breeze blowing off the Atlantic Ocean, which felt clean and refreshing as we climbed out of the car and headed toward the house. When we climbed into bed that night, I placed my head on Lee's chest and began to softly nibble on his nipple. Then for the first time since our love making began, Lee became the aggressor. He gently placed his hand on the back of my head and began to forcefully guide my head down the length of his body until my lips reached the head of his wet, throbbing, manhood. I became so excited by his show of sexual aggression and manliness that I devoured him until his body became electrified. He held my head and rammed his hips forward, burying himself deep within the warmth of my longing lips. He screamed out in ecstasy as he exploded again and again flooding my sense of taste with his nectar.

Shortly after our love making, I felt that the time was right to finally question Lee on certain issues. So as he held me in his arms I softly said, "Lee, I want to ask you something. Do you remember the bill I told you that Frank will be trying to pass in the Senate this year?"

He gently stroked my head, "Yes, I remember. Why do you ask?"

I positioned myself to gaze into his eyes and with curiosity asked, "Just suppose that bill passes and a corporation like Powers Incorporated tried to take controlling interest of Bradford Computers from you. What would you do?"

With a slightly arrogant tone, "First of all, Powers Incorporated couldn't orchestrate a corporate takeover of Bradford Computers, because it's not established enough to do so."

I gave him a cocky smile, "What if it was? What would you do?"

He chuckled, "You still couldn't do it."

"Why not?" I protested with frustration.

He laughed at me, "Because I wouldn't let you get away with it. I'd stop you first, that's why."

I gently bit his nipple, "You're still not answering my question smart ass. How would you stop me?"

"Okay! Okay!" He answered, as he pulled away from my teeth. He rolled over on top of me and proceeded to give me three scenarios of how someone might try to take over the corporation if the law were to pass. He told how he would stop each one. I listened ever carefully as he explained each maneuver he would take to stop a corporate takeover. As he talked, I was amazed at how sharp this man's mind truly was.

The week we spent in New Hampshire together was the most romantic time I'd spent with anyone since Tony. We laughed, played, and had fun. It was as if we were children again, and we enjoyed one another as we basked in each other's growing love. Then with the blink of an eye, I realized one day, that it was working. I had finally overcome the devastations I had suffered over the past three years of my life, and I was excited to be alive again. I decided at that moment, Lee and I would truly live in the White House one day, and I was going to see to it!

As soon as we arrived back home, it was straight to work. We had two months to get things in New York settled with both our companies, before taking on the Washington life style. So we busted our buns together to get the job done. Before we started our new dual residency life style, between New York and Washington, D.C., we knew everything there was to know in order for either one of us, to run the other's companies'. Lee was a genius at saving time, money, and manpower, in the way he ran Bradford Computers. I took every advantage of his expertise, and implemented many of his corporate secrets straight into Powers Incorporation. Lee and I also decided to enter a joint business venture together, separate from our parent companies. I took two of my eighteen buildings and equipped them to produce computer components to supply Bradford Computers directly from our own subsidiary.

December 10th, we celebrated my twenty-fifth birthday by opening the new offices and home of Powers Incorporated to the business world. After two and a half months of hard work and two-billion-dollars in the red, my complex was 76% in use with a staff of six-thousand employees. We had films underway and records being produced in one of the main hubs. We had one hub strictly for producing computer components with research labs adjacent to the manufacturing buildings. I also decided to create a chain of corporate owned radio stations, which would link the entire country directly to me. There was no way my music would ever be taken off the air before its time again, and I was going to make sure of that. I knew that with my new business endeavors I could pay off the debt in two years. Then, I would see the real profits of my soon to be Mega Empire. This knowledge helped to make my party that evening the most exciting birthday party I'd known in years.

After my party, it was off to Washington, D.C., where Lee and I began to make ourselves familiar with the Capital region. We bought a modest, but elegant brownstone in Georgetown. We made it a point to get acquainted with a number of influential, political, operatives as we plunged feet first into the Washington scene. You see, I knew I had four months to muster all the support necessary in the Senate to offset Frank's expected assault, and I was wasting no time in getting that support. NO MATTER WHAT THE COST!

I worked us extra hard and it took us about two months to learn the Washington ropes. And when we did, we were great at it.

Lee and I were racing the clock in an attempt to be sure footed before April 1st, 1981, arrived; which would be the date when Senator Welm would introduce Frank's-sponsored bill to the Senate Floor for a vote. Senator Welm was only giving the senators one month to study the bill, which would be brought to 'the floor' for a vote on April 23rd.

April 15th, rolled around faster than we could imagine. Lee was scrambling around the senate floor all that day in a desperate attempt to estimate the final outcome of the vote. When Lee and I met at home that evening it was around 9:00pm. Just as we sat down for our normal late dinner, he said, "Well, I have a final count on next week's vote." My heart began to pound as I anxiously asked, "So, what is it?"

With a frustrated tone he continued, "With all our joint pull, we are still down by one swing vote."

"One vote, it's that close! There must be someone's vote we can swing!"

Lee answered guardedly, "Tom Kenney's I thought, but when I approached him about it, he turned me down flat."

With a sense of optimism I replied, "I know Tom, I met him a few years ago. I'll try to speak with him tomorrow."

Lee had a concerned expression, "I wish you wouldn't do that, he has a reputation with women."

I confidently chuckled, "Lee, you're talking to *Christina Powers*, there's not a man alive I can't handle."

He began to shake his head 'no' as he spoke in a demanding tone, "I know Tom too, and I don't want you to speak with him at all. It will look as if I sent you to him."

With a surprised expression, "Lee, don't be ridiculous. You know as well as I do what Frank will do to Powers Incorporated if this law passes."

Lackadaisically he cockled, "So what, I have more than enough for both of us."

I became instantly outraged by his chauvinistic reply and I showed it sharply, "Why you snob! What a selfish thing to say. I've worked my fingers to the bone to build Powers Incorporated and I'm not letting anyone take it from me! So I'm sorry if I blemish your ego, but I can't let this bill pass! Now, I am calling Tom tomorrow because he is a friend of mine, not because you are sending me. Even if you were sending me, we would be doing the same thing we've been doing since we got married, which I thought was working together to accomplish a mutual goal."

His attitude resembled Frank's as he shouted, "If you go, I will be very upset with you, Christina!"

I immediately stood up from my seat, "Oh really! Well that's your choice honey, but I must do this and you, as my husband should understand that!" With that I stormed straight to the bedroom, grabbed his pillow, a blanket, threw them at him just as he reached the door, slammed it in his face and locked it.

The next morning I called Senator Kenney's office and I was immediately transferred directly to Tom. He answered the phone, "Christina Powers, it's so good to hear from you. I've been hoping to run into you now that you're living in town."

With a pleasant tone I answered, "Well thank you, Tom. I'm sorry it has taken me so long to give you a call, but Lee and I have been very busy since we arrived."

"I know, I've been watching you from afar and I must say you're quite an impressive woman. You jumped right in the first day and made yourself right at home here in our nation's capital with no trouble at all."

"Now I'm impressed, I had no idea you were such a fan of mine."

He chuckled a little, "I've been your biggest fan since I first met you, Christina. Maybe even 'bigger' then your husband."

I chuckled first then seductively, "Tom that could be interpreted in many ways. But that's not quite why I called you. I really need to speak to you in private as soon as possible. Can that be arranged?"

With an excited tone he assured me, "I can arrange almost anything I want to, how about this afternoon for lunch?"

"That would be wonderful."

"Why don't you meet me at my private suite at the Radisson, suite 1210. Say promptly 1:30. Will that do?"

"That will do nicely Tom, I'll see you there," I answered, with a slightly seductive tone.

That afternoon as I rode the elevator to the 12th floor, I told myself, "Whatever happens here today, just remember its only business. As long as you can stop Frank, you do whatever you have to."

I wore a bright smile, as Tom answered the doorbell, to match my bright spring colored outfit. As I entered Tom's suite, I spotted one of my bodyguards standing by the elevator and I felt like I was being spied on instead of guarded, but I still gave Tom a big hug when I saw him.

Over our lunch, I told Tom exactly what I wanted from him and he was not surprised. As we finished our lunch he said, "Christina, your uncle would become quite upset if I did what you're asking of me."

With an air of confidence, "You're a big boy you can handle a little heat from Frank. He'll get over it the next time he needs your vote." I reached across the table, took his hand and seductively added, "Tom, this means much more to me than it does to Frank, and I promise I will remember the favor graciously."

His eyes lit up and I could see him start to sweat as he tried to calmly say, "Please allow me to inquire just how important is this to you?"

I looked him dead in the eyes, and turned up the heat with a sensual, "It's very important to me Tom, so let's not play any more games. If your appetite for me is worth your vote, then I will completely satisfy that hunger." Tom took me in his arms, and the moment he did I screamed in my mind, "Lord, God, forgive me!" Then, I proceeded to earn his vote, as once again I degraded my flesh to save my ass from Frank. I did not think of Lee once as I had political, animalistic sex with my biological uncle. I told myself, it's strictly a smart business agreement. The kind my men always keep. When I left Tom's office, I left with his vote, but I sure didn't feel like celebrating. I was sick to my stomach. 'Oh by the way!' Tom wasn't as 'big' a fan as he professed to be.

That evening when Lee arrived home from work, he was definitely not himself. He acted as if he knew exactly what had happened. But I held my cool. He was not going to see the guilt in my eyes, no matter how hard he stared at me over that speechless dinner. I was a Hollywood Queen; I couldn't believe he even tried. No one has ever been able to read me unless I let them, and I was not letting him in my mind this time. I could tell by the way he was acting, if he ever found out, it would destroy us; so, I decided at that moment I would have to lie to him if he should ever ask. Finally he spoke up, "So tell me, how did you make-out with Tom today?"

Nonchalantly I volunteered, "Very well thank you, he is going to give us his support."

This time he asked point blank, "Did you sleep with him?"

I became offended, "Don't ever ask me a question like that again."

He stood up from his seat and yelled, "I can't believe this! It's true! You're nothing but a sick, painted up, lying, slut."

I leaped out of my seat and slapped him across his face with the might of my anger, as I viciously shouted, "Don't you dare speak to me like that! You knew how much that vote meant to me; so, if this was some stupid bet between the two of you, then you lose. And you think I'm the sick one! Well look again you egotistical prick. I can't believe a man with your character would place his wife in a position like that, and then call me the sick one for doing what I had to do to save my corporation. Lee, you would have let me lose everything just to save your ego. I think that's what's sick, not what I did!" I grabbed my bag and headed for the door.

When I reached it, Lee yelled with a demanding tone, "Where do you think you're going?"

I stopped, turned to look at him and sarcastically yelled, "Oh go fly a kite, asshole!" And I walked out.

Two days after my victory over Frank by the defeat of his bill on the Senate Floor, Lee and I were back together. We decided that our love would overcome our faults. Only Lee was never quite the same with me again. He refused to see his own part in the whole thing and he never truly forgave me. As for me, my image of Lee being my knight in shining armor faded fast. We still kept up the appearances of the happy newlyweds, at least for the public. Oh, we tried, but every time we had the smallest spat he would throw it up in my face again.

We lived like this until November 13th, 1981. I could take the fighting no longer, so I decided to move back to our home in New York. I figured we needed some space and time to try to mend this marriage. Besides, my new manuscript 'The Innocence of Deceit' was finished and Powers Incorporated was also in need of a financial shot in the arm, so it was time to go back to work. I grabbed one bottle of champagne and it was back to New York, only by myself this time.

November 13th, turned out to be another one of those days I would never forget, for many reasons. I got off the plane at 7:00pm that night at Stewart Airport in Newburgh, and the weather was cold to the bone and rainy. As soon as I entered the airport, I was met by Mickey Winslow. He was Lee's vice-president at Bradford Computers. He handed me an envelope, "Christina, Lee needs you to call him at this number from a pay phone before you leave the airport."

I opened the envelope and there was a phone number on a plain white sheet of paper and another with a list of accounts receivable. I looked up at Mickey, "What's this all about?"

With a mysterious tone he spoke under his breath, "All I know is I was to give this to you personally; then disappear." Then he looked at me as if I was stupid, "So you haven't seen me, understand?"

I looked at him as if he were an ass hole, "Not really, but you can disappear now."

I headed for a phone booth, dialed the number and Lee answered with a mysterious nervousness to his voice, "Christina, is that you?"

"Of course it's me Lee, what's going on?" I answered slightly annoyed.

Still with the nervous voice, "I had you call me on a public phone just in case my lines are tapped."

"Tapped, why would the lines be tapped?"

This time his voice began to shake, "Listen to me. I'm in a little trouble and I really need your help right now."

Immediately, I became concerned, "This sounds serious, what's wrong Lee?"

I could tell he was trembling, "I've just found out that all my financial records will be subpoenaed first thing in the morning by a Grand Jury, appointed by the Ways and Means Committee. They're investigating my personal and business finances and there is one item I can't afford to have them find. Christina, I have to be able to trust you completely before saying anymore"

With an annoyed baffled tone, I sharply reminded him, "Lee, this is me you're talking to; I shouldn't have to say any more."

Nervously he began, "Okay, I need you to go to my office at Bradford Computers. Go in my safe and take out the black leather binder. Take the binder and hide it until I ask you for it. Christina, don't have anything in your hands when you sign in at the security office, or going out. You will probably be questioned as to why you were there, so I am asking you to lie for me, if you're called before the Grand Jury." Neither one of us said anything for a moment, then he added, "Will you be able to do this for me?"

I swallowed hard, "Yes Lee, I will lie for you."

With a sigh of relief, "Thank you Christina--you're saving my ass. Okay, there is a list of accounts in the envelope Mickey gave you. Take them and update the files in my office. This will give you a reason for having been there. I know it's a shabby alibi, but it will do. Then, hide the binder on your person and get out with it. Christina, before I give you the safe number, I'm asking you to trust me with one more thing?"

I answered reassuringly, "Lee, you don't have to say it again, I'm here for you."

With an obvious tone of self-shame he continued, "Whatever you do, don't open the binder. It's something I don't even want you to know about."

With an uneasy tone and a feeling of apprehension, "All right, Lee. I'll do exactly what you ask." Then I hung up the phone and it was off to Bradford Computers.

I climbed into my rented town-car and drove through the downpour of that dark, cold, night until I reached the Corporate Headquarters where I proceeded to follow Lee's instructions to the 'T'.

As I drove through the rain with Lee's binder in my possession I thought, "If this thing is that hot, I can't hide it in my office. Where the hell am I going to hide this?"

I was on route 9W heading north from Newburgh to Milton, and the road was wet and slick. As soon as I left the city limits of Newburgh, the road seemed to become desolate and it was only 8:00pm. From out of nowhere a bright set of headlights began to blind me from behind and I thought, "What the hell is this asshole doing?" just as it rammed me in the ass end and my head jerked forward. My heart instantly began to pound as I received a second jolt. The vehicle started to pull up along-side of me and I heard, "Bang! Bang!" I screamed as my side window shattered.

I screamed again as I floored the car and swerved toward what I could now see was a large pickup truck. I smashed its front quarter panel with the rear of my car in an attempt to force it off the road. It crashed back into me as we both accelerated. We were reaching speeds of 80 miles an hour, as we rounded slippery curves and past other vehicles. We reached a stretch in the road where it became a four-lane highway and I pushed the-peddle to the floor! My blood was racing through my veins as this truck attempted to pull up alongside of me at a 100 miles an hour. I turned to glance at it quickly and I could see the barrel of a large gun pop out of the passenger side window. I screamed and began to swerve the car from side to side. With fear in my eyes, I glanced down at the speedometer and even at 110, I still could not get away from this truck. Then, I caught the flashing of headlights in my rear-view mirror, so I slammed on the brakes and screamed as the car spun out of control. I struggled with the wheel until I finally regained control of the vehicle. I was shaking like a jack hammer as I brought the car to a stop. My heart froze again as I saw both the other vehicles whip around in the road ahead of me and start speeding right toward me again. I screamed in horror, "Oh God!" as I popped the car into reverse and spun around. I threw it in drive and hit the gas just as these two speeding vehicles slammed into the back of my car, causing the three vehicles to become wedged together as we all spun off the road.

I was freaking when we all came to a stop together. I grabbed the black leather binder, opened the door of my car and started to run away as fast as I could. Then, I heard someone holler, "Mrs. Bradford, get down!" I stopped running, turned to look behind me, and saw four men climbing out of the other two vehicles. One of the men from the pickup aimed a shotgun at me. I screamed in utter terror as I immediately threw myself onto the wet grass, trying not to be shot. Just as I hit the ground I heard, 'BANG' as one of the men from the car shot the man from the truck, just before he shot at me. The driver of the truck pulled a pistol from his pocket and began to shoot at the man who just shot his partner. As he was shooting, the other man from the car jumped out from what seemed like nowhere and landed on top of the man with the gun. I was shaking so badly, I could not move as I watched this take place right in front of me. I could see them fighting horribly, until finally the man from the truck was lying unconscious on the ground. When the fight was over, this man hollered over to me, "Mrs. Bradford, are you all right?"

I ran to the man who had just finished fighting for my life and I leaped into his arms crying. I was so shook up, I could hardly think of what to do next. I managed to get a hold of myself with the help of this extremely handsome man and I was finally able to say, "I hope you guys work for me?"

The man holding me smiled and said gallantly, "Yes, Mrs. Bradford, we're part of that team of pesky shadows you have lurking in the background."

I kissed his cheek gratefully, "Well, I'm sure glad you were here tonight."

Confidently he replied, "I'm Michael Gillespie, I've been your chief security agent for six months now, and it's nice to finally meet you."

A little more relaxed I smiled, as I saw the lights of police cars coming down the road, "I'm glad you're in my shadows, Michael." I turned to them both, "You guys do your jobs very well. It's reassuring to know my money has been well spent."

Just as the Troopers pulled up, I slipped the binder under my clothing concealing it, and it was off to the State Police Barracks.

After we were questioned by the State Police, I called James to come pick us up. He took the three of us to the Powers Complex. As we drove, I thanked Michael and his partner John once again for saving my life. I had James take us to the main garage, and give Michael the keys to one of the corporate cars. As the two men began to climb out of the limo from the other door, I felt myself compelled to reach out and embrace Michael one more time, and in that one more embrace, I felt as if I never wanted to let go of this strong, handsome man. After our embrace, I thought, "I wish I didn't have to let this one get away." Then he was out of sight.

He was adorable. Every inch of his five-feet-ten-inch tall, one-hundred and seventy-pound, firm strong body, was all man. He had well-trimmed blond hair, beautiful blue eyes and a splendidly shaped face. His lips looked moist and hot, the kind that I knew could melt a girl's heart.

James turned to me, "Are you ready to go home now?"

"Take me to my office first James."

When I opened the door to my office at Powers Incorporated, I turned on the light, walked over to my desk, and sat down. I slipped the black leather binder out from under my clothing, at which time I opened it and there were some papers and a computer disk. First, I began to read the pages which had a list of top-secret government accounts with billion-dollar figures written next to each one. I made copies of the papers, after which I tried to access the disk, but it kept asking for a password code. So I tried to copy the disk onto an identical one, and it seemed to work. I took the original papers along with the copied disk and placed them back in the binder exactly the way I'd found them. Then I sealed the binder in a large envelope.

When I returned to the limo, I had the binder and three other envelopes. I climbed in and I told James to take me to the bus station in Kingston. As he started the car I said, "James, take this envelope and keep it in a safe place." I grabbed his hand before he pulled away from the curb and with a desperate tone, "You must never let anyone know you have this." Looking uneasily into his eyes, "James, the only thing I want you to do with this is to see that it gets to the FBI if anything strange should happen to me."

He looked at me with concern as he swallowed hard, "God forbid anything should happen to you Christina, but I will do exactly as you wish."

He took me to the bus station, where I had James rent two lock boxes. I instructed him to place the now sealed binder in one box and the other envelope in another. Then, I had him take us to Jimmy's. As we drove, I thought, "Holy shit! I can't believe Lee would actually do this. This is the kind of information people in the business world would kill for, but what's on this disk," I wondered. Then I thought, "God! I hope I get away with this one!"

James dropped me off at the front door of Jimmy's place around 11:40pm that night. He was living at the home I had built for him and myself on the grounds of the Powers Complex. We named it 'Executive House.' I was truly looking forward to seeing Jimmy and everyone else. Although I had been in touch with Jimmy over the phone on a daily basis, I had not seen him or any of my staff since my birthday. When Jimmy opened the door and I saw him, my heart was struck with fear. You see, the entire time from the day I went on the campaign trail with Lee to that very minute, I had not thought of, or even mentioned the 'gay plague' once. I pushed it out of my mind and totally forgot about it! It was as if it never existed until I saw how ill Jimmy was when he opened the door.

Jimmy looked terrible. He was thin and he had the same skin blotches on his face that Bobby had when he died. I immediately dropped my hand bag and hugged him. I started to cry, as my heart pained, "Jimmy, why didn't you tell me?"

We were holding one another in the large open foyer of the Executive House, when Jimmy's voice began to break up, "Christina, I'm scared!" crying as his fear burst out from the depths of his soul, "I don't want to die! Christina, I still love life too much. I don't want to die! Not now! Not like Bobby did!" He became hysterical and screamed out, "Please don't let me die like I let

Bobby die." Looking straight into my eyes as he cried out in anguish, "Christina, please kill me before it does!"

I grabbed him tight and with our pain and tears merging as one I cried and shouted, "No, God! Please don't take my Jimmy from me, too!"

I looked at Jimmy who now looked so much like Bobby did just before he died, that it was killing me. I screamed out again, but this time with anger, "No! God! No! This time I won't let you take him from me." From somewhere I've never touched before inside myself I felt a burst of 'Power' come over me. I shouted with authority as I placed my hands on Jimmy's head, "In the name of Jesus Christ! I command you to be healed!" As I held my hands on Jimmy, I could see a light beginning to glow from over our heads. I gazed up and the light was becoming brighter. As the light grew, I could feel the 'Power' of its pureness filling my body. The light and the feelings of awe and fear, all increased to an intensity which caused me to begin to shake and lose my balance causing both to fall to our knees. The light grew so intense that I thought I was going to die from the pure 'Power' of this Heavenly Presence and I screamed, "God! No! I can't take any more!" instantly it was gone.

I was shaking to the core when Jimmy grabbed me, slapped my face with all his might and shouted, "Christina, snap out of it!"

When I began to come around, I said, "Oh my God! Jimmy, do you think that was God?"

With a frightened expression, "Do I think what was God?"

I looked at him as if he were stupid, "The light you idiot! What else?"

His face turned white, "I didn't see any light, Christina."

Then my face turned white as I exclaimed, "Don't tell me you didn't see that light, it was all over us!"

With an honest expression he replied, "I swear, Christina, I did not see anything, no less a light."

I shook my head in disbelief as I replied with an eerie tone, "This stress is either getting to me Jimmy, or I think I'm going mad." We got off the floor, walked over to the sofa, and fell asleep in each other's arms.

The next morning I called my office and had a one hundred thousand dollar bonus placed in each of the pay envelopes of the two heroes who saved my life.

I thought of calling Michael Gillespie, but I decided that there were more important things to do then get involved with my own bodyguard right now, so I did not call.

When Jimmy woke up he wiped the sleep from his eyes and said, "I'm starving, I feel like I could eat a cow."

I looked him straight in his eyes, "Maybe it has something to do with last night, Jimmy."

His eyes grew wide, "Oh my God! I don't know what to think Christina, but I do know I feel better then I've felt in months. Could it be?"

With a spooked expression, "Never mention last night again, all right?"

"Why?"

"Because I said so," slapping the back of his head, "Go ask Carman to fix us some French toast and bacon. I'm starved too." With that Jimmy went to the kitchen and I called Lee.

When Lee answered the phone, I told him about my little run-in with my two friends from the pickup truck, and of Jimmy's condition. I had him give me the number of the director of the CDC who was a friend of his. After which I said, "Lee, I truly do care for you. If you would just stop looking at your hurt, then maybe our love will survive."

With a sincere tone, "You know I want you here with me Christina, but I'm not going to try to force you."

"Let's plan on talking this out when you come home for Christmas." Then, we said our goodbyes and I hung up the phone. I picked it right back up again and called a Mr. Chuck West, the Director of the CDC. After we chatted for a few moments, I made an appointment to meet with him for the following afternoon.

I then called Dominick Giovannetti on his private line in Rome. When he answered the phone, I said, "Hi Dominick, its Christina. Dominick, someone tried to kill me last night and I'm not sure who, or why. Can you help me?"

His Italian temper flared his anger with a heightened sense of outrage as he said, "Tell me what happened!"

I told him what took place the night before, then I said, "My security man killed one of them and the other is in the Ulster County Prison. He swears he and his partner were just disgruntled fans out for fun. The police might buy that, but I sure don't."

He replied with an authoritative tone, "I'll see what I can find out from here and I'll get back to you."

With an appreciative tone, "Thank you again, Dominick, I knew I could count on you." With that we promised to see one another soon. We said our goodbye's and I hung up the phone.

I called Dominick because I knew that as far as Dominick was concerned, I was his very special mistress. He would not let anyone get away with trying to kill me and I knew it. I was also aware if it turned out to lead back to Frank, it could cause an all-out international underground war between the two most powerful 'Mafia' leaders in the world. But, that was the chance I had to take. I had to know who ordered the hit on me. This way I could deal with them in my own way. As I was feeling this anger straight to my core, out of nowhere I once more thought about the light I thought I saw the night before and I thought, "I think I may be losing my mind!" I shrugged my shoulders to accompany my thoughts, "Oh well! I'll figure it out tomorrow!" With that it was off to the kitchen for breakfast. At least I hadn't lost my appetite.

The next morning on my office desk, I found an envelope from my insurance company, Allstate. When I opened the envelope, I discovered that their investigation into the fire was completed. There were also two checks enclosed. One was for the fire and the other was Joy's life insurance policy. They totaled thirty-two-million-dollars, and I just tossed them into my purse like pocket change. I was not ready to think about the past at that moment. I called all my best people into my office and put them to work on my soon to be fourth film, 'The Innocence of Deceit.' Then it was off to Atlanta, Georgia, and my 4:00pm meeting with Mr. Chuck West of the CDC.

I walked into Mr. West's office, exchanged greetings, sat down and I got right to the point, "Mr. West, please tell me exactly what is being done to stop this disease from killing more people?"

Bluntly he replied, "Mrs. Bradford, on the record I won't talk to you, but off the record I will."

I was surprised by his response, "Please call me Christina, and start talking off the record."

He began with a tone of urgency, "We think it is a sexually transmitted virus of some kind, but we have still not been able to identify any new virus as of yet."

I was taken back with his reply and it showed on my face, "If you know that it is transmitted sexually, then why has no one in the public been told about it yet, and what's being done to find this virus?"

Shaking his head in disgust, "You have to look at your current administration to find the answer to those questions."

"What do you mean?" I asked with a puzzled tone.

Sounding completely frustrated he answered, "The Feagan Administration has put a lid on all out going information from this place. It has also cut our budget so badly we can't even purchase the type of highly sensitive electronic microscope which is needed to even try to find the virus."

With a tone of shock I swiftly replied, "Do you mean to tell me almost a year has passed since the elections and no one has made any progress at all toward finding this disease?"

His expression turned sad, "I hate to say it, but as long as it's only killing gays, the funding is not coming from this administration to find it."

Immediately I opened my purse, pulled out thirty two million dollars in insurance checks, signed them, handed them to Chuck, "Use this to buy what you need. I'll make a deal with you; you find this killer and stop it. As for me, I think it's time to move some political mountains."

As I walked out of Chuck's office, I decided it was time to declare **war on this unknown killer**.

CHAPTER 15. TRUE SOUL MATES

The pace of the next few years was incredible! Between work, a long distance marriage, my all-out attack on the government for not being truthful to the nation about this dreaded disease, my frequent FBI questioning and numerous days of sitting in front of a Grand Jury, I thought I was going crazy. When I wasn't in a Washington Court House, I was in an Ulster County Court House testifying against the man who tried to kill me. How I made it through those days only God knows. Not only did I go out on the limb with the Grand Jury for Lee, but I also put the financial holdings of Powers Incorporated on the line for him as well. The day the Grand Jury probe was announced Bradford Computers stock began to plummet. I had to personally guarantee Bradford Computers stock holders, Powers Incorporated would cover all losses which might result from any negative publicity due to the Grand Jury probe. This was the only thing which kept most of them from panic selling. It was so intense; I hardly had any time to breathe. Whenever I tried to sneak off to collect my thoughts, I would be swamped by the press. As hard as I looked in those days for a place to find some peace, there was none to be found. I was being pulled in so many directions; I don't know how my nerves held up, especially since I chose not to fall back on my old friend, cocaine.

The only time I found any sense of sanity at all was when Lee and I were alone, which was not very often. You see, when Lee and I spent that Christmas together in 1981, just after the FBI began to come around, we had finally decided we were truly in love and that our marriage could survive anything as long as we continued to love one another. That Christmas, Lee was back to his wonderful loving self. He told me he was wrong and sorry for what he had done. He asked me to forgive him and I did the same. After that Christmas, I had my husband back and I knew it. He promised, together we will make it through the Grand Jury probe, and onto the White House. It was at that point we went from this warm, loving, Christmas, straight into the **Fires of Hell**.

Although the years between January 1982, and January 1985, were hectic, there were still some very good things happening. **First** and foremost, Jimmy's health slowly began to improve and with pressure from the American people, along with Lee and me, the 'gay plague' was finally given a name on January 4th, 1983. It was called, 'Acquired Immune Deficiency Syndrome,' 'AIDS' for short. Then, in October of `83, the AIDS Virus was discovered and shortly after a blood test to detect the HIV antibodies in the human body was developed.

Jimmy took the test on February 6th, 1984, and on February 16th, Jimmy and I both went to find out the test results together. To our complete amazement and relief Jimmy's test results were negative. As we hugged each other and jumped up and down with joy, neither one of us mentioned that night in November of 1981. We were just grateful for an answered prayer!

Second, my career was soaring. I had written and starred in three blockbusters, which I rode all the way to the bank. I also released six platinum albums and I had created my own cable television network called, 'Radio, Video, TV.' When videos first came out onto the market, I decided to record live performances and air them twenty four hours a day over my new cable network. It was a long shot, but I was a gambling woman. My personal financial success helped Powers Incorporated get back in the black again. We managed to pay off our debts as I planned, but it wasn't as easy as I thought. By January 1985, our cash holdings had only grown to three billion dollars. But as I said, we were debt free.

Third, lucky for all of us, I found out in March of `83, that Frank had nothing to do with the assassination attempt on my life. According to Dominick Giovanetti it was not meant to be an assassination attempt at all. Dominick discovered Senator Tom Kenney was somehow aware that I was taking documents out of Lee's office that night, and he wanted those documents. Dominick also discovered it was Tom, who orchestrated the Grand Jury probe in the first place. It seemed he was trying to get even with Lee, for what, he had no idea. Dominick also said, "Christina, don't forget, we're talking about a famous U.S. Senator here, so think carefully before you tell me how you would like me to handle this delicate situation."

"Dominick, I love you and thank you for what you have already done, but I want to take care of Senator Kenney, **my way**. But as for this **pain in the ass** court trial, it's driving me crazy! I'm constantly being bothered with it. Is there anything you can do to speed this trial up somewhat for me?"

Without hesitation, "I'll take care of it tonight."

Quite sincerely, "Dominick, thank you again, and as soon as I can come to Rome to see you and thank you in person, I will."

The next day the man who tried to kill me was found dead in his cell and the trial was over. This was not quite what I meant, but it taught me to be very specific when it came to asking Dominick for favors.

Fourth, I received a call in June of '83, from Detective Fred Ulrich. He told me he had found and arrested the arsonist. Then he said, "He's a tough nut to crack, he's not talking. I'm trying to have him tried on first degree murder. Hopefully when he realizes he's going up for the next twenty-five-years, he'll accept our plea bargain and start talking. I'm sure he'll lead us back to Frank."

"Do you have any solid proof to connect Frank to the fire at all?"

Sounding determined he swiftly replied, "Not one bit, but I'm not giving up. I'll get this guy to talk, even if it kills me."

"Thank you Fred, you're doing a great job and I'll be waiting to hear more."

Unbelievably on January 16th, 1985, the most drawn out Grand Jury probe in history, finally dropped their investigation against Lee. When I heard that news, I thought, "Thank God! Now maybe my life can begin to return to its normal pace."

The press finally stopped hounding me and the stress created by this whole mess, which Lee pulled me into was gone for good. That was when I was finally able to breathe again. That night, Lee took me out for dinner to celebrate our victory over the Grand Jury probe. After dinner, we went home and the rest of that evening Lee was full of manly testosterone, as he obnoxiously gloated, from his personal triumph over Senator Tom Kenney. He proceeded to become aggressive in a way which was not flattering. I knew it was his way of showing me he was superior to Tom, and because I loved him, I allowed it to take place. I managed to make it through that night of tasteless sex, but I protested strongly the next morning. After that one outburst of aggressiveness, he was back to his normal laid back approach.

It took about two weeks for the residual effect of the end of the Grand Jury probe to affect my life in a real way. Like breathing, eating, sleeping, you know, all those everyday things. It felt good to eat a large bowl of pasta again without having to eat a handful of antacids first, because my nerves were shot.

All of a sudden, like magic, I had some free time for me. I took advantage of that time and with half of it, I plotted and schemed my revenge on Frank; with the other half of that free time I not only fought AIDS, I began to publicly fight every injustice I saw in the world. I was so loudly critical of the Feagan Administration and the reaction of our nation's response to human rights issues for all people and all nations, that the Republicans coined a phrase at my expense. They began to publicly call me, 'The Queen of the Bleeding Heart Liberals' even though I was married to a Republican Senator.

By 1987, I was bad news in Washington. First, the Feagan Administration tried to hog-tie my mouth shut through Lee. When that didn't work, they tried to blacklist me throughout Washington. Needless to say, they knew I was too visible and powerful for them to quiet me in the conventional ways, and after the Grand Jury I was squeaky clean, so they couldn't go from that angle either, so their only hope was Lee. Since that didn't work, Feagan and I found ourselves at a stalemate for the first few years of his term on every issue that I condemned his administration.

The tension I created between 'yours truly', and the administration, ended up becoming a personal battle between President Feagan and myself, for the public's approval rating. So, as he fought presidentially against me, I fought my way. I not only talked about the issues publicly, I contributed millions of dollars toward each one publicly. Then finally the public pressure which I rallied began to give me some leverage. This pressure caused the Administration to finally begin to bend a little. I became so good at burning the Administration I was nicknamed by the press, "Feagan's Wild Fire!"

Lee and I managed to be happy together until the summer of 1987, June 3rd, to be exact. That was the day Lee had me return the black leather binder to him. When I handed it to him, he said, "Tell me the truth Christina, did you open this?"

I looked at him innocently, "I did exactly as you requested, Lee."

With an air of relief, "That's good!" He kissed my forehead, "You really saved my neck by sticking with me, and I will never forget it. I thank you from the bottom of my heart."

I returned his kiss, "You're welcome Lee; just remember I did it because I love you."

Shortly after our exchange of the binder and our tender moment, Lee changed. The thoughtful, loving, concerned man I went through hell for, became a 'Doctor Jekyll'. The personality difference was unbelievable. At first I wondered what I had done to provoke this change, but I could not think of a thing. Then I thought maybe he knows I switched the discs. When I finally asked what was wrong, he acted as if I was imagining it. I put up with his verbal and mental abuse for a whole fucking year, just because I kept telling myself I loved him and I was not going to fail at this marriage. I had been a failure with my personal life for so long now I just had to make this marriage work.

On June 11th, 1988, Lee finally threw the straw on which broke 'this' camel's back. The scenario went like this. I had just finished shooting my sixteenth and most sensual film to date, entitled, 'Family Love Affair.' I was tired from work and I had not seen Lee in six weeks. So, I took the rest of the month off to be with him. That night, after six weeks of not being together, we laid in the bed naked with candlelight and soft music. Needless to say, I was feeling very amorous as I once again became the aggressor. To my amazement, as hot as I was that night, Lee couldn't get an erection. Believe me, I tried everything and it stayed limp, so I said, "Do you feel all right Lee?"

With a disgusted tone he rattled, "I just don't feel like making love is that all right with you?"

I thought to myself as I laid there feeling rejected, "What the hell is this?" With that thought in mind I flew up out of the bed, grabbed my robe, covered myself quickly and shouted at him, "Screw you, Lee! I have had it! Do you realize who I am? I'm *Christina Powers*, a thirty-four-year-old sex goddess!" I was so mad I grabbed a book from off the dresser, threw it at him and shouted, "There is definitely something wrong with this picture! If I wanted, I could give every man on this planet a freaking hard-on, but I can't give my own, forty-eight year old husband one." **STEAMING** I stormed into the bathroom, got dressed, stormed back out to find him still lying in bed just glaring at me. His superior expression made me even angrier, "Lee, I'm leaving and I'm not coming back. You will hear from my attorneys, because I want a divorce." I took off my wedding ring, threw it at him and stormed out. I headed back to New York that very night.

The next morning, Tuesday, June 12th, I was having coffee in the kitchen, when Jimmy walked in and said with surprise, "What are you doing here? I thought you were in Washington?"

Over our coffee, I told Jimmy what had happened and he leaped up into the air and shouted, "It's about fucking time! I have never said one word to you about him since you told me you married him. But now I can, and I'm gonna let you have it with both barrels! That guy is a fucking brainy, know-it-all, asshole. I will never know how you slept with that dweeb in the first place."

"Give me a break, would you please?" I answered defensively, "I'm feeling bad enough as it is. Do you think I'm happy my marriage broke up?"

Starting to laugh, "Christina, let me give you some news. Give it two hours of real thought and you'll be jumping for joy that your marriage **from hell** broke up." We both laughed, then Jimmy added, "Please do me a favor and don't get married to anyone without talking to me first!"

We laughed again and I promised, "You have my word on that one, but don't worry, I'm never getting married again. I've had it with this crap!"

Smiling, and **with the flick of that wrist**, he chirped, "If there is one thing I know, girlfriend, **you never say never**." Getting up from his chair, "I have to go to work; I don't get the luxury of staying home, like some of us do."

I chuckled, "That's right, I'm a slave driver. Now go make us some money."

Grinning from ear to ear he chortled, "Christina, I have a date tonight. His name is Tom LaChance. We're going out for dinner, than dancing at a local gay nightclub called, 'The Prime Time'. Why don't you come with us?"

I replied excitedly, "Are you kidding? You have a date? I wouldn't miss the chance to meet your first date since Bobby's death for anything. What time do you want me ready? And what the hell has taken you so long to date again anyway?"

He answered with a wink, "You, you bitch! Now that you've led me to Christ, I realized meaningless sex is not fulfilling. I figured if God wants me to have sex then he will bring the right person into my life. And this might be the one, so meet us here at 8:00pm girlfriend!"

"I'll be waiting!" I replied, as he kissed me goodbye and left the room.

After Jimmy left for work, I decided to take a walk outside. The morning was delightful, and I wanted to be part of it. I was once again back to my cut off blue jeans, tee shirt, sneakers, and it felt great. It was around 9:00am when I came back from my walk and I climbed right into my new Cadillac convertible and went riding with the top down. As I drove all around the Hudson Valley that day with the fresh spring air blowing through my hair, I realized Jimmy was right. I was free and it felt like a ton of weight had been lifted off my shoulders. This was going to be my time. I was not going to even think of having a man in my life. I was done with love and as I drove over the Mid-Hudson Bridge on my way into the city of Poughkeepsie, I could feel something in the air that morning. It was as if the day itself was telling me something wonderful was going to happen.

As I wound my way through the unfamiliar streets of Poughkeepsie, I found myself at a beautiful park right on the river. It was called Kale Rock Park and it ran along the river right under the bridge. As I parked the car, I looked up at this magnificent bridge, which towered the span of the river to connect the two mountains on either side. It was a beautiful sight to behold as the noon sun glistened on its silver arches. I climbed out of the car and started to walk the trail which ran along the river bank. As I walked, I was daydreaming to the peaceful sounds of the waves slapping the shore line. I began to focus my eyes on a man wearing a tight fitting jogging suit. As he gracefully approached me, his firm muscles were rippling with every movement. I could not stop staring at his body. It was so sexy! With every step he took closer my heart began to pound, and it felt exciting. It was so exciting it was almost frightening. My body was beginning to quiver and I hadn't even made eye contact yet. As we came within a few feet of one another, I timidly gazed up into his beautiful blue eyes and I was stunned! It was Michael Gillespie, my bodyguard, whom I had not seen since the night he saved my life.

I stopped dead in my tracks and with a pleasantly surprised tone exclaimed, "Michael! It's so nice to see you!"

His eyes lit up, "Mrs. Bradford! It's good to see you too. How are you?" Then he looked at himself with the sweat dripping from his brow, and apologetically added, "I'm sorry you're seeing me like this."

I smiled nonchalantly, "Don't be sorry Michael, and please call me Christina. Besides, I'm sure you're not working, are you?"

He chuckled, "Sure, I go to work like this every day! Don't you remember? I was sweating bullets the last time we met." He chuckled again, as he added, while pointing toward some townhouses, "No, I'm only kidding. I live on the other side of that hill over there."

I looked in the direction he pointed, "Are you in a hurry, do you have time to talk?"

"No, I'm not in a hurry. As a matter of fact, this happens to be the start of my two-week vacation."

With amazement I replied, "You're kidding, what a coincidence. I just started my vacation today as well."

"Well I'm just going up to my place to take a shower and have some lunch. Have you had your lunch yet?"

I answered with a friendly smile, "No I haven't eaten yet and I'd love to have lunch with you; so lead the way."

We talked about the weather as we walked to his home together. As we entered his three-bedroom quaint, clean townhouse, that overlooked the river and the bridge, I commented, "This is a very nice home you have here, Michael." Then I walked over to the glass doors which led out onto the balcony, gazed out at the splendid view, "Michael, I never took the time to truly thank you in person for saving my life; so, I would like to say it now, seven years later, thank you Michael."

He replied sincerely, "I would also like to thank you. If it were not for your kind generosity, we would not be standing in a debt free home right now." Then he placed his keys down on the big captain's desk, which was placed in the living room beside the brick fireplace, "If you don't mind I'll let you make yourself comfortable, and I'll go take a quick shower and remove some of this sweat."

I smiled warmly, "No I don't mind at all."

He smiled back as he turned to leave the room, "Great! Then I'll be back in a flash."

I watched as Michael walked out of sight and I thought, "Holy shit! This man is incredible! Just look at how his tight, round, firm buns move as he walks. I can't believe I waited seven years to look at those buns again." He was hot! Then my mind wandered back to the night he held me in the pouring rain, just after saving my life, and I remembered how magical his embrace was that night and my body became warm with the memory.

As I walked around his home I noticed there was a small home gym in one room and a library in another. When I walked into the library, I could not help but notice most of the books were on the subject of spirituality. There were some on God, Jesus, Angels, Heaven, life-after death, and understanding the spirit world. As I glanced through the books, Michael came into the room with a gorgeous skin tight, pullover, short sleeve, navy blue shirt on with tight fitting, black denim shorts, white socks and Adidas sneakers. I found myself once again quite impressed with his beauty. He walked over to me as I glanced through one of his books, "Come on with me, we can talk in the kitchen while I fix us a chef salad for lunch."

I followed him into the kitchen and offered, "Please let me help. I really can slice up a head of lettuce, no matter what you may have read about my cooking. It's all lies."

He laughed as he handed me a head of romaine lettuce and a knife, "Here you go! Now I'm gonna take your word over the Inquirer's and leave you on your own with this, so try not to cut yourself 'cause the proof is in the pudding."

I chuckled, "You're not only a chef, but you're a smart-ass too. I like that in a man." We both laughed some more, then I said, "Michael, may I ask you something?"

"Sure, ask whatever you'd like," He sweetly answered. "I'll be honest."

"I noticed all the spiritual books you have in your library. Are you a very religious person?"

He smiled boyishly as he glanced into my eyes and replied mischievously, "Yes I am, but not in the normal sense of the word."

"Ahh," I said suspiciously. "Now that was an interesting answer, what do you mean?"

As he was slicing up a tomato, "I believe in God with all my heart, and I try to live my life in a way which I feel is pleasing to God and that is usually how I please myself."

I looked at him strangely, "You must be a unique character then, because I've tried to live my life in the way the Bible says we should and it wasn't pleasing to me at all; as a matter of fact it almost drove me mad. I couldn't live up to God's expectations, no matter how hard I tried. I failed every time, which only made me feel worse, so I just gave up trying." I spoke as I tossed the lettuce into the bowl with Michael's sliced tomatoes, "Michael, I'm not putting you down when I say this, but I know in my heart there is no way any of us can keep the laws of the Bible, no less keep them and be happy doing it. It just can't be done, we're too imperfect not to fall into the trappings of certain sins no matter how hard we try, it's just not possible. That's why I have to disagree with you."

As Michael served the chef salad, "I respect your right to disagree with me, but at the same time I respectfully disagree with you. I'm not saying I'm perfect, all I'm saying is I try my best to follow my heart with everything I do. Since I believe I am one with God, then the desires of my heart will always lead me closer to the Lord. But I think you have a more traditional Christian belief, which usually teaches fire and brimstone instead of love and forgiveness. If you look at God as a condemning heartless Father, then you're absolutely correct, not one of us will ever live up to the Christian world's teachings of what God expects of us as his children. That's because they put too much emphases on the sin, thus helping to keep people trapped in their sin. That's one of the reasons why I enjoy worshiping God in a corn field, better than I do in a church. I look at the earth, animals, trees, flowers, myself, and God differently than most churches do today. I believe I am part of it all."

With a doubtful tone, "Flowers and trees, I can see the beauty in them, but I can't see myself as being part of them."

He chuckled innocently, "I see it like this. When God created it all, he put his life force into every living atom and as long as God's life force is in that atom, that atom sustains life. Do you understand what I'm saying?"

I looked at him with amazement, "Yes I think I do, I never thought about it like that before, but I can understand the concept of it."

He smiled in a way which told me he was pleased, "So when I think of God, I think of myself and everything around me as being one with God. I try to live my life in harmony with the earth and every living creature, because if everything is from God and part of God, then I must respectfully treat everything and everyone with the same divine respect and love as I would myself."

In awe of his spiritual intelligence, yet at odds with it, "That sounds great, but it also sounds like you're saying you are God. Isn't that blasphemy? Didn't Jesus say there was only one God?"

With all sincerity, "Yes Jesus did say that, and that's exactly what I mean. Jesus taught there is only one God, yet he said, 'He was God' thus making Himself equivalent with God. Jesus also said, 'If I am one with God and you are one with me, then God lives within you.' I believe Jesus was saying we are all equal and divine in nature, meaning we are part of God the Father. So, whether we believe it or not, the unconditional gift of love Jesus gave us all when he paid the price for sin on the cross, gives us all the opportunity to have a love relationship with God, despite our sinful nature. Now, if God dwells within us; we are one with Him, which makes us divine beings despite ourselves. Once one reaches that level of spiritual understanding, sin will eventually lose its power over your life as you begin to move closer to Jesus' teaching and being Christ like." He looked at me with true passion in his eyes, "Don't you think if everyone would just stop looking at their sins and the sins of others, and start looking at themselves as being part of God, there would be a lot less judging of our neighbors and a lot more loving of our neighbors, as Jesus taught?"

I was surprised by his spiritual wisdom and it showed on my face, when with amazement I said, "That is so profound Michael, and very beautiful. But I've found when I tried to live my life by the teachings of the Bible it put my entire life at odds with God's will. When I gave my life over to God's will, to do what I was told God wanted of me, which was to teach the will of God to everyone, those same church leaders who told me that, would never let me address the public alone because I was a woman. They said it would have been a sin. So as far as I'm concerned I will love God in my way, and until I see the churches begin to bring the world together instead of dividing it, I will never become a member of any organized Christian group again."

He was surprised by my bluntness, "Well, you need to understand something about most Christian organizations and the Bible, and that is the Bible was written for a different time, place and people, with a lesser scientific mentality and spiritual knowledge. Churches are still stuck there. What really happened was that in time as mankind's knowledge and intelligence grew, so did his spirituality, and the churches ignored that. That's why I believe, as the soul of each of us departs from God to become a child, its goal is to bring our conscious mind and physical body to a higher awareness of our own divinity; which comes back to our own individual oneness with God. If we believe we are one with God, through Christ Jesus, Buddha, Allah or whomever one's higher power is, then our conscience, which is guided by the Holy Spirit, is always there to guide our hearts on the choices we make in life; thus, we are given the ability to judge our own actions accordingly, and at the same time we're taught by Jesus not to judge our brothers."

With that I interrupted, "How does anyone ever really know if they've made the right choices or not?"

He smiled like an angel and replied as if it were as plain as the nose on my face, "You know, if your choice brings you to a closer feeling of oneness with God. You will feel good about what you have done and it will bring you eventually, to a higher awareness of your own divinity in God. That's when you will have the power to move mountains in your own life and others. So, if the churches choose to continue to teach us to look at ourselves, as weak failures in God's eyes, because we continually fall short of what they want us to believe is important to God, then that is what we will be, failures. But, if we look at ourselves as God sees us, which is a divine child or part of God's own essence, then we open ourselves to the mysteries of Heaven through God's eyes within us. But this knowledge only comes from true spiritual growth and the choices we have made throughout our lives."

"Whoa! That is heavy Michael. I never looked at God with such a broad aspect before. It's an incredible theory."

He gazed at me with sadness in his eyes, "That is all it will ever be to you Christina, until you allow yourself to touch a little bit of your own divinity."

"Please don't think I was putting you down, because I wasn't. I find what you are saying to be very enlightening; I just don't know how it all connects to my fundamental beliefs in Jesus Christ as being my God in Heaven, not in me."

He softly smiled, "First of all, I didn't think you were trying to put me down and I hope you don't think I was putting you down either. What I meant was, one day you will realize even though we all battle our own dark side and many times lose, you can still live as Jesus taught. It is not our job to condemn the world or ourselves, it is our job to save the world in its sin, not from its sin, because Jesus already did that. So if we can see that, yes, God does reside in Heaven, but it is His life force the 'Holy Spirit' which gives us every breath we take. When we truly realize that, we will know God lives within us. Then sin will no longer be an issue in our lives. I believe once the human race as a whole stops looking at the sins and differences' of others, and starts looking at their own oneness in God, then mountains will truly be moved."

"Michael that is beautiful, but how will the world ever reach the point of moving mountains, without Christ's physical presence?"

His eyes radiated wisdom, "Listen to your question, then try to think as I believe and answer the question yourself."

I thought for a moment, "Do you mean that because God lives within us, it will be the human race as a whole, who will make a heaven on earth and that Jesus will not be coming from the heavens to take away the pain and tears himself."

Calmly he replied, "Not exactly. I believe Jesus will return someday. But until he does, we are the Christ every eye shall see and it's up to us to fight the battle against the darkness in our own lives, as well as in the world, not through condemnation, but through the unconditional love which Jesus has shown for us. Then one day, we will all dwell in the light of the Lord forever. But until He comes, we are that light and each one of us must use the light of God which is within us, to light the path of love for others."

Once again, I was amazed and it showed on my face, "Michael, I can really relate to what you're saying, but it sounds like you're asking for a one world belief in God and I don't think the human race will ever reach that level of understanding."

With an alarmed expression he quickly replied, "No I'm not. I'm asking for a one world belief, which will allow for all beliefs, because I believe all faiths will one day lead the world to the truth Jesus taught, which is that through His teaching we are all one with God and God is one with every living thing. So, if we don't start looking at ourselves as one with God, then we will not recognize the **evil one** when he begins to mislead the human race."

I chuckled, "Now you sound spooky."

Looking very seriously, "You can laugh, but some people believe that somewhere on this planet right now, is the living Anti-Christ. Many people across the world have received spiritual messages from the angels of God. Many of these angels speak of a demon, which has taken the form of a human, and is now rising in the world arena somewhere. No one will know he is evil until he strikes out. It is up to us to become aware of the power of our own divinity now, so we may stand strong against this **evil one** when he emerges. These spirit guides, as some people call them, say the human race as a whole is either coming to the true knowledge of our own divinity, or else we're coming to our own destruction on this planet. But that may be a little too much to swallow over a chef salad. So, how would you like to go for a ride with me?"

I smiled, "That sounds great, let's go," and with that we headed back out into the warm sunshine.

As we walked out of Michael's home that early afternoon I said, "I have my car in the park, do you mind if we take it?"

"Not at all, have you ever seen the Catskills on a beautiful spring day before?"

I looked at him with admiration in my eyes as we walked toward the car, "No I haven't, but I'd like to."

He smiled again, "Great, I have a family home up in Tannersville, which is a hamlet of Hunter Mountain. It's beautiful up on the mountain this time of the year would you like to see it?"

"I'd love to." I answered with an excited tone, "But only if you don't mind driving?"

He replied, with a boyish smile, "No, I don't mind at all."

I tossed him the car keys, and we climbed in. We drove out of the park and Michael casually waved to his two co-workers, who were on duty guarding me, as we drove past them, then he turned toward me, "Christina, I hope I haven't given you the wrong impression of myself. There happens to be a lot more to me then my spirituality. It's true I have a strong faith, but I am still learning every day, just like everyone else."

I slapped his leg in fun, "Don't become self-conscious on me now, I have been enjoying the real you."

Within what seemed like minutes, Michael was skillfully handling the curves of Route 23B, as we wound our way up the mountain. I was in my glory watching the beauty of the Catskill Mountains go by, as Michael told me how he, his parents, his one brother, and three sisters, all grew up on this mountain top. He spoke of his family life and growing up on this mountain, with such fondness I almost felt envious. Those were the kinds of memories I never had, but it was still wonderful hearing Michael's. He was actually charming as he shared some of his childhood antics with me, but the best was when he said, "I've got to tell you this one. One day when I was about five years old, my seven-year-old sister Jody was teaching my three-year-old sister Michelle and myself, how to ride a two-wheel bike. First, I held the bike for my sister Michelle and let her roll down the hill to where Jody was waiting to stop her and keep her from falling. Michelle did great, then it was my turn. Well I climbed on the bike, got my balance just like Jody told us to do and off I went. I began to pick up speed as I raced toward the place on the hill where Jody was waiting to catch me, and as I reached her, she screamed and jumped out of the way, letting me roll right past her. As I continued to fly down the hill, I realized Jody never told us how to stop the bike. So I went flying off the road, over an eight-foot embankment and landed face first into the ice cold creek at the bottom of the hill."

I laughed so hard when he told that story I nearly wet myself, "I wish you had told me I'd be meeting your family, I would have changed first."

"You're not. No one lives in the house anymore; we only come up here to get away or on holidays. We all moved away after my father Joe passed away in 1976. I had a home built for my mom in a new development, near where my sister Jody and her family now live. It's in the village of Ravena New York, which is about forty minutes north of here."

With a smile of relief, "That's good, not that I wouldn't like to meet your family, I'd just like to dress for the occasion first."

Just then, we turned onto Gillespie road and drove up a winding, wooded driveway, until we reached a large three story white wooden colonial home. On the wood trim over the front porch were the words, The Dellwood House. As we climbed out of the car and headed up toward Michael's prestigious looking family home, I asked, "Michael, why is the house named Dellwood?"

He opened the gate to the white picket fence for me, "It was once a hotel called The Dellwood, back in the twenties. Some say the gangster Jack-Legs Diamond once stayed here with his mistress, Kiki Roberts. That was the big buzz on the mountain for years."

I laughed as we walked up the steps of the porch. Michael took me inside of this true country style home. He showed me his childhood bedroom, then we went up to the third floor balcony and I could not believe how beautiful the view was. I took a deep breath of the fresh mountain air, "This is fabulous Michael." I pointed toward a bridge we could just see from our vantage point, which crossed the river, "What bridge is that?"

"That's the Kingston-Rhinecliff Bridge. That bridge happens to be more than 50 miles from here and we have the best view of it on the mountain top." He replied proudly.

Taking in the beauty all around me, "It must have been magical, to grow up in such a beautiful place."

He looked at me with fondness in his eyes, "It was." He grabbed my hand and as we stood next to each other gazing out over the horizon, "Would you like to take a walk to see the beaver pond? I think you might enjoy it."

I turned toward this extremely interesting and adorable man, "I would love to see it."

As we walked through the woods toward the beaver pond, Michael told me how he and his siblings would swim in the pond when he was a child, and how he and his whole family would come into these woods every Christmas Eve together to pick out their Christmas tree. As we walked, I grabbed his hand squeezed it gently for a moment, "Your family sounds wonderful Michael, now I'm sorry I'm not meeting them after all."

Just as I finished speaking, we reached a clearing in the woods and there it was! It was absolutely fabulous. It was a beautiful crystal clear pond, nestled at the bottom of three large mountains. From off of one of the mountains, a small waterfall fed the pond on one side, and there was a large beaver dam on the other side, with two large beavers chasing their three babies all over the dam. Quietly we watched the five of these beautiful creatures playfully splashing together in the pond and I felt as if I were becoming a part of that peaceful display of mother-nature. It was truly a spiritually moving experience.

It was 4:00pm when we headed back to Michael's home in Poughkeepsie and by that time we were both totally enchanted with one another. As we caught the Thruway in Saugerties I said, "Michael, I really enjoyed our afternoon together and I don't want it to end just yet. So would you please join me and some friends of mine this evening for dinner and dancing?"

He answered with an enthusiastic smile, "As long as I can go home and change first, I'd like that very much." With that he quickly glanced into my eyes and with a look of honesty questioned, "But I must ask one question first, before I accept. What will your husband think?"

I smiled, "I have asked him for a divorce. I plan to file for it on Monday, so it doesn't matter what he might think."

His whole body seemed to light up with his smile, as if his heart were suddenly filled with joy, "Wow! That's phenomenal news, and someone would have to kill me to keep me from going out with you tonight."

I chuckled as I felt myself compelled to reach out, take his hand, "I'm glad my bad news pleases you."

First, we drove to Michael's home, so he could shower and change. Then we went to my home, which was Lee's home in Gardener, where I showered and changed. From there it was off to meet Jimmy and Tom for our 8:00pm meeting at the Executive House. After we were all introduced, Michael suggested going to the Mariner Harbor Restaurant in Highland. Jimmy took Tom in his car and followed Michael and me in my car to the restaurant. When we arrived at the restaurant, we found ourselves right down on the river bank. It was quite romantic with the lights of the City of Poughkeepsie glistening on the beautiful, peaceful, Hudson River. As we entered the restaurant, Jimmy and I immediately noticed the thirty foot lobster tank. I looked at Jimmy and smiled, "It looks like we're at the right place."

He laughed, "Please don't try to eat a five-pound lobster this time. I almost threw up just watching you the last time."

We all laughed and I added, "I'll stick to my normal three pounder this time, okay?"

The four of us had a lovely candlelight dinner that night as we dined in the shadow of the city. Jimmy and I approved of one another's dates and we both knew it without saying a word. We had grown to read one another quite well, and we knew we were both having the first good time we'd had in years. After our meal, it was off to The Prime Time Disco, where I was going to dance for the first time in more than eight years. When I realized how long it had been, I was amazed.

When we pulled into the parking lot, Michael parked the car beside Jimmy's and we all went in together. The four of us had the best time, and Michael turned out to be a great dancer. It felt good to be out on a dance floor again with the hot music and flashing lights. My sensual feelings were stimulated in a way I hadn't felt in years, as I watched Michael move so manly across the dance floor. I found myself deliberately trying to entice and seduce him with every move I made as we danced.

It was around 1:00am when Michael and I said our goodbyes to Jimmy and Tom, and left them at the nightclub. When we climbed into the car Michael looked at me with a gleam in his eyes, "Would you like to go back up to the mountains with me tonight?

It's a clear night and you would be amazed at how many stars you can see from out on the balcony on a night like this."

With a sincere tone and a sweet smile, "There is nothing I'd like more right now, then to be with you Michael."

He leaned over and kissed me gently, "Thank you, Christina." And it was off to the Catskill Mountains again.

When we arrived at The Dellwood, we went straight up to the third floor balcony. Michael left me there as he went to fix two White Russians. I was caught up in the beauty of the starry sky when Michael returned with our drinks. We sat down side-by-side on a two person redwood recliner lounge chair. As we sipped our drinks, we were gazing out at this awe inspiring view and feeling totally at ease with one another. Michael turned to me and said softly, "Christina, have you ever had an out of body experience?"

I gazed inquisitively into his eyes, "No I haven't. I have heard of the term before but I'm not sure what it means. Why do you ask?"

He smiled innocently, "Well, it's when you use your mind to allow your spirit to leave your body, so your spirit may soar anywhere in the universe you choose."

I laughed a little in disbelief, "It sounds like a wonderful fairytale Michael, but I don't believe it can be done."

With an air of confidence he replied, "If I could prove to you it's possible, would you try it?"

I looked at him a little doubtful and smiled, "I'll try anything once."

He smiled again, only this time it was a mischievous smile, "Good! Then will you allow me to lead you into a meditation?"

I reached over and gently touched his hand, "I trust you enough Michael, to let you try."

He started with a soft, soothing, voice, "Then just lay back, close your eyes and begin to feel your body relaxing. Allow your mind to let go of all your concerns and fears. Now, take a slow deep breath filling your lungs completely. Very slowly, begin to allow yourself to completely exhale. As you continue to breathe like this, I want you to visualize in your mind's eye the light of God entering your body with each breath. Allow the light to totally fill your lungs and radiate throughout your entire being, so every single cell in your body is glowing with the white light of God, and warmed with unconditional love. Slowly begin to fade deep within yourself, as your body becomes limp and free. Now, go deeper and deeper within yourself and when you're completely relaxed, I want you to open your mind's eye and look for me. I will be there waiting to help you."

I could no longer hear Michael's words, but I could still feel myself drifting deeper within myself. Somehow, I could feel my body become lighter as my spirit began to slowly rise. Within my thoughts, I could see my body lying beneath me and as I gazed at my physical being in awe, I felt a cooling touch on my back. I turned quickly to see Michael's silhouette floating right beside me. I looked around us at the stars as we weightlessly floated in the air together. What I was feeling at that moment was totally wondrous and spiritual. Michael then took my hand and I could hear his thoughts in my mind, "Come with me, Christina."

We began to fly through the emptiness of space together. It was incredible and we were truly soaring up toward the stars and straight into the heavens. In complete awe, I went to squeeze Michael's hand, but I couldn't apply pressure until I felt it in my mind. I gazed at him and noticed we were both glistening like gold star dust which seemed to follow us wherever we went, yet keeping us connected to our bodies in some way.

He then put his arms around me, pulled me close to him in the heavens, and he began to kiss me. As he did, in my mind I could hear him say, "Christina, I have dreamed of making love to you like this and I have known our destinies would bring us here since the first moment our eyes met."

At that point, our spirits merged as one. It was phenomenal! I felt the scorching of our souls as our life forces mingled. It was pure heavenly ecstasy and we became one as we soared through infinity together. There was no actual sexual contact between our physical bodies at all. It was the fire of our souls which became one in the heavens that night and yet, it was the most pure feelings of ecstasy I had ever reached. It surpassed every feeling of love I had ever felt with anyone before. After what seemed like a lifetime of pure divine love making, Michael began to bring me back to the balcony and I could hear him in my mind, "I want you to very slowly re-enter your body now and when you're able to, slowly open your eyes. I'll be waiting for you."

When I opened my eyes, Michael was leaning over me and asked as I looked into his eyes, "Are you a believer now?"

With gratefulness I smiled, "Michael that was incredible!" I slowly ran my fingers through his golden hair as I pulled him close to me, and feeling more love and passion then I had ever felt before for anyone, I kissed him, "Thank you Michael that was the most extraordinary experience I've ever had."

He returned my kiss, "I love you Christina, and I want you to be mine. I know we're meant to be together."

Somehow, I found myself saying, "Michael, I love you too and I want to be yours."

We embraced and Michael laid his warm body on mine. As he tenderly kissed my face he kept softly repeating, "Christina, I love you." He gently began to undress me and caressed my breasts with both hands as he exquisitely slid his tongue down to my naval, where he began to lick my entire body. My body was being stimulated to the point of melt down when he pulled himself back up to once again consume my lips in his. I reached down, took hold of his hot flesh and gently placed him at the quivering opening of my starving body. I placed the palms of my hands on his muscular buttocks and slowly began to push him just within me, as we devoured each other with our tongues. As we kissed, he plunged forward and I mounded in ecstasy, "Oh Michael take me." as our bodies caught up with our souls. The love we made that night was beyond words.

As we lay in each other's arms, I realized Michael was right. I truly believed I was part of God and I would continue to give my life, meaning my flesh and my soul totally to Jesus Christ, despite my sinful nature, until I reach that higher consciousness when I would know and feel my divinity in Christ. Somehow, I also knew I would spend the rest of my life with this man.

The next morning I woke and kissed Michael until he awoke, "Michael, do you have plans for your vacation?"

He began to kiss me all over, "Nothing I can't change."

As I returned his kisses, "How would you like to hop in the car with me and just drive until we feel like stopping?"

He looked at me with wide eyes, "Let's go!"

We washed up, put our clothes back on, and hit the road, destination unknown. As we drove, we talked and talked. We talked about our lives, our dreams, our past lovers, and about God. One thing Michael said which struck a cord within me was how he sees the future, "Christina, I believe the earth and the human race is heading for a cataclysmic change. But after that, there will be a new birth, a new beginning in God, for the new earth and the new human race which will emerge from the ashes, will be superior to this old one. People will know what it means to live in the Light of the God, because the human race will truly be living after God's own heart. We will all finally understand that the Omnipotent God of the universe's Life-Force is within us and we are an extension of God. Then, we will learn to communicate through thought and all things shall be known. There will be no room for hatred and deceit, for all feelings and emotions will be open for all to see. Love, understanding, kindness, oneness, and true harmony, will be the new way of life. One day families will live together as one, in unconditional love. Acceptance of each other's individual differences will be the natural way, not the exception."

With that thought I replied, "Michael that is beautiful. Now if it could only be true."

It was as if we were spiritually becoming one while we rode and talked for hours, of what our spiritual purpose might be. We only stopped driving long enough to eat, gas up, and use the rest rooms. We didn't stop to take a room until we reached St. Augustine, Florida.

We checked into a hotel at 11:00am on Monday, June 14th, and we went straight into the warm Jacuzzi, where we began a five-hour marathon of incredible romantic love making. After which we collapsed and we didn't wake up, until 10:00am on Tuesday, June 15th, and we immediately made love again, then it was off to the closest diner. We ate, and then hit the malls to do some clothes shopping. When we returned to the room, it was

6:00pm and I said, "Michael, why don't you shower first and I'll call Jimmy. If we get in there together, we might not come out."

He chuckled, kissed me, "I'm going, but I'm gonna miss you."

I slapped his buns as he walked away from me, then I picked up the phone to call Jimmy.

When Jimmy answered the phone, he sounded concerned, "Where the hell are you? I haven't heard a thing from you since Saturday night."

Enthusiastically I answered, "Jimmy, Michael and I have driven to Florida."

Immediately he interrupted, "Let me get this straight. You're in Florida, with a man you just met, while your stupid husband is breaking my door down looking for you." Then he started to laugh, "Why am I not surprised, Christina? You will never stop amazing me no matter how long I know you. I guess that's one of the reasons I love you so much, girlfriend. So start talking, is he hot?"

I laughed at Jimmy's reply, then abruptly quibbled, "If you would let me speak, I'll tell you."

"Okay, who's stopping you?" He answered in only the way he could. I laughed a little more, then cleared my voice and with a tone of sincerity sighed, "He's a dream Jimmy, and I'm truly madly in love with him."

With a caring tone he blurted out, "Oh my God girlfriend, how you fall in love at the drop of a dime, I'll never know? Is it truly love this time Christina, or is he just another rebound?"

"Jimmy, I have never felt like this. Not even with Tony, or Johnny." I felt a hot flash shoot through my body when I heard myself say the name, **Johnny**. Then I thought, as Jimmy went on speaking, "Oh my God! I haven't thought of him in years, and just saying his name still makes me feel the effect his touch had on my life. Could I still be in love with Johnny?" Just then Michael burst into my thoughts and I realized, "Yesterday is gone with the wind. All I know is what I am feeling right now, today, and Michael, you're the one I'm dreaming of."

When I came back from my thoughts, I stopped Jimmy's babbling by saying, "Jimmy, Jimmy, Jimmy!" "What?" He screeched, as I said, "I don't care what Lee wants, just please don't tell him where I am. I also need you to do me a favor, call Lesley Stein and tell her to file divorce papers for me."

Michael and I spent eight glorious days in St. Augustine, and we were totally in love every minute of every day. We spent our time going to the beach, fishing, boating, water skiing, dancing, eating in restaurants and most of all love making. We were having a spectacular time which we wished would never end, but our last day did come. That night we walked from our hotel, to a restaurant recommended to us by the bellhop. It was located in the quaint Spanish section of town which was on the other side of a beautiful old draw bridge. After dinner, we each ordered pumpkin pie for dessert. As we ate to the wonderful sounds of the piano player, Michael took my hand, looked deeply into my eyes and placed a ring in my hand, "*Christina Powers*, will you marry me?"

I became so excited I dropped the ring right into my pumpkin pie. I started to laugh as I picked it up, licked off the pie, and with tears of joy escaping my eyes said, "Michael, yes! I will marry you." Then I slid it on my finger.

Michael immediately jumped up out of his chair and shouted, "Yes! I love you, my little Pumpkin pie." We both started to laugh and cry at the same time. Then, because everyone was looking at us, Michael shouted again, "She just said she'd marry me." Everyone began to applaud.

I was so happy; I went up to the piano player and asked him if he would play a song for me. I told him the song and he said he could. I took the mike, "Michael, I love you baby and I'd like to sing a special song to you."

The piano player began to play and I began to sing, Karen Carpenters song, 'We've only just begun.' As I sang to Michael that night, I was singing from the depths of my heart and he knew it. After we left the restaurant, we began to walk arm-in-arm back to the hotel. When we reached the draw bridge, it began to go up. As we held each other and watched this bridge begin to rise, on that beautiful Florida night, I kissed Michael, "I wish I had told you the night you saved my life that I loved you, because I knew it then."

With his heart in his eyes, "I knew I loved you even before that night. But, I guess all things happen in their own time."

The next day, we were on our way back to New York and we were determined to make a new life for ourselves together. We knew it was our destiny to be together. Michael summed up our feelings when he said, "I love you. These three words will change our lives forever and I promise I will always be here for you Christina, until the end of time."

I kissed him, "Michael, right here with you is where I want to stay. I thank God he has brought us together, and I know I will always love you."

As we spoke of our love and future dreams together, we totally forgot one thing Michael said, and that was, "**All things happen in their own time.**"

CHAPTER 16. THE POWER OF UNCONDITIONAL LOVE

When we arrived back in New York, we went straight to Lee's home in Gardener. Once there, I proceeded to pack two suitcases, grabbed one singed bottle of champagne, and I was off to live with Michael in his Poughkeepsie town house. I was so in love with Michael and I wanted to be with him. I was tired of fighting the world alone, and living all by myself without the affections of my true soul mate. Now that I had found him, I wanted to spend every minute of my life with him. I longed for just his slightest touch on my flesh. Michael had the bravest of hearts and the strongest of souls. He was the light of my life and the place I wanted to call home. He was the one man in this world I found myself living for, and I would lay down my life for the power of his love.

It was Monday morning at 8:00am when I asked Michael to leave his position with the security firm and come join me as my private, personal, bodyguard. He replied, "Let me have some time to think about it before I answer. But for now, I have to get back to work."

"Well after you clock in or whatever you do, just come in the house with me. You can guard me from in here."

With a chuckle he replied, "Christina, I haven't been assigned to your case in two years. They have me assigned to Donald Stump."

"You're kidding!" I replied, with alarm. "You mean to tell me I've had a false sense of security for two years now. I thought you were out there, somewhere watching over me."

Laughing, he kissed me, "Well Punkie, I have to go to work and I won't be home until Friday afternoon around 5:00."

With a disappointed tone I exclaimed, "Friday afternoon! Michael, I didn't know you were not going to be with me, how can I stay here by myself?"

He laughed again, "I love you Punkie, and I'll miss you like crazy, but for now I have to do my job. What else can I do?"

I held him tight as I kissed him, "I understand Michael, and I'll be waiting for you to come home to me." I watched him leave and I felt sad when I realized I was alone again.

Once he was out of sight, I grabbed a pen and paper, and began to write my feelings of love for Michael. By 2:00pm that afternoon, I had composed the lyrics to nine dynamite singles. Six of them, told my fans a different story of the feelings I'd had from my break up with Lee, to my meeting and falling in love with Michael. Three of them were from the purest essence of my love for my Michael. I became so excited when I read my finished works I climbed into the car and went straight to the studio, where I immediately put my favorite crew right to work on the melodies.

When I checked my messages at the office, there were eighty two of them from Lee. According to Jimmy, Lee had come into his office twelve times, pleading with him to tell him where I was. Jimmy was adamant, "Christina, you're going to have to call him. He is half out of his mind trying to find you. The only reason Lee doesn't have a nationwide manhunt out looking for you, even after he received the divorce papers, is because your security people informed the FBI you didn't want to be found."

I lackadaisically replied, "What do you mean he's half out of his mind?" Just assuming Jimmy was over-dramatizing the situation.

But I became concerned when melodramatically he said, "Just what it sounds like. He was acting crazy, and he made no sense at all."

Becoming alarmed I asked, "When did you see him last?"

"He was here acting like a nut just this morning."

As soon as he said that, I instantly thought of Tony and was hit like a bolt of lightning, with terrifying images of the last second

I saw Tony alive. With that, I dashed to the phone and began to dial Lee's number. Somehow, I knew something was horribly wrong. The phone rang ten times and just as I was about to hang up, I heard the line pick up. I waited for someone to speak, but no words came, "Lee, is that you?"

I heard him mumble, "Christina, I love you."

Then, I heard the phone drop and I screamed, "Oh God, no! Lee, answer me!" There was nothing but dead silence. I immediately slammed the phone down, dialed 911, and told the woman who answered, "My husband is lying unconscious in our home." Then I shouted the address and the woman said, "Okay ma'am, now I want you to stay on the phone with me, to make sure we find the right place."

I shouted at her, "To hell with you! I'm going to my husband!" I grabbed Jimmy's hand and shouted again, "Come with me. Lee is killing himself."

We ran out of the office and down the three flights of stairs to the parking level. When we reached the car, I hit the hazard lights then I hit the gas. We made the fourteen miles to Gardener in nine minutes, beating the rescue squad. I slammed on the brakes, throwing dust twenty feet into the air. When we finally stopped, we both jumped out of the car and ran to the front door. I tried to open it, but it was locked. Jimmy yelled, "Unlock the fucking door already!"

With a panicked tone I yelled, as I started to bang on the door, "I left the keys here. We'll have to break in."

That's when Jimmy and I both began trying to break down the door. After we almost broke our shoulders, I shouted, "**The hell with this**! Watch out, Jimmy!"

I ran to the car, which was still idling, threw it into drive and drove right through the front door. As I climbed out of the car and ran into the house looking for Lee, all I could see flashing through my mind was the blood stained hands I had on that God forsaken night Tony took his own life. I screamed, "Lee! Lee," as I frantically ran through the house looking for him. I charged up to the bedroom with Jimmy right on my tail. When I flung open the bedroom door, my heart almost stopped. I saw Lee's lifeless body lying on the floor and I screamed again, "Lee," as I raced across the room to his side. I grabbed him and began to slap his face as I screamed and cried, "Lee! Wake up! Don't do this! Wake up Lee, wake up!"

At that moment the paramedics came running into the room and began to try to resuscitate him. Jimmy grabbed hold of me as I cried desperately for Lee. Jimmy stroked my back, as I buried my shaking body into his arms. I whispered as I cried, "No Tony, no."

Jimmy whispered back, "I know, baby. I know. But this is Lee not Tony, and he is going to survive."

That's when one of the paramedics shouted, "Clear," as he used a defibrillator on Lee's chest. Then he shouted, "We have a rhythm here guys, let's move fast."

Jimmy drove as we followed the ambulance to Vassar Brothers Hospital in Poughkeepsie. All the way there, all I could do was pray for Lee to survive. When we arrived at the hospital, he was rushed straight into the emergency room. Jimmy and I answered their questions, then we waited in the waiting room for word on his condition.

After six hours of waiting on pins and needles, a doctor finally came out to speak to us. Without introducing himself he said, "Mrs. Bradford, your husband is in stable, but guarded condition in the Intensive Care Unit."

Distraughtly I asked, "What happened to him?"

"Your husband had a heart attack, brought on by alcohol and barbiturates."

With that news I immediately took on an air of authority, "I assume you are aware of how much my husband, Senator Bradford and I have contributed to this hospital. So I will also assume you will delete the second part of that diagnoses from my husband's official record. I hope there is no need for me to express how disconcerting it would be to me personally to have this information made public."

Appearing nervous he quickly replied, "I understand perfectly Mrs. Bradford, and let me assure you that you have no need for concern."

I smiled courteously, "Thank you, doctor," as I moved his stethoscope, just enough to read his name plate, "Slater, I will see I do not forget your helpfulness in this matter." After our discreet conversation, we followed him to Lee's room.

Jimmy left when visiting hours were over, but I stayed with Lee all that night, just holding his hand. I felt so horrible every time I thought of Lee trying to take his own life because of me. As I looked at this man I once loved, my heart went out to him.

Sometime around 4:00am I gently kissed his hand as he slept. With tears in my eyes I whispered, "Lee, I do love you and I can't stand to see you hurting like this, but . . ."

As I spoke he slowly opened his eyes, gazed up at me, gently squeezed my hand and in a half-conscious state said, "Thank you, God." He slowly pulled my hand up to his lips and kissed my finger-tips, "Christina, as I swallowed the pills, I told God I did not want to live without you. I said to God if you want me to live then bring my Christina back to me. And here you are." After that, he drifted back to sleep. Needless to say, I never finished my sentence.

Later that morning, I called Michael's superior and asked him to inform Michael that I had to go out of town, and I would see him Friday afternoon when he returns home. He said he would give him the message as soon as we hung up. I did not know how I was going to handle this situation with Lee yet, but I sure didn't want Michael knowing that I was with him. I knew Michael would ask me to leave Lee and I just couldn't do that yet. You see, as Lee said those words, I realized I still had a love for him, and the fact I almost caused his death, ripped my heart apart. I had to help Lee through this, and I now also had to re-evaluate my own feelings of love, which I felt for these two men.

Lee was discharged from the hospital on Friday, July 3rd, and I was going home with him. I knew Michael would be coming home that afternoon, and I had still not said anything to Lee about Michael yet. In four days, I could not find one opportunity to tell him. It was 12:00pm when Lee and I sat down on the sofa in the living room of his Gardener home. We sat there speechless for the longest time. I was trying to get up the courage to tell Lee, I was in love with another man, and I couldn't stop loving this other man just because I still had a love for him. As I was having these thoughts, Lee turned to me and said, "Christina, I love you and I promise to never treat you badly again. I will give my life up for your love." He grabbed my hand, "Why don't we go get your stuff from his place before he comes home."

Instantly, I felt my face turn white, at the same time, I felt the blood draining from it, "Do you mean to tell me, I've been tormenting myself for four days over how to tell you, and you already knew?"

He slid over to me, "I didn't know how to say it, Christina. You're my wife and I love you. Let's not throw our dreams away. Together our love will take us to the White House. Think about how we will be able to help the people of our nation if we stay together. I offer you the power to really change the country for the better."

When Lee spoke of truly helping the people of our nation, my heart raced with a force I had never felt before. Somehow, at that very moment, I knew there was a higher purpose for my life. I looked at him and thought, "Could my destiny truly be with Lee?"

Damn it! I did it to myself again! **Without a second thought**, I leaned over, kissed Lee, looked deeply into his eyes, "I love you Lee, and I will go get my belongings right now. We will put this one behind us with all the others and head to the White House together."

I got up and went straight to Michael's town house; where I packed my belongings, grabbed one bottle of champagne and sat down to compose a **Dear John** letter to my beloved Michael. As I sat at the mahogany reading table in the library of his home, with the shadows of his essence all around me, all I could do was cry. The magnitude of my decision had engulfed my soul and my heart bled as I wrote these words;

"My Dear Beloved Michael, I am leaving you this letter, because I cannot speak these words to you in person. I must leave you; my destiny calls me in another direction. Michael, my love, my tears stain this paper as I tell you I can never see you again. I love you too much to ever look into your eyes and

know our souls shall never soar through the heavens together again. Michael, remember what you taught me, cross roads have a way of leading us to our final destinies. Thanks to you, my beloved soul mate, the course I must take to reach my destiny has been revealed. I will love you through all eternity, my Michael. Forever yours, Love, your Punkie."

I kissed the paper leaving a deep red impression of my lips, and the pain shot right through my soul. My heart broke, as I gently placed the letter on the reading table. I placed my ring on top of the letter; picked up my belongings, turned and cried as I walked away from the most incredible lover I had ever known. As I drove away, I was completely enveloped in warm thoughts of Michael. I remembered our nights of pure unadulterated passion, our romantic talks and peaceful walks.

My heart ached as I pulled into Lee's driveway. I parked the car and climbed out, leaving my belongings still in the car. It was 5:00pm when I slowly walked up the sidewalk to the newly repaired front door. My eyes were still blood shot from tears of pain when Lee opened the door. Lee hugged me as I entered the foyer and said, "Where are your things?"

"I left them in the car, I'll take them out later."

He closed the door, and held me close to him, "Christina, I love you. I'm so happy you're home with me and I will never let you down again."

He began to gently kiss my neck as he nestled his erection against my waist. As he kissed me, I thought, "Is my destiny truly with this man I once loved? Is this the man I will spend the rest of my life with?" He kissed me deeply then he began to lead me up stairs to the bedroom.

As we reached the bedroom door I stopped, "I'm sorry, but I can't now Lee, so please don't ask me." I pulled my hand out of his and went back down the stairs. I went into the kitchen and poured myself a glass of orange juice.

As I sipped the juice, Lee entered the kitchen and walked over to me, "I'm sorry, Christina."

As Lee continued saying something, I felt out of place and I thought, "Oh God! Yes I still love this man, but it's not like the love I have for my Michael."

Then there was a knock at the door. Lee looked out the front window where he could see who was at the door. His face turned red with anger and he shouted, "What the fuck is he doing here?"

My heart leaped as I instantly knew it was Michael. I watched in horror as Lee dashed to the desk drawer and grabbed his gun. I ran to him and shouted, "Lee, no! Put that gun away."

Michael began to bang on the door as he shouted, "What the fuck is going on in there? Christina, open this fucking door now before I break it down."

I pulled the gun from Lee's hand and took out the bullets, "Stay here, I'll ask him to leave."

With my heart in my throat I opened the door, stepped out and looked into his eyes, "Michael, I told you I could never see you again." I started to cry, "Please leave now, Michael. I must stay here with Lee. My destiny is here with him."

He grabbed me and with tears in his eyes, "No my Punkie, you're wrong! Your destiny lies with me Christina, in my arms, not his."

I pulled myself from him, "Michael, listen to me. Lee tried to kill himself because I left him. I can't let that happen again." Then I turned, "Goodbye my love," as I walked back into the house, and closed the screen door. I watched as this powerful man I loved with all my heart and soul staggered away from me like a brokenhearted little boy.

I closed the door, leaned up against it and began to shake. Lee ran to my side and the moment he grabbed me, I heard the most heart wrenching cries my ears have ever heard.

"Christina! I love you! Please Punkie! I'm dying out here! Please save me!"

With pain shooting through my heart I screamed, "Oh my God! Michael," as I burst into tears.

I opened the door and Lee fell to his knees in front of me and pleaded, with tears pouring down his face, "No, Christina! Don't leave me! I love you, Christina!"

I shook my head and screamed, "Noooo! Stop this!" I ripped myself from Lee's clinging arms and ran out of the house and down the driveway. When I reached the street I was shaking, I turned back to see Michael leaning up against his blood red Saab convertible shaking as hard as I was. My heart pained from the sight of this beautiful man, suffering because of me. I ran back to him with tears of love in my eyes. I placed my hands on the shoulders of this beaten, brokenhearted man and sobbed, "Let's go home, my Michael."

He gazed up at me and his pain filled eyes began to glisten with a look of gentle, unconditional love. I gently helped him into the passenger seat of his car, "I'll be right back, Michael." He said nothing to me at all as I walked back toward the house. When I reached Lee, who was sitting on the sofa in a state of confusion I simply said, "Lee, I care about you, but I'm no longer in-love you with. My true destiny lies with Michael. I'm sorry, but I must leave."

I turned, walked out, and headed over to the car where my security guards watched this whole display of hysterics, and asked one of them to take my car and follow us. I went back to Michael's car, started it and headed for Michael's family home in the Catskills.

As I drove, I held Michael's gentle quivering hand and neither one of us said a word for the longest time.

Then somewhere on Route 299, between Highland and the Thruway entrance in New Paltz, Michael slowly placed my ring back on my finger and with a soft broken voice, "Punkie, will you marry me?"

I pulled the car over on the shoulder, took Michael into my arms and with tears of joy running down my cheeks whispered, "Yes, my love! I will marry you. And right here, right now, I pledge my undying, eternal, love to you my soul-mate." I looked right through his eyes, straight into the depths of his soul and whispered, "I will never leave you again my love, so gently close your eyes now and please take me as my spirit soars with yours."

With our bodies embraced as one, our spirits exploded with the passion of angels for what felt like a lifetime of ecstasy. The power of the love between us that night was beyond human explanation.

We pulled off the road around 6:30pm and we did not come back to our bodies, until we were abruptly drawn back, by the continual banging on the car windows by my bodyguards sometime around 10:00pm. I took a few minutes to compose myself, before pulling back onto Route 299 heading to the Thruway.

As we drove north, Michael had his head on my shoulder and at one point he said, "Christina, did you sleep with him?"

I squeezed his hand, "Michael, I love you with all my heart, you're my angel and the answer to your question is no. I did not sleep with him and I tell you right now, I am yours baby, body and soul. I also promise you I will never give you a reason to ask me that question again because we will always be together." He tenderly nestled his head into my breast and he stayed there until we arrived at his family home in Tannersville.

We held each other up as we slowly walked to the house. When we entered it, we went straight up to Michael's boyhood bedroom. As soon as we walked in, Michael, took me into his powerful arms, drew me passionately into his all-consuming embrace and said, "You are my life force, Christina."

I looked up into his tearing eyes as his lips met mine with the power to enslave my heart for all eternity, and all I could say was, "I love you too, baby. I love you too."

He slid his tongue to my ear and softly whispered, "I love you my sweet Punkie, and I place my heart into your hands. Christina, I know I could face anything this cold world may throw at me, but life without you, would be a travesty." He gazed passionately into my eyes and with his heart in his hands, added with quivering lips, "Baby, please don't ever leave me again. I don't think my heart could take this again."

With the passion of undying love flowing through my being, I pulled his head back to mine and began to softly make love to his lips. Our physical passion that night had an aura of tenderness which neither one of us had ever reached before.

Upon our simultaneous explosion of ecstasy, Michael completely collapsed on top of me and we drifted off to sleep. The next morning, I woke up with my body so close to Michael's he was still buried deep within me. As soon as I kissed his lips, he instantly began to throb. My body flared, with the desire of pure love and we were thrust right into the fires of our passion again. After our exquisite encounter, I showered and dressed, then floated straight to the kitchen to fix my man his breakfast. This time, I was truly in love. Everything about Michael was beyond my dreams. I was just putting two plates of pancakes with bacon on the table, when my Michael walked into the kitchen. He was wearing blue jeans and a tight fitting, Italian tee shirt, which enhanced the beauty of his physique. He looked like an angel as he came toward me with open arms and I melted into his embrace.

After our passionate embrace, we sat down to eat our breakfast and Michael said, "If it's all right with you, I made plans for the day for us. I tried to call you last week to ask you about it, but you were out of town."

I mischievously smiled, "Whatever you would like to do will be fine with me, because I'm not doing anything without you."

He leaned over, kissed me and with an excited tone said, "Great! Then you will be meeting my family today. My mom is having a Fourth of July barbeque at her house at 1:00pm this afternoon. After that we have a honeymoon suite reserved on the 15th floor of the Omni Hotel in downtown Albany. I made sure our balcony would be situated precisely where we can see the fireworks go off."

I smiled, "That sounds wonderful, Michael." And we were off to Ravena, to meet my future in-laws.

As we drove to Ravena, I said with a slightly nervous expression, "Am I going to be meeting all of your family?"

"Don't be nervous you silly goose, my family will love you, and they'll all be ecstatic for us when we tell them we are going to be married."

He drove with the top down so I cuddled close to his shoulder, "I love you Michael, and I can't wait to tell your family with you. Do they know I'm coming?"

He casually replied, "No, I haven't said a word to any of them about you. It's going to be a complete surprise to them all."

The weather that day was made to order, as we basked in our love on the road to Ravena. When we pulled on to Magnolia Circle in the heart of the quaint little village, Michael took his arm from around my shoulder, "We're here, Punkie." Then he parked in front of a two-story colonial and we climbed out of the car and headed up the driveway toward his Mom's home.

As we walked toward the house, we passed another Saab in the driveway. As we did, Michael pointed to it and said, "That's my sister Jody's car. She's the one who turned me onto Saabs. She's also the star of the Dumpetts."

I looked at him strangely, "Is she a performer?"

He laughed, "No! Jody and my other two sisters, Connie, and Michelle, would always take our father's old pickup truck to the dump every weekend. So one day, the three of them were all in overalls and on their way to the dump when I was coming into the house with some friends and said, "There go the Dumpetts' and all my friends laughed. The next school day the whole high school began calling them the Dumpetts. The title stuck with them for the rest of that school year."

With that, I started to laugh, and I was in hysterics when Michael's mother opened the door. She gave me a strange look, as if to say, "who is this person laughing uncontrollably at my door step". Then she looked at Michael and after a few seconds of watching me, as I struggled to stop laughing, finally said, "Where did you get this hyena from?" and I really lost it. I felt like a fool, as his whole family came running to the front door, to see what the commotion was. If I could have crawled under a rock, I would have. I just knew they thought I was crazy. I could see it in their eyes. Finally, with some help from Michael, who had just stopped laughing himself, I was finally able to stop. But by that time, Michael's whole family was in the front yard, where I was just catching my breath.

No one had any idea where I even came from, no less who I was when Michael shouted into this commotion, "Since we're all here, may I have your attention?" Once everyone calmed down,

Michael began with, "I would like to introduce my fiancée to all of you."

Their faces showed their shock, joy and surprise, as they all welcomed me with open arms into their loving close knit family. His mother Tess turned out to be one of the most interesting women I had met in a long time and some of the 'mountain stories' she told were hilarious. His entire family was precious as well, from his oldest brother Jay, to the Dumpetts and straight to his niece, Mary. That day turned out to be wonderful and after our visit that Fourth of July, I knew I had finally been accepted into a loving family, which I could truly call my own.

We left Tess' home around 8:00pm and headed straight to the Omni Hotel in the heart of Albany, the beautiful Capital City of the majestic State of New York. We checked into the honeymoon suite under Mr. and Mrs. Gillespie, and the bellhop took us straight up to our suite on the 15th floor. When Michael opened the door, he picked me up, carried me over the threshold, and stood me up in the center of the room. He went to tip the bellhop, closed the door, turned and headed straight for me with an air of sensuality in every movement. I could feel myself beginning to melt with every step he took closer. As he reached me, we embraced into an explosion of light and sound from the open balcony directly behind us. That night we embraced in the shadows of the fireworks, which exploded over the beautiful Capital Buildings of the Empire State Plaza, in the heart of Albany.

The passion I felt with every kiss I placed on his flesh was electrifying. As the colors of the explosions filled the skies, the sparks united the flames of our souls.

Michael took my heart and soul, as he touched the deepest depths of my flesh with his. I screamed out in ecstasy, love, and passion, "Oh God! Michael! My love! Please, baby! Give me your child." And as he devoured my essence in the midst of the grand finale, I knew I had conceived my **beloved Michael's child.**

CHAPTER 17. SHOWDOWN ON WALL STREET

Michael and I were happier than two people could ever hope to be. So happy, we decided to plan a wedding fit for royalty, just as soon as my divorce was final. Michael also decided to leave his position with the security firm after all. He made his decision on July 6th, 1988, as we walked hand in hand down Gillespie Mountain Road. It was a beautiful, sunny morning, and as we walked I just stopped, and shouted with excitement! "Yes!" I turned to Michael with a gleam in my eye and added, "Let's go to the casinos in Atlantic City. It's only about a five-hour trip from here by car, and I haven't been gambling in years."

He kissed me in the midst of his amused chuckle, "You know, I have to take your job offer Punkie." He took me in his arms, shook his head, looked into my eyes and smiled, "Little girl, you need to have me around. You're just too damn impulsive for your own good for me to leave you alone for any more than ten minutes unsupervised." I laughed as we lovingly embraced and it was off to Atlantic City.

On our triumphant ride home from Atlantic City later that night, I snuggled close to my angel and said, "Michael, I love you baby, and I don't want you to just come work for me, I want to give you half of everything I own. I'm not just giving you my love; I'm giving you everything I am. Baby, I want you to come run Powers Incorporated with me. It's ours Michael, and I'm praying with all my heart that you truly want to become part of my very existence. I know I can no longer reach my dreams without you." I moved up to kiss his cheek and with tender passion pleaded, "Please baby, I need to know the oneness we have in our souls can be obtained in the flesh as well."

He tenderly kissed my forehead as he drove, and softly said, "Punkie, I will go to the ends of the galaxy with you."

The way Michael said those words shot passion right through me. I became so excited I slowly and lovingly began to ravage his flesh, as we sped north on the Garden State Parkway. It's totally amazing we survived that ride. I had Michael in a state of ecstasy, he was screaming and humping with such force, the car was rocking. Our passion was so intense, by the time we both reached our points of ecstasy, we had to pull the car off to the side of the road and recuperate in each other's arms for ten minutes.

We laughed as we pulled away from the shoulder, because Michael said, "Whichever crew is on duty tonight, is going to have a lot to talk about tomorrow."

On Monday morning July 13th, Michael came into the office with me and it was straight to a prearranged board of directors meeting. I introduced Michael to all of my personal friends, and colleagues, all of whom, were personally appointed to their seats on the board of directors by 'yours truly'.

After Jimmy called the meeting to order, I stood up and addressed them like this, "Hi everybody, before we dive into business, I would like to introduce my future husband, Michael Gillespie." I turned to Michael who was seated beside me and said with a joyful smile, "Come on Michael, stand up and meet my family."

Michael stood up, "Hi everyone, I've heard so many wonderful things about every one of you that I feel privileged to be finally meeting such a highly respected group of people. I know you're all wondering where the hell did he come from, so I'll turn you back to Christina for that." Everyone was laughing as Michael turned the meeting back over to me.

I smiled as I stood up, "Well guys, not to anyone's surprise, I'm divorcing Lee. Just as soon as that divorce is final, Michael and I will be inviting you all to our wedding. I love him, gang! Now, I know I am going to embarrass him just a little, but that's because he's not truly aware of the relationships we all have in this room." I raised my right hand into the air with my fist closed and thumb up, "He's wonderful gang, and I know you will all love him once you get to know him. Now I am going to ask all of you to once again trust my judgment, because I am giving Michael 50% of everything I have. I would also like to make Michael Co-President of Powers Incorporated. This will mean, the ultimate decision making power, will now lie with Michael, Jimmy, and myself. I believe the record shows at least 99% of my decisions have been on the mark since we all created our corporation. Well, I truly believe this decision is the wisest one I have made to date, so out of courtesy of our camaraderie, I am putting my wishes up for a democratic vote. I also promise you I will abide by the majority decision." We finished the rest of our business and Michael was unanimously welcomed as Co-President of Powers Incorporated. From that day forward I began to teach Michael everything I knew about running a major corporation. I also began recording my next album entitled, 'The Power of Love.' I was so inspired by the power of Michael's love that I got right to work on my next screenplay entitled, 'Torn between Two Lovers.' I knew it was going to be hot! I had just lived it.

On August 6th, my marriage with Lee came to a mutually agreeable end. On that very day, Michael and I sent out five thousand wedding invitations. We set the date for December 10th, 1988, which would also be my thirty fifth birthday. Oh yes! Let me tell you. The press had a field day with this one. The headlines read, **"The Queen of Hearts, *Christina Powers*, Slays another One! Leaving Senator Bradford devastated, for the love of a man seven years her junior."** The tabloids ran stories similar to this about my divorce, for the next month. It seemed my public was eating it up.

It was on August 12th, when I received a call from another very busy woman, whom I never got to see enough of; you guessed it. I answered the phone to this, "Shit girlfriend, can anybody keep up with you?"

I chuckled, "Well, I guess you received our invitation."

She laughed, "Don't you ever give that *cat* a rest."

I started to laugh, "No more than you do, smart ass!" When I stopped laughing, I added, "So how the hell are you, Barbara?"

She answered with a serious, "I'm fine, but if you're having a real wedding, then I'm guessing he is some stud-puppy."

With a purely sensual tone I purred, "The best, sister, the best!" We laughed, than she told me she wouldn't miss my wedding for the world. We stayed on the phone for two hours, just talking like two silly school girls, who were best of friends.

Barbara and I finished our conversation around 11:56pm. Just as soon as I hung up the phone, I turned my full attention to my Michael. He was doing paper work through most of our conversation, but for the last ten minutes he had been lying on the bed beside me, and I had been massaging his erection with the soul of my foot the whole time. I did enjoy my conversation with Barbara, but after ten minutes of lusting for Michael's beautiful body, I lost all self-control. It didn't matter whom I was talking to with a man like mine beckoning to me, I had to go. We made passionate love and fell asleep in each other's arms. After sleeping for I'm not sure how long, we were awakened by the ring of the phone.

Michael answered it, handed it to me as he said in a groggy state, "It's for you, Punkie."

I took the phone, still half sleeping, "Hello! Who's this?"

To my surprise I heard, "Hi Christina, its Barbara."

"What time is it?"

Her reply sounded quite serious, "Its 4:00am your time, sorry for waking you but this can't wait."

Sensing the urgency of her tone, I quickly sat up in the bed, "What's the matter, Barbara?"

Excitedly, she replied, "Hold on to your covers baby, because I've just discovered something you need to know."

I listened with a heightened sense of curiosity, "This sounds intriguing already. So what did you overhear this time?"

"Just this! Your dear Lee Bradford is getting ready to stab you in the back. He's joined forces with Frank to crush Powers Incorporated."

Shocked, I replied loud enough to startle Michael, as well as wake the dead, "Holy shit! Why that rotten bastard! Do you know what they're planning?"

Just as Michael sat up in the bed and started looking at me like, 'what the hell is going on' Barbara replied, "As a matter of fact, yes I do. Frank is having Senator Elms, resubmit the stock market bill for a vote in October of this year. Lee is going to help push the bill through, so President Feagan can have the pleasure of signing it into law, just before the November elections. The bill will go into effect on November 1st, 1988. After that, any corporation which falls under the guidelines of the new law will have to become compliant on or before midnight December 1st. This means Powers Incorporated will go on the public stock market at 9:00. Then on December 2nd, exactly at 9:30am, Bradford Computers and Salerno Incorporated plan to jointly attempt to take-over Powers Incorporated."

With that news I took a deep breath and exclaimed, "My God! You weren't kidding when you said I needed to know this. I won't ask you where you got your information but give that angel a kiss for me whoever it is."

"I will, but are you going to be able to handle this?"

I chuckled, than lackadaisically replied, "You know me, I'll always rise to a challenge. Thank you Barbara, once again you're saving my ass, and I will never forget it. I love you, girlfriend."

We said our goodbyes and I immediately told Michael everything. I pulled out my personal phone book and called my attorney, Tom Davies at his home in Manhattan.

When he finally answered the phone, I said, "Tom, its Christina. Sorry to wake you, but I need you to cancel everything you're doing and get some information for me."

With a concerned tone he replied, "This sounds serious, just give me one minute, Christina."

The phone went silent for a few moments and when Tom came back on it he said, "I'm sorry Christina, please go on."

Feeling slightly suspicious I said, "Before I go any further Tom, I want to tell you something. I trust you, so if you're not with me then you'd better tell me now."

Sounding slightly offended he swiftly replied, "Of-course I'm with you, Christina! Have I ever given you a reason to ask me that question?"

Carefully studying the tone of his voice I said, "Only one; what were you doing when you just left me on the line?"

He replied with a tone of sincerity, "Just going to the bathroom, boss lady."

I chuckled a little from my paranoia, "I'm sorry Tom, I'm just being cautious. I called because I need to have you come up to my office as soon as you can get here. When you come, bring me all the stats you can dig up on Bradford Computers, Salerno Incorporated and Kenney Baby Foods. We have to plan some heavy duty strategies."

Curiously he asked, "Can you tell me what this is about?"

My reply was blunt, "The sooner you get here, the sooner you'll find out."

"Okay, boss lady," he remarked with an assured tone. "I'll see you later this morning."

The moment I hung up the phone, I started to pace the bedroom floor. As soon as I did, Michael climbed out of bed and left the room. He returned with a cup of coffee, just as I reached my maximum state of thought and said, "I figured you could use this." I smiled appreciatively as I kissed his cheek, took a sip and went right back to pacing. As I paced my mind started to spine so fast and it wasn't stopping until I'd spun a web I knew none of them would escape.

It was 11:00am when Tom Davies arrived at my outer office and I had still not been able to organize my thoughts. As soon as Tom entered my office I said, "Tom, do you have what I asked for?"

He handed me three 12/14 manila envelopes, "All the financial dirt on the big three, are in those envelopes."

I took them from him intently, "Great! Come on and sit down with me for a few minutes, while I look these over." Then I looked at him, "Fix yourself some coffee, it's over there on the counter and I'll be right with you."

I buzzed my new personal secretary Terry Baggatta and said, "Terry, please notify everyone I will be ready for our emergency board meeting at 1:00pm." I handed the Bradford Computers envelope to Michael and the Salerno envelope to Jimmy.

I took the Kenney envelope as I thought, "This one was just for me! I didn't forget someone tried to kill me without meaning to, and since it's time for the payback, you might as well get yours now too." Then I said, "Dig me out all the information on cash holdings and I need to know who holds the majority of their stock." With that we went right to work.

By the time we were ready for the meeting, I had all the information I needed to begin to truly develop strategies. We all said our normal greetings when we entered the conference room. Then I got right to the point, "Okay guys, I called this meeting because Powers Incorporated is under siege. We are in a dire situation which will take the wits and cooperation of every single one of us in this room, if we hope to emerge victorious from our upcoming battle." I took a sip from my orange juice then continued, "It's like this, Lee Bradford is going to help Frank Salerno pass his new stock market bill through the Senate." I filled them in on how they planned to achieve this, then said, "Now, depending on how much damage Lee has already done with other senators, I might be able to change Mr. Bradford's mind, thus once again, temporarily solving the problem until the next time. But I think there may be another way of handling this."

I began to slowly pace back and forth on the speaker's platform as I said, "I think if we let them pass the law, then we may be able to strike a sneak attack on both their corporations. But, before I suggest it, I first need to tell you if we go through with my plans and fail, then we may eventually lose Powers Incorporated."

Joe Cole stood up, "Christina, may I speak?"

"Please do, Joe."

"All I want to know is, will we finally get out from under the thumb of Frank Salerno? We go through this with him every year, and every year we go crazy trying to defeat this damn bill. So, if you have a plan you believe in then please tell us about it. I think it's about time we kick some corporate ass, and take care of this problem once and for all!"

Everyone began to clap, so I said, "Okay guys, I said I had a plan. However, I didn't say it was going to be easy, but here it is. As it stands, if we were to go on the open market today our stock would be selling at sixty-two dollars a share. That's not high enough. When we hit the market, we have to be over one-hundred dollars a share. Now that point leads into this one: right now Powers Incorporated has cash holdings totaling sixty-three-billion dollars. Bradford has two-hundred and forty-four-billion dollars, and Salerno Incorporated has one-hundred and seventy-six-billion-dollars. This leaves us the financial weakling compared to our opponents. So the first thing we need to do is to increase our income substantially and fast. This will also bring up the value of our stock, and we will have to keep them up, as we try to knock our opponents stock down. Now, I will handle the value of our opponent's stock come D-day, but I need you guys to bust some ass with me and build up our stock." 'Privately, I discovered Kenney Baby Foods had a cash value of seventy-eight billion dollars. I had to calculate all my figures to the penny, if I were to be successful.' I continued; "First, we need to have the album ready to be released as soon as possible, like tomorrow. Second, we have two weeks to set up a six month, seven day a week, nationwide concert tour, beginning in September." I turned to Jimmy and added, "Jimmy, I want my December 2nd, performance to be in Las Vegas."

That's when Joe interrupted, "A seven day a week tour, will the crowds come every night?"

Confidently I answered, "I haven't performed live in more than ten years Joe; they'll come. Once we announce the tour, our stock will begin to climb and once the cash from the concert tour begins to pour in, I think we'll be solving both our cash and stock problems at one time, but it has got to be a super-hot tour. So guys, you have got to make it hot. We are going to have to start finishing up the album tonight, because I will be going out of town for a few days, at the end of the week."

Anxiously Jimmy said, "You have two weeks to get in shape for a six-month concert tour, and you're going out of town for a few days?"

I shook my head at him disappointingly; then reassured them all, "In order for all of this to work, I have to. I'm not leaving you guys in a sinking ship. I know what I'm doing. So as soon as I come back, I'll start rehearsing."

It was straight to work and we worked all day long. When Michael and I arrived at our new home on the complex grounds, overlooking the river it was 1:00am. We walked in the door and went straight to the showers. Afterwards, we laid in bed together and Michael began to gently massage my shoulders as he said, "So where are we going?"

I turned to look him in the eyes, "Michael, there are some things about myself which I have never told anyone, and I've always handled things my way. But now I'm in a dilemma that I'm not sure how to handle." I looked up at him as if to say help me, as I struggled with my words.

Michael, seeing my distress took me in his arms, "Christina, I love you and if you're having a problem telling me something, then don't be, I will be beside you no matter what you've done."

I thought very seriously for one moment, "Michael, I've got to be truthful with you no matter what the cost. I have been the mistress to one of the most powerful mafia leaders in the world for years now. I have only slept with him twice in my life, but as far as he's concerned, I will always be his special secret lover. He lives in Italy and I need to go see him. He is the only man on this earth right now, with the power to help me."

Michael looked at me strangely, "Punkie, I can handle your past, but I hope you're not thinking of sleeping with him again?"

I pulled Michael on top of me, kissed him and replied, "Michael there was a time I would have just gone off and do what I had to do. But I can't do that anymore, that is why I'm telling you this. I need his help, but even if I come out of our meeting in a **box**, I will not sleep with him. I believe I can now make him understand that."

This time, Michael looked deeply into my eye, "I trust you, Punkie." Then he kissed me, "So when are we going; because I'm still coming with you."

I kissed him again, "Friday. But first we're going to Washington on Thursday."

With a curious look on his face he asked, "Why are we taking all these trips anyway?"

I answered cautiously, "Michael, I love you, but if I tell you and my plan fails, then I might be spending a few years in San Quentin."

"San Quentin! What the hell are you up to?"

My expression was more than serious, "Michael, the less you know about it the better your chances in a court of law would be, if it comes to that. So please don't ask me anymore."

"Fuck that!" He swiftly replied, "I want to know what you're planning before I decide whether we go through with it or not!"

With that remark I began to get a little hot under the collar, "Now just one minute, who do you think you're talking to? You're going to decide?"

"Hold on before you get upset Christina, and look at it from my side. What if I just told you everything you just told me? What would you say?"

I thought about it for a moment, "Okay, Michael, you're right."

I told him every detail of my plan and he said, "That is pure genius and ruthless, besides. How the hell did you figure that out?"

I smiled deviously, "I'm a fucking genius, that's how. And I can't believe I just let you into my darkest thoughts."

With an amused look on his face he said, "Baby, I love you, and as devious as your plan is, I give you my blessings. I just hope no one gets hurt."

Don't worry no one will get hurt, except the three snakes." I looked very seriously into his eyes, "Michael, I hope you know I would never do this if I didn't have to, my hand is being forced."

Tenderly he kissed me, "I know that Punkie, and believe it or not, it makes me love you even more."

He kissed me passionately and we ended that night the way we've ended every night since we moved in together, in the heat of our passion. We just couldn't get enough of each other.

First thing I did the next morning was to place a call to Senator Tom Kenney. He would be my first pawn in our game of corporate chess. I told him I would be in town in two days and I needed to meet with him. We set an appointment for 1:00pm on Thursday, August 10th, at his office in Georgetown. My next call was to Dominick Giovanetti. I told him I would be arriving in Italy that coming weekend, and I desperately needed to see him. He told me to let him know when my flight would arrive, so he could have a driver waiting for me. He also said he would cancel whatever he was involved in, as soon as I arrived.

We ended our conversation, and I thought, "Dominick's assistance is absolutely crucial right now for my scheming to be foolproof. Now, if I can only talk him into helping me without the sexual favors, I'll be doing really well." Then I thought, "What if I can't control him?" With that I shrugged my shoulders and thought, "Oh well, I'll figure it out tomorrow." Then it was straight to work on the recording of 'The Power of Love.'

By Wednesday night we had finished recording and it was ready for mass production the next morning. After Michael and I tied up a few loose ends at the office on Thursday morning, we went straight to Stewart Airport in Newburgh.

On our flight to Washington, Michael and I were discussing our plans and I said, "Michael, I don't want you to be upset, but when we arrive at Senator Kenney's office, as well as Dominick's office, I will have to speak to them alone."

Immediately a strained look came over him, "Christina, I don't know that I can let you do that. Besides, I already know everything you're going to say."

I kissed him gently and with all my heart said, "Honey, I know how you feel about me doing this by myself, but just because you know everything, doesn't mean you can be present when I speak to these men. They must believe no one else knows what I will be asking them to do for me. I need to have their utmost confidence in my ability to pull this off, with no one knowing. Besides baby, I really am a big girl and I can handle myself quite well." He kissed me and reluctantly agreed.

When I entered Tom's office, I immediately gave him a warm embrace, just to remind him with whom he was dealing. After we exchanged greetings, he gestured to me to take a seat beside him on a large vinyl sofa. As I did, he gazed at me as if my presence alone made his blood begin to race to all parts of his body, as he said, "Christina, it's been so long and you're still as lovely as ever."

I softly smiled and graciously replied, "Well thank you, Tom. You're still looking quite good yourself. But this is not a social call, it's strictly business. I happen to have in my possession some information on a mutual friend of ours. I believe this bit of information would be very useful to a man in your position."

I knew I caught his interest, just by the way he tried to hide his enthusiasm as he casually said, "Christina, I have no idea what you're talking about."

I smiled again, but this time a little more sensually. Then I gently placed my hand on his upper thigh and seductively said, "What if I told you, if we worked together we could politically, and professionally, slit Lee Bradford's throat."

Immediately the lights in his eyes said it all and 'I knew I had him.' With that, he grabbed my hand and said, "Just how do you plan to pull this off?"

I gently squeezed his hand and began to tell him my part, in my plan of revenge on our mutual adversary. I told him what I had and what I planned to do with it. A look of delightful wickedness grew on his face and he said, "It sounds too devious not to work, so what's my part in your little scheme?"

That's when I told him what I wanted from him, as well as exactly when and how I needed him to deliver.

After carefully absorbing and analyzing my every word he asked, "How can I be sure, I'll get what you say you can deliver, when you say you will deliver it?"

With utmost confidence I replied, "Tom, think about it. Do you really think I'm just out for personal revenge? Well I'm not. I want the world to know what kind of a thieving bastard Lee Bradford, truly is." With sincerity I stood up, took a few steps away from him, turned back and added, "Tom, you were right all along, Lee

Bradford does need to be brought to justice for his crimes, and I'm the only person who can help you do that!"

With a look of sweet revenge in his eyes, and a smile on his face, "I'll do it!" he replied with enthusiasm.

By the time we finished our meeting, I had Tom drooling from the mouth, with just the anticipation of the thought, of the kill.

Michael romantically wined and dined me that night, and somehow in the midst of the beautiful city of Washington, D.C., we totally forgot our impending crisis and once again we were young lovers. This was the way we truly wanted to spend every moment of our lives, immersed in each other's love, not battling for our corporate survival against two evil men, who were so arrogant they believed they could destroy innocent lives at will just to obtain and maintain their corrupt POWER!

That night after love making, I laid in Michael's arms and thought, "I will let no man ever destroy me again, and may God forgive me, but if I have to, I will KILL THEM BOTH before they get a chance!" Then I drifted off to sleep in Michael's strong arms.

The next evening we were both a little nervous as our plane approached Rome. I had just finished saying, "Michael, whatever you do, always treat Dominick with the utmost respect. You will see his presence alone commands it."

Before we knew it, it was 7:00pm Rome time and we were climbing into the limo Dominick had waiting for us at the airport. The driver told us we would be having dinner with Dominick at his mansion in the city, and off we went. Dominick was aware my future husband would be arriving with me. I didn't want to surprise Dominick with trivial things at our personal meeting. I also hoped this information would help to calm his appetite some. I knew it really wasn't going to hold any water with Dominick at all, but I was still glad Michael was with me.

When we entered the formal dining room, Dominick warmly embraced us both with a strong, Italian, bear hug. To my surprise, we were also meeting a small group of some of Dominick's very close friends, who had been anxiously waiting to meet me. After our cordial introductions, Dominick led us to the green dining room where we proceeded to have a wonderful dinner, with what seemed to be an older and more-gentler Dominick. He was absolutely charming, and he treated Michael more like a son, then the lover of his 'lover.'

Sometime after dinner that evening, as we all chatted in the informal golden living room, Dominick excused us from the rest of his guests' and led me to his private library. I winked at Michael as I left him with the others, then I took a deep breath as I followed Dominick.

As we walked, I began to pray in my thoughts. I was scared shitless! The last thing I wanted to do was to be forced to sleep with him in order to obtain his help." When he closed the library door, I swallowed my heart and thought, "Oh God! Help me with this one." With that, I turned to Dominick, went right into my performance and truthfully, but dramatically said, "Dominick, I'm here because I am fighting for my life, and I won't be able to survive without your help."

He hugged me gently and took me by the hand. My heart pounded like a jack hammer within me, as he led me to a love seat. Then he sat me down beside him and said, "Now calm down, you can ask me anything. If I can help, I will." He kissed my forehead and with sincerity continued, "Now tell me all about it and we'll decide how to handle it together."

I proceeded to tell Dominick everything, including my whole plan to remedy the situation. He was the only other person I told besides Michael, because when dealing with Dominick, one had to be totally honest.

He gave me a surprised look, "Do you really think you can pull this one off?"

I looked confidently into his eyes, "With your help, I know I can, Dominick. Once the smoke clears I will only be battling Salerno Incorporated who will be weakened, but so will Powers Incorporated. Now if I could only come up with that one missing piece of the puzzle."

Dominick shook his head and smiled suspiciously, "I'm sure you're going to tell me what that piece is."

I took his hand and smiled, "I need one more board to pull out from under Frank's feet to make him unstable enough to fall with the rest of them."

Dominick stood up, pulled me into his arms and kissed me, "Christina, do you know what intrigues me the most about you?"

I smiled sweetly, "No, but I hope you will tell me."

With a loving expression, he kissed me again, "You are the most magnificent **'black widow'** I have ever laid my eyes on." He began to lead me over toward a large sofa on the other side of the room, and as we reached it he said, "I can help you with Kenney, but as for Frank, I'll have to do some fancy side stepping when it comes to him, but I'll see what I can do." Then, he took me into his arms and began to passionately kiss me.

I gently tried to pull out of his clutches and with the deepest sincerity said, "Dominick, please listen to me before we go any further. I must tell you something."

He slowed his passion, and said, "I'm sorry Christina, I thought we were through talking, please continue."

Cautiously I replied, "Dominick, I do love and admire you with all my heart and I would never turn you away. But I must tell you, I am truly in love with Michael, and if I sleep with you it would kill him. Please, I love Michael too much to do that to him." I began to tear up as I grabbed his hand, "I'm begging you not to ask me to sleep with you."

His eyes began to tear with mine as he kissed me again, "I'm not a groveling man Christina, but if I hold you any longer I will be. So please take my love with you and may God bless your future." He squeezed me gently, kissed me one more time as he looked deeply into my eyes, "I will always remember you Christina and I'll be cheering you on from the sidelines," as he slapped my ass, "Now get the hell out of here, before I change my mind."

With tears of joy and relief in my eyes I whispered, "I love you too, Dominick." Then I turned graciously and victoriously walked away.

On Monday, August 13th, it was straight into rehearsals for my just announced Ten Year Anniversary concert tour. The tour was scheduled to open at Yankee Stadium that coming Friday August

17th. That gave me four and a half days to get ready for the hottest concert I had ever given. I was a little rusty at thirty-five-years of age, but I still had it and once again the financial stability of Powers Incorporated depended upon it. As you know, the schedule was going to be beyond intense, but we had no choice if we were to be ready for D-day. I decided to hire a small army of security staff to accompany us across the country. I knew if any of my opponents got wind of my plans, there would be a good chance I might become the sight at the end of a sniper's barrel. And I sure as hell didn't want that.

When the morning of August 17th came I found myself a little nervous, to say the least. All day long the pressure grew inside me. You see, I had still not heard from Dominick, and I had everyone I trusted looking for the last piece of my puzzle on Frank, **with no success**. I believed I could defeat Salerno Incorporated in an all-out battle, but if I had that last piece of the puzzle, I could do it with little or no bloodshed at all to Powers Incorporated. And to top my day off, I started to get my normal pre-performance jitters.

The show time was scheduled to begin at 9:00pm and by 8:00pm that evening I was freaking. I waited in my dressing room alone, trying to psych myself up for my performance. As I paced the floor, I glanced up at the clock on the wall and it read 8:15. I stopped pacing and headed straight for Michael and Jimmy who were taking care of some last minute changes I had asked them to make on the stage props. When I found them, they were out on the stage and I could hear the crowds filling the auditorium just behind the curtain. I went straight to Michael, wrapped my arms around his neck and began to cry.

Michael lovingly embraced and tenderly said, "I love you Punkie, and you're going to be great tonight."

Michael kissed me as Jimmy walked over, "I told you she'd be crazy by show time." Jimmy wrapped his arms around Michael and me, "Listen to me guys, as long as the three of us stick together we can make it through anything." He kissed our cheeks, "Christina, when you go out there, you will be taking the strength of three with you. Now all you have to do is go in that dressing room and come out the great, *Christina Powers*."

I wiped the tears from my cheeks, kissed them both once and replied, "I love you two and you're both right." I slid out from between them, "Well I'd better go get ready." At that I swallowed hard, turned and walked back to my dressing room.

When I emerged, I was once again *Christina Powers*, the world's most famous and hottest sex symbol. And I looked like a **goddess** in my red satin skin tight gown. The gown flowed down to just past my calves, with my famous slit up the middle, to show my million-dollar legs, red heels and silky clear stockings. I thought I was going to have to pick Michael up off the floor, when he saw just how beautiful his future bride could truly be.

In awe, he embraced me and bellowed, "I have never seen anything as radiant as you are at this moment." He kissed me passionately, "Take our passion for love with you and knock them dead, Punkie!"

I returned his kiss, "I love you too, Michael." It was at that moment, the lights flashed, signifying the opening act was finished and it was now my turn. I kissed Michael one more time, turned and walked over to get ready for my cue to go on stage. As I anxiously waited, I said a little prayer to myself.

I took a deep breath when I heard my cue and sensually danced my way out onto the stage, to the screams of one-hundred and fifty-thousand fans; all of whom actually had to fight for each one of their tickets. This was the biggest concert crowd to ever attend one performer's show and I immediately began to give them their moneys' worth. I went right into a medley of all my hottest past hits, straight into singing the singles from my new album, 'The Power of Love'. In between sets I stopped three different times to chat with the crowd. In the midst of the final chat, we were laughing and having a great time, when someone shouted out, "Christina! Please do 'Halloween in Hell' for us." As soon as he did, the crowd went wild with cheers and chants for 'Halloween in Hell'. When I was finally able to calm them down, I said, "Friends, I haven't sung a cut off that album since the night I lost my daughter, Joy. So please forgive me, but I must say no. You see, I promised myself I would never sing one of those songs again."

The crowd cheered even louder as they shouted, "We love you, Christina!" I stormed right into the rest of my performance and after being absent from the stage for more than ten years, I had them screaming in the aisles and my show that night was a smashing success!

The next morning the critics wrote, "**Christina Powers showed New York why she's the Queen! Her performance was spectacular!**"

We were full steam into our tour, when finally on September 26th, I heard from Dominick!

I anxiously grabbed the phone from Michael's hand, in our hotel room in Atlanta, Georgia, when he said, "It's Dominick."

"Hi Dominick, I've been going nuts waiting to hear from you."

Chuckling at my anxious tone he replied, "Calm down little girl, I told you I'd get it."

With excitement in my voice I asked, "You got the piece I need on Frank?"

This time there was no chuckle, "First, I have Senator Kenney covered for you." Then he took on a serious tone, "Now listen, I don't want you going off the deep end, but here it is. As for Frank . . ." as he continued, he told me something which made my blood boil from the pain which shot straight through my soul.

"Dominick thank-you; I promise I will never forget what you've done for me. You've been my guardian angel for a long time now and I love you for it. As for what you just told me, **I will make it work**." We ended our conversation and it was now time to begin to implement phase two of my counter strategy.

By the time the Senate passed Frank's bill on October 6th, I was well on my way to finally catching up with the two financial giants I would soon be doing battle with. My concerts were bringing in huge crowds every night and with no seat selling for less than one hundred dollars, the money was pouring in. When we added in the sales from the album, we were grossing a phenomenal ninety-million dollars a week, worldwide. Not only that, but I finally had Powers Incorporated in full swing and our grand total per week was reaching the three-hundred-million dollar mark. I was jockeying into position as fast as I could and our stock showed it. The value for one share went up to a hundred and two-dollars on the market. We were doing so well, that by the time I decided to pay a visit to Lee, on November 30th, Powers Incorporated had a cash net worth of ninety-eight-billion dollars and rising fast! That fact helped me feel more then confidant I would be victorious. But the best thing of all was as of yet, none of my enemies had any idea what was coming.

9:00pm on November 30th, I knocked on Lee's door at his home in Gardener. I knew he was home and I had plenty to say. I was looking very good and Lee was quite surprised when he saw me standing there.

As he opened the door, I casually said, "Hi, may I come in? I'd like to talk with you."

He gestured me in and as I entered, he arrogantly said, "Christina, come on in. Hmm, I wonder what brings you to my door." Then he gloated as he looked at me, "Maybe I should guess. Let's see, maybe you're here to grovel on **your knees, this time**. As a matter of fact, I'll bet you're thinking just maybe I can seduce and deceive Lee into saving my desperate little ass, just one more time before I destroy him again!"

I turned to him and with a disgusted tone reeled, "Lee, no matter what happened between us, I would have never betrayed you. The one thing you will never understand is even though we are no longer together you will always have a place in my heart, whether you want to be there or not, and I won't change the kind of person I am just to suit you." I took a step closer to him, looked earnestly into his eyes, "Even though that's all water under the bridge now, I still care about you and that is why I hate to say what I am about to, but Lee, you gave me no choice."

I told him what information I had on him and what I would do with this information, if he did not do exactly what I wanted him to do, when I wanted him to do it, and precisely how I wanted him to do it." I completed my instructions with a sarcastic, "Who's groveling now Lee?"

He turned so red I thought he was going to burst. He reluctantly agreed to my terms then said, "Do you destroy all your ex-lovers?"

I gave him a disappointed look, "Only the ones who betray me." I walked away feeling horrible for what I had just done, but as I drove away I thought,, "Oh well, I'll figure it out tomorrow."

On December 1st, 1988, at 3:00pm Powers Incorporated became compliant with the new federal guidelines which governed the stock exchange. Powers Incorporated was now also, completely ready for our December 2nd showdown on Wall Street. When D-day arrived Michael and I were going over every detail for the one-thousandth time in our suite at Caesar's Hotel and Casino, in Las Vegas, Nevada, and it wasn't even 6:00am yet. I was so psyched I couldn't wait for the 9:00am bell to ring on Wall Street. We had the entire suite setup with computers and phone lines, so we could monitor every movement the stock market made. I also had a small army of phone operators who would be in constant contact with my hand chosen stock brokers, all waiting for me to send them into action.

At 8:00am, Eastern Standard Time, 5:00am Pacific Time, I called Detective Fred Ulrich at his home in Los Angeles, California and said, "Hi Fred, its *Christina Powers*. I'm sorry to wake you, but I have to talk to you now."

He perked up, "You sound serious. Have you come up with something?"

With a positive tone I answered, "I sure have, Fred." I proceeded to painfully tell him what I had discovered. After which I asked him to keep this information to himself, until I called him later that morning. When I hung up the phone, I thought, "Finally all the pieces to my puzzle are in place, and I am more than ready to play the game with the big boys."

On December 2nd, at 9:00am, Eastern Standard Time, the bell rang on Wall Street. The market opened like this: Powers Incorporated, one-hundred and four-dollars per share. Salerno Incorporated, one-hundred and twelve-dollars per share. Bradford Computers, one-hundred and twenty-six-dollars per share, and Kenney Baby Foods, seventy-six-dollars per share. Frank's plan was to begin his joint corporate attack along with Bradford Computers, at 9:15am on Powers Incorporated. So I'm sure he was shitting when Bradford Computers waged an all-out corporate take-over attempt on Salerno Incorporated at 9:05am. By 9:15am I began to smile as I watched Salerno Incorporated shift gears from Powers Incorporated to a full-force retaliation against Bradford Computers. Their stock soared so fast that by 10:00am each corporation had committed more than twenty-five-billion-dollars cash toward the destruction of the other.

As I had counted on, by 10:30am Lee was showing all his might as he began to over-take Salerno Incorporated with a seventy-six-billion dollar commitment. I knew Frank would be afraid to invest any more than seventy-five-billion dollars, even to save his empire. So, I made my first phone call to Tom. The entire stock market was going crazy as these two giants forced all the stock to begin to climb with them. Then, just as Frank was about to concede, Tom jumped into the game. Kenney Baby Foods offered to join forces with Salerno Incorporated against Bradford Computers, and they would divide up the spoils. Once again, just as I hoped, Frank jumped back into the game. I sat back and watched the markets go mad, as these three giants of the business world did battle. I watched in complete satisfaction as these three men committed most of their cash holdings into this battle. Finally at 1:00pm Bradford Computers had committed two-hundred-billion dollars to the battle. Salerno Incorporated one-hundred and fifty-billion dollars and Kenney Baby Foods sixty-eight-billion dollars.

That's when I made my second call and once again it was to Tom, and at 1:05pm the United States Congress, announced a warrant for the arrest of Senator Lee Bradford, on the charges of conspiracy and espionage. Ten minutes later Bradford Computer's stock began to drop like a sky diver without his chute. At 1:20pm I made my third call, this time to Detective Fred Ulrich, and at 1:26pm an arrest warrant was issued for Frank Salerno, for conspiracy to commit murder. I was ecstatic by 1:40pm when Salerno Incorporated stock began to drop almost as fast as Bradford Computers did. Then at 1:52pm I made my fourth call, this one was to Dominick, and at 2:11pm the CDC recalled two-million cases of Kenney baby foods for possible food poisoning. And guess what! Kenney Baby Food's stock began to plummet faster than the other two combined. The last minutes of the day, the stock holders of all three companies, scrambled to sell their plummeting stock with no buyers to be found anywhere. I laughed with a sense of pure satisfaction as I watched all three of these corporate giants begin to crumble.

By 2:30pm not one of them had enough capital left to save their own asses, no less try to take-over the corner drug store. So, at 2:35pm as each of their stock reached the lower double digits, I started shouting out orders left and right to my phone operators to start buying.

At that, I swept down and devoured the aftermath and by 3:00pm December 2nd, 1988, with the help of my colleagues, we had taken control of 79% of Bradford Computers, 92% of Kenney Baby Foods, and 96% of Salerno Incorporated. By 3:05pm the whole business world was reeling in the aftermath of my day of vengeance. By 3:15pm Eastern Standard Time and 12:15pm Pacific Time, I was on my way to the headquarters of Salerno Incorporated to claim the spoils of my victory, and to spit in Franks face. I could not wait to watch Detective Ulrich and the Nevada State Police arrest Frank for the murder of my baby. As our caravan headed to the headquarters of Salerno Incorporated, we drove through the worst storm front the Nevada desert had seen in ten years and my blood raced in anticipation with every mile.

When Michael and I arrived at Salerno Incorporated we came in with an entourage of staff to go right in and monitor all aspects of the corporation until I could formally take over.

As I walked down the hall to Frank's office I thought, "This is it! My moment of sweet victory; which I had fought sixteen years to achieve."

We reached Franks outer office and I was surprised to see Detective Fred Ulrich and the Nevada State Police were not there yet. But that was not going to stop me from throwing Frank the hell out of his own office.

I walked up to Carroll, Frank's long time secretary, "Carroll, I'm sure you know why I'm here. Now where is Frank?"

Nervously, she answered, "Wait one minute Christina, and I'll let him know you're here."

As Carroll began to buzz Frank, I barged into his office with Michael and three bodyguards right behind me, "Well Frank it's funny seeing you here in my office, I thought you'd be in jail by now."

In reply to my sarcastic words, he shouted out in rage, "Get the fuck out of my office right now, before I throw you out!"

With an air of superiority, I threw a fax of the final Wall Street count of the day's games into his face and viciously shouted back, "Looks like I win Frank, read them and weep, you bastard. Now get your ass the **fuck** out of my seat because the state police will be here any minute to arrest you, and I don't want to look at a baby killer any longer than I have to."

He seemed to calm down some as he replied, "I'll leave, but at least give me five minutes to talk with you alone before the police come. It's about your parents."

I looked at him with hatred in my eyes and with curiosity in my heart said, "For some reason I want to know what it is you have to say to me Frank, so I will grant you a private audience." I turned to Michael and my bodyguards and added, "Please give me five minutes with him alone and wait in the outer office for me."

Michael interjected with a suspicious tone, "Christina, I don't trust him, let me stay with you."

Sarcastically Frank asked, "Is this the new fiancée everyone is talking about? Funny, but he looks a lot like someone else we once knew, doesn't he, Christina?"

Angered by his innuendo I turned to Michael and with a forceful tone said, "No, Michael! Please wait outside! Besides, you'll only be on the other side of the door."

Michael shook his head reluctantly, and turned to Frank, "Okay, but I'll be right outside this door."

When they left, I said, "Okay Frank, start talking, your time is limited."

He stood up from his chair, "You think you have destroyed me, don't you?"

I smiled deviously, "I don't think so, I know so. So what's your point?"

With evil radiating from his eyes he answered, "My point is this, Christy. Your mother tried to destroy me once and I had her killed. Your father tried to destroy me, and I had him killed too. You just insulted me, and I had your child killed. So what makes you think you can do what a President couldn't do?" With that he pulled out a hand gun, as he hit the button on his desk, which locked the large doors to his office. My mind and blood began to race as Frank pointed the gun at me, "What a shame it turned out like this for us, Christy. I would have loved you and given you the world. But now I have to kill you."

I looked at him with utter sincerity, "Before you pull that trigger Frank, I want you to grant me one last thing?"

I knew he could sense my desperation, "You're not in the position to ask for anything, but I'll let you speak."

I slowly began to sensually move toward him, "Frank, those doors are thick and no one is getting in here too soon." As I reached him, I carefully brushed my fingers through his hair and very sensually said, "Frank, make love to me just once, before you take my life."

He took me in his arms, "This is what you needed sixteen years ago."

As he kissed me deeply, I kneed him right in the nuts as hard as I could, at the same time I grabbed the gun still in his hand, and as he yelled, "You fucking bitch!" I yelled, "Michael, Help! Help me!"

We began to fight for control of the gun as I continued to scream, "Help! Michael! Help!"

I screamed as our bodies smashed into the large book shelves sending the books hurling to the floor, "Michael, help me!"

I could hear Michael banging on the door when the gun flew out of both our hands as we fought and it landed on the desk. Frank grabbed me as I tried to run for the gun and flung us both to the ground. I could feel my breath being taken from me with Frank's weight landing right on top of me. I screamed and struggled to escape him as he reached for my neck with his hands.

I had just made it to my knees, when Frank belted me right across the right jaw, knocking my head back against the corner of the desk so hard it split the back of my head open. I could feel the blood begin to rush down my back, as I struggled to catch my breath. Seeing Frank coming toward me on his knees, I sprang my knees back and with all my might pushed up with both feet, hitting him right in the chest. As he went flying over backwards, I climbed to my feet, grabbed the gun and ran for the door. Just as I reached the door Frank leaped at me and once again grabbed the gun as I held it in my hands, only this time it went off **'Bang!'** I screamed in terror, as I let go of the gun.

I watched in horror as Frank began to fall to the floor with blood gushing from his chest. Then "**Bang!**" came the second shot, this time I grabbed for my abdomen as the pain shot through my body. I began to stagger, than I fell to the floor with blood pouring from my open stomach. When I hit the floor, I could see the figure of a man and I could hear him talking to someone. I felt a cold feeling in my hand and I began to fall backwards as if I were falling right through the floor. I kept falling back into the mist of a dark, bleak, nothingness. As I fell into this cold emptiness, I could see the spirit of my unborn child begin to leave my body. This gentle, soft, pure soul began to beckon me toward a speck of light in the distance.

This beautiful little spirit took my hand, and I instantly felt the bond of love only a parent could feel for their child. Joyfully I floated along with my child toward what was becoming a brilliant, bright white light. As we reached this magnificent light we were filled with the presence of the love of God. Just before we entered the warmth of the light a beautiful golden winged angel came to us. This beautiful being took my precious child from my arms and said, "It's not your time my child. You have much life to live yet."

Saddened I replied, "Then let me have my child."

This beautiful angel seemed to look through me as she said, "This spirit has fulfilled its destiny, but you haven't."

I cried out, "How could my child have fulfilled its destiny? It was never born!"

I heard, "You will understand in time my child."

Once she stopped speaking to my thoughts, they both began to fade away into the light, leaving me alone in the darkness. As they vanished, I desperately began to scream and cry, "My baby! I want my baby!" Then they were gone and **everything went dark.**

CHAPTER 18. CHRISTMAS FROM HELL

When I came out of that horrible darkness, I opened my eyes and the first thing I saw was Michael asleep in a chair beside my bed. All of a sudden, a sense of disoriented urgency came over me. I quickly gazed around the dimly lit room, then to the IV lines which led to my arm, and I realized I was in a hospital bed. When I tried to move, I felt a sharp pain in my stomach and I moaned. As soon as I moaned, Michael's eyes popped open and instantly met mine. Like a flash of lightening he sprang up from his chair and dashed to my side. He gently took my hand through the safety bars on the bed, softly kissed my forehead and with tears welling in his eyes gently whispering, "Christina, oh baby, I love you. I thought I had lost you. How do you feel Punkie, can you tell?"

I lovingly gazed back into Michael's tearing eyes, "I feel horrible Michael, what happened?"

A look of surprise immediately came over his face as he replied with concern, "Don't you remember what happened?"

I thought about it for a minute, "The last thing I remember is arguing with Frank, then everything went black."

Michael gently kissed me again, "Let's not talk about that now, its 4:00am we'll talk more later. Do you need anything for pain?"

With a groggy tone I replied, "No, I'm just tired, baby."

Michael gently slid the side railing on the bed down and carefully crawled in beside me. Very slowly, I laid my head on his chest, and as he gently held me in his arms' he said, "I thank God you're okay, Punkie. Now, lie still and just let me hold you." And that was the last thing I heard before I drifted off again.

It was some time around 7:00am when Michael was sternly ordered out of my bed by a large black nurse who said, "Mr. Powers! Get out of that bed right now! Don't you realize your wife is in a coma?"

Startled I lifted my head from Michael's chest and said as this nurse's mouth dropped open, "She looks like she means business, honey you'd better get out of the bed."

As Michael climbed out of the bed she immediately came to me and began to take my vital signs as she said, "Welcome back Ms. Powers, we were all worried about you."

I looked at her earnestly, "I'm starving, may I please have something to eat?"

Giving me a big smile, "You've been unconscious for three weeks, you can't eat yet, but I'll have your doctor in here pronto."

She turned to leave the room and as she closed the door behind her, I turned to Michael, "What was she talking about? Have I been unconscious for three weeks?"

Michael sat on the bed beside me, took my hand in his, "Punkie, you really don't remember what happened?"

"No, Michael!" I answered nervously, "I still don't remember. Will you please fill me in on what's going on?"

Looking at me sincerely, yet tenderly, "Christina, you were shot. When the ambulance arrived with you here at the hospital, you were clinically dead. When they brought you into the E.R., the doctor wanted to pronounce you dead on arrival, but I started ordering them to resuscitate you, so they tried. Five minutes later, they got vital signs. Once you were stabilized, they took you right to the operating room, where they removed a bullet from your uterus." He gently held me, "We lost our baby, Christina."

I immediately started to cry, "God! Not our baby! I wanted to have our child so badly!"

Michael tenderly embraced me, "Christina, I just thank God they were able to save you. After the surgery, you were in critical condition for a week. I thought I was going to lose you too. My heart was breaking every minute you were in the intensive care unit hooked up to all kinds of tubes. They finally stabilized you enough to take you off the respirator, but you still wouldn't come out of the coma. The doctor who saved you in the O.R., a Doctor Sonne, thought the coma may have been brought on more by a mental trauma, rather than a physiological one, since physically you began to do better. But, they still couldn't get you to come out of the coma, until you woke up this morning."

I was totally overwhelmed and it showed on my face, "Michael, how did I get shot?"

Michael took my hand, "I was hoping you could tell me that. What can you remember about the fight you had with Frank?"

I shook my head, "All I remember is asking you to leave the room, because Frank wanted to tell me something in private. Somehow we started to fight. Oh God! That's right! I remember! Frank pulled out a gun and we fought over it. I knew you were trying to get in, so I ran to the door and that's when everything went black. Oh my God! Frank must have shot me! Where's Frank, now?"

Puzzled Michael looked straight into my eyes, "Christina, Frank is dead! By the time we broke the door down two shots had already been fired. When we finally entered the room, you both had been shot and you had the gun in your hands. The Nevada State Police have been waiting for you to come out of the coma so they could question you."

All of a sudden I began to feel weak, "Michael, I'm not feeling too good. Please call someone I think I'm going to pass out."

Michael immediately pulled the call button out of the wall and within seconds, two nurses came running into the room. Michael told them I was feeling faint so one of the nurses put smelling salts under my nose and I began to come around. Just as I caught my breath, a distinguished looking tall man with graying hair, wearing a three-piece blue suit, walked into the room. When he reached my bed, the nurses backed off a little as this man said, "Hi, I'm Doctor Sonne, it's about time you woke up sleeping beauty."

I replied with a grateful smile, "Hi Doctor Sonne, I hear you had a hand in saving my life. I'd like to thank you. Now I'd like to know what day it is and when may I eat?"

Doctor Sonne chuckled, than with a look of amusement said, "Today is Thursday, December 19th, and all you can have are clear liquids. We'll see how well you tolerate them, before we serve the fillet mignon. Now, I want you to rest for a couple hours, then I'm going to have the nurses walk you every four hours. We have to start building those muscles back up."

Gratefully, I shook his hand, "Thank you once again, but before you leave, I do have one more question."

"You may ask me whatever you need to."

With nervous concern I inquired, "Michael told me you had to take our baby because the bullet entered my uterus. All I want to know is, do I still have all my womanly parts?"

He shook his head sadly, as he spoke with a tone of authority, "I was going to wait to tell you this, but since you asked, the answer is yes. But Christina, your uterus suffered some severe trauma and I don't believe you will ever be able to bear a child again. I hate to tell you that, but that's my professional opinion."

I swallowed hard, "Well, I can at least thank you for being honest. Now I think I'll try to get some rest, before I have to go jogging."

After he left the room I turned to Michael, "Did you already know I could no longer have children?"

"Yes Punkie, I knew," he answered sadly. "But, I was going to wait until you were feeling a little stronger, before telling you."

With anger in my voice I yelled, "That **fucking,** Frank! He deserved to die! This is the third child he took from me and now they're telling me I can never have children again!" My tears began to fall as I added, "I didn't mean that Michael, no one deserves to die. I just feel so sick inside. I wanted us to have a family so badly."

Michael held me oh so tenderly and with his voice full of compassion said, "Punkie, I love you no matter what! And even though we can no longer have our own children, we can still have a family. There is no reason we can't adopt."

I looked up at him through my tears, "I know we can adopt and God willing we will. I just wanted to bear your child, Michael. Now, we can never have a child of our own."

That's when Michael began to choke up, "Punkie, I love you more than life itself and there is nothing more I'd like then for you to bear my child; but, it's not the end of the world. So for now, let's get you out of this hospital, then we'll talk about how we'll have our family." As he finished speaking, Michael tenderly took my hand in his and held it until I fell back to sleep, which only took a few minutes.

Jimmy flew in from New York as soon as Michael called him, and he started to cry the minute we saw one another. Later that evening over my clear broth dinner, Jimmy filled me in on what transpired after my so-called death by saying, "Christina, it was crazy! 3:00pm that afternoon when the closing bell rang on the market, our stock closed at one-hundred and thirty-six-dollars a share. But the next morning, after the news hit you were shot and might not survive, our stock began to plummet with all the others. When Dominick saw what was going on, he called me and offered to help. He gave us a ten-billion dollar shot in the arm. After his generous loan, we were able to stabilize all four corporations, and right now Fortune 500 has declared you the most ruthless and richest woman in the world! Christina, thanks to your brilliant maneuvering, the size of the Powers Empire is now **second to none**." Then with pure excitement in his mannerisms he yelled out, "Christina, you have become the tenth richest person on this planet. Can you believe that? In thirteen years, you took us from a basement apartment in Rome, to this. You are truly remarkable Christina, and I thank God you're still with me, because girlfriend, I'd have to kill you if you left me." With that, I held my stomach to help control the pain, which shot through me the moment I started to laugh.

I quickly stopped laughing and asked curiously, "If Dominick gave us a ten-billion dollar loan; how can I be the richest woman in the world?"

Jimmy laughed, then with that flick of his wrist said, "First girlfriend, no one knows where the money came from. Second, two days after you left Wall Street reeling, the Senate reversed the decision on Frank's Stock Market Bill; thus, leaving you the right to be the sole owner of the whole kit and caboodle. Do you realize what our holdings are now? We own an awful lot of stuff and now that we've moved in with stage three of your plan all four corporations are on their way back up. As a matter of fact, just today from the news of your recovery, our stock are back up to one-hundred and twenty-six-dollars a share. Not only that, but the Senate also passed a new law which states, 'all future multi-billion dollar corporate takeovers must apply for Congressional approval first."

With that news, I asked the million-dollar question, "What happened to Lee and Tom after they lost everything?"

Jimmy smiled triumphantly, "Lee is once again fighting a Grand Jury Probe, but without the evidence you were going to give Senator Kenney, they still can't prove anything. As for Kenney, he went running home to his family with his tail between his legs. You really caused an-uproar this time, let me tell you."

Immediately a pleased expression lit up my exhausted face as I looked at Jimmy and Michael, "Well guys, that's great news, and I love you both with all my heart for being here for me, but I think I'd better get some rest now." I kissed them both and they left the room together.

The next morning I had two poached eggs, toast and O.J. for breakfast and I devoured it all. Shortly after my second walk of the morning, I received a visit from a Detective Jeremy Jones from the Las Vegas Homicide Division. After he introduced himself to Michael and me, he very bluntly said, "Ms. Powers, I just need to ask you a few questions on exactly what transpired the day of the shooting. Do you think you're up to it?"

I answered politely, "Yes, I think so. Go ahead and ask your questions."

He pulled out a pen and pad as he began, "What I need to know is how you both got shot?"

I shook my head in bewilderment, "I have been trying to remember as much as I can." At that, I proceeded to tell him everything I could remember about the fight, and after which I added, "I don't know how we both got shot, but I do know Frank pulled a gun on me and tried to kill me."

With a superior attitude he pressed on, "Well Ms. Powers, your story has a few things which don't seem to jive, so please try to remember everything you can. It would sure help us solve this case. I will be speaking to you again before you leave the hospital. Oh yes, please don't try to leave the state, or we'll just have to bring you back."

Curiously Michael asked, "Can you tell us what it is that doesn't 'jive', with Christina's story?"

He abruptly answered, "No, I'm sorry sir, I can't do that right now. I have to wait until all the evidence is in first." Then, he thanked us for our time, and left.

After he left Michael said, "I think we better call Tom Davies before you talk to him again."

With a concerned look I asked, "Why? Do you think I'm in some kind of trouble?"

Michael hugged me, "I don't know, I just didn't get a good feeling about the way he was questioning you. He acted as if he didn't believe you."

Feeling totally exhausted and overwhelmed, I sighed with frustration, "Then would you call Tom Davies and Lesley Steine for me? They're the two best attorneys we have."

Michael kissed me, "I think I'll go do that right now. Why don't you try to get some sleep before your next walk." He kissed me again and headed for the door.

As he left my room I could tell he was concerned and I thought, "Oh, God! I pray I didn't kill Frank." I started to laugh to myself, "Oh well, if I did kill Frank, then he asked for it and if I didn't, I wish I had."

Finally on December 24th, at 11:00am I was getting ready to be discharged from the hospital. I was going to be out of the hospital for Christmas, but I was still under a court order not to leave the state. Michael had just gone down to make sure the limo was waiting as close to the front entrance as possible, while I dressed in a two piece, white business suit, with a knee length skirt, 'V' neck and matching jacket. We knew the parking lot was full of reporters, and fans. I also knew I had to face them, so I decided I wanted more of the sexy business woman look, rather than my standard superstar look. I was well aware my public was worried about me by the millions of telegrams and letters that were sent, all wishing me well. So I had to speak to them, but at the same time I wanted to make it as short as possible.

Michael and my sweet big black nurse arrived with a wheelchair to bring me downstairs and the nurse said, "Okay Christina, your ride out of this joint has come and I'm taking you to sweet freedom."

I happily took my seat, "Let's go, because I'm sure ready to get out of this place. Not that you guys weren't great, I just need to get out of here."

She laughed, "I don't blame you. You've been with us longer than most patients."

As we were getting ready to leave Michael said, "The place is mobbed worse than I thought it would be. There are camera crews from all over the world out there, all waiting to give the world just a glimpse of you." He knelt down in front of the wheelchair, "Punkie, are you sure you're ready to face them all? I can still get you out the back way."

I leaned forward and kissed him, "How do I look?"

He took a double take, "Great! I love the suit. Why?"

I smiled confidently, "Because I'm dressed to impress baby. So let's go do some impressing and get it over with."

He returned my kiss, "Okay, let's go get 'em, little girl." And off we went.

When we reached the hospital entrance, I climbed out of the wheelchair, opened the door, and with Michael and three bodyguards beside me, proceeded toward the large concrete staircase, which led down toward the front parking lot.

As soon as we came out from under the canopy which covered the front entrance, we hit the sunlight and were immediately swamped by the press and the clicking of their cameras. Then came the shouts of "We love you Christina," from my fans, who were being held back by Security Guards on both sides of the path to our limo.

From out of the crowd of reporters Connie Chuck yelled, "Christina, how are you feeling?"

I smiled, "I feel great! Don't I look it?"

She laughed, "You look as good as ever."

Kan Alh asked, "Christina, can you tell us how it feels to be so loved on Hollywood Boulevard and so feared on Wall Street?"

I smiled graciously as I triumphantly replied, "I love being loved on Hollywood Boulevard and I love being feared on Wall Street. So, I guess the answer is they both excite me."

Heraldo Saiviera shouted, "Christina, did you kill Frank Salerno?"

You know that saying, 'if looks could kill' well, if it were true, Heraldo would no longer be with us. Sternly I answered, "No! I did not kill Frank Salerno! Now, I think that will be enough questions, thank you very much Mr. Saiviera." Then I ended the press conference and began to head down the steps.

Just as I took my first step down I watched in shock, as ten state police cars sped up to the front of the hospital with lights on and sirens blaring. It looked as if two-hundred state police officers jumped out of the ten cars, and they all came running toward me.

I thought I was going to die, when one of them said in front of the whole world, "*Christina Powers,* you are under arrest for the murder of Frank Salerno." Then, as he placed my hands behind my back and began to put handcuffs on me, he read me my rights. I was horrified as they led me away from Michael and straight through the shouts of the press and cries of horror from my shocked fans.

There I was '*Christina Powers*', "*America's Sex Goddess*" in handcuffs for the entire world to see and being carted off to jail!

When I arrived at the Las Vegas County Court House and Jail, they took a mug shot, fingerprinted me, and put me in a holding pen until I could be brought to the judge for a bail hearing. I sat in that jail cell by myself, from 11:45am that morning, until 3:45pm. That's when Michael, Tom Davies, and Lesley Steine, entered my cell together. As soon as they did, I hugged Michael and said, "I have got to get out of here, or I will go nuts for sure."

Lesley hugged me, "Christina, I have been getting the run around all afternoon. The judge finally agreed to set your bail hearing for 4:30. What I could gather from my questioning is not too good. It appears Frank Salerno was well liked in this state. Everyone in political office, from the Mayor of Vegas, to the

Governor of the State of Nevada have been put there by Frank, and it sounds like they all want to see you hang for his murder."

I looked desperately at them all, "This can't be happening! I couldn't have killed Frank, I was shot remember. How the hell could I have killed him?"

Tom hugged me warmly and said, "As Lesley was trying to get a bail hearing, I was trying to find out what evidence they had to charge you with."

Anxiously I quickly replied, "What did you find out?"

He shook his head in dismay as he glanced at me, "Well to start, forensics shows Frank took the first shot fired from the 22 caliber hand gun found at the crime scene. There were also gun powder burns on the palms of both his hands. This shows when the gun was fired he was trying to take it from your hands. The second shot fired was at close range to you. The prosecution is going on the assumption; this is a failed, murder/suicide attempt." Then he took a breath, "To top it off, there are no other fingerprints on the gun but yours, and they still can't trace the gun back to its original owner, the serial number was illegible."

When he finished talking, my legs began to give out from under me, and I grabbed for Michael as I began to collapse. After he caught me, he helped me sit down on the small cot, and with a nervously excited tone asked, "Are you all right, Punkie?"

I slowly regained my composure, and with tears of fear filling my eyes pleaded, "Please guys, you have got to get me out of here! I know Frank had the gun, so if someone is saying mine were the only fingerprints on the gun, then they're lying." I stood up and with panic in my voice cried out, "Oh, God! Somehow, someone is trying to set me up!" Then, I turned to the three of them, "I'm afraid if they try to keep me here tonight, I might not be alive tomorrow!"

Michael immediately took my hand, "Christina, we have a bail hearing in fifteen minutes. No judge in his right mind is going to keep you in jail on Christmas Eve. Not with the world watching. It would be political suicide."

I looked dead in his eyes and with a fearful tone said, "Michael, you don't know this town like I do. If someone in high places wants me dead, the Las Vegas County Jail is the place they would want me to be. Don't you see? If they're saying it was a failed suicide attempt, then there is a good chance you're going to find me hanging from a sheet in the morning."

Sternly, Lesley replied, "Christina, we are going to need you to be calm if we're going to get you out of this place. So please try to pull yourself together, and let's go see the judge before we all become hysterical." She then called for the guards and off we went.

The flashes of the press cameras were blinding as we reached the waiting area of the judge's chambers. I held my head high as I was led in handcuffs, by two female police officers past the furor of the press, straight into Judge Edward Homble's chambers, where I was taken to the defendant's chair, un-cuffed and asked to be seated. Michael took a seat behind me in the public seating section, as Lesley and Tom sat to the right of me at a narrow, six-foot-long table, which sat twelve-feet from and two-feet lower than Judge Homble's throne. Judge Homble was a gray headed, fifty-eight-year-old, right winged radical, who was appointed to his seat by Frank himself, and to add to my 'favor', he was a self-proclaimed bigot. The first thing he did was to order all the reporters out of his court room. He took one quick glance at me through condescending eyes and I knew I was in trouble. I watched in horror as he swiftly began to dispute both my attorneys' requests for bail.

After about twenty minutes of this, Lesley visibly frustrated said, "But Your Honor, my client just this morning, was released from the hospital. She is not physically capable of staying in custody. She also happens to be a World-Renown Figure, and she has no intention of breaking bail."

With that, the prosecuting attorney for the state of Nevada said, "Your Honor, I can bring witness after witness who will testify they heard the defendant state on numerous occasions she was going to kill Frank Salerno. Because of that, the state is seeking murder one in this case sir, and we also feel the defendant is more than capable of fleeing justice, if she so desired. So with these points in question, the State requests a denial of bail."

All at once, with a voice that thundered throughout the room, Judge Homble shouted as he slammed his gavel down, "The court hereby denies the defendant's request for bail. The defendant will remain in custody without bail until the completion of a trial by jury."

He stood up and began to step away from his throne and I shouted, "What the hell kind of bullshit is this! Do you know whom you're dealing with my dear Judge Homble?"

In reply he shouted, "Counselor control your client, or I will hold her for contempt as well."

I felt fire in my eyes and I knew for sure I was fighting for my life, so I shouted, "To hell with you, Judge! Do you really think I'm going to let you have someone put a noose around my neck and get away with it?" I shook my head, "It's not going to happen asshole. You should have looked really close at '*Christina Powers*' before you decided to try to railroad me you stupid ass!" Two police officers once again handcuffed me and pulled me away as I shouted, "I'll be out of this place in two hours, Homble. And when this is over I'm coming after your career, you bastard!"

With anger in his voice, he turned to me, "Ms. Powers, I know damned well who you are and even you fall under the law of the land. So you're not going anywhere."

Even madder I shouted, "I am more than willing to come under the same law which governs us all your Honor but I will not unjustly be prosecuted by **NO MAN**!"

By 5:10pm I was back in my dirty little cell, but I was determined not to stay there. I had Jimmy call Dominick, Michael call Barbara, and Tom Davies was trying to reach President Feagan himself. I figured among the three of them, someone would get me out of this place. Finally around 9:45pm after the clamor from the crowds in the streets began to subside, I heard the sounds of footsteps echoing in the brick hallway. The sound was growing louder, the closer they came to my cell. My heart began to pound as thoughts raced through my mind, "Is this my way out or is this someone who is here to kill me?" When the sound reached my cell, I was stunned to see the vice-president of the United

States, who was also the new President-elect, George Rush, standing on the other side of the bars.

Although I was shocked I did not allow my face to show my surprise as I said, "George, it's so good to see you again."

George smiled sweetly, "Christina, it's wonderful to see you looking so well after your narrow escape. And you'll be happy to hear I have come to personally release you on your own recognizance." Then, the guard opened the door and out I walked through a back entrance with George, to three waiting limos. We climbed into his limo and off we went.

George and I had locked horns over political issues in the past, but as for our personal relationship, we had always treated one another with the utmost respect. Although I didn't always agree with George, I did however trust him; that is why I climbed into his limo without asking where we were going, or why he came in person. I was just glad to see him.

As we sped away from the courthouse, George said, "Christina, this is not just a one purpose trip for me. I have come to get you out of jail, but I have also come for something else as well. You happen to have something I would like you to give to me."

I smiled seductively, then innocently glanced into his eyes as I said with a chuckle, "George, I'm flattered, I didn't realize you cared so much." He began to blush, so I kissed his cheek and added, "All right I'll stop the joking, and be good now. So, how can I help you Mr. soon to be President?"

He wiped the perspiration from his forehead, "Woah! I almost forgot what I was talking about."

I smiled again as I took his hand, "You were about to ask me for something, and I was about to say thank you for rescuing me from that horrid place." I let go of his hand and continued, "If I can help you George, I will, so please go on."

Looking dead into my eyes and with a completely serious tone he said, "It has come to my attention you possess some very damaging information on Senator Bradford. Well, I am going to be blunt. I need that information."

I looked at him strangely, "Are you aware of what is contained in the information I have in my possession?"

Still with a serious look he answered, "I am well aware of the content, that's why I do not want this information made public. If this information is leaked, it could jeopardize the security of our nation."

I looked at him and wondered, 'How could this information jeopardize National Security?' as I said, "You're the President, George. Who am I to jeopardize our nation? You will have the one and only copy of this information in existence in two days and I will never speak of the matter again."

A look of relief came over him as he smiled, "That's a very wise decision Christina, and I thank you myself, and for the President."

When the limo arrived at my hotel, George took my hand and said, "I hope everything works out for you with the case, Christina. And if there is any way I can help you again in the future, please let me know."

I tenderly squeezed his hand as I softly kissed his cheek one more time, "Thank you George, and I wish you all the best with your 'Presidency' as well. I would also like to extend the same courtesy to you, if you should ever need my help in the future, please call."

I climbed out of his limo and was escorted by three secret service men to my suite at Caesar's Palace Hotel and Casino, which by the way, now belonged to me.

As soon as I opened the door I was greeted by the worried loving hugs of Michael and Jimmy. The first thing they both asked was, "What happened?"

Excitedly Jimmy said, "Tom Davies already told us George Rush was going to be bringing you home himself. So what did he say?" I told Jimmy as much as I wanted him to know. Later that night while in bed, I told Michael everything which transpired between George and me.

At 9:30 on Christmas morning I was informed by Tom Davies, via a phone call that a jury would be picked after the first of the year, and the trial date was set for January 21st, 1989, at 9:00am. All that day Michael, Jimmy, and I tried to have a Merry Christmas, but none of us could get the murder trial off our minds. Then I got sad because Michael and I had missed our wedding; and to top it off, when we exchanged gifts around 7:00pm that evening, I didn't have one thing to give either one of them. So, I raised a toast with my tenth cup of coffee and said, "I wish the best to the two most important people in my life on this Christmas day. May I also say, please don't expect much from me this year, I was on vacation and it slipped my mind."

I began to laugh and as I laughed, Jimmy handed Michael a gift, turned to me and with the flick of that wrist said, "Sorry, girlfriend! We didn't think you were going to be with us this year, so we didn't get you anything either." With that we lost it! We laughed so hard, we all went running for the bathrooms!

I received a call at 10:00pm on Christmas night from Dominick Giovanetti. He was calling in response to Jimmy's call for help. When Michael handed me the phone, I said, "Dominick, thank you for calling, and thank you for saving Powers Incorporated. I'll never know how to thank you enough."

Dominick's voice cracked emotionally, "Christina, I'm just pleased you're still with us. After Jimmy told me what happened, I made some calls. I found out a few very interesting things. First, no one has tampered with the gun at the forensics lab. Somehow, between the time you were shot and the time Michael broke into the room, someone either wiped off Frank's fingerprints and put the gun in your hand, or you had the gun all along little girl."

Urgently I replied, "Dominick, I swear I did not have that gun."

With a concerned tone he said, "Then someone is setting you up. I'll continue looking from my end, and I'll keep you informed. But, we now have a wild card thrown into the works, which you're going to have to watch out for. It seems Anthony has taken control of his father's position as head of the Salerno Family. Word on the street is he has blood in his eyes for you."

Frustrated I said, "Great! What's next, a round of machine gun fire as I'm driving down the road?"

"All I'm saying is increase your security, at least until I can try to get a handle on this." Then, with that deep Italian accent of his, "*Abafangul* girl, when you start shit, you really start shit."

I laughed a little, "Thanks for the vote of confidence."

As soon as I ended my conversation, I called Tom and Lesley, whose rooms were on the same floor as our suite and had them come in to meet with us right away. They arrived together at around 11:00pm and I told them, along with Michael and Jimmy, exactly what I had just learned from Dominick.

Tom said, "It could have been done. Lesley and I were at the crime scene just two hours ago, and there is a back entrance into Frank's office." He turned to Michael and added, "Michael, how long after the second shot did you and the guards break in the door?"

Michael scratched his head, "I'd say two minutes."

Tom snapped his fingers together, "That's it! Two minutes would have been more than enough time for someone who could have possibly been in the next room, to come in right after the second shot was fired. How long could it take for whomever to take the gun out of Frank's hand, wipe the prints off and place it in your hand? Except this time, the only prints on the gun would be yours. Then they could have slipped out of the room with no one seeing them."

"But who?" I asked with intensity.

He smiled confidently, "There can't be too many people with access to Frank's private entrance. All we have to do is find out who had that access, and then start eliminating suspects."

The next few months the craziness started all over again. I had so many psychological and physiological evaluations by the time the trial started, I felt like a guinea pig. Then once again the press was up my ass twenty-four hours a day, and once again I was going crazy. You'd think I would have handled the pressure better by now, but this time it was my neck on the line. The trial was delayed for weeks, as the attorneys from both sides, struggled to select an impartial jury. On April 21st, 1989, a jury was finally chosen and a new trial date was set for May 2nd.

By the time the trial date came around, the whole world was anticipating the Frank Salerno murder trial, "Starring 'yours truly'!" My attorneys and I had been over every detail of my case, at least one thousand times, by the time we entered that Las Vegas

County Court House, for the first day of what would captivate the entire world for eight grueling weeks of my life.

The prosecution for the state was District Attorney Samuel Perry. Sam was a short fat pudgy nosed, twenty-eight-year-old tiger, who was going to make a name for himself by frying my ass. Sam was playing for keeps and he came out swinging with both fists, with his opening statement to the Jury; as we sat in front of the, oh so humble, Judge Edward Homble, with the eyes of the world upon us.

Sam waddled up to the Jury Box with his hands behind his back, "Ladies and gentleman of the Jury, the people of the State of Nevada intend to prove, beyond the shadow of a doubt, that the defendant, *Christina Powers*, is a calculating cold blooded killer, who ruthlessly planned the demise of her Uncle's fortune. Then, she took his life upon the news he would soon be in custody for the murder of her daughter. I must remind you now no matter what the circumstances, you must remember, no one is above the law. We cannot allow the driven passions of a grieving mother, to take the law into her own hands and commit cold blooded murder. We are going to show the defendant and the victim, have been consumed by a personal vendetta toward one another for the past sixteen years, which culminated with the murder of Frank Salerno and a failed suicide attempt by the defendant, *Christina Powers*. Now, I thank you for your time and I ask you to judge this case by the law, not by the emotional pleas you will receive from the Defense Counsel." Then, he nodded to the Jury, turned, and waddled back to his seat.

We had no proof of our suspicion I may have been framed, so we were forced to plead self-defense.

At that point, it was Lesley Steines turn. She was the one we chose to give the opening address for our side. She was a tall, slim, dark haired, thirty-six-year-old, Jewish girl from Queens. She had enough spunk and mental sharpness, to be the envy of most female attorneys, and I liked that. Lesley appeared more than qualified, as she confidently approached the jury, and she looked very professional in her custom made, dark blue designer suit.

As she reached the Jury Box she stopped, and slowly turned her head to gaze into each one of the juror's eyes, as she said, "Ladies and gentleman of the jury, the prosecution made a very good point when he used the words, 'beyond the shadow of a doubt;' because that is the key to justice in our nation's judicial system. You must be convinced beyond the shadow of a doubt, that the defendant you are being asked to convict for murder in the first degree, is guilty of murder in the first degree. We, the members of the Defense intend to show there are too many shadows in the prosecution's case, to ever seriously consider prosecuting our client. The first question to be answered should be whether this is truly a murder case, as the prosecution believes, or was it actually a case of self-defense? We intend to show the court our client was brutally beaten by the so-called victim, before our client ever pulled the trigger on the gun which took the life of the man who was trying to kill her. Now, I would like to ask you individually and as a group, to consider this possibility as the trial proceeds. I also thank you all for your time and I ask one more thing as the evidence unfolds. Please remember, guilt must be proven beyond the shadow of a doubt." She nodded her head to the jury, walked back to her seat beside mine, and the trial of the century began.

From that moment on May 2nd, and day-after-day, there were numerous witness testimonies and cross examinations by the prosecution and the defense. The prosecution brought in every person who knew anything at all about my dispute with, and distaste for, Frank. And let me tell you, God knows, enough people knew. We spent the first four weeks of the trial just questioning personal character witnesses. I was so drained by the time the trial finally got around to forensic evidence; I hardly knew what the hell they were talking about. Lesley and Tom decided not to put me on the stand, unless I could remember something more substantial. They felt I would give the prosecution more help, then I would be worth in my own defense. So I sat there day-after-day, all day long, just listening and watching as so much evidence piled up against me that eventually, even I was starting to believe I killed him. By the time the eighth week arrived, things were looking pretty bad for my case. It seemed no matter what angle we would take with the case, the prosecution kept coming back to their one hard piece of evidence, the gun with only my fingerprints on it.

On June 27th, at 10:00am we finally got around to the eight people subpoenaed from Salerno Incorporated who had access to Frank's private back entrance. Tom Davies called his first witness of the day, Kathy Brown, to the witness stand. Kathy glided to the witness stand, just like a perfect lady should. She raised her right hand and swore on the Bible with her left hand, to tell the truth and nothing but the truth so help her God. Kathy seemed somehow fragile looking as she climbed on the witness stand, but when she sat facing us and started her testimony, she became what she was, a lying, scheming bitch.

As I listened to her lying, I became angry and I thought, "Why you no good, bitch!" Then I thought, "Who are you to judge! You're looking at her is just like looking in a mirror!" After I chastised myself, I felt utter disgust for my own actions and I thought, "Dear God! Is there any hope for any of us here in this life?" As Kathy answered the questions to the best of her recollection, I closed my eyes and began to drift away.

As I drifted off into a dream state, I felt myself lifting out of my body. I began to gently float above the drama being played out in the court room. As I began to soar through the skies, I was praying for my memory to come back. As I searched through the stars looking for an answer to my prayer, I noticed a bright light glistening off in the distance through the darkness of space. I soared toward the warmth of the light with every drop of strength I had. When I reached it, I was greeted by a golden winged angel and I found myself in awe of her impressive beauty. As I gazed at her, she reached out and without saying a word took my hand and began to lead me into the white light. She took me to an enormous emerald mansion in the heavens, where she led me into a large diamond-glistening room. She placed my hands on a beautiful tear drop shaped crystal which was suspended in the center of the room. As I held my hands on that crystal, its reflection showed everything which happened that fateful day of Frank's death, like a TV screen.

When I opened my eyes, I was once again in the court room and I was stunned to see Anthony on the witness stand.

I caught my breath, stood up, pointed at Anthony, as Tom questioned him and shouted, "I remember it all now! You did it, Anthony! You cleaned the fingerprints off the gun."

Judge Homble shouted, "Order in the court! Counselor control your client," as Anthony shouted, "She's crazy! I don't know what she's talking about!"

Tom came to me, "Do you want a recess?"

"No! Put me on the stand now!" I demanded. "I remember what happened."

He nodded his head, "Your Honor, I am finished with this witness for now. At this time I would like to call, *Christina Powers* to the stand."

You could hear a pin drop as I walked up to the witness stand, swore on the Bible and took my seat. Tom approached me, "Ms. Powers, would you please tell us in your own words what happened on December 2nd, 1988?"

I took a deep breath, "When I went into Frank's office with the others, I didn't expect to see him. When I did see him there, I began to order him out of the office. I told him the police were coming to arrest him for the murder of my baby and I couldn't stand to look at him anymore. Then, he asked to speak to me in private and when I accepted, I asked to be left alone with Frank for five minutes. As soon as everyone left the room, Frank pulled a gun out and said he was going to kill me. We began to fight over the gun and somehow, I got a hold of it. I ran to the door with the gun still in my hand, and Frank jumped me again. This time the gun went off and as soon as I heard the shot, I let go of the gun and screamed. As Frank began to fall backwards he pulled the trigger of the gun, which was now in his hand and shot me. As I was falling, I saw Anthony come into the room through the back door. As I lay on the floor bleeding, Anthony took the gun from his father's hand, wiped it off and placed it in my hand."

With that Anthony immediately stood up and began to leave the court room. As he did Judge Homble sternly ordered him, "Mr.

Salerno, please don't try to leave just yet. I'm sure the counselor will want to recall you to the stand."

Anxiously Anthony said, as a Court Guard approached him, "I don't know what she's talking about and I'm going to call my attorney."

Instantly I added, "There was also a witness to this scene your, Honor!"

Then in front of the eyes of the entire world, Kathy Brown stood up and shouted, "Christina! I'm sorry! He said he would kill me if I told!"

Just as soon as she said those words, Anthony pulled the Court Guard's gun out of its holster and shot, "**Bang!**" killing the guard instantly! He turned toward Kathy and in the midst of the screams of the court-room, **'Bang'** he shot again, hitting her right between the eyes. I watched in horror as he took aim at me this time, **'Bang'** came a third shot only this one came from a guard who shot Anthony dead. I screamed as I watched this nightmare unfold in front of my eyes. I jumped off the witness stand and ran to Michael crying hysterically.

My mind and body were totally numb when Michael and Jimmy helped me walk out of that Las Vegas County Court room on June 27th, 1989. As Michael pushed our way through the midst of the frantic pace of the police and emergency medical crews, all I could think of was Kathy and the horrible way she had just died. Then like a slap across the face, we walked right into the press with their cameras and a million questions and I couldn't utter a word. As stunned as I was from my emotional trauma, when we reached the madness of the cheering crowds out in front of that courthouse, I emerged a **vindicated woman and a national hero**.

That afternoon I was on the front pages of every newspaper in the world, and for the next two weeks I had top billing on every news broadcast in the country. The headlines read, **"Christina Powers, found innocent in the most dramatic court trial in history."**

After the chaos started to slow down, I thought it was finally over, but little did I know, **'it was just the beginning'**.................

CPSIA information can be obtained at www.ICGtesting.com
Printed in the USA
LVOW07s2236080515

437610LV00003B/3/P